Praise for *Into the Broken Lands*

"Huff's natural dialogue, her eye for the practical, ground-level details, the interaction of her characters, lends humor and wit to the gravity of the whole." —*Fantasy & Science Fiction Magazine*

"If you like your adventure fantasy spiced with a good dose of introspection and plenty of intelligence then this book is for you." —Blogcritics

"I picked up *Into the Broken Lands* because I knew Tanya Huff would never let me down and, lo and behold!, she did not. This is a character-driven fantasy at its best." —Tea Leaf Reads

"Intriguing and thought provoking. [*Into the Broken Lands*] is what true fans of fantasy or science fiction long for, a book that questions, makes you consider the answers and think through what the novel is trying to say . . . I found this one compelling and masterful." —The Nameless Zine

"*Into the Broken Lands* is a great pair of stories interwoven to become something better than the sum of its parts." —Game Vortex

"Huff is an author that has never let me down no matter the genre . . . . *Into The Broken Lands* meshes these stories and characters into a wonderful picture that brings the world to life and makes me sad that it's a standalone novel. Not because this story doesn't end with a nice sense of satisfaction but as I really found the world so intriguing." —SFcrowsnest

The Finest in Fantasy and Science Fiction
by Tanya Huff from DAW Books

THE PEACEKEEPER NOVELS:

AN ANCIENT PEACE (#1)

A PEACE DIVIDED (#2)

THE PRIVILEGE OF PEACE (#3)

THE CONFEDERATION NOVELS:

A CONFEDERATION OF VALOR

Valor's Choice/The Better Part of Valor

THE HEART OF VALOR (#3)

VALOR'S TRIAL (#4)

THE TRUTH OF VALOR (#5)

THE SILVERED

INTO THE BROKEN LANDS

THE ENCHANTMENT EMPORIUM (#1)

THE WILD WAYS (#2)

THE FUTURE FALLS (#3)

BLOOD PRICE (#1)

BLOOD TRAIL (#2)

BLOOD LINES (#3)

BLOOD PACT (#4)

BLOOD DEBT (#5)

BLOOD BANK (#6)

THE COMPLETE SMOKE TRILOGY

Smoke and Shadows/Smoke and Mirrors/Smoke and Ashes

THE COMPLETE KEEPER CHRONICLES

Summon the Keeper/The Second Summoning/Long Hot Summoning

INTO THE BROKEN LANDS

TANYA HUFF

DAW BOOKS
New York

Cover design by Adam Auerbach

Cover images: archway by Susanitah / Shutterstock;
ravens by Marcin Perkowski / Shutterstock

Interior design by Fine Design

Edited by Sheila E. Gilbert

DAW Book Collectors No. 1921

DAW Books
An imprint of Astra Publishing House
dawbooks.com
DAW Books and its logo are registered
trademarks of Astra Publishing House

Printed in Canada

ISBN 978-0-7564-1526-6 (trade paperback)
ISBN 978-0-7564-1525-9 (ebook)

First edition: August 2022
First paperback edition: August 2023

10 9 8 7 6 5 4 3 2 1

For Sheila . . . who waited and waited and waited.
And who was understanding about delays. Thank you.

We left behind a land given over to chaos, a destroyed city,

and uncounted dead.

✦

Those of us who survived the terror and the pain will make a new life here.

We will never go back.

—FROM *THE CAPTAIN'S CHRONICLE*

"Nonee! Nonee!"

Darny's cry shattered the silence wrapped around Arianna's deathbed. Squatting close beside the bed, cradling the thin hand of her first friend, she raised her head at the call, shifted in place, and winced as her bulk caused the bed to rock. All but one of Gateway's inhabitants called her Nonee, and had for long enough she'd accepted it as her name. It wasn't the name she'd given herself, but other people wore the names they'd been given, why shouldn't she? Only Arianna refused to use it.

"Nonee!" The timbre of Darny's voice changed as he entered the herbarium and grew louder as he approached the private rooms at the back. "Nonee! They're coming!" He rocked to a halt in the open doorway. "Oh. I forgot. Is she dead?"

"No." Barely louder than her labored breathing, Arianna's voice held as much conviction as it ever had. "I'm not."

Not yet. Nonee carefully tightened her grip around loose skin and swollen joints, holding on. Not ever, had there actually been gods who listened.

Darny kicked the threshold. "Sorry, Healer. Sorry, Nonee. But they're coming!" He lowered his voice when Nonee glanced over and frowned, resenting the need to shift her attention from Arianna even for a moment. "They're coming like you said they would."

"Now?" She could hear the anger in her voice.

But Darny had known her for his entire life and merely blew out an annoyed huff of air. "No, I just thought I'd practice running and yelling. Of course now!"

Of course now. When all she wanted to do was be with Arianna, to sit beside her bed and guard her from the inevitable. She needed . . . She shook her head. She needed to be here, but she also needed information. There'd been four of *them* the last time. This time . . . What if they'd come with an army? What if there'd been enough change at the other end of the road that they'd come to try and dig destruction out of the ruins?

This was *not* the time!

Arianna nodded when Nonee's gaze returned to her face and her slack lips twitched, the closest she could come to a smile. "I'm not . . . not going anywhere yet."

She searched for a clever response, something Arianna could answer with wit or sarcasm, a moment's banter to delay the inevitable, but Arianna had too few words left to waste any on foolishness. "How many?" she asked Darny without turning.

"Seven riding. Four in leather and scale, two in fancy clothes, with like embroidery and stuff. The seventh isn't in a uniform and he's not so fancy dressed as the rest. And they have two people wearing all blue riding in a wagon. They've got round hats on, sort of like what Mam wears in the sun but not really, and the hats are the very same blue. So," he declared after a moment, "nine I could see."

"A wagon?" That was unexpected. They might have come for trade if they came with a wagon.

"Yeah, hard to miss. And I only *saw* two people on the wagon, but it's big and covered over so there could be more soldiers hidden inside."

"Guardians."

"What?"

"They call their soldiers guardians. Why do you think they'd hide guardians inside the wagon?" she asked, as Arianna's lips twitched again. Their arrival had given Arianna a chance to smile twice. For that, Nonee might forgive the interruption.

"They could want to sneak more people inside the wall. People that we didn't know about, to take us by surprise. It's a big wagon," he added defensively. "With two big horses!"

Except for the hand cradled in hers, the clever fingers still and damp and so cold it was clear they'd never be warm again, Nonee might have smiled as well.

A long, long time ago, when Arianna's hair crowned her head in a gleaming tangle of chestnut curls, when her eyes were bright, when she could beat all challengers in a footrace, Garrett, Heir of Marsan, had stopped at Gateway on his way to the Broken Lands with his ancille, his best friend, and his best friend's ancille. The ancilles had been barely more than boys, boys from the Five Thousand learning to be men at the side of those older and possibly wiser. *"A small party can move fast enough to survive,"* Garrett, Heir of Marsan, had said. *"The smaller the party, the faster it can move.*" Nonee looked down to see Arianna's eyes dancing and knew, the way she always knew, that Arianna was thinking of the heir as well. The healer had disapproved of Garrett Heir in the beginning, but had come to like him well enough by the end.

Arianna's fingers twitched. "He brought you . . . here." After so many years together, teaching and being taught, living in each other's head went both ways.

He'd have mocked a party of nine. Maybe he *had* mocked it. Arianna and he were of an age, he could still be alive.

Garrett Heir hadn't brought a wagon, but he had brought the only one of the six great mage-crafted weapons to survive the war. This new company riding—and rolling—up the Mage Road to the Broken Lands would want to claim it.

She could hear Darny's bare feet scuffing against the worn stone floor. "So, are you coming, Nonee?"

"No."

"But you need to talk to them! You know they're gonna want . . ."

"Later."

"Not long . . ." Arianna sighed.

She could feel Arianna's pulse fluttering in her wrist like a small bird throwing itself against the bars of a cage. Would it help if she thought of Arianna's spirit fighting to be free of the cage that age had made of her body?

No.

"Much later," she said.

Arianna managed to find the energy for both a snort and an eye roll.

"Much later," Nonee repeated. Belief wouldn't slow the inevitable. For all her familiarity with death, for all she was, for all Arianna and others had taught her over the years, she couldn't stop time. But she refused to surrender.

"So what do I tell the gate guards if you're not coming?" Darny demanded.

"Has the council been told?"

He snorted dismissively. "Well, yeah. Shalla was hanging around, so they sent her to tell Sa Oryn while I ran for you."

Oryn Archivist would be the easiest of the council to find; some nights he slept at the archive. "Go to Oryn Archivist. Tell him the council should stay clear until we have more information, that they should send Gils Trader to deal with them. He'll know how. Then go to the gate. Tell the guards Gils Trader is on his way and that he has the final word on whether or not they open the gate."

"You mean I should tell Sa Oryn that Nonee says to send Gils? And then tell the guards that Nonee says Gils has the final word? And then run around the walls because I've run out of other places to run to?"

"Darny." She rolled his name out of the depths of her chest, the sound as much a rumble of displeasure as a word.

"Fine. I'll run. I'll tell them." She heard him turn, pause, return. "Nonee? I'm sorry Ari's dying."

She closed her eyes. Heard him turn again and leave. Opened her eyes a long moment later.

"Everyone dies," Arianna murmured. "I shouldn't have to . . . tell . . . you that."

Nonee carefully brushed a thin strand of brittle, white hair back off the high arc of Arianna's forehead. "Not you. You don't die."

"Also . . . me." A shallow breath struggled to lift the sunken chest. "Come . . . closer. Don't make me . . ."

A group of children ran past the herbarium, shrieking with laughter.

". . . come up . . . there and . . ."

Off to the east, a cow bawled for her calf.

". . . get you. You know I . . . will."

The remains of Arianna's imperious expression pulled Nonee in until they breathed the same air. The dying woman's breath smelled faintly of vinegar as her body devoured itself. They held the position for what seemed like a year or two, although Nonee knew it couldn't have been more than a moment.

Another labored breath. "Clo . . . ser."

"Ari."

"Don't be . . . a . . . afraid of your . . . self. I trust . . . you."

"Yes, but . . ."

"You can't . . . refuse it . . . now . . . stubborn one. Last re . . . quest." Fingers twitched within the cage of Nonee's hand, brushing against her palm like the wings of a mayfly. "Closer."

She closed the distance. Felt her heart shatter as the first person to ever care for her gave her one last gift as she died.

RYAN.NOW

"Do you know who I am?" Ryan yelled up at the two archers on the battlements. "Do you?"

"Said you were the Heir of Marsan," replied the taller. She turned and added something quietly to her companion, who laughed.

Ryan stiffened in the saddle. His horse stepped back two paces, dark ears flat. Forcing himself to relax before Slate scaled up his objection, he scratched at a dapple-gray shoulder and reminded himself he was used to laughter. First from his brothers, then while trying to take his brothers' place. But these people were laughing at the Heir of Marsan. At the title, not at him. That wasn't supposed to happen.

It wouldn't have happened to Donal.

"It's like they're not glad to see us." Keetin moved Thorn, his gelding, in close enough for the two horses to bump haunches, the contact calming Slate enough that he stopped shifting in place.

"I don't care how they feel about us," Ryan muttered. "I just want them to open the flaming gate."

The gate should have been opened to the Heir of Marsan.

The gate remained closed.

He lifted his chin and met the archer's gaze. "How long do we wait?"

She glanced to the west and shrugged. "B'in fore dark."

The sun showed red between the trees. Daylight lingered in midsummer, especially this far north, but dusk had crept closer than expected.

"Before duck?" Keetin muttered. "What's duck got to do with it?"

"Dark."

"No, she said duck."

The local accent made shared words sound like another language. Ryan dragged the reins across Slate's neck, wheeled the horse around to the left, and charged back toward the wagon. Slate complained about the sudden start and stop by bucking before he settled, but it was a perfunctory protest at best.

When he became Lord Protector, he'd expand his influence north. Gateway had been a traders' town, according to the Captain's Chronicle, a point of contact between the mages and the greater world, with scholars and artisans and merchants gathered together to create a city of unparalleled beauty and advancements. Most of the Five Thousand who went south with Captain Marsan were from Gateway: five thousand survivors of the Mage War who'd had brains enough to realize they couldn't live in the wreckage.

Those who'd stayed behind, like the ancestors of the archer, had been too stupid to realize their lives had irrevocably changed. They'd clearly bred that stupidity into their descendants.

Slate danced sideways. Ryan forced himself to relax. The guards on the gate were being cautious. It wasn't personal. No matter how it felt.

Lyelee was standing when he reached the wagon, ready to dismount. He'd gotten used to seeing her in regular clothes, but during a quick late afternoon stop, before they'd started out to cover the last bit of road before Gateway, both scholars had dressed in full regalia. Robes. Stoles. Even the ridiculous flat hats. She was no longer his family—the two of them closest in age among the cousins so expected to get along in spite of differences—she was a scholar novitiate.

The scholars didn't answer to the Lord Protector and they certainly didn't answer to the Heir. According to their Charter, they were directed only by scholarship and were above the day-to-day distractions of commerce and politics. They were to be scholars before anything else.

No one had expected the Lord Protector to give them permission to take the Mage Road north. Scholars were revered, venerable, wise, not sent into certain danger. In the end, for that permission to be granted, they'd had to agree that safety would overrule scholarship until they were back in the Scholar's Hall. During their travels, the Heir of Marsan would have the last word.

Ryan hadn't yet tested the strength of the agreement, and he was well aware that Court and the Scholar's Hall had both assumed the last word would actually come from Captain Yansav.

"Lyelee . . ." He paused as her brows rose and she twitched a fold from her robe: a fabric reminder that she had an audience now. He stifled a sigh. "Scholar Novitiate Marsan, please remain in the wagon."

"Why?"

He glanced at the streaks of orange above the horizon. "We need to be ready to move when they open the gate."

"How long do you think it takes me to get back into the wagon?" she demanded.

Scholars never asked rhetorical questions. If they asked a question, they expected an answer. Over the last twenty-eight days of travel, the non-scholars in the company had learned they could be knocked off the scent with a return question, and on the days the scholars had been particularly *scholar-like* they'd taken a petty pleasure in winding them up until annoyance turned to affronted silence. "Do you want to have to scramble back on board when the gate opens? With that lot watching?"

Head tipped back to lift the angle of her hat, she glanced past him, up at the archers, and he hoped the need to been seen as in control would outweigh a scholar's need to be right every single time. He breathed a sigh of relief when she sat.

"So." She shot him a narrow-eyed glare from under her hat. "What are we waiting for?"

"Possibly a duck." Keetin reinserted himself at Ryan's side.

Lyelee glanced between them, frown deepening. "A duck?"

"A sacrifice perhaps," Scholar Gearing suggested from the other side of the wagon seat, back straightening, the chance to lecture easing his exhaustion. "Some primitive peoples read entrails when they require . . ."

"There's no duck!" Ryan snapped. Slate bucked again. He shifted his weight into the movement and used it to turn the horse to the left until they faced Captain Yansav and the three guardians at the rear of the wagon. "Gateway wants us to wait," he announced, pitching his voice to carry over the scholarly *discussion* on what exactly constituted entrails and why they couldn't be referred to in the singular. "As we haven't much choice in the matter, we wait."

They needed to enter Gateway. They needed the weapon. Both the Lord Protector and the Heir's Chronicle—the record of the trip the Lord Protector had made sixty-three years earlier—had specifically said that no one could enter the Broken Lands without the weapon and expect to survive.

"Not that the weapon guarantees survival." The Lord Protector had blinked rheumy eyes more or less in Ryan's direction. *"Raises the odds though."* He'd coughed, spat, and added, *"To about fifty-fifty."*

Even with the weapon, half the people accompanying him would die. Four of the eight.

Ryan had been able to bury that number and the terror it evoked under the monotony of the road. Riding, walking, eating, sleeping, then doing it again and again and again had made the concept seem unreal. Here and now, off the road, with night approaching and the Broken Lands in sight, he used the irritation of being kept waiting, of not being acknowledged as Donal would have been, to shove it aside.

Donal would face it, acknowledge it; he'd do what he had to to keep moving.

Captain Yansav narrowed her eyes and studied the archers on the wall, her expression suggesting she, not they, had the advantage. "Do you expect trouble?"

"No." He could recognize asshole behavior when he saw it, flame knew he'd seen it often enough. "But we should stay alert in case that changes."

"Sir."

Promoted out of the Lord Protector's Guard, Captain Yansav could have taken advantage of her position with the new, inexperienced heir, and everyone in the Citadel was aware of it. Half the Court expected it, and Ryan hadn't helped by spending the first days after being publicly declared heir in a near panic, looking to her for orders. She'd finally broken him of that during their first ten days on the Mage Road by forcing him to make every single decision no matter how inane until he'd ordered her to stop. He may have continued to ask himself *what would Donal do*, but as she hadn't known, it hadn't mattered. During the next ten days, he'd learned she wasn't a morning person, her first name was Coree, and she'd been driven from her native land by a political coup. That Shurlia had also been Captain Marsan's native land had no doubt been a factor in her choice as the new Heir's Captain.

Also, his brother's captain hadn't wanted the job.

Ryan thought both he and the captain had made the best of having been pitched into not just the unexpected inheritance but the sudden departure for the Broken Lands. At this point, given a choice between Captain Yansav and an officer he could choose himself, he'd stick with the captain. He wanted to believe the captain would stick with him.

He didn't. Not entirely.

In creating the new Heir's Guard, Captain Yansav had ignored guardians who'd been in service to his oldest brother, not giving them their captain's chance to refuse, and had chosen the guardians to accompany them from outside the political appointees serving at the Citadel. All three had at least ten years on Ryan. Vaylin Curtin-cee had nearly fifteen. Curtin and Calintris Servan-cee were of the Five Thousand—the formal "cee" matronym, dropped after introductions but never forgotten. Borit Destros and the captain were not. All three were decent shots, but Servan was the best archer Ryan had ever seen. On the road, her bow had supplemented dried and salted meats with ducks, geese, rabbits, and once, a yearling buck.

None of them had bonded or children back in Marsanport, which said more about the captain's understanding of this trip than Ryan found comfortable.

"Sir?" Harris appeared from behind the wagon. Cloud, his mare, stopped a body length away and shot Slate an eloquent *don't try anything* look. "Do we consider this a rest stop?"

Do I light the kettle and make tea?

Ryan took another look at the angle of the sun, half inclined to have Harris boil some water and show Gateway how little he cared about their insult, both to him and to Marsanport. "No need," he said instead, turning Slate back toward the wall and raising his voice. "We won't be out here long."

The two archers had been joined by two more. At least he assumed they were archers from the similarity of clothing. If they had bows, they kept them out of sight.

The lower levels of the wall had been cobbled together from the rubble left behind by the Mage War—described in the Heir's Chronicle as the result of panicked survivors piling the stone from shattered buildings into a barricade. The upper levels, built sometime in the last sixty-three years, had a familiar silhouette. It looked as though Gateway had copied the wall surrounding the Citadel, although Ryan had no idea how. Only a single family of Marsan traders had been allowed contact. Traders, not masons or artists.

Seven people now watched from the top of the wall.

Eight.

Nine.

That was more people than he'd seen in one place since they'd left Marsanport. His back ached, and he wished he could relax the rigid posture the Heir of Marsan was expected to maintain in public.

They wouldn't have made Donal wait.

Donal would have been there eleven days earlier, into and out of Gateway, and into and out of the Broken Lands by now.

According to the Heir's Chronicle, it had taken seventeen days to ride from Marsanport to Gateway. Seventeen. Ryan's company had been held by the wagon to the same pace as Captain Marsan's walking wounded, who'd taken twenty-eight days to limp, stagger, and crawl from the destroyed city to Marsanport after the war.

The Court had protested the time the wagon would add when the Lord Protector granted the ridiculous petition from the Scholar's Hall to study the Broken Lands, but the Lord Protector, in full possession of his mind for that moment at least, had swept his gaze around the chamber, locked eyes with Ryan, and dismissed the protest with a curt, *"They go for the good of Marsan."*

For the good of Marsan.

The scholars sought knowledge.

Knowledge was power. Everyone knew that.

Knowledge traveled too flaming slowly.

When he became Lord Protector, the scholars would stay in the Scholar's Hall.

Yeah, he didn't believe that either.

"Sir."

Captain Yansav's quiet voice stopped his spiraling thoughts and drew his attention back to the wall in question. Two of the nine archers were gone; four of the remaining seven leaned far enough out to look straight down.

The door cut into the left half of the gate opened.

The man who stepped out had straight dark hair, cropped short, and a full beard braided with copper beads that glinted in the sun. He was darker than Lyelee, but not as dark as the captain or even Ryan himself; the heavy black lines of tattoos spiraling around both arms were visible at a distance. He didn't have the heavy muscle of a physical job, the bearing of a guardian, or the confidence of a politician. He wore loose trousers, a sleeveless tunic, and sandals—all in shades of brown.

Except for the beads, he could have stepped through the gate from a working-class street in Marsanport. Ryan picked at a loose thread on the edge of his saddle. To be fair, beads *might* be popular with the working class in Marsanport. He wouldn't know.

The man didn't look like a fighter, but the archers above the gate meant he didn't have to.

He knew the crest on Ryan's tabard, his eyes drawn to it before his gaze rose to Ryan's face. He frowned. "Your pardon, but I've seen the heir and you are not he."

Grateful that the man spoke slowly enough to be understood, Ryan moved Slate up beside Captain Yansav. "When did you see the heir?"

"Six years ago, when the Lord Protector granted me permission to remain in Gateway."

A lot had changed in six years.

A lot had changed since the Water Moon.

"You saw my brother Donal. He died. As did my brothers Corryn and Josan. They drowned. All three of them. Together." When it rained and the water ran into his eyes and his clothing got soaked through, he could hear his father howling as croppers pulled the bodies of his three oldest sons from the lake, the lake pulling back at their sodden clothing.

"Apologies, Lord Marsan. And my condolences on your loss." He raised his right fist to his chest and bowed his head. "I am Gilsin Yeri-cer."

Yeri. The trader family. Emphasizing their weak connection to the Five Thousand by using the patrilineal *cer*. Had the Lord Protector inserted Gilsin Yeri-cer into Gateway as a spy? Six years ago the Lord Protector's mind had still been sharp. Had he planted one of his own within Gateway to keep an eye on the weapon? "We're not here to trade . . ." Repeating the patronym would mock the trader's weak lineage. Donal had excelled at mockery. In this instance, Ryan realized, he didn't care what Donal would have done. ". . . Gilsin Yeri."

"I'm aware of that, my lord." The beads flashed when he smiled. "You've come, as the Lord Protector did when he was Heir, because the Black Flame's fuel is nearly spent and, before you enter the Broken Lands, you need the weapon. And, very probably, to receive a report on how conditions in the Broken Lands have changed over the last sixty-three years." He paused and asked, "You'll be trading for supplies?"

"We will." Ryan knew he sounded defensive when he should have sounded assertive.

Gilsin Yeri didn't appear to notice. "Any chance you've brought anchovies in oil? Love the little buggers and I always run out before my family returns." He smiled so broadly the corners of his mouth disappeared into his beard. Then he stopped smiling. "I'll need to have a look at the wagon. This close to the Broken Lands, we have to be careful of what we allow within the walls."

That seemed too reasonable for Ryan to deny him. Too reasonable for

Ryan to ask him what wasn't allowed. Or should he assume the answer was obvious, given Gateway's proximity to the Broken Lands?

He rapped his knuckles against both water barrels, and dribbled a thin stream of water onto his palm and then onto the ground. He examined the underside of the wagon . . .

"Mage Road's easy on the rig, I'll give it that." He winked at Harris, who rolled his eyes.

. . . then untied and flipped up one of the canvas sides. Even with the trade goods, the scholar's supplies, bedrolls, cooking gear, and the like, the wagon was nearly empty.

Ryan could see the questions as Gilsin Yeri stepped back. "It was full when we left Marsanport," he said. "Food. Grain for the horses. Other things we might need on the road."

"Looks like you needed all of them."

"We've been traveling for twenty-eight days," Gearing snapped, having apparently heard insult rather than observation.

"It's always twenty-eight days, Scholar," the trader/possible spy said flatly. "It's a mage road."

"It is?" Sarcasm dripped from the question. "Would that be why they call it *the Mage Road* then?"

"Yes." The scholar seemed taken aback by the flat answer and hadn't yet recovered when Gilsin Yeri added, "It takes twenty-eight days because they built a full turn of the moon into it."

Keetin nudged his horse forward. "The Lord Protector took only seventeen days."

Within the depths of his beard, Gilsin Yeri's mouth twisted. "I've read the Heir's Chronicle."

"And what is that supposed to mean?" Lyelee's scowl looked capable of physical damage. Beside her, Gearing seemed to have sucked the overhang of his mustache into his mouth.

"It means that the Mage Road always takes twenty-eight days from Marsanport to Gateway, Scholar."

Like everyone in Marsanport, Ryan had been taught that scholars always had, always would have the last word. Both of them would have plenty to say in response to the lack of respect, and Ryan had been raised to let them say it. But they needed to be behind the wall before dark. He'd opened his mouth to try and stop the lecture before it began when Gilsin Yeri leaned back far enough to get a better angle on the battlements, cupped his hands around his mouth, and yelled, "I speak for the Heir of Marsan and his party, Clea. Open the gate."

Metal groaned behind the slabs of wood.

At Slate's shoulder, far enough away he'd clearly taken the horse's measure, Gilsin Yeri met Ryan's gaze. "The Trader's Hall is being prepared, my lord. Beds made up, kitchen stocked. If you've been traveling since your evening meal, you'll want a bite. There's stabling and a turn-out for the animals once the sun's up again." He cocked his head at Ryan's frown and added, "It's late. Representatives from the council will meet with you tomorrow."

"Of course." He'd assumed they'd do it all tonight—resupply, accept the weapon, collect information—and leave at dawn, but admitting that would be admitting how little he understood what was happening. Donal would've known.

"Follow me." The trader/possible spy turned toward the open gate. "And stay on the road. We're almost positive we've located the last of the cellars, but we'd rather you not risk it."

No need to ask what Donal would have done. Donal would've taken insult at being commanded by a mere trader. He'd have sent someone to find a cellar just to prove who was in charge. Ryan, who'd been told how dissimilar he was to his stronger, smarter, better-prepared-to-be-heir brother half a hundred times his first day in the Citadel, preferred not to fall into a cellar.

He settled back into the saddle and met Captain Yansav's eyes. Did she know the spy? Had she been assigned to him to keep him from accidentally giving Gilsin Yeri's position away? Would she tell him the truth if he asked? Would it matter? He already missed the monotony of the road, where he'd come to know the answers. Was this a trap? No, that was a stupid overreaction. Gateway wanted trade with Marsanport and they'd agreed to help when the Black Flame flickered. "We follow the trader, Captain, and we stay on the road."

"Sir. Curtin, take point."

"Captain."

The guardian passed so close, Ryan could have effortlessly clapped him on the shoulder, and it was luck as much as skill that kept their knees from cracking together. Suspicious by nature and raised to believe in guilt by association when it came to mages and mage-craft, Curtin wouldn't be distracted.

LYELEE.NOW

Lyelee understood why they had to enter Gateway.

But once within the walls, what then?

Trust Ryan not to have asked how long she'd have to wait before they moved on into the Broken Lands.

She'd been planning for this expedition—although absent the presence of Ryan and Scholar Gearing—since she was a child. A thousand questions had pushed against the inside of her ribs for as long as she could remember. They'd driven her into the Scholar's Hall, and finally, into this wagon.

For the last few nights, she'd dreamed of the Broken Lands as they had been, filled with lost wonders. History waiting to be reclaimed. On the approach to Gateway, she'd been able to see the foothills from her dreams climb to meet the purple smudge of distant mountains, and the urge to take the whip to the horses and race toward the greatest mysteries that scholarship could ever hope to unravel was almost unbearable.

But right now, she'd have to settle for Gateway, the point of entry to the territory the mages had controlled. For hundreds of years, it had supplied the mages with mundane necessities while the mages supplied it with the crumbs of arcane knowledge they'd been willing to share. According to documents in the Scholar's Archive, Gateway had been the *only* point of entry—which was both ridiculous and illogical. The maps of the Broken Lands had been drawn years after the war, and, even if failing memory hadn't shifted borders, not one of the fleeing Five Thousand had known the full extent of the mages' combined territory. It had been large, that they'd agreed on. And if they were correct, why would the mage furthest from Gateway—historically equal in knowledge and power to the mage closest to Gateway—agree to such an inconvenient distance when they also shared a border with the outside world?

Logic answered that they'd create their own trade town in a more convenient location.

The original Captain's Chronicle, safely preserved in the Archive, said they hadn't.

There was only Gateway.

Gateway has been destroyed, said the Five Thousand.

Green flame engulfed the temple of Gani Hav. The walls melted as though made of butter.

Stones fell from the sky and crushed my mother's house and all my family.

Lyelee had read everything in both the library and the archives, from family histories filling multiple journals to illustrated manuscripts to scraps of paper with yellowed edges still stained with soot and faded brown smudges of blood. She knew what to expect.

There'd be ruins inside the walls: the remnants of an ancient civilization taken down to bare bones at the edge of a magnificent destruction. If forced to wait, she could fill a few hours with study.

Lyelee shifted forward on her seat as they passed beneath the gate, readying herself for the first glimpse of the city her ancestors had fled.

When the wagon emerged back into the sunlight, she stood, braced herself against the curved frame supporting the wagon's painted canvas top, took a deep breath, and looked around.

There were no ruins.

"How dare they!"

"How dare they what?" Gearing asked, his attention on the horses.

"The ruins of ancient Gateway have been removed! The history erased!"

"The history we're concerned with remains within the Broken Lands, Novitiate. Now, sit down."

She remained on her feet, the only protest she could make.

A circle of grass paralleling the wall was obviously used for common grazing. Given the amount of wool the traders brought back to Marsanport, there had to be grazing outside as well—to the west, she assumed, given the position of the road and the Broken Lands. The open area was most likely a part of Gateway's defenses. Allowing structures to be built against a defensive wall was a documented bad idea, although very few cities managed to prevent it. Had Gateway's council used the weapon to keep the area clear? Lyelee wondered. Historically, the possession of a weapon resulted in the use of that weapon.

Beyond the inner edge of the grass, the only ruins she could see had become part of the new Gateway—broken walls still high enough and stable enough to pen livestock, blocks of dressed stone used to build a patternless jumble of small houses and barns. History disrespected by expediency.

Trees made it difficult to see if the entire ancient city had been repurposed.

The wagon bounced. She twisted to keep her balance, and saw, off to the left, the upper story of a row of tenements rising above the trees. Her fingers tightened around the strut. The roofline matched rooflines in the sections of Marsanport first rebuilt by the Five Thousand. Did the roof still protect an intact building from before the Mage War?

Did the people of Gateway have some small awareness of what was actually of value?

On both sides of the road, children and dogs gathered sheep into small groups. If the inhabitants of Gateway hadn't found all the cellars, they were remarkably careless about both their livestock and their children.

Unless the small, random piles of rock scattered through the grass warned of danger below.

The children shouted as they passed the wagon, the spill of high-pitched words too fast for Lyelee to understand.

The mixed sounds of people and animals came nowhere close to the roar of Marsanport outside the buffering walls of Scholar's Hall and Citadel. She could smell sausages and honey cakes. And sheep. There'd been plenty of time for crowds to gather, but except for those few who'd joined the archers on the wall, no one seemed to care about their arrival.

"Government repression?" she wondered.

"A reasonable explanation for the apparent lack of interest our arrival has generated," Gearing allowed, understanding her question without it needing to be expanded.

The people of Gateway were acting as if scholars came through the gate every day.

"Whaha lukin fa?"

Lyelee jerked around and stared down at the boy keeping pace beside the wagon. "Where did you come from?"

"Me?" He made a face that suggested she was a little slow. "From here."

He had the medium-brown coloring dominant in Marsanport—the blend of a trading city evident on Lyelee's skin as well. His hair was thick and dark, his feet bare and dirty, and his homespun tunic and trousers declared farm not city. He looked as though he was waiting for a response, although his reply had been a statement, not another question.

Ah, Lyelee realized. He waited for a response to his first question.

"What am I looking for?" An exaggerated eye-roll confirmed her translation. "Evidence of the days before the Mage War."

"He might be sensitive about that," Gearing muttered.

He didn't seem to be. But why would he? The Mage War had happened long before he was born.

"All the ruinser outsye th'all on th'ay ta th'ine."

"Outside the wall? On the way to the line?"

"W'else?" He slapped his chest with an open palm. "I's Darny. Who're you?"

"Just Darny?" That gave her very little information.

"A'yea. You?"

"I am Scholar Novitiate Kalyealee Marsan-cee."

Dark eyes widened. "S'truth? Marsan like at the gate?" He slowed his voice down to a close approximation of Ryan's. "I am the Heir of Marsan!"

Lyelee rolled her eyes. The respect due a scholar was of considerably more significance than the respect Ryan thought should be due declaration of the family name. "The Heir of Marsan is my cousin."

"You a Heir of Marsan too?"

"Not while the current Heir lives."

"You plannin' t'off 'm?"

"No." She planned to remove herself from the line of succession the moment her novitiate ended and legality allowed. Knowledge was power and the actual power in Marsan lay with the scholars.

He flashed a pair of dimples. "You d'it, you'd b'eir."

"Not where my interests lie."

Gearing cleared his throat. He either disapproved of the discussion or he'd swallowed another insect. Lyelee ignored him.

So did Darny. "Is novisheet like a 'prentice?"

Would he know what *essentially* meant? Unlikely. "Sort of."

"Aren't you abbotol to be a 'prentice?"

Abbotol? Ah. A bit old. "No."

Darny studied her face, apparently unconcerned with where he put his feet in an area of potentially undiscovered cellars. "Takes that long, does it? How much longer you got to be a novisheet?"

"I'll be a full scholar later this year."

"If you defend your thesis," Gearing cautioned.

"F'in you don't die in the Broken Lands," Darny added. "That's where you're going' right? 'Cause the Black Flame's goin' out and you gotta get more fuel 'cause if you don't no one'll be scared of you even though my mam said that's a load of ratshit."

"Daaaaar-neeeeeeey!"

He jerked, stared into the direction his name had drifted out of, then threw her a grin. "S'my mam. Think she knows when I'm talkin' 'bout her. Gotta go. My turn to gather the chickens and bring 'em in. The chickens hate me," he added and broke into a run, racing diagonally through the sheep, lambs scattering like balls on a game table, the protests of the children who'd been gathering them drowned out by his bellowed, "Coooooom-ing!"

"The point of that conversation?" Gearing muttered as Lyelee sat and arranged the folds of her robe.

"Children lie less often than adults do. Prevarication is a learned behavior."

"Granted. And what did you discover?"

"That a scholar is less important to him than a chicken."

"Chickens. Plural." He twitched the reins. Dusk and Star continued to follow the horses in front of them as they had since leaving Marsanport. "The boy suggested our business here is common knowledge."

"Ryan's business, not ours." Let Ryan retrieve the fuel; she'd retrieve their past. The shadows lengthened. More adults called out, more children responded—not only sheep and chickens were being gathered in for the night. "The Heir's Chronicle referred to Gateway as a surprisingly thriving community."

Gearing snorted. "I don't doubt he was surprised, given that the Five Thousand believed they'd left behind fire and ash."

Lyelee waved a hand at the low buildings, at the trees they hid among, at the pockets of density further in from the wall. "Fire and ash aside, I wouldn't call this thriving. Before the Mage War, the people of Gateway had access to mage-craft. They had lights that burned without oil. They had heat without fire. They had . . ."

"Death and destruction raining down from the sky."

It always came to that, as though death and destruction wiped out everything that came before. And yes, it had—literally—but she referred to knowledge, to wisdom, to craft.

As though he knew her thoughts—and he very well could, their argument was an old one—her mentor made a noncommittal sound and turned toward her, the reins loose over the swollen knuckles of his left hand. "In comparison to nonexistence, I have to agree with the chronicle's assessment of thriving."

She gestured toward the sound of a protesting rooster. "Chickens and sheep."

"Eggs and fiber and meat."

"Government repression."

"Or a complete lack of curiosity."

"Which indicates a population focused solely on survival. Consider the resources that have gone into that wall—not only building materials, but the hours of work taken away from actual progress. No wonder the people are at a chickens-and-sheep level." She leaned out and twisted around to peer back the way they'd come. Two silhouettes were barely visible against the sky over the gate. Where had the other watchers gone? "During her tenure, the sixth governor of Midlake wrote and enforced two hundred and sixty-three different ordinances and lived in luxury while her people starved," she continued, facing front again. "How many ordinances did it take to build the wall?"

"That Darny boy didn't seem to be starving."

"Granted. But it would've been useful had the Lord Protector included specifics in the Heir's Chronicle about how this rebuilt Gateway was governed. And if not that, had he remembered enough to speak to me about it before we left. Although, had he retained his memories . . ."

"If his advanced age hadn't weakened his memory of his journey to the Broken Lands, we wouldn't have this opportunity," Gearing interrupted. "The Court would never have agreed to fund scholarship if they'd been happy with the details at hand. If anything, we should be thankful for the Lord Protector's lack of specifics."

And that Ryan's brothers drowned, Lyelee added silently. Gearing disliked her treating the tragedy as though it were any other mitigating factor. She didn't understand his objection; the deaths hadn't occurred in his family. And he was ignoring the way the accident had become the default conversation throughout the entire protectorate. *Nice day. You're looking good. Did you hear about the accident?* The ripples of losing the childless heir and his two closest brothers would continue for generations.

Donal had been Heir of Marsan for seventeen years, since his mother had died of sepsis when Donal was fourteen and Ryan just two. As the Heir's Journey to refuel the Black Flame would one day need to be made again, the Lord Protector had gifted his eldest great-nephew with all he knew of the Broken Lands and the ancient weapon. It was knowledge meant for the heir, but Lyelee bet Donal would have shared what he knew with Corryn and Josan, because the three were inseparable. Everyone knew that when Donal went to the Broken Lands, the twins would be going with him.

Donal's bonded had quite a bit to say about how inseparable they were at the funeral, emphasizing that they'd learned to sail at the same time and that clearly the person who'd taught them was an idiot.

The point was—and Lyelee had made it countless times on the road—Ryan's brothers drowning and the information lost with them had more to do with the Court agreeing to advance scholarship than the Lord Protector's advanced age.

She'd barely to had remind her Uncle Heath that Scholar Gearing, her mentor, held the Scholarship of the Broken Lands before her uncle had begun leaning on the Court. It didn't matter that Uncle Heath—and her mother—thought they were arranging things so she'd be available to bring the fuel home and claim the Lord Protectorship should Ryan not survive. After all, her uncle had announced—with heavy emphasis—it was to be a dangerous trip. Lyelee had smiled and nodded and let them scheme. Eventually, she'd been granted time with her great-uncle, had held his hand and answered a hundred and one questions about her studies—roughly seventy-five percent of them multiple times. In a moment of clarity, when his eyes had locked with hers, she'd pointed out that the knowledge trapped in the Broken Lands was just that, knowledge, neither good nor bad in and of itself, and it should not be abandoned as though it had personally been responsible for the destruction. After a long moment and a mournful expression, he'd tightened his grip and said, *"I suppose you'd better go, then."*

It wasn't a ringing endorsement, but it had been enough.

Watching Dusk's tail sweep from side to side, she wondered if Gilsin Yeri-cer, who'd stayed in Gateway for *love*, even considered how close he now was to the greatest cache of lost knowledge that had or likely ever would exist. Had he ever crossed the Broken Line? Or had he wasted his time with chickens and sheep?

Then the light of a lamp shone through a distant window. And another. And another. Sometime in the last few minutes, without her noticing, the sky above had taken on the brilliant sapphire of pre-dark. "Do they have to build the Trader's Hall before we can spend the night in it?" she asked, scratching at a line of raised welts on her shoulder. "What's taking so long?"

"Patience . . ."

She locked her response behind her teeth.

"I understand your frustration." Gearing shifted on the seat. He'd lost weight during the journey and he hadn't been well padded when they'd started. "We have the opportunity to create a new framework for Broken Lands Scholarship that generations of scholars will use." He gestured toward the far curve of the wall as though he were in a lecture hall, the motion shifting the reins lying slack on the horses' haunches. Dusk tossed his head. Star ignored him, her head down, checking the ground for food. "You and I, Novitiate, are very close to true history. Close to uncovering the truth buried in five thousand and one highly subjective memories. We've been given an opportunity we must make the most of."

Five thousand and one. Captain Marsan had led the Five Thousand, not been a part of it, although her memory had been just as subjective. Gearing had declared multiple times that they must make the most of the opportunity. Lyelee had decided repetition number thirty marked the border between scholarship and obsession and had stopped counting. He'd continued to make the declaration regardless.

At the front of the line, Gilsin Yeri-cer pointed left toward a two-story building, the nearer side separated from the grazing lands by a single tree. The angle prevented her from seeing an entrance, but when Curtin dismounted, walked left, and disappeared, she had to assume one existed or acknowledge that if Curtin had walked through a solid wall, enough mage-craft had survived in Gateway to justify Marsan's concerns.

"If that's the Trader's Hall . . ." Gearing paused, as a distant, angry voice ran words together into incomprehensible disapproval before stopping abruptly. ". . . we'll find nothing of worth in it even should it be as old as it looks. Everything of value will have been either removed or its provenience destroyed."

The building—a stone rectangle with narrow windows on both the floors she could see—might have been pre–Mage War; its architecture was too basic for her to be sure of age at a distance. The enormous tree between her and the building didn't help. Nor did the loss of light.

Ryan and Captain Yansav moved forward when Curtin emerged. The guardian remained a careful distance from Ryan's obnoxious horse, and appeared to speak to them both—even though everyone but Ryan knew he spoke to the captain. After a moment, the captain beckoned them forward.

Lyelee clutched the wagon seat, practiced now at keeping the initial lurch from toppling her backward. Glancing down, rubbing her ankles together, scratching welts with welts, she realized her feet were so dirty her sandal straps were barely visible. She suspected the rest of her body matched. Cutting her hair off short before they'd left had been a brilliant idea, but the curls had grown long enough to mat together with sweat and dust, tipping her hat to the right. Servan had offered to take a blade to them or roll them into short locs, but she'd watched the guardian shave Destros's head and refused. Her clothing hadn't been properly washed in twenty-eight days and although she hadn't worn her robe since the barrier, it still smelled of sweat. As a Marsan, she was self-aware enough to realize, she'd never been hungry or cold or dirty unless she'd chosen to be, and while she'd most definitely chosen to travel to the Broken Lands— the prologue to the chronicle *she'd* write would include a few more mundane details. Bring twice as much soap. Half as much salt fish. Build inns along the road and staff them with guardians to keep scavengers from the Broken Lands—there was no reason that scholars should have to travel like barbarians.

In the Heir's Chronicle, the Lord Protector noted that he'd been able to bathe in Gateway.

A dribble of sweat rolled down Lyelee's side, the salt burning in an insect bite she'd dug open. She could almost reach out and touch the history she'd spent a lifetime working toward, and having to stop in Gateway to make nice with the natives made a mockery of scholarship.

Her tongue dragged through grit as she wet her lips.

However, if the Traders Hall provided her with the chance to study large amounts of hot water, she'd try and cope with the delay.

RYAN.NOW

Ryan glanced around the courtyard, aware of Lyelee and Gearing arguing about delivery areas and warehousing in the ancient city. He paid little attention to the spill of words. For all those two were always talking, they covered a limited number of topics and always ended up at *Oh woe. So much knowledge lost in the Mage War.*

Although *oh woe* had never actually been said aloud.

The back wall of the courtyard rose two full stories where it attached to the stone buildings and dipped to barely one story in the center. Whoever'd capped the brick against the weather hadn't bothered to even out the damage. The wall had clearly been part of a third building; even in the dusk, Ryan could see where windows had been filled in. Had it fallen during the Mage War, the brick less able to stand against mage-craft than stone, or had it been a newer build that had collapsed on its own, evidence of how Gateway's post-war population had degraded?

The windows in the hall that opened out into the courtyard had shutters, not glass, and the wooden door had been patched into a larger opening. The surviving color suggested it had once been painted a deep yellow-orange.

"They're not exactly attempting to impress the Heir of Marsan, are they?" Keetin murmured, moving up to stand at his left shoulder.

Ryan had been thinking the same thing. Aloud, it sounded significantly less justified than it had inside the confines of his head. "No reason they should. At this point, the Heir of Marsan will be impressed by a bath and a mattress."

"There's a good-sized copper in the hall, my lord."

He flushed as he realized the trader had heard him refer to himself by his title. If the man *were* a spy for the Lord Protector, would he include that trivia in his report? Could he be convinced not to?

"I had them light the fire, so the water should be hot by now. The stable . . ." Gilsin Yeri leapt back as Slate snapped at his outstretched arm.

"Hey, you. Don't be rude." Ryan lightly smacked the big horse's shoulder while backing him away from further temptation. "You startled him," he explained.

Keetin snorted. "You gave the bad-tempered sack of dog meat an excuse," he amended. "I have a scar," he added, before Ryan could protest.

"You don't . . ."

"Half-circle hollow on my shoulder." Keetin patted the body part in question. "The big brute has taken a bite out of everyone in the company but Servan."

"He's exaggerating," Ryan told the trader. "His shoulder was barely bruised. You were about to say?"

Gilsin Yeri shot a narrow-eyed look at Slate and took another step back before answering. "There's plenty of hay, but not much of last year's grain. Use it if you want to, my family won't be returning until after the harvest." He nodded toward the painted door. "Beds are made up, kitchen's been stocked, you should be good for the night. Anything else, we'll deal with tomorrow."

A line of sweat dribbled down Ryan's side. "The weapon . . ."

"Tomorrow," he repeated, as though it were nothing to interrupt the future Lord Protector.

I am the Heir of Marsan, I don't answer to you. Except it seemed he did. He suspected a demand for immediate access to the weapon would lead to a flat refusal, shredding any pretense of authority he might have. Donal wouldn't have stood for it. "And if we want to leave the hall tonight?"

His lips twitched, but Gilsin Yeri's tone remained even. "You're not a prisoner, my lord, but wandering about in the dark would be unwise. Not only are you likely to get lost, but some of the nocturnal shattered fly, and back during the Milk Moon, we lost an archer off the wall."

"*Shattered* is a local reference to a creature from the Broken Lands," Lyelee called from the wagon seat as though Ryan had never read either chronicle. "Was it killed?"

"It was."

"Did you keep the body?"

"It was back in the Milk Moon, Scholar. No," he added hurriedly as Lyelee opened her mouth, proving to Ryan's satisfaction that however long he'd been in Gateway, he remembered how to deal with scholars. "We didn't keep the body."

"Keep the next one." The failing light hid the nuance of Lyelee's expression, but her tone split the difference between thwarted scholar and Ryan's ten-year-old cousin denied an exploratory trip into the Citadel's chimneys. "I want to study it."

"We," Gearing called. "We want to study it."

Lyelee rolled her eyes, the motion so extreme the gathering dusk couldn't hide it. Ryan noticed she replaced impatience with a neutral expression before she turned toward her mentor. "You've never cared about anatomy before."

"The anatomy in question has never originated in the Broken Lands before."

Ryan shook his head as the scholars began debating the descriptions of shattered in the Captain's Chronicle that only marginally matched those in the Heir's. When he noticed Gilsin Yeri watching them, arms folded, brows drawn in, he said, "They're Scholars of the Broken Lands. This is their first chance to do actual research." When arms remained folded and brows down, he added, "They're historians, mostly."

"Dissolving precludes descendants!" Lyelee snapped.

Who or what, Ryan wondered, had been dissolved? He'd clearly missed that particular shattered in his readings.

"Will they be crossing the line with you?" the trader asked over Gearing insisting the chronicles' timelines had been misinterpreted.

Ryan snorted. "We may have to lock their doors tonight to keep them from crossing before us."

"They won't be allowed outside the wall, but please try to convince them it's a bad idea."

"Scholars." Ryan shrugged.

"A very bad idea."

"I'll do what I can."

"All anyone could ask. I leave you to your rest, my lords."

"You're not staying?"

He spread his hands. "The Hall has everything you need and I've a home of my own." With a quick nod in Ryan's direction and a wary eye on Slate, he walked around them and sidled past the wagon that nearly blocked the entrance to the courtyard. He turned right, Ryan noted, taking the road back toward the wall.

"There used to be gates closing the courtyard off," Lyelee called. "The hinges left discoloration on the stone, there . . ." She pointed. "And there. And if you'd get off your collective asses and stable your horses, we'd be that much closer to hot water and beds and a dawn departure."

"Should I be pleased you've noticed my ass?" Keetin preened.

"You should get your ass off your horse," Lyelee replied flatly.

"Come on." Ryan flicked the ends of his reins at Keetin's leg. "The Scholar's Hall has the last word."

The courtyard barely held four horses and a wagon. Had the captain not already hustled the guardians' mounts into the stable, the wagon would still be out on the road. Ryan swung out of the saddle, the soles of his feet buzzing at the impact with the cobblestones even through the soles of his boots. It seemed darker at ground level. He grabbed for Slate's bridle as Destros and Curtin emerged, heading purposefully across the courtyard toward the painted door.

Destros paused long enough to say, "Captain Yansav asks you to wait to enter until we've checked the building, sir."

"I can do that."

Harris followed close behind the two guardians. "I'll examine the food and drink before preparing a light meal."

"Do you expect them to poison us?"

"I was thinking more of checking the available quantities, my lord, but I'll keep the potential for poison in mind."

"Is he serious?" Keetin murmured, pushing up against Ryan's side so as not to be overheard.

"Isn't he always?" Keetin had called Harris "mother" the first three days of the trip. Then he'd been shown the folly of annoying their only retainer. Among other things, Harris did the cooking. Ryan shoved his friend toward the stable doors. "Get moving or I'll take Slate in first."

Slate kicked. And his back end was harder to control than his front.

The stable was as deep as the courtyard, at least twice as wide, and un-expectedly well lit. Half of the space had been divided into ten box stalls, the five against the far wall already occupied. Lattice-work bins filled the other half, bulging with sweet-smelling hay. Slate tried to push toward the familiar scent. Ryan braced himself and pushed back against his chest. "Not yet."

"I wonder what they're burning?" Keetin reached up and poked one of the lanterns, setting it swinging. "That can't be oil, not throwing that much light."

In the nightly arguments around the fire, Lyelee had insisted that the mages, and therefore Gateway, had lights that burned without oil, al-though Ryan couldn't remember reading about their presence in either chronicle or the traders' reports. Lyelee could have settled the matter by reading the relevant passages aloud—the scholars had copies of both chronicles with them—but she'd declared his memory wasn't her prob-lem. Gearing hadn't seemed pleased, although Ryan hadn't been able to determine which of them he'd been displeased with.

"It's oil." Captain Yansav descended a broad flight of stairs that looked too ornate for a stable and were probably left over from what the stable had been *before*. "It's been filtered so it burns cleaner. I don't know how they do it here, but we had clear-burning oils back in Shurlia. Olive mostly. Not usually in the stables," she allowed after a moment. "The upper floor is trade storage. Outgoing currently, mostly fabric, some bales of wool. Given the size of the tables, I expect they divide the incoming goods up there as well. No sign of the weapon."

"Good." The word slipped out before Ryan could stop it.

"Good?"

"Well, it's late, right? I should be rested to deal with it." Ryan hustled Slate into a stall and reached for his cinch.

"Granted." She pulled off her helm and ran a hand over her short, tight curls. "But I wouldn't have been surprised to find it ready. I very much doubt Gateway's council wants us hanging around."

"But . . ."

"Every city has secrets, my lord, and Marsanport is not Gateway's friend."

"The Lord Protector has allowed trade . . ."

"And continues to maintain the barricade. More importantly, with the city this close to the Broken Lands, they won't be happy about us taking the weapon and a vital protection away."

"The Lord Protector said . . ."

"It's been sixty-three years, my lord. With all due respect, he has no idea how Gateway feels about the weapon now. And the traders," she continued before he could raise the point, "are not guardians. Their reports reflect that."

"Do you think there'll be trouble?"

"Of course." She smiled and stepped aside as Lyelee coaxed Dusk over the threshold. "That's my job. Servan drew stable duty. She'll take care of feeding and watering."

"Good. Slate . . ."

"Slate and me are buds, sir," Servan called from the shadows where she pulled a fork-load of hay from one of the bins. "He doesn't bite me, I don't bite him."

The stable door looked as though the hole had originally been smashed through the wall rather than cut. Small pieces of stonework filled the space between the shattered edges of the blocks and the wooden beams.

"Nice work." Keetin patted it as he passed.

"Like you care." Ryan glanced toward the entrance as they crossed the courtyard. In the gathering dusk, the patches of rust looked like bloody shadows on the stone. At least they weren't locked in. Then he remembered the archers on the wall.

Keetin leaned in and bounced off his shoulder. "Trouble?"

He nodded back toward the light. "Where do they get the oil from?"

"Where does anyone get oil? Maybe they grow olives."

"Enough to waste the good stuff in the stables?"

"Maybe they grow a lot of olives."

"They don't have the space."

"Plenty of space outside the wall. Maybe the olives suck up mage-craft and glow in the dark and that's why the lanterns are so bright."

"Shut up." Ryan ran a hand back over his hair, scratching between his short locs. "The Heir's Chronicle includes more about the Broken Lands than about Gateway."

"The Broken Lands are more likely to kill us."

"You don't know that."

"Well, aren't you a flaming bundle of joy." Keetin's hand lay hot between his shoulder blades. "You should be happy we're off that boring-ass road."

He suspected he should. Except . . . "Why do you think there's been a big chunk taken out of the road? It stops just before the gate, then starts up again at the edge of the grass."

"Probably damaged in the war."

"I think the break is deliberate. I think they want to control what comes up the road."

"A theory without evidence is an opinion."

"You sound like Lyelee."

"Now *that* was uncalled for."

Behind the once-yellow door, the entire first floor of the Trader's Hall had been opened up into one large room. Scattered posts supported the beams that held the second floor and a kitchen took up most of one narrow end, divided from the rest of the room by a long table with ten chairs. Stairs drew a diagonal line across the wall facing the kitchen.

Destros knelt by the fireplace in the long wall opposite the door.

"It's high summer," Ryan reminded him. "Do we need a fire outside the kitchen?"

"Securing the chimney, sir."

"From what?"

"From whatever can get down it," the captain informed him, emerging from the door to the right of the kitchen. "Storerooms through here. Facilities beyond that."

"Facilities?" Keetin asked. "Like . . . shitters?"

The captain opened her mouth. Ryan cut her off. "The facilities are inside?"

She stared at him for a long moment, shot Keetin a look that should've had his balls perched on his shoulder, and finally said, "Yes."

Fancy. Even the Citadel used cloisters. He drew in a deep breath, nostrils flaring. Inside, but no stink.

"There's a bathing room as well," Harris announced, emerging through the same door. "The water is hot and I've filled the tub, my lord. You'll have time to bathe before the food is ready."

Ryan could hear Lyelee's voice out in the courtyard. Her half of the familiar cadence rising and falling; Scholar Gearing's responses too low to hear. The scholars would raise the only real opposition to him going first, and if reminding him of the rights of scholarship didn't work, Gearing would play the age card while Lyelee stressed the obligations of family.

Fumbling with the laces of his tabard, he headed for hot water and soap.

"Hey, where are you going?"

He raised a fist and flicked open his fingers, flashing fire over his shoulder at Keetin. "Rank. Privileges."

"Asshole."

"I can live with that."

<hr />

The bathing room held a tub, a tank, a bench, and a high, narrow window filled with a fancy metal grill. His clothes hit the floor in a cloud of dust and he shoved another two pieces of wood into the fire under the refilled tank before sliding into the tub. Eyes closed, he sighed and sagged back against the heated metal, immersed in hot water for the first time in twenty-eight days. The steam smelled of mint.

The water had become opaque and begun to cool when the door opened and Lyelee dropped a pile of cloth on the bench. "Harris borrowed some clothing for us. Get out."

Muscles that had begun to relax tightened again. "Lyelee . . ."

"The water you're soaking in is now cool enough to support visible mold growth. You should see what Scholars of Nature can grow from bath water. Filaments," she added when he tried to ignore her. "Filaments writhing into your body through the opening in the end of your . . ."

"Enough!" He heaved himself up onto his feet, water slopping over the sides onto the slate. "You play dirty when you want something."

"Knowledge is power."

"Good thing you're a scholar," he muttered, reaching in to pull the plug. "You're too flaming mean to be in charge."

She threw him a soft cloth with one hand and dragged her robe over her head with the other. "From your mouth to the Court's ears."

"No, it's simpler than that." At the other end of the table, Servan waved a forkful of egg. "The pump in the corner . . ."

Ryan frowned around a mouthful of dark bread. He didn't remember having seen a pump in the bathing room, but he'd been fixated on the tub of hot water.

". . . brings water in from the well. Pipe from the well to the pump, pipe from the pump to the tank. No one has to go outside with a bucket."

"How do you know so much about pumps?" Keetin asked her, piling another helping of peas and onions onto his plate.

"They installed a system sort of like this in the barracks," Curtin answered as Servan chewed. "Five, maybe six years ago. Traders must've brought the plans back from here." He sounded like he didn't approve.

Keetin, on the other hand, sounded indignant. "You have pumps in the barracks and it's a bucket brigade to fill the tubs in the east wing? How is that fair?"

Destros frowned thoughtfully. "Well, sir, could be 'cause you've got more servants than us."

"And the Gears weren't sure it wasn't going to explode," Servan added.

"Scholars of Mechanics," Gearing muttered, not quite under his breath.

Clean, full of scrambled eggs and fresh vegetables, on an actual mattress however rustic, Ryan expected to fall instantly asleep. He watched the moonlight through the shutters make patterns on the whitewashed ceiling, he picked at the callus the reins had rubbed into his right hand, he heard the Traders Hall grow quiet and the sounds of Gateway devolve to a distant cat fight and a few barking dogs.

Finally, he heard only the leaves rustling outside his window.

He had a room to himself. Keetin had offered to stay, but after so long without a door to close, he'd wanted to be alone. Given the multiple small rooms on the second floor, the traders who made the same journey twice a year felt the same way. The scent of mint dominated the scent of fresh hay rising from the mattress as he thrashed. Right side. Left side.

Maybe he needed a rock in his back.

Or the pungent smell of summer days spent in the saddle.

Or the high whine of insects.

He scratched at an insect bite. Pressed the lump hard enough his fingers dimpled his flesh.

When he closed his eyes, he could see the Black Flame flicker and go out. See the other trading cities on the Great Lake forget the danger the Flame had warned of and mass fleets to attack, drawn by the stories that filled the Broken Lands with forgotten treasures rather than the death and destruction the Five Thousand knew as truth.

They'd sack Marsanport, tear the barricade apart . . .

He almost hit the wall with his feet when he swung his legs off the bed. Fortunately, when he opened the window, the single shutter swung out because both he and the shutter wouldn't have fit in the room.

The moon spilled silver from behind the Hall, but all Ryan could see was the flickering dark/light of the enormous leaves that blocked his view. Windowsill digging into his stomach, he leaned out to pluck one from the tree and froze.

A light shone through a dome at the end of the road.

There was a dome on both the Citadel and the Scholars Hall, but light sure as flame didn't shine through them.

❧

Bare feet silent against worn floorboards, Ryan crept down the stairs and across to the door, stopping and starting to the rhythm of Destros's snoring. A guardian on a pallet by the fireplace had been his security compromise with Captain Yansav, and the big axeman had drawn the short straw.

In the Citadel, the guardian on duty fell into step behind him whenever he left his rooms and stayed there until he went through another door they could stand outside. With his guard unformed, he'd had to use Donal's, and compared to his father's resentment, their reaction that he lived while his brothers were dead had all the substance of smoke.

Opening the yellow door just enough to squeeze through, he closed it softly behind him and headed out to the road. The borrowed clothing, trousers and tunic, had paled with many washings, and he felt like the reverse of a shadow as he stepped away from the building. He glanced toward the gate and realized that making camp on the grass would've been the only way they could have been less inside Gateway while still inside the wall.

To be fair, they *had* smelled of days on the road.

Walking toward the dome, he could hear only the soft pat of his soles against pounded earth. He could smell smoke, and livestock, and mint . . . but the mint might be him.

The road wrapped around the dome, enclosing a small plaza between the circle and the circular building. The area was open, flat, and exposed. No trees. No pillars. Nothing to break up the moonlight. Nothing to hide him from curious eyes. If he crossed to the dome, he'd be seen.

Did it matter?

They hadn't been locked in.

The building might not have looked out of place in the city Gateway had been, but it was too large, too . . . *other* for the remnant remaining. Pale gray walls rose higher than his head, the curves pierced with arches that could have been doors. The dome rose twice that high again, and were it not impossible, he'd say it looked to have been made from a single piece of frosted glass. The lamps within turned the silver moonlight to gold.

"I should go back to bed," he told a small toad watching him from the top of a lichen-covered rock. Or maybe it was just a lichen-covered rock and he'd imagined the toad.

Shoulders squared, chin up, Ryan strode across the open ground to the closest arch.

NONEE.NOW

Nonee didn't think Arianna looked peaceful. Or like she was sleeping. She looked dead. Only the dead lay on a bed of sweetgrass and yarrow, yellow and white purkin flowers over their eyes and their heart and in their hands. Only the dead lay between six pillar candles made of purkin-scented beeswax, guarded by smoke and fire.

For the first time in over sixty years, Nonee couldn't protect her from what might come out of the Broken Lands.

She knelt at Arianna's feet, outside the circle of crushed crystal, maneuvering carefully lest she create an air current and blow out the nearer flames. The Initiates had laid out the body, touched them both with gentle fingers, and left. They understood. For longer than many of the Initiates had been alive, she'd been by Arianna's side. Now she'd keep watch, to see with her own eyes that Arianna would be buried untouched by shadows.

Let the new heir arrive with his wagon.

Let him demand access to the Broken Lands.

He could wait.

He would wait for the next three days.

She'd obey the Last Command when Arianna lay safely in the ground and not a moment before.

RYAN.NOW

Ryan shuffled forward only a body-length before a stone wall stopped his progress and he had to turn either left or right into a dark passage toward distant, identical spills of light.

Left or right?

Did it matter?

Right, then.

Keeping as far from the passage walls as possible, he lifted each foot and set it silently down, heel to toe. Not sneaking about as his brothers had often accused him of; walking carefully.

The light spilled from an arch identical to the one he'd entered by. They'd built a circular wall within a circular wall, the entrances offset. Donal would call it smart defensive positioning. If the building predated the Mage War, what had they been defending against? Ryan stopped short of the light and listened.

Nothing.

Smelled candle smoke.

And mint.

But, again, probably him.

Barely breathing, eyes squinted nearly shut, he stepped forward, and leaned head and right shoulder out past the edge of the inner arch.

The space beneath the dome was a single room. Hanging lanterns, more ornate than those in the stables, hung from narrow metal crossbeams. The light from the lanterns was a familiar soft yellow. Candles surrounded a pile of cut plants on a central dais and on the plants lay a . . .

A body?

Someone sleeping?

A mannequin?

A sacrifice?

He couldn't tell. Neither the Captain's Chronicle nor the Heir's Chronicle nor the Lord Protector himself had detailed what the inhabitants of Gateway worshipped or how they worshipped it. The Five Thousand had given up faith when their world had burned.

A woman knelt at the far end of the plants, head bowed. She wore a pale yellow shift, and a pale green headscarf, and the difference in size between her and what he could see of the body made him think the body had to be a child, or a mannequin of a child, the proportions were so off.

The skin on her heavy, muscular arms looked gray.

Ryan opened his eyes wider as they adjusted to the light.

Still looked gray.

He recognized the curve of her neck and the line of her shoulders. His father had held the same position, had fought the same battle against collapse, as his brothers' biers passed. She grieved. Perhaps the body had been her child.

He couldn't see her face.

The hand against his chest shocked him into a sudden breath. He choked on spit, and found himself pushed gently back into the passageway as he coughed.

"This isn't for you," a woman said softly when he finally quieted.

She was almost as dark as the captain; not as tall, much wider. Her body flowed from one curve to the next and her hair had been twisted into multiple small puffs. Ryan noticed her hair only because he was staring past it, staring into the room under the dome. The angle lined up his view of the woman standing in front of him with the woman kneeling. The proportions were still off. But now he knew why.

"This isn't for you," the woman in front of him repeated, speaking slowly and carefully to be sure he'd understand. Her hand pressed harder against his chest, her palm a warm brand, her fingertips individual points of pressure.

He wondered if she could feel his heart pounding. Faster. Harder. This *was* for him, in a way. He swept his tongue over dry lips. "What's happening?"

"She guards her dead against shadow taking control."

"Shadow?"

"In from the Broken Lands."

"Taking control?"

"Of the body. Of her dead."

"That happens?"

"It has. We'd rather it never happened again so we guard against it." Her voice was kind, but firm, as though she spoke to a child. "Go back to the Traders Hall, Ryan, Heir of Marsan."

She knew who he was.

Of course she knew who he was. He'd announced it at the gate, and the absence of crowds didn't mean an absence of gossip.

The pressure of her hand pushed him back a step, and then another. He looked down at her face as he lost sight of the interior of the dome. He was at the arch, then the plaza before he could find words. It seemed to take less time going backward than it had going forward.

She met his gaze in the moonlight. "If you hear what sounds like wet sheets blowing in the wind, lie flat. It makes it harder for them to catch hold."

Was she kidding? She didn't sound like she was kidding. "I need to speak with . . ."

"Three days." And she was gone.

He turned and looked along the moonlit road and realized he had no idea how wet sheets blowing in the wind sounded.

LYELEE.NOW

Lyelee's dreams had been filled with voices calling her from the Broken Lands where gold and crystal towers rose to touch the sky and history lay spread out for the taking. Books and art and shattered wonders that she knew she could rebuild if she only had the time.

The feeling of frustration, of time running out, lingered and grew stronger when she realized she was almost the last to rise and Harris hadn't finished preparing breakfast.

"Eggs and ham and biscuits," he said when she asked. "As well as fresh vegetables, fruit, and cheese. Gateway has been very generous."

She picked up a small piece of cheese, sniffed it and put it down again. "What do they want for that generosity?"

"They haven't said."

"Scholar."

He looked up from his kneading, brows raised.

Lyelee sighed. "We're no longer on the road. We need to be precise in speech so the people of Gateway avoid bad habits based on observed familiarity."

The corners of his mouth twitched, but he folded and rolled the dough twice before replying. "They haven't said, *Scholar*."

She approved of him taking the time to think. However . . . "Sarcasm, Harris?"

"To a scholar?"

Not an answer. Weighing the formal respect due scholarship against a delay in acquiring breakfast, Lyelee poured tea from the familiar metal pot into an unfamiliar heavy clay mug and stepped out into the courtyard. Tucked up against the rear wall, Captain Yansav was tearing a strip off the Heir of Marsan.

". . . and ignoring Gilsin Yeri's warning of potential attacks."

"I didn't ignore the warning." Ryan had his arms crossed and his mouth flattened into his *stop picking on me* expression. "I took it into account."

"That is, if anything, worse, Lord Marsan-cer."

"No, it's not."

Lyelee rolled her eyes. If he continued defaulting to childhood responses, he'd be as much of a flaming tragedy when he became Lord Protector as her mother'd predicted. "What did you do, Ryan?"

"That is not your concern, Scholar." The captain met her gaze and held it.

"I wasn't speaking to you, Captain." Lyelee smiled. "Ryan?"

"It's nothing, Lyelee."

"I'm a scholar. I seek knowledge."

He shook his head and echoed the captain. "It's none of your concern."

Back in Marsanport, he'd have told her. Back in Marsanport, the captain wouldn't have dared keep knowledge from her. Another example of how travel with such a small company had worn away deference due—but with Captain Yansav in a mood, it was best to let it go. The captain hadn't been raised in Marsanport and that raising had negatively influenced both attitude and actions toward scholarship. Lyelee swept her best disapproving gaze over the two of them and continued to the stable.

"The Heir went for a walk last night."

She turned to see Curtin sitting on the stairs, left hand pressing a wet rag to his right arm.

"All the way to that domed building at the end of the road," he added.

"Curtin!" One hand rubbing up under her gelding's mane, Servan glared across the stable.

He lifted the cloth and peered beneath it. "You answer scholars when they ask a question."

"She didn't ask *you* a question."

They were both right.

With perspective on the captain's anger, Lyelee vowed that the first chance she got, she'd smack her cousin to remind him of his responsibilities. If he died and she ended up carrying the fuel for the Black Flame out of the Broken Lands, she'd have to fight both family and council to remain out of the succession. Her uncle and her mother might have assumed she had her eye on the Protectorship when she'd maneuvered them into supporting the Hall's bid to accompany the heir to the Broken Lands, but Lyelee considered their political ambitions to be slightly ridiculous. Useful, but ridiculous, and nothing to do with her.

Political power was ephemeral compared to the power she could gain uncovering the history of the Broken Lands.

The mages had respected knowledge.

She took a sip of tea and changed the subject. "Did you pull double stable duty, Servan?"

"Not exactly. Slate took a bite out of Curtin this morning, so . . ." Servan spread her hands and laughed when Akart lipped at her hair, protesting the sudden cessation of attention.

Slate had bitten everyone. Lyelee's head still ached where he'd pulled a clump of hair out and she'd have turned him to dog meat had that hair not grown back. Running through the available information again, she found a piece missing. "Servan, has Slate ever bitten you?"

"No. Animals like me. Always have."

"Always?"

"Pretty much."

Lyelee had assumed Servan had exaggerated when telling stories of the cat who hated everyone but her. Glancing over at Slate, who curled his lip, exposing slabs of yellow teeth, she was no longer so sure.

"My mam used to say some folk just smell right." Servan returned to scratching Akart's neck. "And he might just remember I gave him my last piece of honey bread. Where are you off to so early, Scholar?"

"I'm going to look around upstairs." There was a chance, albeit a small one, that historical significance had escaped renovation on the trading floor. "Is there a problem?" she demanded when Servan frowned.

"Sorry, Scholar, but Cap says no one goes up. She doesn't want us blamed if something of value goes missing."

"Think she meant us, not the scholar," Curtin grunted, heaving himself up off the step.

Servan shrugged. "She said everyone."

Lyelee weighed the odds of anything worthwhile remaining on the second floor against having to defend her actions to Captain Yansav, who had taken the scholars' agreement to defer to her in dangerous situations to mean she could apply inconsequential rules. Lyelee'd had to argue the point countless times on the road and, quite frankly, she was tired of it. Not to mention that the captain was already in a bad mood. She took another sip of tea. "Any sign of the weapon?"

"Not yet, Scholar."

Flame forbid Ryan actually attempt to command compliance with their needs. An opportunity to examine the weapon before her attention became focused solely on the Broken Lands would be invaluable. Had sixty-three years in Gateway damaged it in any way? Had proximity to the Broken Lands made it more or less efficient? She'd reviewed all the information available in the Scholar's Archive—including a very dry and badly thought-out dissertation on what its existence said about the mage who'd created it—had sifted through the speculation of her companions on the road, and now needed to perform comparison studies.

It seemed, thanks to Ryan's poor grasp of what being the Heir of Marsan involved, she'd have to split her focus and do those studies as they traveled.

With both the trading floor and the weapon unavailable, she glanced toward the rear of the stable. "The trader said there was a turn-out. Have you checked it?"

"Not yet." Servan's shoulders relaxed. "Wasn't sure when it'd be safe."

"The sun's up. I'll have a look."

"Thanks, Scholar."

Thanks for not arguing. Thanks for not heading up the stairs and forcing the guardian to choose between the rights of scholarship and the captain's orders. It took so little to keep people amenable, and amenable people were significantly more useful.

Lyelee pushed the back door open far enough to slide through, and stepped outside.

The sun hadn't risen high enough to have burned off the dawn palette, and the air remained comfortably cool. Although her observations so far this morning suggested they'd still be here wasting time when the temperature began to rise.

The corral had been constructed inside the ruins of the building that had once extended from the back wall of the courtyard. Sturdy rail fencing filled in the two and a half sides where the walls had entirely collapsed. An enormous tree on the far side of the southern wall provided shade, and water filled a stone trough by the stable wall. Eroded corners suggested the trough was old, but Lyelee'd seen similar troughs in Marsanport. Its historical significance was minimal.

She squatted to examine the lower, less exposed stones in the south wall. These stones had been here before the Mage War. These stones had survived the Mage War. This was history. She rubbed a finger over the discoloration, licked it—after a hundred and sixty-three years, it tasted of finger—and then rubbed the damp skin over the same area to no effect. Using what remained of her fingernails, she scraped up a bit of the surface.

"If stone could talk . . ."

Based on the small amount they knew the mages were capable of, the mages might have been able to make stone talk—if not participate in an actual conversation, at least surrender its secrets. "Think of what scholarship could expose if that was an option," she muttered. How had they done it? What else had they been able to do? How much had been lost?

"Dasa falere fuputard."

By the time she'd risen and turned, wiping stone dust off her fingers onto borrowed trousers, she'd pried the words apart.

"Da says it'll fall over if you push too hard."

The three children on the other side of the fence had skin ranging in shades from Ryan's to Servan's—nothing as dark as the captain nor as pale as Keetin. Unfortunately, with so small a sample size, it was impossible to determine if the extremes had been bred out of a small, static population. All three were barefoot, wearing sleeveless tunics belted with a strip of cloth. Hems flapped around dirty knees. Frayed edges and patches indicated either a lower economic level than Darny had shown, or parents who recognized how destructive young children could be and dressed them accordingly. The clothing was too simple to be historically relevant.

All three stared at her with wide, brown eyes.

Lyelee sighed and made the first move. "Hello."

The child with the long, dark braid yanked the smallest child back and made a garbled announcement.

Lyelee understood two words—*not* and *you*. Although *you* sounded more like *yee*. She raised a hand then lowered it, palm toward the ground. "Speak slowly."

"*Slur* not *slur* to talk to you."

"Once more."

The braided child rolled their eyes. "Wore nog alloo ta take ta yee."

But Lyelee now had sufficient samples to work her way around the accent. They weren't allowed to talk to her. "Are you allowed to be here at all?"

They exchanged glances, then the braided child said, "No."

"Then you might as well talk to me if you're going to be in trouble anyway."

After a moment, all three nodded. Scholars, past and present, agreed that children responded to logic better than many adults.

"Are you here to take Nonee?" the braided child asked.

"Nonee?" This was the first Lyelee had heard the name. Was Gateway intending to supply a guide?

"She said you'd come."

"The olders watch for you." The palest of the three told her. "Out there." A grubby finger pointed toward the wall. "We're not old enough."

The braided child picked at a scab on the back of their hand.

"Open it and you open the way for infection," Lyelee warned. "Is Nonee in charge?" she added when the child flicked the scab away and sucked at the wound.

"No." The smallest child shook curls cut as short as Lyelee's own. "Auntie Raych."

"Your Auntie Raych is in charge?"

"Uh huh. Till frost. But Nonee's best!" The smallest child clambered up to sit on the top rail of the fence. "She brung all the stones for our house from houses what fell down."

"She brought the pole for the hall out of the forest."

"She found three lost sheep who were almost at the line and fought off a grr to bring them home." Dark brows drew in. "One died. My da made sausages."

The braided child wiped their nose with a bit of tunic and said, "She tells the best stories."

More nodding from the smallest. "The flying pig!"

If it was the story of the flying pig from the Captain's Chronicle—and how many flying pigs could there be—Lyelee suspected Nonee had not told these children the ending. The pig had exploded. On the other hand, they didn't seem too upset about the loss of the sheep, so maybe she had. Lyelee made a mental note to find this Nonee and see if she knew *why* the pig had exploded. Neither the chronicles nor the Archives had included what was inarguably an important detail. "What's a grr?"

"You know." The braided child raised both hands to shoulder height and curled them into claws. "Grr."

"A type of shattered?"

"Yeah." The child wore a look as scornful as any elderly scholar. "A grr."

"If Nonee saved the sheep from a grr, does she go into the Broken Lands?" A positive response would support the theory that Nonee was intended to be their guide. Ryan needed all the help he could get.

"She goes all the time."

"You don't know that, Jisper!"

"Do."

"Don't. You only know she goes outside the wall. Lot of people go outside the wall!"

The braided child sighed again and gave both companions a silencing shove. "Can we pet your horses when they come out? The traders let us pet their horses."

"We won't be here long enough to turn them out."

All three arranged their faces in exaggerated expressions of disappointment.

"Scholar!"

Lyelee turned to see Servan leaning out the stable door.

"Food's ready."

The two children still on the ground rose up onto their toes as though standing a fraction higher would help their eyesight.

"Is that your mam calling?" the smallest child—Jisper—asked.

"No." She thought of her mother with her rosewater and unguents and political ambition being mistaken for a common guardian and grinned. "I need to go."

"You in trouble?"

"No. But if I'm late, I won't get any breakfast."

They nodded in unison. That was a consequence they understood.

❧

"Three days?" Standing by the empty fireplace, Lyelee glared at Gilsin Yeri-cer. "We're to stay here for three days? No. That's unacceptable."

Yeri-cer glanced over at her, then turned his attention back to Ryan, still seated behind the table, fiddling with a broken bit of biscuit. "Our eldest healer has died, and we mourn."

"That has nothing to do with us. Trader!" Lyelee snapped the word out like a whip. When scholars spoke they were *not* ignored and Yeri-cer knew that. He hadn't been gone from Marsanport long enough to forget. "Are we being held prisoner here?"

He turned reluctantly, but he turned. "No, of course not, Scholar. You can leave whenever you want."

"Even to the Broken Lands?"

"Yes, but . . ."

Ryan cut him off. "But the weapon mourns as well."

"Mourns?" Lyelee glanced around the room. Captain Yansav maintained her professional, blank mask, but Keetin's brows were up. Gearing looked as incredulous as she felt. A clang of pans in the kitchen broke the silence and she shot a glare at Harris. Ryan had sounded as if he *understood*. "The weapon mourns? For the healer? Are you aware of how ridiculous that sounds?"

Yeri-cer met her gaze with a directness he had to have learned in Gateway. No one in Marsanport would challenge a scholar so blatantly. "And yet, she mourns. For the next three days, she guards against the shadows."

"The weapon guards against the shadows?"

"Yes, Scholar."

"Shadows from the Broken Lands?"

"Yes, Scholar."

Lingering mage-craft, Lyelee realized. Making the best of a bad situation, she reached into her satchel for her notebook. "Describe them."

"The shadows?"

"Yes."

He shook his head. "I've never seen them."

"Has anyone? Have they an actual physical presence?"

"Lyelee."

"What?" She turned far enough to glare at her cousin.

"The shadows have a physical presence."

"And did you learn this during your nocturnal wandering?"

"You don't put that much destructive force into . . ." Ryan tipped his chair back and waved, as though he could pluck the words from the air. "Into guarding against nothing."

"That's what religion is," Gearing pointed out calmly. "Nothing. And how much destructive force has been wrapped about religion over the years?"

"Plenty," Keetin answered.

Gearing nodded approval. "Exactly."

Lyelee seethed. How could he be so calm? They were Scholars of the Broken Lands and they were being denied entrance to the Broken Lands. "Go to the weapon and tell it . . ."

"Her." The front legs of Ryan's chair thudded to the floor.

"What?"

"Not it, her."

"It's a weapon. The last great mage weapon."

"She's the last great mage weapon."

"The chronicles . . ."

"I don't care what the chronicles say. She's not a thing."

He was clearly going to be obstinate about it, but Lyelee had a more important point to argue. "Fine. Her. Go to *her* and tell *her* that we leave immediately. If necessary, use the Last Command."

"Command her to stop mourning her dead?"

Lyelee rolled her eyes. "She's a weapon. *Her* purpose is death."

He rolled a bit of biscuit between thumb and forefinger, his gaze unfocused. "That doesn't negate her grief."

He was thinking about his brothers. Lyelee couldn't understand why; they'd never liked him and their deaths had catapulted him into responsibilities he had neither training nor aptitude for. Logically, he should resent them. Unfortunately, when he retreated to their memory, there was no point in arguing. "Then we leave without the weapon. You can command *her* to catch up."

"Leave without the weapon . . ." Yeri-cer stepped forward, the movement drawing Ryan's attention. ". . . and after the three days of mourning, she'll retrieve your bodies from the Broken Lands."

"We're not entirely defenseless," Ryan snapped, pulled out of memory by pride.

Lyelee hid a smile. The trader couldn't have made a better argument in her favor if he'd tried.

Yeri-cer's brows drew in. "Due respect, my lord, but you have no idea of what to defend against."

Ryan shook his head. "The Black Flame has flickered. We can't wait."

Excellent. Lyelee headed for the stairs.

"If you leave without the weapon, you'll die."

She paused, and turned back toward the others at the certainty in Gilsin Yeri-cer's voice.

The trader stepped closer to the table and leaned in, as though he spoke to Ryan alone. "She won't leave for three days. You need to wait."

Lyelee waited for Ryan to tell him where he could stuff his three flaming days.

Ryan, surprising no one, refused to show backbone. He sighed and said, "Then we wait."

"I do not agree to this," Lyelee snarled, heading back to the table. "You're deliberately delaying scholarship."

"Then study the burial practices of Gateway."

"I am a Scholar of the Broken Lands!"

"Then maybe you should broaden your focus." Ryan dragged his hands back through his hair. "If we *all* die, we can't bring the fuel back to Marsanport."

She wondered at his emphasis on the obvious, discarded it as unimportant, and jabbed a finger toward him. "Then if I have to waste my time, I want access to the tenement in the west, near the wall."

"You want to study the warren?" Yeri-cer asked after a moment. "How do you . . . ?"

"I'm a scholar, Trader. I make it a point to be aware of my surroundings." There was something there, she knew it.

He spread his hands. "The warren is abandoned. It's been empty for years. I don't know if it's structurally safe and . . ."

"We can determine that ourselves," Gearing interrupted. He closed both hands around the strap of his satchel, folding the leather. "If we must delay, and it seems we must, we'll use the time to secure knowledge."

For all the years he'd been in Gateway, Gilsin Yeri-cer had been raised in Marsanport. His shoulders slumped. "As you wish, Scholar Gearing. I'll find you a guide."

Gearing shook his head. "No. A guide will distort research with *common knowledge.*"

"Unfortunately, the warren is . . ."

"If we must have a guide . . ." Lyelee cut him off, unwilling to waste yet more time on pointless arguments. ". . . then Darny will do. Early teens, thin, straight dark hair cut short, medium complexion. Chickens dislike him. I spoke with him yesterday," she added. "On the way in from the gate."

"He's young enough to obey instruction," Gearing contributed. When Lyelee glanced over at her mentor, he shot her a look of bland agreement that covered both the boy and the pointlessness of arguing with a mere trader.

"While you're arranging for Darny," Ryan pushed his chair away from the table and stood, "I'd appreciate it if you could find a second guide. I'd like to take look at the Broken Lands. From the wall," he added, before anyone could protest. "Unless your council wants to speak with us this morning?"

"Given they have the time, they thought tomorrow would be best, my lord."

They want to take your measure first.

It was some of the loudest subtext Lyelee had ever heard. Did Gateway's council think scholars wouldn't realize what they were doing? She folded her arms and barely kept from tapping her foot as Yeri-cer thought things through. "As Darny has already spoken with you," he said at last, "there should be no problem having him accompany the scholars. As for the Broken Lands, my lord, I'll escort you to the wall."

Because we want to minimize your contact with our people.

Ryan had the analytical abilities of a gnat, but Captain Yansav's expression suggested she'd also heard what Trader Yeri-cer was saying and wasn't happy about it.

Isolationist cultures always had a reason—historical if not current. Lyelee knew it could be as subconscious as *we don't want you to lead another five thousand away* or as immediate as *we're hiding something.* The weapon must have a certain amount of control over Gateway if they'd risk three days of potential contamination until it . . . she was willing to leave.

RYAN.NOW

Ryan listened to the sound of Darny explaining an unlikely shortcut fade into the distance, and thought the boy might actually be up to spending the day with two scholars. He was smiling at the thought of Lyelee having to answer a thousand questions for a change when Gilsin Yeri-cer stepped out onto the road.

Yeri, Ryan corrected his mental voice. *Call him Yeri, as you call the guardians by their family names. Even if he is the Lord Protector's spy, he has no more rank than they do. And using his full name, even only inside your head, is ridiculous.*

"Whenever you're ready, my lord." Wire woven into his beard glinted in the sunlight.

Donal had worn jewelry in his beard. Only a single pearl had remained when they pulled his body from the water.

Ryan had taken a blade to his beard upon rising, shaving off the messy edges he'd allowed to grow in on the road, his skin dark enough the difference in color where the sun had been blocked barely showed. He trimmed back the remainder until it covered just his upper lip and chin, forgetting it was a style portraits showed the Lord Protector had favored in his youth until Keetin reminded him.

"My lord?"

He fell in at the trader's right, willing to be escorted, not led. Keetin and Captain Yansav fell in behind. The Mage Road was wide enough they could've walked abreast an arm's length apart, but, in spite of a lack of obvious threat, he felt more comfortable with the captain at his back. Not guarding necessarily; just *there*.

In the dark, focused on the dome, he'd missed the small, empty spaces where city land had been repurposed. From one of those spaces, a trio of shaggy, red, long-horned cows watched them pass. Just beyond the cattle, three adults leaned on a fence and watched them with the same intensity. Wearing his own tunic and tabard, the seams still damp, but both pieces miraculously cleaned, there could be no doubt of who he was. He didn't want them to doubt who he was. He didn't *think* he wanted them to doubt who he was.

"Not much of the original city left in these parts," Yeri told him, following his gaze and misinterpreting his expression. "Little use for the surviving buildings, so they came down. Got repurposed. The few remaining get used for storage, salvage mostly, though some hold goods, waiting for trade to pick up."

"Trade goes through Marsanport," Ryan reminded him before he realized how pompous that must sound. It was truth, though. The Mage Road ended at Marsanport and there was only one road.

Yeri waved a hand and Ryan stiffened at having his point dismissed. "Someday, the Lord Protector may open the road."

"Marsan has excellent trade relations all around the Great Lake," Keetin pointed out. "Why would we expand toward the horror stories of our past?"

"Things change," Yeri said, and glanced at Ryan.

A dribble of sweat ran down Ryan's temple although the day wasn't particularly hot. He wasn't Lord Protector yet. He wouldn't ever be if he didn't return with fuel for the Black Flame. And lately, he'd experienced as much change as he wanted to cope with.

A black pig ran across the road followed by a trio of shouting children.

The last building before the dome had folded open the walls facing the road and the plaza, exposing six weavers, four non-weaving adults, and assorted children inside. The three looms were the largest Ryan had ever seen. Granted, his exposure to looms had been limited, but the size certainly explained why fabric was Gateway's most popular export.

How did the looms not shake apart?

He wondered if he could convince Lyelee to study a little of the present. Doubtful.

When he was Lord Protector, he'd send a couple of Gears north with the traders and then find a way to convince them to share the knowledge found.

They passed unnoticed until a toddler pointed, shouted, and raced toward them. Ryan smiled, turned to face the child, and found himself facing Yeri instead. His cheeks heated as an old woman caught and dragged the excited child back.

The steady beat of the looms stopped.

"Trader?" The old woman stood at the exposed edge of the floor.

"We're to the wall," Yeri called back, speaking so quickly Ryan struggled to understand. "The heir wants a look at the Broken Lands."

He understand none of the old woman's answer. The laughter, though, that sounded like the laughter he'd heard all his life.

The looms began to beat again.

Using the memory of laughter as a counterpoint, Ryan fought to keep from matching his stride to the rhythm. "What if I wanted to speak to the weavers?"

"Do you?"

No. He had nothing to say to weavers. "That's not the point."

"They're working. From their perspective, the Heir of Marsan has nothing to say that's more important than making the cloth that'll keep us warm this winter. Or be used in trade for anchovies in oil."

Ryan thought of pressing the point, but couldn't chance the weavers not wanting to speak with him. He didn't return Yeri's grin. He wasn't sure what Yeri was grinning about.

Three black-faced sheep, recently sheared, cropped the grass around the dome. In daylight, Ryan could see the stone walls were made of vertical blocks, his height or a little taller, as smooth as the marble flooring the Lord Protector's father had imported from Triess.

If the scholars had wanted to study a pre–Mage War building, there was one a lot closer to the Trader's Hall than the tenements.

Of course, they hadn't known.

And he hadn't mentioned it.

Keetin moved up to Yeri's other side. "This is where Ryan wandered off to, right? Where the weapon is? Can we go in and get a look?"

"She's guarding her dead," Ryan said before Yeri could.

"So looking . . ."

"No."

"Okay." Keetin waved at the dome. "That roof? That's flaming impressive. Is this a temple? It looks like a temple. I saw temples in Midlake," he added before Ryan could ask how he knew what a temple looked like. Marsan had scholars, not priests.

"Yes," Yeri told him. "It's a temple."

"Thought so. What do you lot worship up here?"

"Lord Norwin-cee."

Ryan flinched, although Captain Yansav's reprimand hadn't been directed at him.

Yeri raised a hand. "No insult, Captain." Just when it seemed that was all he had to say, he answered the question. "Most of Gateway's beliefs come from before the Mage War."

"From before the Mage War?" Keetin lengthened his stride again, until he could turn and walk backward, pinning Yeri with a laughing gaze. "Belief in an invisible, unquantifiable power didn't protect those believers when the mages cut loose."

"Maybe not," the trader allowed. "But it was the survivors who continued to believe."

Behind them, the captain snorted, amused, as Keetin protested. "They thought their belief saved them? You can't prove cause and effect."

"Are you sure? No one's tried."

"Fair enough." He stumbled, recovered, and continued walking backward. "And your bonded? She . . ." He raised a brow and continued when Yeri nodded. "She's descended from those survivors; what does she believe? And do you believe it with her?"

"Kee!"

"He said no insult."

Ryan frowned. "I don't care. You sound like Lyelee."

"Again?" Keetin fell back into step on Yeri's left. "I'd be insulted, but, you know, I could've been a scholar."

"If that's true, my lord, then standards have fallen since I left Marsanport."

Hand over his heart, Keetin stumbled again, dramatically declaring, "I am slain."

Ryan pasted on a meaningless smile as they laughed.

The dome defined the edge of the southeast section of Gateway, not the center of the entire enclosure as Ryan had assumed. By the time they reached the fountain in the center of a small, circular market, the sun had risen significantly higher above the horizon and they all needed to stop for a drink.

"They like circles," Keetin observed.

"Harder to spring a trap in a circle," the captain murmured, moving closer.

It hadn't been a wealthy neighborhood before the fall, the buildings were too small and too close together, but neither had it been a poor neighborhood. Had there even been poor neighborhoods in Gateway before the fall? Ryan hated to admit it, but Lyelee was right about the amount of knowledge lost.

He wasn't as sure about her desire to reclaim all of it.

Neither buyers nor sellers came closer. No one yelled questions. Or comments. Or insults. They weren't overtly ignored, but neither were they acknowledged. He could see babies and toddlers, but no children. Were the children at lessons, or had they been hidden? And if they were at lessons, who taught them when Gateway had no scholars?

The sparse, graceful lines of the original fountain had been nearly entirely obscured by clumsily ornate restructuring and Ryan thanked the flame that Lyelee wasn't with them. She had *opinions* on modern abominations replacing historical landmarks. Lifting one of the metal mugs chained around the fountain's outer edge, he bent over the middle tier, and found himself staring at a carved squid, arms appearing to writhe with the movement of the water. Each arm wore a light coat of fuzzy green that matched the tint of the liquid. Considering the heat of the season, Ryan had seen worse. But why squid? No squid larger than his palm had ever been seen further north than Midlake. Fisherfolk netted them, dried them, and sold them up-lake. They'd had a packet in the wagon when they left Marsanport.

As he drank, he could see the leg and elbow of a woman on the other side of the fountain. Could hear her in conversation with another. Could hear them greet a third as he stepped aside so Captain Yansav could drink. Most of the words flew past too quickly for him to catch, but an accusation ending in ". . . yesterday!" and an indignant rather than apologetic response suggested the third had arrived a day late through no fault of her own. When the captain finished, he wiped the sweat off his forehead, and stepped in to pick up the cup again.

The water was clear. And cold.

Clear enough to see the individual suckers carved onto one arm of the squid. Cold enough his teeth ached.

He spat the mouthful out.

"Bug?" Keetin asked.

Ryan locked eyes with Yeri. Watched the trader scoop out another cupful of water and drain it, movements deliberate. Was suddenly conscious of the weight of eyes watching *him* from all around the market.

Donal would have demanded answers.

Replacing the mug, Ryan circled the fountain, stopped and stared at the three women filling containers at a spout protruding from the open mouth of a stone lizard-thing. The tallest of the women had leaves tattooed around her arm, sweat making the skin beneath them gleam like brushed copper. She met his gaze and raised a brow. The eldest, gray curls cut close to her skull, exchanged an empty container for a full one, her expression making it clear she had no intention of interrupting her work for him. The third woman had a cloth bag hanging from her shoulder, one hand pressed protectively over the bulge made by its contents.

"Ry?" Keetin stopped by his side, smiled, and bowed extravagantly. "Well met. If the Heir of Marsan has offered to help," he continued as he straightened, "I add my offer to his."

The background noise of the market dropped off until the sound of the fountain filled the space where it had been.

The tallest and the one with the bag exchanged a look, then the tallest sighed. "We've no need of help." She spoke so slowly, consideration nudged at insult. "But thank you."

"If you're sure." Still smiling, Keetin bowed again and turned to go.

The tallest cocked her head at Ryan in a silent, *well?*

Ryan glanced around the market and half a dozen heads turned away. No one was watching, but everyone was paying attention. He opened his mouth, closed it again, and shrugged.

The eldest might have clucked her tongue.

It might have been a chicken, he wasn't sure.

Passing between a building with colored glass windows and the welcome shade of a large, broad-leafed tree, Ryan wanted to ask about the water. To ask how it had grown cleaner and colder after the third woman had arrived.

He didn't want to be lied to, so instead he asked, "Why have people been told to keep away from us?"

Yeri snorted. "They haven't been."

So much for not being lied to. "Evidence suggests otherwise."

Keetin snorted. "Now you sound like Lyelee."

"Keetin."

"Shutting up."

Yeri sighed. "They're afraid you've come to take Nonee away, so they're keeping their distance."

"Nonee?"

"You call her the weapon."

"The weapon has a name?" She had no name in either the Captain's Chronicle or the Heir's. But then, she'd been referred to as *it* in both.

"Most legendary weapons have names," Captain Yansav said dryly.

They walked in silence while a woman with a scythe over her shoulder and a black and white dog at her heels passed as far from them as the width of the road allowed. The dog glanced over. The woman didn't.

Nonee. Ryan repeated it silently. She had a name. Of course she had a name. "Tell me about her."

Yeri exhaled audibly. "I am of Gateway now, my lord. You don't command here."

You don't.

You aren't.

You can't.

His brothers' voices.

Aware the trader hadn't objected to the question, only to his manner, he considered asking rather than commanding. He didn't.

"What do those mark?" Keetin broke the uncomfortable silence, pointing toward a trio of metal stakes in among shorn sheep grazing in the grassy band between the last building and the wall.

Yeri glanced toward them. "I've been told that's as far in as the worms got."

"Worms?"

"Worms. About as big around as your thigh." He cupped an impressive circle of air between his hands.

Keetin turned to stare, brows nearly at his hairline. "Is that why you told us to stay on the road?"

"Because of the worms?" The trader snorted. "Nonee dealt with them years ago, when my bonded was a child."

It might have been an invitation to speak of the weapon. Captain Yansav clearly thought so, given her expression when Ryan refused it. "Why did they stay?" he asked instead. "The survivors. The city was in ruins. Why not leave with the Five Thousand?"

"Why should they leave? Broken though it may have been, this was their home."

"Worms as big around as my thigh," Keetin reminded him.

Yeri shrugged. "Not until years later."

This was their home. Isolated. Damaged. Ryan watched two small children chase a lamb back toward its mother. More, he thought, for the pleasure of chasing it than because it had gone where it shouldn't. He caught Yeri's gaze. "Why did you stay? Why not bring your bonded back to Marsanport?"

"She wouldn't have been happy there. This is *her* home. And I," he added as they reached the wall, "am happy where she is. The Broken Gate, my lord."

Ryan wouldn't call it a gate, more a door. It was no wider than the spread of Destros's shoulders and three metal bars in heavy brackets secured the banded wood. Had additional defenses been added after the worms? he wondered. No, that was stupid. Worms wouldn't use a gate.

On either side, protruding, diagonal stonework acted as stairs. The top of the wall had chest-high crenellations. Three corked, green-glass bottles of water had been tucked into a triangle of shadow. A fourth, empty, lay on its side in the sun.

"The archers keep moving." Yeri nodded toward the two walking away to the right, bows in their hands. "No point in tempting any of the shattered that've come in close."

"They cross the line?"

"Some live between us and the line."

"Are you saying that creatures shattered by the Mage War live between the Broken Line and Gateway?" Ryan didn't much like the way his voice rose at the end, but he continued, "If the shattered live beyond the line, what's to keep them from spreading over the entire world?"

"According to Nonee, the shattered have to live close to the Broken Lands. It sustains them somehow."

Grinning, Keetin shook his head. "Considering that your Nonee spent over a hundred years in Marsanport, that's not as reassuring as you think."

"Nonee is the last great mage weapon," Ryan reminded him. "She wasn't shattered, she was built."

Keetin gestured expansively toward Yeri. "So you're on his side now?"

"Do *we*, like the archers, need to keep moving?" The captain's tone added, *If so, why are we standing still?*

"We're safe enough." Yuri moved closer to the exterior of the wall. "This is the most direct view."

Distinct enough to indicate fairly frequent use, a path wound away from the wall, crossed a bit of grazed land, and cut through a tangle of briars. Beyond the briars were ruins, impressive if only for the amount of land each squatted in. The wealthy had lived in this part of Gateway. Ryan could see his family home, down-lake from Marsanport, in the destruction. There, the base of a tower almost entirely dismantled. There, the stumps of trees recently cut and already showing new growth. There a pile of rubble so huge and so covered in vines it looked at first glance to be a hill. There a probable carriage house, the blocks of stone melted into grotesque shapes.

Melted stone. A visible effect of the Mage War. Lyelee would have gone over the wall.

Looking beyond the ruins, Ryan could see trees in full summer foliage, the darker shades of evergreens, and the land rising toward the mountains. The Heir's Chronicle placed the Broken Line less than a day's travel away. If he looked toward the line or the Broken Lands beyond, they weren't obvious. Shouldn't the scars of a Mage War that melted stone be obvious?

"It doesn't look so bad," he said as he turned.

"No, it doesn't," Yeri agreed.

"Have you been to the line?"

Yeri looked past Ryan's shoulder. "No. Got a babe and another on the way and no reason to risk it. Others have, though. Scavengers. And line scouts. They watch to be sure nothing new crosses."

"I want . . ." Ryan paused. Reconsidered. "I'd like to speak with some of them, if they're available."

The trader's gaze shifted to Ryan's face and Ryan fought to keep from fidgeting under the weight of his regard. After a long moment, Yeri nodded. "If the council allows, I'll arrange it, my lord." Then he smiled and waved a hand, scattering the almost tangible *something* between them. "I'm a bit surprised the scholars didn't change their plans when they heard you were heading for the wall."

Ryan had been a bit surprised himself, but Lyelee had clearly wanted to investigate the tenements, and when she made up her mind, she was almost impossible to shift. The tenet that scholars had the last word had just reinforced her childhood belief that she was always right. She'd been destined to be a scholar. Even Gearing, her mentor, knew when not to push.

"Good thing they're not here." Keetin stepped close enough to nudge Ryan's shoulder. "One look and they'd have gone over the wall. And you've been here too long, Yeri, if you've forgotten how fond scholars are of *look don't touch*. Which is to say, not at all."

Yeri huffed out an acknowledgment. "If they touch what's out there, they could lose more than a finger."

"Wouldn't stop them," Ryan sighed.

And Keetin added, "I've always wondered why there aren't more nine-fingered scholars."

Ryan noticed Yeri checked his surroundings before laughing. He hadn't been that long from Marsanport, then.

"Why did they enclose so much land?" Ryan asked, turning inward toward fields and farmsteads and the small sections that remained a town. Historically, according to both Lyelee and Gearing, walled cities were cramped, crowded, stinking places.

Yeri shrugged. "The way I understand it, it was panic, not plan. My guess is that the survivors were trying to hang on to as much of the old Gateway as they could. Nonee strengthened the wall's rubble base and added the second level."

With reclaimed blocks and a gate that looked like the gate leading into the Citadel. Had the weapon built the Citadel wall as well, or merely copied the only wall she'd known? Ryan turned to stare along the curve. "The archers keep moving, right? Then why are there two archers stationed over the gate facing the road?"

"Nonee's suggestion. The council usually follows Nonee's suggestions in matters of defense."

"Defense?" He frowned. "She thinks the greater danger will come from Marsanport."

"I don't know what she thinks, my lord."

"Are you frightened of her?"

They all turned to face Captain Yansav, who met their surprise with a bland stare.

"At first," Yeri admitted reluctantly. "But after a hundred children have told you to *stop staring, it's rude* . . ." He spread his arms. ". . . you realize she's Nonee."

"She's safe." The captain didn't sound happy.

"No. But to be fair . . ." He swept his gaze from her sword, to the long knife on the other side of her belt, to the short knives sheathed on the outside of her greaves. ". . . few people are."

"I, personally, could take down an army with my manly musk." Keetin pulled his tunic out from his chest, the fabric visibly damp. "We're almost to the mountains. Shouldn't it be cooler h . . ."

A shriek cut him off. A second cut the silence into jagged pieces.

Mouth dry, Ryan drew his sword and jerked around to face the ruins, Keetin to his left, Captain Yansav to his right. The patrolling archers were too far away to help and Servan was back at the Trader's Hall.

None of them had crossbows.

They should have been carrying crossbows.

Half of the people who traveled with him would die in the Broken Lands.

"It's farther away than it sounds."

If Yeri had sounded amused, Ryan would've run him through. Tried to run him through. He swallowed twice before his throat was wet enough to speak. "It sounded like it was on the wall."

The grass remained empty. The brambles and the growth over the ruins lay still. He shuffled two steps forward, felt Keetin's welcome warmth at his side, and looked down at empty stone.

"Some of the shattered are flaming good at staying unseen."

Captain Yansav snorted. "You're not helping, Trader."

Ryan turned in time to see Yeri smile and Captain Yansav shake her head. They were of an age, he realized. He must seem young and naive to them. Even Keetin's three years had given him more time to learn how the world worked.

Donal had been thirty-two when he died.

Yeri swatted a bug, checked the mashed body, and said, "We should keep moving."

"You said it wasn't close." Ryan hated how unsure he sounded.

"It isn't, but Lord Norwin-cee's right." Yeri nodded at Keetin. "It's hot in the sun and all this pale stone makes it hotter still. We should find some shade."

Sheathing his blade, Ryan swept his gaze over the ruins out to the Broken Line and beyond. Get the fuel, get it home.

Simple.

If he laughed at the thought, if he burst into laughter here on top of the wall, they'd think he was crazy.

LYELEE.NOW

Lyelee stopped and folded her arms. "This isn't the fastest route."

"How do you know? You just got here."

"I'm a scholar. And I have eyes," she added. Gateway didn't have scholars. He wouldn't understand what it meant.

"It's not the straightest route," Darny allowed, turning and walking backward along the top of the rail fence that defined the left side of the barely visible path. "But it's faster than having to stop and answer questions every two steps."

"And you were told to keep us away from people asking questions."

"Yep."

She'd heard people—rather too much about a distant someone about to do something dangerously stupid—but seen no one since they'd left the Trader's Hall. "What doesn't Gateway want us to find out?"

"Dunno." He balanced on one foot. "I figured it was 'cause you were in a hurry. I bet you'd get some pretty stupid questions."

He wasn't wrong.

"Stupid questions that'd take a lot of time to answer," he added.

They had the time. They had three days. Three days before they could enter the Broken Lands. Her teeth ached. She had to stop grinding them.

"We ask the questions." Gearing pushed his way up beside her, shoving her closer to the fence. "We are Scholars."

"Yeah, I *know*. That's why . . . Pippa! No!" Darny leapt off the far side of the fence and lunged at the small brown and white goat with the hem of Lyelee's robe between its teeth.

Lyelee began to point out she was in no danger when a sudden yank slammed her sideways. The goat—Pippa, she assumed—darted left, then right, avoiding Darny's grasp while maintaining a grip on the fabric. The pressure suddenly released. Lyelee grabbed the top rail to keep from toppling backward, and the goat raced toward a small shed, a triangle of blue fabric flapping in her mouth. "What are you doing?" she demanded as Darny returned to the path side of the fence. "Harris can't make repairs without that piece!"

"Yeah, well, she'll have swallowed it by the time I catch her." Darny shrugged philosophically and set off, once again, along the path.

She'd have stood her ground, but Gearing passed her and she wasn't walking behind him; something he'd had for breakfast was leaving a scent trail. "Do you expect me to wear a torn robe?" she demanded of the boy's back.

"You don't have other clothes?"

"The robe identifies us as scholars," Gearing huffed behind her.

"So? Why do people have to know you're scholars?" Darny jumped a narrow ditch and turned.

"Knowledge is power," Lyelee told him. Breathing through her nose, she hiked up her torn robe and stepped across.

"Okay." He waited until Gearing had safely reached the other side before walking on. "So scholars are special where you come from."

"Scholars are respected everywhere," Gearing declared.

Darny snorted. "Not here."

"Tell me about Nonee," Lyelee commanded before Gearing could respond. If she was to gain any information from the boy, she couldn't allow her mentor to dominate the conversation, where conversation meant *interrogation* and *dominate* meant bore to tears.

"Can't."

"Why not?"

"My mam told me not to. She's on council. I wasn't supposed to talk to you yesterday, but I did, so I got to help today." He darted to the right, swung up into a tree, and held out a handful of cherries when he returned. "Besides, I can get anywhere inside the wall faster than anyone." A muffled bellow came from inside the house the cherry tree stood closest to. Grinning, he offered her some of the fruit.

"Did your mother say why you weren't to talk to us about Nonee?"

"Nope." No surprise. Adults seldom explained their decisions to the young. "But it's chicken duty until the next moon if I do."

"And the chickens hate you."

He flashed a grin over his shoulder, pleased she'd remembered. "I'm guessing you don't wanna climb over fences, right?"

The ice in Gearing's voice should have dropped the surrounding temperature from high summer to midwinter. "I am a scholar."

"And you're old. Okay, then . . ." He stepped back and swept Gearing with a critical gaze. ". . . no fences. Bit longer without them, but we're good. Come on."

The lane he led them to held no farm animals. Or fences. They were heading west. The Broken Lands were to Lyelee's right. They'd been in front of her for so long, it felt wrong.

"So if knowledge is power," Darny said thoughtfully, dropping back to walk by Lyelee's side, "then you're powerful where you come from?"

"Yes, and . . ."

"We are respected." Gearing cut her off. "We are the final word."

"On what?"

"On the scholarship we master."

"Scholar Gearing is the Master of the Broken Lands," Lyelee explained.

"Not even," Darny scoffed. "He's never been there."

"But he knows what there is to know." Her silent *for now* was as obvious as possible without being spoken aloud. Gearing scowled at her, but Darny flailed the hand stained with cherry juice, drawing their attention.

"So, if he says some stuff about the Broken Lands, everyone just thinks he's right all the time?"

"I am right."

"You've never been there," Darny pointed out again. "And if he doesn't come back . . ." He turned to Lyelee. ". . . then everyone'll think you're right all the time?"

"Yes. I'll be the new Master of the Broken Lands."

"Not until you defend your thesis."

She glanced over at her mentor. "Who to, if you don't come back?"

"If you're the Master of Chickens," Darny continued, ignoring them, "then everyone believes you're right about chickens all the time. Right?"

"Yes."

"So what if you're wrong?"

"Scholars are the final word," Gearing repeated.

"Yeah, but what if it's the wrong word?"

"A scholar who is the Master of a Scholarship is the definitive word."

Lyelee could almost smell the smoke as Darny turned that over. "So," he said, "you define what stuff means?"

"Within the parameters of our scholarship, yes." Gearing shot her an intrigued glance. "The boy is quite intelligent."

"But what if you're wrong?" Darny insisted.

Bushy eyebrows rose. "I rescind my opinion. He's merely stubborn."

"If you're the only one who knows stuff about stuff, no one would know if you were wrong." He poked a grubby finger toward Lyelee. "You trying to tell me, you never thought he was wrong?"

"He's the Master of the Broken Lands." Which would satisfy her mentor, if not the boy. Time to change the subject. "The healer that Nonee's mourning . . ."

"Arianna."

"Arianna, the healer from the Heir's Chronicle?"

"I don't know about no chronicle—this way." He tugged on her sleeve, pulling her between two low buildings. "That way's got about a hundred fences."

"Was she old?"

"She?"

"Arianna."

"Almost as old as Granny White. So, yeah, old."

The temperature barely dropped in the shade between the buildings. The path was disgusting. There might not be farm animals on it now, but there certainly had been in the recent past. Darny didn't seem to notice.

The Lord Protector was Arianna's age, and he still lived. The recently dead Arianna could easily be the Arianna from the chronicle; the probability of *two* aged healers connected to the weapon was low.

The death of Arianna raised another question. "Darny, who controls the weapon?"

"You mean Nonee?"

"Yes, Nonee, the mage-crafted weapon."

He shrugged, apparently unconcerned that a creature designed to destroy had nothing calling it to order.

"The weapon is under no one's control?" Gearing surged forward until he could grab Darny's arm. "Do you know how dangerous that is?"

Darny looked down at the clutching hand, then pointedly yanked his arm free. "Not very."

"Not very what?"

"Not very dangerous." He rolled his eyes. "It's Nonee."

Gearing stood staring at the boy's back. Stood until Darny stepped out between the buildings and back into the sunlight. Head up, jaw tight under his beard, he strode forward. "I'm sure Ryan Marsan-cer knowing the word will be a great comfort to those the creature destroys before he gets close enough to use it."

"What word?" Perched on the edge of a water-trough, Darny cocked his head. "The last word scholars have?"

"No," Gearing snapped. Squinting in the sudden bright light, Lyelee wondered what she'd seen flash across her mentor's face. "This word controls the weapon and has been passed from Captain Marsan, through the Lord Protectors that followed, to Ryan Marsan-cer, the Heir of Marsan."

He jumped down. "The guy with the fancy vest, who was all *do you know who I am* at the gate, right? Does he think he can tell Nonee what to do because he has this word?"

"Of course!" Gearing snapped.

"Not likely."

"Why not?"

Darny grinned. "Told you, can't talk about Nonee. Tell you this much, though," he added after a moment, "everyone's talking 'bout you two."

Gearing waved it off. "As I said, scholars are respected everywhere."

As he said, not here. But Lyelee kept that observation to herself.

❧

A section of cracked and broken road separated a small field of drying peas from the tenements.

Lyelee dropped to one knee. "This is mage-crafted. Like the Mage Road." She plucked a small piece free and ran her thumb over the smooth surface. During the first week of travel they'd tried everything they could think of and had been unable to break off a piece of the road.

"Mam says the whole place used to have roads like this. Then . . . WHAM! Mage War."

"I doubt it was that simple," Gearing declared.

Darny shrugged. "Wasn't there. Don't know."

"The Mage War involved pitched battles, the mages throwing both followers and mage-craft at each other. Twisting the earth and the water and the sky to prove which of the six was the most powerful, only to end in the death of all. It can't be summed up by *wham*."

Darny shrugged again. "Sure it can. Wham. Mage War." He squatted by Lyelee's side. "What's the sticks for?" he asked as Lyelee pulled her sample sticks from her satchel.

"I use them to retrieve uncontaminated samples."

"The what?"

"If I touch a sample, I leave evidence of that touch behind." Using the sticks, Lyelee picked up a piece of the road a little smaller than the first she'd handled and twisted to drop it into the linen sample bag Gearing held open. Then she picked up a second piece for herself.

"You know that's a road, right?" Darny watched her with an intensity that might have sent him to the Scholar's Hall had he lived in a civilized city. "Been worse things on it than fingers. And yours are mostly clean." She blocked his view into her satchel and with an amused huff, he straightened. "You're not supposed to take pieces of it away."

"I'm a scholar," Lyelee reminded him.

"Sure, but council talks about making the warren some kind of memorial thing. It never got touched, not even a little, even though all around it did, and lots of people lived here right after Gateway got squashed." Darny stepped out onto a large, angled piece of pavement. "Talk. Talk. Talk. Nothing ever happens. It'll fall down before they do anything, probably."

Four sets of steps rose up from the edge of the road; the Warren was one long building in four sections. Not particularly warren-like from the outside. Similar buildings in Marsanport ranged from slums to opulent apartments—although the Five Thousand had them built originally to house the Northport survivors. Practical, cheap, and contained.

While Gearing sat to fix his sandal—to catch his breath, he wasn't fooling anyone—Lyelee sketched the intricate carvings over all four upper door casings. The detailed vines and birds carved into the slightly paler stone of these lintels were evidence that either the menial workers of old Gateway had coin to spare—an argument against mages being the auto-cratic tyrants history painted them as—or the building had been built for them by someone who considered them worth the adornment—she drew a line to her previous note about the mages. Two solid theories.

"Roads and buildings," she muttered. "Supporting my thesis that mage-craft had its uses."

"Uses." Gearing spat the word loudly enough to stop Lyelee's pencil. "You persist in arguing against the words of the Scholar's Charter. *The attempt to control forces never meant to be controlled corrupts and irrevocably leads to the desire to control further power unto the ultimate destruction of all involved.*"

"I'm arguing against the word *attempt* and the phrase *never meant to be*. The first is imprecise and the second is opinion."

"An opinion of mage-craft based on observation."

"Roads and buildings," Lyelee repeated.

"That's where it starts. Captain Marsan and the Five Thousand had good reasons to ban mage-craft, reasons that left scars on flesh and spirit. Do not, in your desire to defend your thesis, ignore everything you've been taught about the Mage War."

Lyelee waved toward the Broken Lands. "What I've been taught is a tiny fraction of what's available to discover."

"Opinion!"

"Based on observation."

"Sa Trace said mage-craft is like holding a boulder over your head. I mean, it's pretty great while you're doing it, I guess." Darny lifted his arms. "Hey, look at me, I'm holding a boulder!" And brought them down again. "But sooner or later, your arms give out and you get squashed flat." When both scholars turned to stare at him, he shrugged.

"Who is Sa Trace?" Gearing snapped.

"Teacher. Well, not anymore, she's old."

"And she taught you about mage-craft?"

"Nope." Darny leapt up onto the thick, stone balustrade. "It's not like we don't know what happens when you drop a boulder on your head. Not a real boulder," he added when the silence extended. "What?"

"You live in the shadow of the Broken Lands." Gearing twitched his robe into place and glared up at the building, clearly declaring the topic closed. "I doubt we'll gather useful information here." He nodded down at the darkened stone at the edge of the road, an almost perfect circle left behind by a recent campfire. "Nothing worthwhile could possibly remain, and we'll find only debris from opportunistic vagrants."

"Don't know what a virgant is, but Mam says if folk make a fire inside, they could gut the whole place and die in a fiery inferno." A nod toward the door. "That's old wood in there."

Gearing folded his arms, chin jutted forward. "This is what happens when there's no oversight by scholars. Significant historical relics should be kept locked."

Darny shrugged. "Good luck with that. The locks were metal, right, and all the metal from before gets used for other stuff. Well, not all the metal, you know . . ." He waved toward the Broken Lands. "There's probably a bunch more out there, but I 'spect Nonee'll get it when someone needs it."

"Nonee . . ."

"I'm going inside," Lyelee interrupted. Three years as a probationary scholar and four as a novitiate kept her from pushing her mentor out of her way, but only just. She could feel anticipation building. She had to get inside.

"Impatience leads to sloppy scholarship."

Lyelee and Darny both ignored the pronouncement—Lyelee from long habit, Darny because he was clearly as smart as Gearing had assumed.

"Mam says the floors are likely all rotted, so she made me say truth to stay out. She says to tell you that if the wood's gone dark, stay off it. Palest stuff's safest."

"I'll keep that in mind." Notebook in one hand, pencil in the other, Lyelee trotted up the steps. Leather hinges had replaced the metal. There wasn't even the security of a nail driven into the casing to hold the door shut.

"Novitiate!"

It seemed years of indoctrination couldn't just be tossed aside. Palm against the wood, she froze.

"You're not a scholar yet!" Robe hoisted almost knee high in one hand as he climbed, Gearing waved her away from the door with the other. "Remember that this isolated example provides no comparisons. We must scrape at the history layered on the interior, sunk into the walls. Everything must be recorded, and you will follow my lead or you will return to the Trader's Hall." The back of his hand against her upper arm, he pushed her aside and, rummaging in his satchel for his own notebook, he stepped over the threshold.

There was very little of the safe, pale wood in the stairwell, although, Lyelee admitted, that might have been the lack of light. It smelled of urine—fresher than she was comfortable with. Five doorways, two on each of the side walls and two on the back, gaped open, their doors long gone. The scars on the floor, the walls, and even the ceiling showed evidence of hard living.

She could see a break in the floorboards through the open doorway to her left.

Gearing barred her way into the room. "We haven't time enough to double what we record. You work from the top floor down." He smiled. "Be careful on the stairs."

He didn't want to share credit for what he discovered. And he assumed she'd make no significant discoveries of her own up where the poorest and most desperate of the tenement's inhabitants would have lived. Flexing his power during the small amount of time remaining in her novitiate.

No matter. She *wanted* to go up the stairs.

Shoulder brushing the wall, Lyelee climbed to the second floor to find a consistent lack of interior doors. Halfway to the third floor, the light spilling down from the fourth illuminated the mud wasp nest before she stepped on it. Not that it would have mattered, there were no wasps. Outside, twigs scraped against the stone. Other people might have allowed their imagination to overrule common sense, but the Scholar's Hall trained imagination out of its acolytes. She stepped over the nest and kept climbing.

The hair on the back of her neck rose as she reached the fourth floor.

With the slate roof intact, the fourth-floor apartments remained in surprisingly good shape. However much they may have needed the slate, the survivors couldn't dismantle the roof while people were living under it, and, logically, once they'd rehoused those people, they had no need of the slate. Plus, she noted silently, moving quickly off a creaking board, there was the proposed memorial. Gateway didn't need scholars to inform them that a roofless memorial would be a foolish idea.

The ceiling of the rear apartment sloped from the entrance to the rear wall, three tiny dormers providing the only light. The windows faced west, not north and east toward the Broken Lands. That was for the best, Lyelee admitted. If she could actually look into the Broken Lands, how could she possibly stay behind that ridiculous wall? As if stone could keep mage-craft out.

She could see a fence, a line of olive trees—near, if not at, the northern edge of their range—two low buildings with thatched roofs, and a hairy red cow with a calf. Beyond that, a strip of the grass that circled Gateway just within the wall. Beyond that, the wall, and if she cocked her head at just the right angle, the edge of a gate.

It didn't look guarded.

She could get out the gate and around the wall and to the Broken Lands . . .

No Gearing. No Ryan. No one to say *this history we save, this history we ignore.*

The soft wood of the sill cracked under her grip, the sound bringing her back to herself.

There'd be time for the Broken Lands later. This was where she needed to be now.

This was where . . .

She frowned, grabbed for the wisp of thought, and lost it.

Fine. Temporarily denied the history she wanted to study, she'd record the history she could access. However irrelevant.

Teeth clenched, she took careful rubbings of the names and crude drawings on the sills, and made note of the carvings intact enough to identify on the walls.

The smallest room had a floor too dark to risk. Given the holes—deliberate holes in spite of visible rot around their edges—she'd have assumed the rooms were latrines, except none of them had been built into an outside wall.

Had mage-craft been so common in Gateway before the Mage War that it had been used to destroy shit?

In what was probably not an answer to her question, someone had carved EA SH T M GES into the short interior wall that cut off the angle of the roof and squared the interior space. Lyelee tapped the end of her pencil against her teeth.

There'd be space behind the wall.

Hidden places meant hidden things.

Shuffling over to the wall's darkest panel, testing each section of floor before she shifted her weight, she kicked at the punky wood. In a few minutes, she'd cleared enough of an opening that, kneeling, she could get her head and shoulders into the space behind the wall . . .

. . . cutting off her light.

The short, fat candles in the scholar's kit fit into a metal holder backed by a curved, polished piece of metal that slid into a track above the handle. She struck flint against steel, and applied the burning taper to the wick, carefully pinching out the taper when the wick caught.

Crawling forward, her left shoulder brushed stone while her right brushed wood. She kept the candle—and the open flame—in her left hand. Had the spiderwebs and insect corpses not already indicated multiple, smaller access points, the flickering would have given it away. The air smelled dry and dusty, the mouse nest piled into the angle of a support strut long abandoned.

She found a second nest tucked up against the stone wall that divided the tenements, this one built by a child. Crude drawings of people, animals, and trees covered the stone. Stains left by puddles of wax marked the floor. The debris included a few scraps of fabric that were almost scholar blue, a cracked pottery bowl, a leather ball, half a wooden cat—or possibly a dog—maybe a horse—and a pile of paper.

No. A notebook.

Scholars used most of the paper produced in Marsan, leaving a very little available for account keeping. Thirty years ago, seditious broadsheets accusing the Scholar's Hall of hoarding knowledge had sent scholars to the Citadel, where they'd convinced the Court to close Marsanport to cheap imported paper. Some still got in, of course, but not so much the Hall couldn't deal with it.

Just after the Mage War, with Gateway in ruins and the people in survival mode, paper had been common enough that a child could own it.

The notebook's binding had rotted, leaving a crumbling ripple along one of the narrow edges where the stitches had been. The paper had yellowed almost to brown and the outer corners had disintegrated. Sitting back on her heels, Lyelee tore a page from her own notebook, slid it carefully under her find, leaned forward to grasp the opposite edge, and raised the fragile relic a finger-width from the floor. To her relief, it moved easily, and she set it down again while she looked for the child's way in and out.

The light in the room outside the crawlspace drew a small, square outline on the wall.

She shuffled backward to give herself room to maneuver. One knee sank into the mouse nest and she sucked in a pained breath. Knee throbbing, she patted the floor until her hand closed around a hard, curved object about the size of her smallest finger. She held it closer to the candle.

"A tooth?" Worn smooth at the wider end, it could have come from a large dog. The bit of familiar, almost-blue fabric wrapped around it suggested it had once belonged to the child. She stroked a finger over the curve. The tooth buzzed against her skin.

A second stroke and she felt only cool bone.

But she knew she'd felt the buzz and scholars never doubted what they knew.

As she straightened, the candle flickered. Guttered. Went out.

Tooth shoved into her pocket, Lyelee pushed open the small, square door, and spilled out onto a patch of floor distinctly darker than the rest.

It bowed beneath her.

Holding her breath, she shuffled around on her knees, leaned back into the crawlspace, and carefully slid the ancient notebook out into the light.

A board cracked.

Her right knee dropped below the surface of the floor.

Her fingers closed around the candle holder—she couldn't count on Gateway to have a replacement—and she threw herself back, rolling left, as the floorboard under her right leg disintegrated. Breathing heavily, she stared at a stain on the ceiling that looked a little like the Citadel and a little like a stack of buns with a knife and a pat of butter. Her stomach growled. Turning only her head, she stretched out her right arm, caught the piece of new paper she'd used as a lever between thumb and forefinger, and tugged the notebook past the broken bit of floor.

"You hungry?" Darny sat crosslegged on the front steps, visible through the open door as she came down the stairs.

Her stomach growled.

"Mam packed us food. Trader Gils said scholars don't think of stuff like that."

Why would they? Her throat felt like she'd been sucking cotton. "Water?"

He held out a waterskin, sides plumped. "Find something?"

"Yes." Turning, Lyelee set her notebook—now protecting the ancient papers closed within it—onto a step. The water was colder than she'd expected, considering the length of time it had been in the skin.

Scholar Gearing was still in the first room.

"Don't worry about him," Darny told her, following her gaze. "He's been in and out. Had a pork bun already."

❧

Gearing glanced up as she crossed the threshold. "What took you so long?"

Lyelee swallowed a mouthful of pork and pastry. "Why are you still here?"

"Not still," he corrected. "I've examined the relevant surroundings and returned. Look here." Beckoning her closer, he used his pencil to point into the hole. "What do you see?"

"Clay pipes."

"Clay pipes." He nodded toward his sketch. "They go through the walls. Darny's mother told him there used to be tanks on the roof and pumps to raise the water up to them. Each apartment had its own lavatory."

"The small damaged rooms." Lyelee frowned. "But they're not on outside walls. At least the rooms on the top floors weren't."

"Nor on the first two. They don't have to be." Passing her his notebook, he indicated a section of parallel lines. "Pipes came down inside the walls, then these pipes carried the waste away."

"Inside interior walls?"

"So it appears."

She leaned forward to take another look into the hole. "What if there was a leak?"

"What indeed."

"Shit in the walls," Darny called happily.

Lyelee straightened. "That's . . ."

"Impractical. I know. Clearly those who lived before the Mage Wars had entirely different standards of sanitation. Not very high standards," he added unnecessarily, rising to his feet.

The water had been colder than expected.

"The well," she began.

Gearing cut her off. "Would be at risk of contamination even considering the timeframe."

"I keep telling you it's clean!" Darny called from the doorway. "You just don't listen!"

"Because your Scholarship in Fluids is unsubstantiated," Gearing snapped.

"You drank water that fish peed in while you traveled here."

"Fish urine is significantly less likely to cause . . ."

"All our water's clean," Darny insisted, paused and added, "Unless, you know, it's in a trough for animals 'cause they slobber. And in the ponds where fish are because fish pee. 'Cept you don't mind fish pee. And frogs. Frogs pee when you pick them up. Did you know that?"

"Yes." The Scholarship of Flesh pushed needles into frog brains so they could be dissected alive. Lyelee found the concept intriguing, and had been disappointed to find it didn't work on more complex animals.

"If we could move on from your fascination with urine . . ." Gearing pointedly turned his attention away from Darny to her. "Did you find anything of note?"

✺

"The poor were literate and paper common enough for poor children's use."

"Or it wasn't the poor who lived here." Lyelee watched as Gearing carefully teased the second page of the ancient notebook up high enough to slide in a new piece of paper. Surface supported, he turned the page. "The apartments aren't small."

"The apartments are a lot smaller, relatively if not structurally, when each of them contains a multi-generational family."

"True."

"I'm pleased to have your endors . . ." He lost the word in a sudden intake of breath.

Time had left the first line of the messy scrawl on the fourth page legible.

"Plant the dragon's tooth to grow a dragon," Lyelee read, shoved up against Gearing's arm when he wouldn't move out of her way. "You have dragons here?"

Back on the balustrade, Darny snorted dismissively. "No." Then added before she could ask how he knew, "Not now, anyway."

"Not now?"

"Well, they had everything before the Mage War, didn't they? And in the stories, one of the mages makes dragons."

"Makes them out of what?"

Plant the dragon tooth to grow a dragon.

"Dunno. It's a story, isn't it?"

After page four, the centers of the next nine pages were essentially legible. The child writer had wanted a dog, and had a brother who'd scavenged in the Broken Lands. Their drawings had no concept of perspective.

The final six pages were as unreadable as the first three.

"It seems the brother was on a salvage crew." Gearing carefully lifted and resettled the pages until page four lay exposed again. "Perhaps he saw a creature in the Broken Lands he erroneously assumed was a dragon. The creatures figure prominently in the stories of Shurlia, and Captain Marsan wasn't the only Shurlian who lived in Gateway. The stories would have spread beyond their original geographic location."

"The captain and the Five Thousand were gone by the time this was written."

"Stories linger." Head turned so as not to breathe dampness onto the delicate paper, Gearing read, *"Bors says he'll bring me some magic dirt next so I can plant the tooth and grow a dragon.* Scholar Maarens will be fascinated by this."

Maarens was a Scholar of Folklore within the Scholarship of History. Lyelee found the lines between folklore and history too blurred to belong to the same scholarship, but her fellow scholars were resistant to change.

Gearing tapped his specimen sticks against his cheek. "If the brother gave his younger sibling a tooth he claimed was from a dragon with the instructions to plant it . . ." He closed the ancient notebook, then closed Lyelee's notebook around it again. ". . . I wonder what happened to the tooth?"

Lyelee pressed her hand possessively against the hard ridge in her pocket. "I expect we'll never know."

RYAN.NOW

Ryan concentrated on crispy strips of thick back bacon while Scholar Gearing informed them of the Scholar's Hall statistics concerning idleness and mischief as though he hadn't brought the matter up every few days while they traveled. Lyelee mouthed the final "learning should be perpetual" along with her mentor. Ryan couldn't tell if it was in agreement or mockery. Given Lyelee, it could be both.

"We haven't been planted on our asses," Keetin told him. "We've been gathering information about the Broken Lands in the desperate hope of keeping you two alive."

Gearing pushed his chair back from the table. "It's been a hundred and sixty-three years, I very much doubt hope is desperate at this point."

"Then maybe you should stay and hear what the council has to say." Ryan folded his arms.

"What could they say that we'd be interested in?" He sniffed dismissively. "They'll choose what you hear and what you don't. We, however, are Scholars of the Broken Lands, and we're here to advance our knowledge. There'll be little advancement if we're hobbled by politically motivated information."

"There'll be less advancement if you're eaten by one of the shattered."

"Then the guardians need to keep that from happening," Lyelee said, rising as well.

She'd worn the same expression at three and seven and twelve and it had held the same meaning. *What I know is more important than what you believe.*

"We're in no danger of being eaten in the tenements." Gearing tugged a fold of his robe out from under the strap of his satchel. "Novitiate."

"Scholar." Lyelee settled her own satchel and followed him out into the courtyard.

"I've just spent a lot, a flaming lot of time in their company," Keetin said thoughtfully, "and I've never seen inside either of those bags. What do you suppose they carry so close?"

"Paper. Pencils. Those sticks they use to pick up samples. Small bags made of paper or waxed fabric. Copies of the pertinent parts of the chronicles. Research that's personally important. Their current notebook. Lyelee's filled three—no, four—since we left Marsanport, which is more impressive when you consider her writing's so small you can go blind reading it. I asked about ten days ago," Ryan added.

Keetin leaned back, eyes narrowed. "And she showed you?"

"No, she told me."

"So, she didn't show you."

"What are you implying, Kee?"

"That they could be carrying . . ." He lowered his voice. ". . . any-thing." After a moment, his lips twitched, his face flushed, and, finally, he laughed. "Your face!"

"Your face," Ryan muttered.

"Lord Marsan." Yeri stood in the doorway, three people visible behind him. "The council has sent representatives."

Keetin straightened out of his slouch and Ryan pushed his chair back far enough to give Harris room to clear the last of the breakfast debris. "Are you staying, Captain?"

"Yes, sir." She left the kitchen to stand behind the chair one away from his. "Servan, on your way to the butts, tell the other two I want to hear sounds of weapons practice from the courtyard."

"Captain." Servan tossed a tomato in the air, caught it, and took a bite before brushing past the ex-trader.

"We accept your trade for food and water." Councilor Rhys leaned back and rubbed at a dribble of sweat running down from the shaved side of her head. "And we'll house you as gesture of respect between your city and ours. Is there anything else you need from us?"

Ryan spread his hands. "Information."

Councilor Tabbin grinned so broadly Ryan could see the gap of miss-ing teeth. "You do need that, Heir of Marsan. You do indeed."

"So you don't actually cross the line?"

"Why would we?" Mirit coughed, and hacked a solid-looking chunk into her empty mug. Disgusted, Ryan shifted away, although he tried to make it look as though he'd merely changed position.

The second scout's expression suggested he hadn't been particularly successful.

"A third, maybe more, of old Gateway's outside the wall. Plenty of places for the shattered to shelter, so if we're on clearances, we stay there. If we're on a line scout, point is to make sure nothing new's come over, not go over after it." Mirit snorted. "No need to risk our skins more than we already are."

Ryan frowned. "But Nonee's crossed the line?"

"Sure. Once or twice."

"Once or twice in sixty-three years?"

Mirit shot him a flat look. "She was busy, wasn't she."

"Doing what?"

"No business of yours what Nonee's been doing." Skye, the second scavenger, rolled broad shoulders and set the multiple feathered earrings they wore swaying. "Knew you lot were coming back, didn't she? Knew that as soon as the flame of yours needed more fuel yin d'brydin'n." They leaned forward, words coming fast enough most were incomprehensible. "Unl'nun pleeceta get it, t'aint tha? Canna lif Marsanport unprota'd, c'you?" Frowning, they sat back, took a deep breath, and continued slowly enough that noises became words again. "Flame g'out and maybe those folk your Captain Marsan had thrown t'the lake try t'take their place back."

"Children of those folk," Mirit corrected.

"Grandchildren, more like," Skye admitted.

"Because *those folk*'d be dead even had they not drowned."

"Or b'killed other ways, right?"

"Killed by the weapon," Ryan pointed out, trying not to sound as annoyed as he felt. Captain Marsan had needed a safe place for the Five Thousand and the Master of North Lakeport had refused them shelter, refused to believe the mages were dead, and was afraid to attract the mages' anger as these walking wounded had. What could the captain do but take what she needed for those she'd saved? They'd given her no choice. "By your Nonee," he added in case they hadn't understood.

Mirit spat again and Skye said, "Yeah, well, she wasn't our Nonee then, and 'sides, she had to do what your captain told her to. Like she was a thing. No choice. She doesn't do that now, d'she?"

Why would she? Ryan asked silently, unwilling to provoke another tirade. *No one has been giving her those kind of orders.* He thought the scouts might ask him what kind of orders he planned to give, but they didn't.

"'Course," Skye mused thoughtfully, "Nonee'd go anywhere Healer Arianna'd go, and word is when t'healer was young, she was always poking around outside t'wall."

"Why?"

"For healing reasons." Their expression clearly added *idiot*, just in case Ryan hadn't heard it in their voice.

"She gave us a list of plants as long as my arm we were t'keep an eye out for." Mirit rolled her eyes. "When we weren't looking for signs of things that could kill us."

"Like some of t'plants," Skye muttered.

Mirit laughed. "Truth. Not so many around now as there was, and those we can't clear are no real danger unless you're careless or stupid."

And you're both.

"We'll tell you what t'watch for, but you'll be with Nonee. Nonee'll take care of you."

Because you're helpless.

Ryan knew he could be hearing things that weren't there. Mirit had no reason to sound like his brothers. And yet . . .

"You do what Nonee says, every time. You might survive." Then Mirit looked past him at Captain Yansav and said something in what might have been Shurlian.

Captain Yansav stiffened and said, "Yes. But, how do you . . . ?"

"We keep t'old languages alive." She met the captain's gaze. "Folk followed the mages t'Gateway from all over."

Ryan unclenched his jaw. "Captain?"

"She asked if the children had to go over the line."

"The children?"

"You and Lord Norwin-cee."

Ryan glared at Mirit, who shrugged, unaffected.

"No one scouts the line until they've had some years closer in," she said. "You two, you especially, you're raw."

"I'm the Heir of Marsan!"

"Doesn't make you less raw. No insult, lad. Just truth."

"The Heir of Marsan retrieves the fuel," Keetin said when Ryan couldn't find his voice. He could always count on Keetin. "We want to be here slightly less than you want us here, but . . ." He spread his hands. "It is what it is."

"It is what it is," Mirit repeated. Then she looked from Keetin to the captain, and unexpectedly smiled. Ryan felt as though he'd passed some kind of test he hadn't known he'd been taking. "We'll tell you what we can t'help keep you alive as far as the line, but seriously, listen to Nonee. She knows what's out there, and any shattered still alive on this side is smart."

"They're survivors," Skye added when Mirit stopped to hack and spit. "Protect yourself, but leave the shattered t'Nonee. Saved my ass once by grabbing a shattered and ripping it in half."

Mirit spat again. "Guts everywhere," she said when she finished. "Whole loop of gut slithered down between my breasts."

"On its own?" Keetin asked.

Mirit frowned. "Don't think so."

"Strangle weed, though." Skye tapped the table with a twisted finger. "You need t'know 'bout that."

Ryan felt both scouts were entirely too cheerful about the possibility of something called strangle weed.

And fire weed.

And saw weed.

"Not a lot of saw weed around these days." Mirit took a swallow from a new mug of chilled tea before continuing, "Always some, though."

"It's a bugger," Skye agreed.

⸗

"There's no roads. The land is *broken*." Yeri clearly couldn't believe he had to point that out. "And if the shattered don't kill the horses, they'll starve. There's nothing safe in there for them to eat."

"We won't leave the wagon." Scholar Gearing drew himself up to his full height.

"Then you won't be accompanying us," Ryan said before Yeri could respond. It was his place to make that decision, not the trader's.

"You can't . . ."

"I can." He squared his shoulders, lifted his chin, and kept his gaze focused just to the left of the scholar's shoulder, lest the habit of obedience that every child in Marsanport had installed by the scholars trip him up.

"Decide what you can't be without and remember you'll have to carry it, as well as some of the food and water."

Gearing's eyes narrowed. "You argued against the inclusion of scholarship from the beginning."

Ryan might have been unprepared to be Heir, but he wasn't stupid. "I argued we could move faster without the wagon."

"And now you're without it. How convenient for you, my lord."

A lifetime of unquestioning respect held, but only just. Twenty-eight days on the road had worn *unquestioning* almost entirely away. "The guardians will help you unload, Scholar."

"The guardians will keep their hands off materials they have no idea of how to handle." Gearing switched his attention to Lyelee. "Novitiate, with me."

As the door closed behind them, Yeri leaned back against the wall and folded his arms. "You didn't seem surprised."

"According to the Heir's Chronicle, the Lord Protector walked," Ryan told him. He mirrored Yeri's position. Except for the leaning. He wasn't close enough to the wall and landing on his ass seemed unlikely to strengthen his authority. "Lord Norwin-cee, Captain Yansav, and I discussed it on the way."

"And yet you didn't discuss it with the scholars, my lord."

"Please." Keetin came out of the kitchen tossing a pair of toasted buns from hand to hand. "Why would we open ourselves up to that kind of abuse?" He sharpened his voice into a close approximation of Gearing's. "We have to take the wagon. We're scholars and we know best. We know about wagons. We know about the Broken Lands. You know nothing. The Lord Protector had no scholars with him."

"And on and on and on," Ryan added, accepting one of the buns. Harris had been taking full advantage of the kitchen while he had it. "Leaving it until the last minute minimizes the arguing."

"Won't stop it." Keetin sighed and stuffed a bun into his mouth.

"True."

"I don't miss scholars." Yeri paused, and Ryan knew he was waiting to be sure the present scholars hadn't heard him. When it seemed they hadn't, he added, "Your horses will be well cared for until you return."

"If we return." Ryan glanced toward the Broken Lands.

Yeri spread his hands. "I guarantee that won't affect how we care for the horses."

The Healer Arianna's burial would happen at dusk on the third day.

"Will you be attending?" he asked, catching Lyelee and Scholar Gearing entering the Hall with armloads of paper, some bound, some loose, all old.

Lyelee rolled her eyes. "We have work to do."

"The dead healer is a stranger," Gearing added, paper crinkling as he shifted his grip. "We have no need to mourn publicly."

"We have a connection to the dead," Ryan argued. "We've been held here for three days because the weapon was guarding her."

"So you want to go and look annoyed at a corpse?" Lyelee cocked her head. "Or did you want to look annoyed at the weapon?"

"I wanted to show respect."

"By intruding?"

"That's not . . ." Or would it be?

"No one expects you and the weapon to be friends," Lyelee added, following her mentor to the stairs.

"Remind me to thank the Lord Protector for sending scholars with us." Keetin's hand was a comforting weight on his shoulder.

"The next heir will need the information they bring back."

"*Your* heir will need the information *you* bring back. The scholars? Even an ancient weapon of enormous power and magical pedigree won't be able to keep them alive in the Broken Lands. I have coin that says they'll have stuck their noses into something lethal by noon tomorrow."

"You're giving them until noon? Generous."

"I can be." He snickered. "Would you think less of me if I tell you that I'd been hoping they'd fall through a rotten floor at the tenements and be just injured enough to stay behind?" Wrapping an arm around Ryan's chest, Keetin pulled him back, close enough to rest his chin on Ryan's shoulder, beard scratching at the side of Ryan's neck. "Don't worry about it. Remind them Gateway still has temples to pre–Mage War gods and this will be their one chance to observe historic burial customs."

The pressure of Keetin's chest plastered Ryan's sweaty tunic to his back. "You're good at that."

"At what?"

"People. They should go to the burial because showing respect is the right thing to do, but they won't." The number of people who shared their grief at his brothers' burial had helped his father find his way back to himself. Had shown him he wasn't alone in his loss. "You've given them a reason they'll agree with."

Keetin shook him gently, then released him. "You're good at people, Ry. I'm good at scholars and politicians and courtiers and courtesans. I know what to say, you know how to feel."

If he didn't find the fuel, he failed. If he died, he failed. If he found the fuel and stayed alive and got back to Marsanport after the Black Flame burned out, he failed. "I feel like I'm in over my head."

"Only because you are."

"Thanks."

Keetin spun Ryan around to face him, spread his arms, and smiled. "You've lived your whole life by the lake. You know how to swim."

He did. So had his brothers.

"Lives for so long and dies the day we arrive, denying us her knowledge." Lyelee twitched her stole straight as their party moved to stand at the rear of the crowd.

Ryan curled his fingers into fists. "I doubt she died to annoy you."

"I don't."

Keetin stepped between them.

The flowers had been removed from the dais and the body wrapped in straw mats secured with tasseled cords. After three days in high summer, covered in flowers that would hasten the rot, that seemed like an excellent idea.

The woman who spoke might have been the woman who'd stopped him that night. Her curves were hidden behind multiple panels of green and yellow fabric that flowed from shoulders to feet. She looked taller than he remembered, but that might have been the calm dignity she exuded. He thought it was the same voice.

"This is who Arianna daughter of Vereen daughter of Mirian was to us . . ."

Arianna had healed a great many people in her ninety-three years and had helped a great many more into the world. Those in the crowd on either list raised their voice to echo the woman on the dais.

The woman on the dais.

Ryan had no idea how to refer to her. Was she a priest? No one had said. He wished he could leave the scholars behind in Gateway; there was so much about the city they didn't know.

The time in the Broken Lands, when Arianna had accompanied his great-uncle to find the fuel for the flame, the journey where three out of five people had died, was barely acknowledged as a part of Arianna's life. The people of Gateway seemed to think that Arianna returning with Nonee was the only part of that story with any importance.

He didn't understand what kind of a relationship the weapon had with the healer.

The weapon had stayed in Gateway because the Lord Protector had ordered her to.

She mourned. He didn't question that. She stood, wrapped in green and yellow fabric at the end of the bier, only her grief visible. His father had looked small and fragile when they buried his brothers. She looked . . .

His memory of his father shifted. A large hand wrapped around his too tightly, his brothers grouped around him, his mother laid into the earth, his father's voice in pieces as he spoke of losing his bonded.

She looked shattered.

❧

The people of Gateway buried their dead in the circular pasture just inside the wall; solemn children and half a dozen dogs kept the livestock out of the immediate area. Arianna's grave had been dug just east of the Broken Gate.

"Watch for shit," Keetin muttered. When Captain Yansav turned toward him, the setting sun burnishing her helm and scale-mail vest with reds and golds, he shrugged. "Those are sheep. I assume there were sheep on this bit. Standing ankle deep in sheep shit respects no one."

Ryan recognized Darny, Yeri, and both line scouts in the procession of mourners who threw a shovelful of dirt into the grave. When it was full, the next group relaid the sod. The last group piled a cairn of rock at the head of the grave. The three rocks on the bottom were large and flat, the rest about the size of his fist.

"So that's what they are. I saw piles of rock when we came in from the gate," Lyelee added when Ryan shot her a silent question. "I theorized they might mark the possibility of an undiscovered cellar."

"What happens if they hit a cellar when digging the grave?" Gearing took a step toward the interment.

Before he could take a second, Keetin grabbed his arm and held him in place. "Not the time to ask."

"But they're . . ."

"No." Ryan added his authority to Keetin's grip and, to his surprise, both scholars subsided, scowling.

"In Marsanport," Lyelee began.

Ryan cut her off. "You're not in Marsanport, Lye."

As the mourners began to leave, Nonee remained at the foot of the grave. Most of those who'd participated in the physical burial had touched her gently on the shoulder when they'd finished their small bit.

When no one stood between them, he took a single step forward.

"Ryan." Keetin gripped his shoulder.

He turned to see Yeri stop a woman from approaching, saw him bend his head and say something quick and quiet by her ear. She looked at Ryan as though his presence confused her, then she nodded and walked by.

"Do you want me to go with you?" Keetin's hold loosened.

"No. Go back to the Trader's Hall with the others. The Lord Protector told me that the first time we spoke, I had to speak with her alone."

"And you're going to speak to her now?"

"Yes." It both did and didn't feel like the right time, but they were leaving in the morning and it was the only time they had.

"Sir." Captain Yansav had moved closer as well.

"Captain, if I'm not safe with her now, we're not going to be safe with her leading us into the Broken Lands."

The silence stretched. Ryan could hear Scholar Gearing muttering, the creak of leather as the guardians shifted in place, and a soft protest from the confined sheep.

"I'll wait at the road, my lord."

As that was as good as he was going to get, he exhaled and nodded. He waited until he heard his people move off, then walked forward, stopping far enough away that he could look the weapon in the eye without having to lift his chin. He'd grown up with three older brothers, he was used to compensating.

She'd grown larger the closer he got to her.

Of course she had.

After a moment, she raised her head, and turned toward him.

There was still enough light to see her clearly.

If he hadn't known what to expect, he wouldn't have been able to stop himself from recoiling.

There were half a dozen paintings of the weapon in the archives. Ryan had examined them until he'd seen them in his sleep. The living weapon's skin was a paler gray, almost the shade of the upper level of stones in the wall, but the wide eyes, the heavy jaw and brow, the short, thick neck were faithful to the renderings. Her brows were less prominent than rendered in the paintings, and not one of the artists had captured the sadness in the pale gray eyes. She was grotesque, but she was also . . . not. Around her neck she wore a string of large, garish beads, each uniquely lopsided as though they'd been made by a child's hands.

Was she waiting for him to speak?

A glance toward the road and he realized the entire company had remained with the captain.

When he looked back at the weapon, she'd followed his gaze to the road.

"They're with me." Taking a deep breath, he squared his shoulders and tried to forget that the first thing he'd said had been so stupid.

"You must forge your own relationship." The Lord Protector rubbed his thumb over a scratch on the head of his cane, eyes locked on the movement. *"Great changes were happening when I left her. Great challenges. Who knows how those have played out."* After a moment his gaze left the past and he clutched at Ryan's arm with thin, palsied fingers. *"Advance alone the first time you meet so that the Last Command will hold her."*

Ryan thought now that he should have asked more questions. Should have risked being seen as unprepared for a position that was never supposed to be his no matter how inadequate that made him feel. He cleared his throat and wiped damp palms against his thighs. "I am Ryan, Heir of Marsan, Heir of Garrett, Lord Protector. The Black Flame is failing and I have come to evoke the Last Command." She remained motionless. Had she blinked? He didn't think she'd blinked. Could she blink? He wet his lips and continued. "As stated in the Last Command, you will guide us into the Broken Lands to replenish the fuel, then guide us out again. This was commanded by the Lord Protector when he was heir." Those were the words he'd memorized, but they were too cold for where he stood, so he added words of his own. "Garrett Marsan-cee is still alive. I'm sorry."

"Why?"

Her voice was deep—deeper than a woman's voice—her grief audible. He nodded toward the grave. "Because the healer Arianna isn't alive, and they were of an age, and you obviously cared for her a great deal."

He couldn't be sure, given the fading light and the gray of her skin, but he thought she closed her eyes. "Arianna . . ." She swallowed, audibly, and tried again. "Arianna made a weapon into a person because she'd seen a person from the beginning . . ."

ARIANNA.THEN

Arianna knew that it was impossible to keep children off the wall after they reached a certain age. She understood the urge to see beyond the barrier, had given in to it herself, but the pieces of shattered buildings that made up the bulk of their defenses weren't merely made of stone. They contained glass and metal and the shards of other things sharp enough to cut into small, bare feet.

"I don't see why it matters what she stepped on." Cleo clambered up the inner slope of the rubble wall like she'd gone up it a hundred times before.

"It matters because I need to know what made the cut in order to treat the cut."

It wasn't the stone or the glass or the metal that concerned her; it was the other things. The survivors had been more desperate than careful when they'd piled the rubble. Mage-craft lingered.

"It was here." Cleo turned in place on a piece of broken colonnade. "No, there." She pointed at a crevasse to the right of where she stood. "Abha was on the top, I was nearly up, and Kasy made that shriek sound she makes and I didn't think anything of it, because you know, Kasy, but I turned round and she was pulling her foot out of that hole and it was bleeding. Her foot, not the hole," she clarified after a moment.

Arianna followed the line of Cleo's finger. Up close, the crevasse was a shallow triangle, barely large enough for a small twelve-year-old's foot. Another stone protruded through one of the inner angles and blood stained the edge. "You wrapped it immediately?"

"'Course. We're not stupid!"

"You're climbing the wall." Arianna took a damp cloth from her pouch and wiped away the blood.

"Everyone climbs the wall."

Hiding her smile at Cleo's dismissive tone, Arianna checked that the cloth had picked up only blood, folded the smear of brownish red onto the inside, and tucked the cloth away. The cleansing she'd already done on Kasy's foot would be enough to keep the wound from infecting and there'd be no need for further treatment. A good thing for multiple reasons; Kasy's grandfather was notorious for arguing about . . .

"Ari! Come quick! There's something on the road!"

Longer legs and arms made the scramble to the top of the wall easier than the last time she'd done it, but there was the same sense of exhilaration as she threw herself flat beside Cleo. It wasn't that they were so high up; they were barely head and shoulders higher than Gregir, the tallest man in Gateway. It was that this view was the view out to the rest of the world.

The trees had turned gold with the change of the season. The sky was an endless arc of blue.

And there was something on the Mage Road.

"I think it's people."

"On horses," Arianna agreed. "Three . . ."

"Four," Cleo corrected.

"Four. And something else."

"A heliphant?"

She grabbed the back of Cleo's tunic and yanked her flat again. "It's *elephant.*" Most of the Records had been saved, but over the last hundred years they'd begun to lose words. They'd have to work harder to keep the old languages alive.

"Mam says . . ."

"She's wrong."

"Okay." Cleo cocked her head. "Could be an elephant lying down."

It could be. Arianna had seen as many of the great beasts as Cleo had, so she couldn't say it *wasn't* an elephant lying down. One of the horses separated from the others, the rider's arm in the air.

"I think they saw us." Cleo twisted until Arianna could see her face. "What do we do, Ari?"

It was the middle of the afternoon. There were no archers on this part of the wall because nothing dangerous came from this part of the world. The nearest archers would be . . .

Too far.

"Find Nica. She's probably at the granary." Nica was the current head of the council. She'd know what to do. Or she'd fake it so well no one would ever be the wiser.

"What are you gonna do?"

The other three horses and riders joined the first. The "elephant lying down" remained motionless. Or what passed for motionless at a distance.

"I'm going to find out who they are."

"I never heard of talents coming in a group," Cleo declared in a tone that suggested if she hadn't heard of it in all her twelve years, it hadn't happened. "Will you stop them from coming in?"

"If necessary."

"By yourself?"

"I'm a healer. People listen to healers."

"But they have an elephant!"

"Probably not. Go!" The outside face of the wall was almost vertical, so she followed Cleo down the inside slope to the ground, her feet remembering the way. As Cleo ran for the granary, thick, dark braids bouncing against her back, Arianna ran for the gate.

It wasn't far. The gate was there for the road and the road was why children climbed that section of wall.

Looking put out at being woken from his afternoon nap, Big Tam opened the right side of the wooden barrier just far enough for her to squeeze through, then slammed it behind her. He asked no questions. She was an adult, could come and go as she pleased, and all the excitement happened at the Broken Gate. Nothing ever happened at the Road Gate.

Well, nothing much, she amended, wiping her hands on the trousers she'd thrown on to climb the wall. She didn't think the riders had moved again, although it looked like the not-an-elephant had shifted, its upper edge now a different curve. Head high, she strode forward.

These horses had longer, more delicate legs than the ponies she saw every day.

They had tidier manes and tails too. She supposed there was little else to do on the road in the evening but groom the horses.

All four riders were bearded—although two were significantly less bearded than the others. Probably men; she wasn't yet near enough to tell for certain, and the first thing a healer learned was not to jump to conclusions. They had a narrow range of coloring, from very dark to not quite so dark. The palest only as light as she was herself, none of the four even as light as Cleo. A half-healed cut that needed cleaning called to her. Their clothes were travel-worn, but then they'd traveled a long way. The records stated that the mages had walked north from Northport at the upper curve of the Great Lake for the full passage of a moon before they founded Gateway, wanting neither neighbors nor random visitors. She'd been a child when Wills had arrived, but in his record he said he'd walked the Mage Road for twenty-eight days.

All the talented traveled the Mage Road for twenty-eight days, regardless if they walked or rode.

She still couldn't tell what the elephant actually was, the horses blocked her line of sight, but every time she got a glimpse of it, the hair rose on the back of her neck. There was something *wrong* about it, and this close to the Broken Lands, she took nothing for granted.

"What is this place?"

The man spoke in a commanding tone. Commanding and suspicious and slow. Arianna didn't care for it. She planted her feet and folded her arms. "Who's asking?"

"What?"

She sighed. "Who. Is. Ask-ing."

He scowled down at her. "I am Garrett, Heir of Marsan."

It had been a hundred and thirteen years since Captain Marsan had taken the people away, and the captain had been at least thirty then. The captain's heir would have long since inherited whatever the death march had left her.

His eyes narrowed as though he followed her thoughts. "The captain, the First Lord Protector of Marsan, was my great-grandmother. Now . . ." He leaned forward, over his saddle horn. "Tell me, what is this place?"

"What did you expect to find at the end of the Mage Road?" she asked as though he were a not particularly bright child. "This is Gateway."

"Impossible! Gateway was destroyed!" His horse danced back, and the elephant rose to its feet.

It hadn't been lying down. It had been squatting, a gray leather cloak and wide-brimmed leather hat shielding it. Standing, it was taller than Gregir and twice as broad. The misshapen hump became a pack under the cloak. The earliest records mentioned a Rock Troll, but the legible parts of the description suggested it was less compact, more a stack of quickened rock the mages had used for heavy lifting.

Arianna took a step closer and tilted her head until she could see the face shadowed by the brim of the hat.

Gray skin, deep-set eyes, and a wide mouth over a heavy jaw. Brows and lashes were scarce and she could see no other hair. Arms were a little long, legs a little short, making the whole shape look top heavy, but Jinny Ivan's daughter Alisinna had been born without a right arm and Tam Two-trees barely came up to her lowest rib, so the gods clearly allowed any number of variations on the norm. The physical signs were almost nonexistent—anyone but a healer would have missed them, but Arianna would bet her own right breast that the . . . the person was female.

There was nothing wrong with her. The wrongness Arianna could feel had been done *to* her, over and over again. Arianna swayed under the weight of the damage she faced. Swayed, recovered, knew it was nothing she could heal, and reluctantly accepted that the way she'd reluctantly accepted her inability to give Alisinna an arm.

"Don't be afraid," commanded Garrett, Heir of Marsan. "It's under my control."

"I'm not afraid." She knew he wanted to say, *you should be.* It was so obvious, a child could have seen it. Leaning in closer to the large person, she kept a tight grip on the healer's urge to touch. "What's your name?"

"It doesn't have a name."

"I'm not asking you, I'm asking her." Flashing the alleged Heir of Marsan her best *I'm a healer, don't mess with me* smile, she turned her attention back to his companion. "Or don't you speak?"

The large person cocked her head slightly.

Marsan bit out a terse, "Rarely."

"Well, why would she, with you answering for her all the time."

The oldest of the other three men barked out a laugh, cut short by a glare from Marsan. Maybe Marsan was the heir, maybe he wasn't. It seemed a stupid thing to lie about, but Wills would find the truth soon enough.

Arianna folded her arms and, when she'd regained the heir's attention, when he once again stared disapprovingly down at her from on high, said, "If you believed that Gateway was destroyed, why are you here at the end of the road?"

"That's no business of yours."

She nodded. "The Broken Lands, then." Not exactly a difficult guess; if the five of them weren't headed for Gateway, the Broken Lands was all that remained. Well, the Broken Lands and trees, but they didn't look like they were after lumber.

"If you think to block our access . . ."

She waved that off. "No need. The Broken Lands takes care of scavengers."

He looked insulted by that. "No scavengers pass the barricade."

"Does your barricade stretch across the world?"

"No . . ."

"Then don't be ridiculous."

"You can't travel the Mage Road unless you start where it begins."

Huh. She hadn't known that. "Well, you're still ridiculous if you think no one has ever slipped past your barricade."

The large person suddenly stood between Arianna and the other four travelers, weight forward, hands out from her sides, a wall built of gray flesh. Her face bore no expression, but Arianna saw a warning in the pale eyes. Not a complicated warning, more a simple *don't*.

The four travelers clutched weapons and peered suspiciously past Arianna, toward the wall.

Arianna heard footsteps.

Without turning, holding the pale gray gaze, certain with no evidence at all that the connection held her motionless, she stepped to the left, leaving the center of the road free. "Nicareei Olan, Voice of the Council, I present to you Garrett, who says he's Heir of Marsan."

She suspected that man who'd laughed before wanted to laugh again. Would have had this not become an official sort of stand-off.

"Marsan?" Nica repeated, her comforting bulk easing muscles Arianna hadn't known she'd tensed. "I see four men. Which one is it then, Healer?"

"Bay horse. Dark blue jacket."

"And the . . ." She paused and waved a hand, thin copper wires knit into the backs of her fingerless gloves flashing.

"The large person?"

Nica's lips twitched. "The large, gray person. You're certain they're not one of the shattered?"

"Yes."

"This is Captain Marsan's weapon!" The supposed heir stood in the stirrups in order to shout over the large person's head. Arianna thought he looked annoyed. Were they supposed to be impressed? "This is the last of the six great weapons created during the Mage War, created by the mages to destroy mages!"

"Wills."

Wills, who'd been standing silently on Nica's other side, twisted both hands in the front of his tunic. Even after living half his forty-two years in Gateway, he remained uncomfortable using his talent. Given the scars on his throat and the damage beneath them, no one doubted he had cause. He wet his lips and whispered, "Truth."

"The Records say the captain carried the weapon out of the Broken Lands." Head cocked, Nica measured the gray bulk. "I doubt she carried that." Generous curves rose and fell as Nica took a step forward. "You, young man, are you indeed the Heir of Marsan?"

"I am!"

"Truth," Wills whispered.

"What is he saying?" Garrett, who it seemed *was* the Heir of Marsan, had his sword in his hand.

"That he believes you."

"Mage-craft!" one of the younger men cried, fumbling for the crossbow tied to his saddle.

"If Captain Marsan's weapon was designed to destroy mages," Nica snapped, "and hasn't yet destroyed us, what does that tell you?" Nica taught the youngest children and the lessons never really left her voice.

The heir *definitely* looked annoyed. "It will destroy what I tell it to!"

"Not an it," Arianna growled.

"Truth," Wills whispered.

Arianna glared at him behind Nica's back. "I knew that."

He shrugged.

"Hush, you two." Nica took another step forward. "Do you see the archers on the wall, Heir of Marsan? They can shoot the shattered from the sky on a moonless night. If I give the sign, they will, albeit reluctantly, shoot you."

"We have business in the Broken Lands." His lips were pressed into such a thin line, Arianna wondered how the sound managed to emerge. "We want nothing from you."

"How could you want anything from people you had no idea existed?" Nica asked him reasonably. "If you want to risk the Broken Lands in ignorance, be our guest. If not, come in. Bathe, rest, and we'll talk."

And we'll try to convince you that you're an idiot. Arianna smiled, hoping the thought showed on her face.

"I don't . . ."

Nica cut him off. "It's clear we all have plenty to catch up on."

"I control the weapon," Garrett declared, rising in his stirrups as though he were speaking to a plaza full of listeners instead of just the three of them. "You cannot defeat it. If you betray . . ."

"Yes, yes, we'll lose." Rolling her eyes, Nica turned toward the gate. "Good thing we have no intention of betraying anyone."

"And they're a person!" Arianna added, as much to the one he called a weapon as to the heir.

RYAN.NOW

Ryan watched the weapon—no, Nonee—stroke the sod covering the grave and wondered if he should leave. Were they done for now? Had they started?

Before he could decide, she tipped her head slightly to the left, and spoke slowly enough to make the local slur of words comprehensible. "You're too young to be Garrett Heir's son, though the healers say a man's seed doesn't wither with age. Grandson?"

"Great-nephew," Ryan replied, mouth moving before his brain caught up. According to the Lord Protector, according to the chronicles, she never spoke more than a word or two at a time. He doubted she'd ever made an observation about a man's withered seed to his great-uncle. They were conversing. He was conversing with the legendary weapon of Captain Marsan. About his great-uncle's seed. Ryan bit back a laugh he feared would have more than a little hysteria in it. "The Lord Protector had no children of his own."

"No one loved him?"

The Lord Protector was ninety-four and there were still those who speculated about his personal life. How much personal life could he have at ninety-four? Ryan had lost a lot of privacy when he became the heir and he hated the thought of losing the rest. "That's none of my business. Or yours."

Nonee huffed out a breath and said, "Perhaps."

And then she said nothing at all. It grew darker. Ryan wondered how long the captain would wait once she lost sight of him. He should command the weapon now, to be certain he could control her when it became necessary. Instead, he found himself saying, "My mother was the eldest child of the Lord Protector's brother. She was his first heir."

Voices called out in the distance, but not for him so he ignored them.

A cow bawled off to his right.

Nonee might have been made of stone, a bulky statue in the near dark.

"I was my mother's fourth child." He wet his lips, unsure of why he kept talking. "I had three older brothers. There was an accident. They died."

Nonee shifted. "Were you a part of it?"

"Was I . . ." He frowned. His heart began to pound as he realized what she meant. "Are you asking if I killed my brothers to become Lord Protector? Are you crazy?"

She shifted again.

Ryan drew in a deep breath and let it out. "No. I didn't. Why would I? I never expected to be heir. I never wanted to be heir."

"Good."

"Which part?"

"All of it." Her silhouette seemed . . . weighted. As though she were judging his fitness to command when the more important question had to be, was she still fit to be called a weapon?

Wearing beads.

Mourning her . . . mourning whatever the healer was to her.

Ryan only hoped that the life she'd lived for the last sixty-three years hadn't destroyed her purpose. They needed her. Marsanport needed her. He squared his shoulders. "My wants and expectations are no longer relevant. I *am* the heir, I've been sent to find fuel for the Black Flame, and as the heir, I command your help."

"The Last Command."

"Yes." The temperature had fallen with the darkness, but his whole body had begun to sweat. Even his shins were sweating. In spite of the heat they'd endured while they'd been traveling, he hadn't known shins could sweat. "I command you to follow the Last Command."

The breath she huffed out sounded almost amused. "Close enough, Heir of Marsan." Then she turned away to stroke the new grave.

Ryan ignored the clear dismissal, pulled closer by the familiar curve of her back. "What was the healer to you?" he asked after a moment.

"A friend."

"That's all?"

"That's everything."

He heard anger and grief and awe in her voice. Softening his own, he said, "Should we call you Nonee?"

The curve changed. Her head came up. "Where did you learn that name?"

"From the children by the Trader's Hall. From the line scouts I spoke to."

It was hard to tell, but he thought she might have laughed. "Yes, Nonee will do."

"I'd like to leave early tomorrow, if that's . . ." He heard sails luffing in the wind, canvas slapping against itself.

He didn't see her move. One moment she crouched by the grave, the next a pile of green and yellow fabric lay in her place and Nonee bent to pick a rock off the cairn.

It wasn't until after he processed the sound of a wet impact and a wetter rain of body parts that Ryan realized she'd taken what he had to assume was one of the shattered out of the sky.

Taken it out of the sky in pieces.

With a thrown rock.

Still a weapon, then.

Good. They needed the weapon.

"But you saw a person," he murmured to Arianna's grave. To honor the healer's life, he'd try to do the same.

NONEE.NOW

"Nonee?"

She brushed her palm over the damp grass. She sat to one side of the grave, as she'd sat to one side of Arianna's deathbed. "What are you doing out so late?"

Darny dropped to the ground beside her. "Mam thought you might stay here all night. So she said I should come talk to you."

"Did she?"

"Mostly. She says everyone's been asked to stay out of sight tomorrow morning, when you leave, 'cause a bunch of people are unhappy about it, about you maybe being in danger, and the council just wants the folk from Marsanport gone without a fight. Then she said the last thing we need are them seeing more stuff. The heir, he was at the big fountain when Sa Viole was there to purify. He didn't say nothing, but Trader Gils said he definitely noticed."

And yet he said nothing. How much had Garrett Heir told him? She stroked the grass again.

"The scholar girl?" Darny continued. "She wanted me to call her Scholar Novitiate Marsan-cee. Stupidly long, right? She's his cousin. The heir's cousin, not Trader Gils's. That would be weird, right?"

"Why?"

"You know, if his cousin just showed up with the heir." He huffed out a breath before she could respond. "Okay, maybe not weird. Do you know what a scholar novitiate is?"

"Yes." Long before Garrett Heir had found her, scholars used to come to speak to her. No. Not to her. At her. Eventually, she'd remained silent, no matter what they did. It was easier.

"Okay. She doesn't want to be heir even though she could be. I think. It was hard to get her to talk about that stuff. She only wants to learn things. But only the before things, because she didn't ask me anything much about now." He stretched out his legs and scratched one ankle with the toes of his other foot, the sandals he'd worn at the burial long since abandoned. Nonee waited. He'd let her know when he was done. "I don't think she cares about now," he said after both ankles had been tended to. "She found papers in the warren written by some kid, about burying a dragon's tooth to grow a dragon, but I guess that only matters if you have a dragon's tooth and Mam says there's none of them around no more. She says that's a good thing."

"Yes."

"I guess. She doesn't listen if you tell her things and she thinks she already knows the answer. I kept telling her the well was good and she kept going on about pipes and seepage and stuff. Mam said not to tell her about the archives. We'd probably never get rid of her."

"And the older scholar?"

"Sort of like Sa Botec. No." His hand appeared in front of her face. Nonee wasn't certain what he thought he was stopping her from doing. "More like Sa Trace. You remember how two years ago she got all, *leave me alone and let me do my work I'm so tired of the lot of you*, even though she was supposed to still be teaching us? Like that."

Trace had been updating the genealogy records. Their population wasn't large enough to let that slide. She'd spent a lot of time with Arianna when she should have been at the school.

Before she'd died of a wasting disease the healers couldn't fix.

Before Arianna had died.

"Nonee?"

How long had she been sitting silent? How much did it matter? She pulled her fingers from the ground. "Go on."

"The old scholar, he's holding something tight inside. I can tell. Like my cousin Mavs when she got with Kirina and she knew the healers were going to yell at her 'cause they told her no more babies. Maybe he's just trying to hide how badly he wants to go to the Broken Lands, you know? They both do. Don't know why they didn't ask to go to the wall. The heir went, but they didn't. I think . . ." He paused and she could hear his frown in the silence. "I think maybe they don't want to tempt themselves? Like if they were that close, they'd go right up and over the wall. Her anyway. She really, really wants to get to the Broken Lands." He snorted and pulled himself up onto his feet using Nonee's shoulder. "She wants to know its *history*."

Nonee almost smiled at his tone. History was all the Broken Lands had.

No.

Not *all*.

She roused herself enough to consider responsibilities. "Can you get home all right?"

"Sure. Clear night." He waved one hand at the sky; the other was still on her shoulder. "And the grrs never fly by twice. Not after they lose one. You going to stay here?"

Yes. No. She liked that he was still young enough to use the children's word for the shattered. She'd lose him in time, but not for a while yet. "Maybe."

Given their positions, he mostly hugged her head. She raised a hand and laid it against the lean, young line of his back as he said, "Be careful out there, okay? And come home."

"Yes."

⁂

She could smell dawn on the air when she woke. Dawn and the lingering scent of purkin blossoms. And sheep shit, but out in the meadow that was a given. Her skin and clothing were damp, the night weeping when she couldn't. Her fingertips traced the joins between the pieces of sod, and the need to see Arianna one last time was so strong she curled her hands into fists for safety. Then almost laughed at the thought.

Arianna would have laughed.

"This new heir is younger than ours," she said softly. "And uncertain of more than the quest he's been given. With luck, Gils can tell me why. He stood here and said he didn't want to be heir and it was truth." Wills had been dead for a long time and none of his children had his talent. Ari had hopes for one of his great-grandchildren. Had *had* hopes. "You should have heard how he said *the Last Command*. Like it was almost a question. His cousin . . ."

The heir's cousin, not Trader Gils's, Darny added in her head.

". . . the scholar novitiate, has been studying the warren. She has eyes like a magpie, looking for shiny things to steal. Where we're going, both uncertainty and avarice could get them killed. Garrett Heir is their great-uncle . . ."

Is their great-uncle. Not *was*.

The new heir was perceptive. Why was Garrett Heir alive when Arianna was dead?

"They have his features," she growled through clenched teeth, anger mixed with grief. "He has Garrett's eyes and cheekbones, she has his nose. Too soon to know their hearts." They'd faced little danger on the Mage Road, lessening their expectation of danger to come. That would make it harder to keep them alive.

She wanted to hear Arianna's opinion on the danger they'd be facing. On the best way for Nonee to fulfill the Last Command. On Garrett Heir's kin. On the seven non-kin with them. Arianna was better with people because Arianna had been a person her whole life. Nonee wanted to hear what she'd say about the horses. The wagon. The clothing.

About anything.

RYAN.NOW

Ryan wished he'd asked Keetin to stay. Company might have kept him from dreaming of a dead woman watching while Nonee threw stones at gulls flying over Marsanport. As her face rotted, Arianna-the-healer kept repeating that he had to remember, but wouldn't tell him *what* to remember. When Harris woke him at dawn, he was slick with sweat.

Had he missed something important?

Scholars said dreams were the brain's way of clearing out old knowledge to make way for new.

Scholars had also said the brain functioned using the movement of spirits drawn in by breathing, and recently they'd had to admit they were wrong about that, so . . .

He'd almost finished dressing when Keetin opened his door holding two scale-mail vests. "Flame it. In daylight this room is smaller than mine."

Ryan nodded toward the window. "Better view."

"Granted. I'm facing the courtyard. Here. Captain says we put them on now. Oh, yay." He dropped one of the vests on the bed, then dropped down beside it. "We going to talk about the elephant in the room?"

Ryan made a noncommittal noise. Harris had trimmed everyone's hair, cutting Keetin's short enough to remove the sun-bronzed curls, leaving only the reddish brown tucked tight to his head. It made him look older. More serious.

"There's mage-craft here, Ry. There's no other explanation for what happened at the fountain."

Tapping a fingernail against the central, largest metal disk on the vest, Ryan sighed. "Do you remember when we saw the elephants?" he asked. "The traveling performers up from Southport? The illusions that looked like mage-craft?"

Keetin met his gaze with narrowed amber eyes. "Is that what you think this is?"

If word got back to Marsanport that mage-craft hadn't died with the mages, there'd be panic in the streets. Mage-craft had destroyed the lives of the Five Thousand, and their descendants had been taught that mage-craft was evil. Chaotically evil. *It can't be understood,* scholars declared. *So it can't be controlled. Mage-craft is like standing on a pile of oil-soaked kindling and dropping a lit taper to see what happens, uncaring of the damage done and the lives lost.*

To the people of Marsanport, the Black Flame was a symbol of how the Five Thousand had survived mage-craft. Although Ryan had heard it said that it was a symbol of how the Five Thousand had *defeated* mage-craft. Usually from the sort of people who puffed out their chests and declared *we defeated mage-craft* even though they were generations removed. He'd heard a few in the Court, a few on the street, and even a novitiate make the claim.

More importantly, if he admitted mage-craft continued in Gateway, as the Heir of Marsan, he'd have to do . . . something, and the archers on the wall would take their shot the moment he said anything as flaming stupid as *give your mages over to my judgment.*

"Ry?"

"I think," he said, slowly, pulling himself back into the conversation, "that the Lord Protector left the weapon here for a reason."

"To stop new mages from rising? Doesn't seem to be working, does it?"

Ryan remembered how the shattered had sounded hitting the ground in moist pieces. "She's not exactly subtle," he admitted.

"Can we trust her?"

"We can trust she'll follow the Last Command."

"Because the Lord Protector told you so?" Keetin huffed out a breath. "No offense, Heir of Marsan, but half the time, the Lord Protector couldn't remember who you were."

"We're here," Ryan said. And meant, *nothing we can do about that now.*

"Yeah." Keetin stood, picked up his vest, and nudged Ryan's closer. "Now it's real. We were riding into danger when we left home, braving the Broken Lands to fuel the Black Flame and keep Marsanport safe, then we spent all that time traveling and forgot that traveling wasn't the point." He shifted the vest from hand to hand, scales hissing as they rubbed against each other. "Can you control her? Nonee?"

Ryan thought back over the single conversation he'd had with the weapon. "I don't think it works that way."

LYELEE.NOW

Lyelee glared around the training floor above the stable. The interior had been as thoroughly gutted as the building across the courtyard; nothing of the time before the Mage War remained.

"Afraid the locals will learn stuff they shouldn't know?" Destros asked as he set the last box sealed with a scholar's blue ribbon on the pile.

"Of course not." Gearing waved him away without looking up. "We're taking *that* with us. You don't hand a child a torch and send it to play in a haymow."

The guardian opened his mouth, closed it again, and headed for the stairs, murmuring, "Well, you're not wrong."

When his receding footsteps told her he'd reached the stable floor, Lyelee unclipped a sheath of papers and fanned them out on the trade table. "These are the pages with the descriptions of the plants and animals the Lord Protector's party was attacked by. Scholar Novitiate Treen did a good job on the copies."

"Her condensed writing is better than yours."

"And yours," Lyelee pointed out. "Shall you carry them or shall I?"

He tapped his nose with the pencil. "You're carrying the copy of the edibles list. I'll take them."

"I'll miss the wagon when we have to carry samples out," she muttered, reaching for his bag.

"Don't be ridiculous." Gearing slapped his palm down, closing the flap before she got it all the way open. "We won't be carrying the samples. Not with four guardians, Harris, and the recorded strength of the weapon." When he realized she was staring at his hand, he added, "On second thought, there's no point in carrying the edibles list. We can't count on what was edible then to be edible now and I don't want to have to explain that every time we stop. Leave it. You'll carry the record of attacks instead."

"We can't count on what attacked the Lord Protector to be unchanged either." She frowned down at the stack of papers, shuffled out the records of attack, and looked up to see Gearing had shifted his bag down the table and out of her reach.

"Avoiding that which we need not avoid has a significantly lesser consequence than eating something we assume to be safe," he said when he saw he had her attention again.

"I could take them both."

"If you're too stubborn to admit I'm right, go ahead."

Not something she was likely to admit—not out loud—but she opened the flap of her own bag and exchanged the documents, wondering what her mentor wasn't willing to share and if he'd found it in the tenements or brought it from the Hall. All she'd seen before he'd reacted was his sample box, his sticks, and his notebook, the corners of a few sheets of loose paper sticking out from between the pages. He had his pencils out on the table, checking the cores were still safely wrapped.

"Do we care if the inhabitants of Gateway read what we're leaving behind?" she wondered, dropping the edibles list into the last open box.

"If any of them can read condensed script, they're welcome to educate themselves." Gearing set one pencil down and lifted another.

About to comment on the apparent lack of education she'd observed, a shriek from the stable jerked Lyelee's attention toward the stairs. It took her a moment to realize the sound was a child's laughter.

"Go on down, then."

"To the stable?" Surprised, Lyelee spun around toward him. "Why?"

"To discover what's going on." Raised brows added a silent *of course*.

She glanced back at the top of the stairs. He waved her on with one hand, the other on his satchel.

It made sense for her to investigate the sudden noise. It would have made as much sense for them to ignore it. He was definitely hiding something.

Two-thirds of the way down, Lyelee froze as a somewhat familiar child offered Slate a bunch of red clover. The big horse dipped his head over the half door, opened his mouth, exposing huge slabs of yellow teeth . . .

And didn't take the child's hand off at the wrist.

"It's okay, Scholar."

Lyelee stared down at Servan, who grinned up at her.

"Jisper's like me," the guardian continued. "Animals love her."

Slate rolled an eye back, but kept chewing, green saliva dripping to the floor.

"That horse loves no one," Lyelee pointed out, stepping down onto the stable floor. "You there!"

The child turned, tiny fingers patting a pale gray nose.

"You're one of the children I spoke to in the corral. Where are . . ."

"Cali! Eril keeps taking the fork and you said I could use it!"

Servan folded her arms as the other two children Lyelee had spoken to ran around the corner. "There's more than one hay fork."

"But this is the best!" The braided child insisted.

The palest child yanked at the perfectly normal-looking hay fork. "And you said I could use it!"

Lyelee frowned as Servan waded into the argument. If the braided child was Eril and the smallest was Jisper, was the palest child Cali?

"Cali! Make her stop!"

Oh. Servan. Calintris Servan-cee. She'd been *Servan* for so long, Lyelee had forgotten the guardian had a personal name.

"Ewww. Horse!" The smallest child wiped their hands on their tunic, adding to the mess already covering it, then turned to look at Lyelee. "Da is helping take care of them while you go away and I'm helping my da."

"Do animals like your da the way they like you?"

"Nope."

"Then remind him that horse bites."

Slate blew out a breath and sprayed the child, who shrieked with laughter and leapt back into Servan's arms.

Servan and Jisper were the only two people Slate hadn't tried to take a piece out of.

⁂

Out in the courtyard, all three children hung off the weapon as though it—she—had been designed for their climbing pleasure. None of them appeared disturbed by her objectively ugly appearance, although if they'd been exposed often enough, they wouldn't be. All three spoke at once, their voices a high-pitched, incoherent noise, and although it was doubtful child comprehension had been included in her design, the weapon seemed to understand what they were saying. As Lyelee watched, the palest child slipped off a broad shoulder, was plucked from the air and set gently on the ground—only to begin the climb again.

The weapon's hands were out of proportion, larger than they should be. The nails almost black. Her body was a thick rectangle—no noticeable breast tissue, no curve of hip. Her bare feet were as out of proportion as her hands. Like her legs, they were thicker and broader to carry her weight. Dust covered her feet and Lyelee couldn't see if the toenails were as dark, but logic said they should be. As much as logic had anything to do with the creature standing in the courtyard.

Her skin was a granite gray, darker and lighter flecks mixed together. Had the mage used stone in her construction? Or had that been an aftereffect of the process? Was the coloring sympathetic to the mage-craft that made her *as strong as stone*? Would the use of sympathetic magic in her construction be a valid hypothesis?

"Just think of what the mages had to do to turn an infant into that," she murmured.

"Nothing good," Gearing said behind her.

Lyelee decided not to argue about it. The weapon was amazing.

That the ancient mages could start with a babe in the womb and create such size and strength by the application of mage-craft beggared
the imagination. There were those among the scholars who argued that
the captain had to have been dealing in metaphor, that no one could have
both the knowledge and the power to do such a thing, not once but six
times. As those who remembered the days when the weapon was kept in
Marsanport grew older and the Mage War moved another generation into
history, the belief grew that the weapons—if more than one existed at
all—had been created by more mundane means. Large, yes. Strong, yes.
There were always those who were larger and stronger. Flesh and bone
encouraged by magics to become what it wasn't intended to be? No. The
paintings were an artist's imagining, and details of the sketches and
the stories had to have been stretched and embellished as stories so often
were.

But there stood the proof.

Big and gray and wearing a sleeveless leather tunic over short, cloth
pants.

"What does the weapon wear?" Lyelee murmured. "Anything it wants
to."

NONEE.NOW

"Nonee! Nonee! Da says I can help take care of the horses! They got a big,
gray horse and his name is Slate and he bites everyone 'cept me."

She glanced down at Jisper swinging off her wrist, bare feet tucked up
so as not to drag on the ground. "You mean he hasn't bitten you yet."

"I don't get bit. I'm like granna." Jasper's nose wrinkled. "Cali don't
get bit either. Is she like granna?"

"Cali?"

Jisper let go and pointed toward the stable.

Nonee turned. One of the guardians paused just outside the stable
door, right hand working the buckles of her left vambrace.

"That would be me." The guardian's throat moved as she swallowed,
but she was calmer than many who saw Nonee up close for the first
time. "Calintris Servan-cee. I said they could call me Cali. It's . . . uh,
shorter."

"Cali! This is Nonee. We told you 'bout her, remember?" Grubby hands on skinny hips, Jisper stared up at the guardian, fearless as only the young could be. "She's gonna bring you back, but you got to do what she says, okay?"

The guardian studied the child for a moment, glanced up at Nonee, then nodded. "Okay."

"Okay," Nonee repeated thoughtfully. This guardian, this Calintris Servan-cee who took the children seriously and showed more caution than fear, she could work with.

"It's time for you three to go." Garrett Heir's great-niece stepped forward, brushing past the guardian without acknowledgment, her magpie gaze locked on Nonee's face. The magpie-who-could-be-heir, Scholar Novitiate Kalyealee Marsan-cee, who didn't so much question as calculate, would bear watching.

"Do we have to go, Nonee?" Playz demanded. "We didn't get to spend no time with you at all."

"We could come with you as far as the wall," Eril suggested, arms folded.

"And how would you get home from the wall?" she asked.

The child's gaze flipped around the courtyard until she pointed at Gils. "He's not going with you, right? Not outside the wall. He can take us home!"

"He is the cat's father." It was something Arianna used to say. Names were important to her. Nonee drew in a deep breath and slowly released it. Grief would be her companion as she dealt with the Last Command.

"Trader Gils!" Eril called imperiously.

"Trader Gils is not your caretaker." She raised a hand and held the trader in place. He was a soft touch with children and these three would walk all over him. "Go home now, and when this is over . . ."

"You'll come play?"

"Yes."

"Promise?"

"Yes."

Jisper pushed past the older child. "Cross your heart and spit in your eye, eaten by grrs if you're telling a lie?"

"Yes." The corners of her mouth twitched. "Now go!"

She bent to accept hugs then watched the children dart back into the stable, heading for the rear corral and the shortcut to their homes. Those in the courtyard watched her. Fear, curiosity, wonder, and more fear. She hadn't been looked at in fear for a long time, but she was sure she'd get used to it again.

Scholar Novitiate Kalyealee Marsan-cee, who-could-be-heir, continued to calculate. Without fear. She had too many names, Nonee acknowledged. Too many names and titles and they'd have to be shortened to define her. The older man beside her, Scholar Gearing, who had only one name anyone used, had his fear tempered by a hungry curiosity. He brought up a distant memory of a gull darting in to pull a prize from a pile of fish guts, darting back before the dog, whose dinner it was, attacked. She'd watch him too.

"We were told to call you Nonee."

"Yes." Her aching heart appreciated how that would never stop being funny. Captain Yansav, who guarded the Heir, stood before her without introducing herself. She wasn't a person to the captain, she was a weapon. An unknown weapon and thus to be wary of.

"I am responsible for the safety of the Heir of Marsan. Do you understand?"

"Yes." She glanced at Ryan Marsan-cer, who was the Heir of Garrett. He was the slightest of the four men she could see, and the youngest, only beginning to put on adult bulk. He looked away when she looked at him. He'd been kind at Arianna's grave. Did they see kindness as weakness? Did he *need* a caretaker?

Why did Marsanport persist in sending children to the Broken Lands?

She turned her attention back to the captain in time to see her chin rise slightly. A challenge, Nonee realized, in spite of the fear. "I need to know," the captain said, "if you can follow orders."

"Yes. And give them too, once on the other side of the wall. Can you follow orders, Captain Yansav?"

Borit Destros, the largest and oldest of the guardians, snorted, the way Blue Jin did when he was amused. Good. They weren't afraid of their captain. Nonee had known commanders who used fear to maintain discipline.

She'd been what they were afraid of.

When the captain realized she was waiting for an answer, her eyes narrowed and her expression changed, expectations beginning to fracture. "You know the Broken Lands."

"Yes."

"I'll take that into account."

"If you want your heir to survive," Nonee agreed. She raised her voice until it filled the courtyard. "The Broken Lands and everything in them were shattered. The residue of mage-craft, with no mage alive to dismiss it, has twisted plants and animals and the stones themselves ever since the war. There's no way to know exactly what you'll find."

"It hasn't faded? Not even a little in all this time?" Keetin Norwin-cee, who was the friend—Nonee's nostrils flared—and recent bedmate of the Heir, spread his hands. He was so pale, she saw no difference in color between the backs and the palms. "Mage-craft that old should be a little tottery by now, shouldn't it?"

The heir's mouth twitched within the shadow of his sparse beard. The novitiate and the scholar whispered about incomplete research. Destros snorted again. Servan frowned and looked as though she agreed with Keetin Norwin-cee. When he noticed her watching him, Vaylin Curtin-cee took a step back, a white-knuckled grip on the hilt of his sword. When describing the company to her, Trader Gils had called Vaylin Curtin-cee suspicious. She saw no suspicion, only fear. And hatred. She could get used to hatred again if she had to.

Except for the pulse beating below the dark skin of her throat, Captain Yansav remained perfectly still.

Nonee lifted her arms out from her sides and spread her hands slowly. As a gesture, to show she had no weapons, it meant nothing at all, but people who didn't think about what it meant to be *the weapon* reacted favorably, so she continued to make it. This time, she mirrored Keetin Norwin-cee, who was liked by everyone in the company. "Mage-craft doesn't get tottery," she said.

"You're not what I expected." Caution had nearly erased the fear on the captain's face, although it lingered below the surface. "But, I tell you now, the amount I listen depends on how much of the weapon remains. We need the weapon. We don't need . . ."

"Whatever it thinks it is," Curtin muttered under his breath when the captain paused, uncertain of how to finish.

"Curtin! Enough!"

"Aye, Captain."

Not a new sentiment, then. Her appearance hadn't caused this, he'd brought it with him.

"The weapon remains." Nonee shrugged. It was one of the first gestures Arianna had taught her. "You look like Captain Marsan. Is that why they sent you?"

Ryan Heir startled. It hadn't occurred to him, but Nonee could see it *had* occurred to the captain.

"I came to Marsanport from the same part of the world as Captain Marsan. I've seen her portraits. The resemblance is . . . minor."

"You believe it's minor because you've only seen the portraits. Not the captain. Although she was taller."

"Most captains are." Captain Yansav's voice was flat, matter-of-fact. She wouldn't defend her lack of height.

Nonee liked her. "Distance weapons?"

The captain took the sudden change of topic in stride. "Crossbows. Servan's our archer. She uses a recurve."

Servan, the guardian the animals liked, lifted a hand.

Her shoulders were broad and her hands steady. "How good are you?"

She opened her mouth. Nonee waited for boasting, but she only said, "Good enough."

A recurve could be fired in time to the archer's heartbeat if the archer was skilled. Faster, if precision wasn't essential. Some of the shattered hunted in packs. Nonee nodded approval, then returned to the captain. "Other weapons?"

"Swords. Daggers. Axes."

"Light weapons only?"

"Destros."

He pulled one of his axes and held it horizontally across his body. The blade was as large as her hand with the fingers spread, a weapon with weight enough to chop through bone. The end of the shaft had been capped with a steel spike. His second axe was small enough to throw. She didn't much approve of throwing weapons away, but occasionally it was the only option. Borit Destros's head would reach her shoulder, a handspan further than any of the others. His shoulders were broad over a barrel chest and thick thighs. He had a braid on either side of his long, oiled beard and wore his hair like the other guardians in a short, tightly curled cap. His eyelashes were thick and his eyes so dark brown they looked almost black.

And the company was waiting for her response. "That's good. The . . ." She waved a hand. "The axe. You'll need heavy weapons."

"I thought you were the heavy weapon?" Keetin Norwin-cee called.

Nonee nodded. "Yes."

The captain's expression suggested he not interrupt again. "Harris was a guardian in his youth. If he has to fight, he uses a mace."

Harris, who took care of the others. He wasn't in the courtyard. "A mix of weapons is good." She jerked her head toward the scholars. "Them?"

"They don't fight."

"Leave them."

"I wish we could."

"Scholarship will not be sidelined! We need knowledge of the Broken Lands. Knowledge," Scholar Novitiate Kalyealee Marsan-cee, who-might-be-heir, added when Nonee turned to face her, "is power."

"Not the kind of power the Broken Lands respects." She turned her back on the scholars, and asked the captain, "When do you plan to leave?"

"We're ready to go," the captain said briskly.

"No."

"No?" Brisk grew cold.

"Not until the packs are checked."

They glared at her again—the scholars, the guardians, the nobles—but couldn't move her. Her skin turned blades. Annoyance could be ignored.

Captain Yansav squared her shoulders. "We need to leave as soon as possible . . ."

"We've already waited three days," Keetin Norwin-cee broke in. "What's a few hours more?" A cheerful question. Good. She understood his function in the company. Arianna would like . . . would have liked him.

"Searching every pack will take too long," the captain continued without acknowledging either the young lord's words or his attempt to break the tension. "We won't make it to the wall before dark, let alone to the Broken Line."

"The packs won't be searched."

Servan held up a hand as though she were in the classroom. "You said checked."

"Yes."

"So you'll just ask us what we're carrying?" Ryan Heir looked confused.

"Yes."

"And if someone lies?" Captain Yansav asked.

"Did you bring stupid people with you?"

The captain blinked and almost smiled. Nonee knew that expression. The captain had begun to see a person. Not all the time. Not yet. But for a moment, at this time. "No, we didn't."

"Good."

⚹

In spite of the wagon, they'd done a certain amount of living off the land as they traveled to Gateway. They needed to get out of the habit. She added more dried meat from the stores the council had sent to the hall. The dried sausages had been made a year ago and needed to be eaten. In balance, there was fresh leather made of this season's berries.

More oatmeal cakes. Less oatmeal.

Harris nodded thoughtfully. "Cakes need less water. How long do you think we'll be in there?"

"As long as needed."

"Can you live off the land?" When she told him she could, he said, "I'd doubted even you could carry enough food to keep you fed."

Even you.

She'd heard those words in the past, said with horror, said with cruelty. From Harris she heard disapproval, although she didn't know what he disapproved of.

He dropped a string bag of radishes back into his pack. "They contain water," he pointed out when Nonee held out a hand.

"They crunch. They'll give your position away."

He tapped a hand against his chest, gaze still carefully averted from her face. "Scale-mail vest. The scholars aren't wearing one, but the rest of us are. And the guardians are armed to the teeth. We're not sneaking anywhere."

She let her hand drop to her side. "Truth."

⚹

"*Three* shirts?" she asked.

"It's hot," Keetin Norwin-cee pointed out as he stared at her. She liked that he didn't try to hide it. He'd never seen anything that looked like her before, why shouldn't he stare? There was no judgment in it, only curiosity. He smelled of clean male, dried mint, and a little of Ryan Heir. "Did you want me to wear the same shirt for however long it takes to find the fuel and get out again?"

"Yes."

"That's not . . ."

"One shirt. Carry more water."

Gils, who'd been close enough to overhear, frowned. "Don't you have . . ."

"Yes." When she let the word hang alone, he moved away. She had a purifier, but there was a good chance these people who lived without talents wouldn't trust it.

Curtin looked past her as he answered her questions, his answers clipped short. Had he not been a guardian and trained to do what he disliked, she knew he wouldn't have answered her at all. He carried most of the company's healing supplies.

Nonee would carry more. Arianna had prepared for a return to the Broken Lands.

The scholars had paper in the bags slung over their shoulders and not enough water in their packs.

"Harris can carry our water," Scholar Gearing sniffed. "Water is heavy."

"Paper is heavy. You carry your own water."

Ryan Heir added his voice, but it wasn't until the captain stepped in that they obeyed.

"The weapon giving orders to the hand that wields it," she heard Kaly-ealee who-could-be-heir mutter, taking two waterskins from Harris.

"You've never wielded a weapon," Ryan Heir reminded her.

She changed little things. Shifted the chance that they'd survive.

"Did you fuss this much over the Lord Protector?" Keetin Norwin-cee asked, leaning against the wall, arms folded.

"No."

"No, I don't expect you would have. I've met the Lord Protector," he added, grinning. "Did Arianna fuss?"

Nonee didn't smile. She knew how the expression upset people who didn't know her. "Yes. Arianna was a healer. Healers fuss."

"Are *you* finished fussing?" Ryan Heir demanded.

"Yes."

"And we can go?"

"Yes."

Both scholars reluctantly shrugged into heavy leather jackets with brass fittings.

She frowned. "It's going to get hotter. This is a uniform?"

"No." Ryan Heir shook his head. "We, Keetin and I, trained on the road wearing the scale and helms, but the scholars don't fight. The leather will help keep them safe."

"In this heat, it'll kill them."

Feet shuffled all around the courtyard, the realization of stupidity set into motion. Curtin glared as though she'd suggested she'd kill them herself.

She sighed, and held out a hand for the jackets. The stitching gave way before the leather, as it should, and she handed them back without sleeves or brass. "Less weight than the armored vests, some protection over organs."

"And if one of the shattered chews my arm off?" Kalyealee who-could-be-heir sneered, holding the leather as though she held the dead animal it had come from.

"You may still survive." Nonee nodded at the guardians' bare arms and vambraces, at the two lordlings' linen sleeves. "The same as the others."

"We're scholars," declared Kalyealee who-could-be-heir.

We're better than they are. Nonee could have heard her actual words even a hundred years ago when subtlety often escaped her.

"We need more protection." Scholar Gearing clutched the strap of the satchel he wouldn't leave behind.

"Do you need to be cooked before you're eaten?" she asked.

Keetin Norwin-cee laughed loudly. The others, even Curtin, smiled.

Lips pressed into surprisingly similar thin lines given the differences in their faces, the scholars reluctantly shrugged into their vests.

"I feel so safe." Kalyealee who-could-be-heir picked at a loose thread.

"Safe from some," Nonee told her. "It's better than nothing," she admitted after a moment. She wore leather from shoulders down to mid thigh, linen shorts to her knees under it, and only because too many were bothered when she didn't. "You should have used the road to gain experience in armor."

"They refused," Ryan Heir told her. "The jackets were a compromise. The Lord Protector wanted everyone wearing a vest. The scholars . . ." His voice trailed off. He sighed and began again. "If the Lord Protector had his way, we'd all be in full armor tucked behind those tall Shurlian shields. He wanted everyone as safe as possible."

"Yes." This time she smiled, unable to stop it. "He always fussed."

GARRETT.THEN

Garrett folded his arms, met the healer's gaze, and said, "We're not leaving the horses behind."

"What part of *the Broken Lands are broken* are you having so much trouble understanding?" Arianna deliberately mirrored his position, dampening enough of the appalling Gateway accent for him to easily understand her. "We won't be following a mage road right to your fuel."

"You don't know that."

"Yes, I do. And there's nothing for them to eat."

"Grass . . ."

"Is broken! Look, they'll be taken care of," she added. "It's not like you'll be leaving them behind to be cooked and eaten."

Garrett ignored Norik's bark of laughter, walked to the far end of the first floor of the small house that had been vacated for them, and returned. Norik and Malcolm were watching the discussion as though they were watching roll-ball. Petre was trying to get a small black cat to take a piece of sausage from his fingers, in spite of Arianna's warnings.

The moment Garrett had moved from her direct line of sight, Arianna had turned to watch the weapon. Understandable. There'd been people watching the weapon when they left Marsanport, even though they'd left before dawn to avoid riots. One of the braver had thrown a broken cobblestone and yelled in triumph when it bounced off the weapon's shoulder. Garrett had held his breath until it became clear the weapon wasn't going to respond. Scholar Meng Wan had insisted it would respond only to his commands, but scholars often had little idea of the distance between scholarship and reality. They'd all watched it on the road until familiarity made it no more of note than their other weapons. Although the weapon wasn't one of the shattered, having been purposefully created before the Mage War, he supposed it looked enough like the creatures that lurched out of the chaos to cause Arianna concern. He only wished he believed that was the reason for her interest.

"I'm not concerned about how the horses will be cared for," he said, forcing calm. "I must return to Marsanport with the fuel before the Black Flame goes out. I haven't time to walk."

Arianna sighed, and shifted her attention back to him. "Did you gallop all the way here?" she asked. "No, you didn't. That would have killed the horses long before you arrived. Over long distances, a person travels as quickly as a horse. More quickly, if you don't care overmuch about the condition you arrive in. Horses need a lot of food and they're fairly fussy about what that is, while people are willing to eat pretty much anything they can get into their mouths. Horses are stupidly fragile in a lot of ways. We have horses here. Well, ponies." She stood and folded her arms, eyes narrowed, and Garrett had to stop himself from taking a step back at the fierce contempt in her expression. "You rode because people of your rank don't walk."

"You're not . . ."

She cut him off. "And you're not listening to me. The ground is unstable and there's no forage, but there are a great many things that'll eat them given half a chance."

"The weapon can protect them."

"And feed them what?"

He didn't want to leave the horses behind. He'd spent most of the Hunter's Moon on the road trusting to Kanalik's strength. He'd slept up against the gelding's side for warmth on the nights a cold wind came down from the mountains. He was one of four among strangers heading into the horror of his people's history, and leaving the horses made him feel the task he faced was impossible.

And people of his rank didn't walk.

Arianna's expression changed and he wondered how many thoughts had shown on his face. She sighed. "All right, if you don't believe me, and to be fair, you have no reason to as you've only just met me, will you believe her?"

"Who?" The healer had come alone. Did she mean the woman from the council?

"Her." Arianna gestured toward the weapon.

"Her?" The weapon squatted, gray and immobile in the corner of the room, oversized hands resting on the floor. When Garrett had found it, deep in the Citadel, it had been in the same position. "How do you get *her* out of *that?*"

"By not making assumptions. I asked her what she wanted to be called."

"You what?"

Arianna frowned. "Do you have difficulty hearing? I may be able to . . ."

"My hearing is fine!"

"All right, then . . ."

He could hear *if you say so* perfectly clearly.

". . . remember that she was there when the Mage Lands broke. Trust her."

"I trust it . . ."

"Her."

". . . to be the weapon it . . ."

"She."

". . . was designed to be." He had to force the words out through clenched teeth.

Arianna sighed again. "Unlike the five previous weapons, the sixth weapon was created to protect the mage who created them. That's why she survived when the five created to attack were destroyed. We have Records here, you know, and I've done some reading since you lot arrived. Trust her to know how to protect you. Ask her."

He knew the weapon could reason, could judge what was a threat and what wasn't. Its orders didn't have to be detailed. According to the chronicles, Captain Marsan had sent it to clear Northport without specifying how. He, personally, felt those orders should have been a little more detailed given the reported number of dead, but that wasn't the point.

"Ask her," Arianna repeated.

Garrett glanced at Norik, who'd been watching their conversation with the same quiet intensity he gave to everything. He hadn't been the only one of Garrett's friends who'd wanted to come—half the young men and women of the court would have ridden north with him—but Garrett's father, the Lord Protector, had refused *"to have him make a production of it."* Norik was strong and steady and he'd reacted to the news that the weapon would be traveling with them the way he'd have reacted had Garrett pulled any other unique weapon from the armory. If it did what it was meant to, he was fine with it.

Here and now, he tipped his head to the side, and raised a brow. *It's your decision. I'll support it.* Then his lips curved within his beard and Garrett added a silent *but get on with it* to his friend's support.

Fine.

The weapon remained in its squat until he signaled that it should rise. Buckets of warm water had washed off the dirt of the road, and whoever had taken their clothing for cleaning had cleaned its covering as well. Aware of its limitations, he searched for the clearest way to ask the question and finally settled on, "Is it safe to take the horses into the Broken Lands?"

It blinked.

After a moment, he turned to Arianna, almost wishing he hadn't been right. "Satisfied? It was taken away a . . ."

"No."

He'd heard it speak before, but it seemed the crushed gravel of its tone had gained subtle differences. "No?"

It blinked again.

"What do you mean, no?"

"Give her a chance." Arianna raised a hand. Garrett wondered what had stained her palm purple. "She's searching for the words."

"How do you . . ."

"My sister's son is almost three. He has the same expression when he's trying to get his point across."

"Broken." It paused, then added, "No safe."

"Are you sure it's not repeating what it heard?" Norik asked softly. "It could have pulled those words from your conversation."

"Where else would she get the words?" Arianna asked acerbically.

Norik nodded, acknowledging the healer's point.

It blinked again.

Garrett waited.

Its dark eyes locked on his face. It had never done that before. It had always looked past him. He could only remember seeing it focus on the animals he'd sent it to kill for food on the way. It had broken rabbits' necks with unbelievable delicacy given the relative sizes. "Protect you," it said. "Horse, no."

"If I order you to protect the horses?"

"Yes." But it didn't seem happy about it. As far as he could tell. "No food," it added. "No horse food."

Arianna spread her hands.

He sighed. "Looks like we're leaving the horses."

They'd traveled as lightly as they could, a change of clothing and an oiled canvas cloak rolled into their bedrolls. They'd have left the change of clothes behind, but traveling in the Hunter's Moon meant a good chance of rain and Garrett needed them all to be healthy when they reached the Broken Lands. They'd each carried a broad, shallow tin cup, two saddlebags of food, and three of them had crossbows and quarrels. Norik had a longbow he'd made himself, steaming the wood, layering the horn, and he'd proven his skill with it time after time.

Everything else, the weapon had carried. Food. Water. Gear. Grain for the horses.

While the big pack hadn't hindered the weapon's movement on the road and it had easily kept up with the horses regardless of their speed, Garrett couldn't afford to count on that once they were in the Broken Lands. It had to be able to move fast and freely.

"Leave the clothing." He tugged the shirt out of Petre's hand. "Food, water, and weapons only."

"Wouldn't we be safer if we smelled less rank?"

"Your smell'll chase them away," Malcolm snickered. "But the kid has a point, sir."

"Six months and four days older does not make you ancient and wise," Petre muttered, thumping Malcolm on the upper arm with the side of his fist.

"We're meat," Garrett reminded him. "We'll smell like food to predators. I assume it can only help if we smell like food gone bad. How long are we going to be in there?" he asked Arianna, who'd just arrived with a basket of supplies.

"No idea." She pulled out a long link of sausages, dried enough that their casings had creased. "I don't know where the fuel is. I'm just there to help keep you alive while we find it."

"No idea?" He glanced at Norik, who shrugged, apparently unconcerned. "If you intend to wander randomly," he said, as Arianna set a net bag of eggs beside the sausages, "we don't need your services as a guide."

"I'm not your guide." She nodded toward the weapon. "She is. But you'll need my services as a healer."

"Yes." It straightened out of its squat.

Garrett turned, finding no more expression on its face than usual. "Yes, we'll need her services as a healer?"

It blinked. "Yes."

"Even with you there to protect us?"

"Alive. Yes." It glanced at Arianna then back to him. "Hurt. Yes."

"You're saying that you can keep us alive, but you can't keep us from being hurt?"

"Yes."

"I'd have been happier if we'd known that back in Marsanport," Norik said dryly. He held up a crossbow quarrel, twirling it between the thumb and forefingers of his left hand. "Could we get more of these? Another ten or twelve for each of them?"

Arianna smiled. "Yes."

Garrett realized she was smiling directly at Norik, that she had a dimple in the right cheek but not the left, and said, "Don't do that. Don't sound like the weapon. And we don't want the eggs. Too fragile."

"Oh, don't be ridiculous, Heir of Marsan. They're hard boiled."

⁕

"Kanalik means One Who Flies. It's Shurlian. Shurlia, that's where Captain Marsan came from before she came here." Garrett pressed his forehead to the horse's then stepped back. He'd been there at the gelding's birth, would have rather not been parted from him, didn't want him injured, would take a blade to the heart were he killed. "Kanalin, One Who Runs, that's a common name for horses. Kanalik not so much."

Arianna shoved her hands into the pockets of her skirt. "We still have Shurlian speakers here."

"Here? In Gateway?"

"Is there another *here*?" The dimple flashed. "The Records are in multiple languages. It makes sense to keep those languages alive to keep the past alive. There's a limited amount even healers can learn from the dead."

Kanalik leaned forward and lipped at his hair.

The dimple reappeared as Garrett wiped a dribble of horse spit off his forehead. "Don't worry, he'll be well taken care of. He'll eat well, he'll rest, he'll have his hooves trimmed, his mane and tail brushed, and when you get back, he'll be able to fly down that road."

Opinion had been split in the Citadel and Scholar's Hall about whether or not the Broken Lands had calmed or continued to roil in mage-created chaos. It had been over a hundred years; Garrett had assumed the destructive mage-craft had begun to wear out. But the undying mage-crafted weapon had called the Broken Lands unsafe. *"When* I get back?" he asked.

"Do you doubt it?"

He looked into her fierce eyes, then past her at where the weapon squatted, reduced pack still rising above its shoulders. "Yes."

She shook her head. "Don't do that."

"Don't sound like the weapon?"

"Don't doubt."

RYAN.NOW

Ryan considered the gaze Nonee swept around the courtyard to be overly critical. He was in command. She needed to remember that, even when he forgot.

"Put the packs in the wagon," she said. "Take them out at the wall."

"No." The sky had turned a clear, bright blue and the sun had risen a measurable distance above the horizon. Ryan raised a hand, holding everyone in place. "Harnessing the horses takes time we don't have."

Nonee heaved her own pack over the side, picked up the tongue, and dragged the wagon forward as though it weighed nothing at all. When no one moved, she sighed. "You *can* carry them."

Lyelee reached the wagon first only because Scholar Gearing had stopped to strip off what was left of his jacket.

Watching the guardians deposit their packs on the painted, wooden floor, Ryan wondered if he should carry his. Thinking of the weapon as a beast of burden would lessen her usefulness and the scholars, at least, would take advantage of it.

"She offered," Yeri said quietly beside him, words pitched under the braiding of voices. "You didn't order her to drag your gear to the wall."

Had he been so obvious a near stranger could see his thoughts? "Does that make a difference?"

"If you can't allow her to make choices now, she'll have a hard time keeping you alive in the Broken Lands."

That made sense, Ryan allowed. He watched Nonee redistribute the weight in the wagon and said, "When you first saw her . . ."

"I almost shit myself." Yeri laughed. "Then my bonded smacked me on the back of the head and told me not to be an ass. No one controls how they look, only how they behave."

As Ryan knew any number of people who worked very hard to control how they looked, he waited for Yeri to finish the story. After a moment, he realized he'd heard everything the trader planned to share. "And that's all it took?"

"The children helped. They adore her." He clasped Ryan's shoulder as though they were friends, not barely acquaintances, and said, "Trust her, my lord. She knows what she's doing."

"That's more or less what the Lord Protector told me."

"He should know."

He should, Ryan agreed silently. "Are you the Lord Protector's spy?" He hadn't intended to ask.

Yeri stepped forward far enough to make eye contact. "No."

"You'd say that if you were a spy."

He smiled broadly enough to curve the tattoos running into his beard. "Probably. They're waiting for you."

They were. Ryan's pack had been moved to the wagon during the conversation. "I need to check on Slate."

"Because we haven't wasted enough time," Lyelee muttered, placing a foot on the step by the seat.

"You're not riding."

"I'm a . . ."

"No." Ryan shot a look at Gearing. "Neither of you. If you can't walk to the wall, you'll never make it as far as the fuel, and we'll leave you here."

Lyelee's brows drew in and she opened her mouth, but Keetin, grinning broadly, cut her off. "Big man with an ancient, mage-crafted weapon at your side."

Ryan flicked flame at him. "Yes, yes I am." That wasn't it. He didn't think that was it. But he was feeling more in control. Maybe because they weren't merely traveling but were actually about to do something. Maybe it was because he had an ancient mage-crafted weapon at his side who'd actually obey him. That was a heady and slightly terrifying feeling. "If you're not off the wagon when I come out of the stable," he told the scholars, "you're staying behind for your safety."

"Sir." Captain Yansav sounded unhappy. "I think . . ."

Nonee folded her arms, muscle bulging. "Garrett Heir took the time to say goodbye to his horse."

"The Lord Protector was able to move quickly, more quickly than we will . . ." Captain Yansav gave no indication she was referring to the scholars, but Ryan could almost hear Lyelee's eye roll. ". . . so he had time he could choose to waste."

"The captain's right." Lyelee's tone was edged. "We don't have time to waste. If the Heir of Marsan fails to get the fuel back to Marsanport and the Flame goes out, catastrophe will follow. Since the current heir has clearly decided his horse is more important than the security of Marsanport . . ." She dropped off the step. "We're leaving for the Broken Lands without him. He can catch up."

Nonee shrugged. "Not stopping you."

"I am a Scholar of the Broken Lands," Gearing began.

Nonee shrugged again, the motion cutting him off. "Don't care."

Ryan watched Lyelee's eyes narrow as she realized scholars didn't get the last word in Gateway. Finally she snapped, "Go see your flaming horse, then!"

～❦～

"She knew my great-uncle when he was young. She knew Captain Marsan. She destroyed enough of Northport it became Marsanport." Ryan pressed his forehead to Slate's, a secure grip on the gelding's halter lessening the odds he'd be bitten. "She knew the mages. A mage created her. She's ancient, and powerful, and studying sketches of her didn't prepare me for the real thing. How am I supposed to command her?" He needed Slate. He couldn't voice his insecurities to anyone in the company.

Slate tossed his head, but Ryan stepped back fast enough to avoid impact.

"Yeah, you're right." He scratched the warm, damp hide under Slate's forelock. "If I can command you, what's a legendary, immortal mage weapon?"

"Hey." The littlest of the three children appeared suddenly by his left hip. She frowned up at him. "Cali says you're the boss. Even of the pretty lady."

The pretty lady? Captain Yansav?

"You got to take care of Nonee and make sure she comes home." She reached up and stroked the side of Slate's face with a grubby hand. Slate leaned into the touch and half-closed his eyes in contentment. "Okay?"

Nonee making it back to Gateway seemed like something Ryan could safely promise. "Okay."

He jerked his arm away just in time for Slate's teeth to snap closed on air.

✦

The streets were empty. Nonee and the wagon were out in front; the rest of them followed behind. Ryan could ignore the absence of Gateway's inhabitants until they reached the market and found it deserted. There were stalls. Produce. Pigeons. A sleeping cat. No people. That was disturbing.

"So no one wants to see us go to our death?" Keetin asked with a laugh that would have sounded less forced had they not been walking through a heavy silence.

"Nonee explained the Last Command," Yeri replied. "They know she has to go, but no one wants her to risk herself."

"She can't be killed," Keetin reminded him.

"The other five were."

"By mage-craft."

"And you're heading into the Broken Lands, where mage-craft makes the rules."

If Keetin had an answer to that, Ryan didn't hear it. He crossed to the fountain and dipped a mug. Three hot days after he'd first tasted it, the water remained clear and cold.

"This is bullshit!" A voice through the open window on a second floor on the far side of the market. "Total bullshit!"

The sound of a scuffle.

Quieter voices.

"So let their flame burn out! Why should we care?"

Quieter voices again.

"Yeah, well, *we* didn't promise the shattered shit anything!"

That seemed to be the last word.

"Come on." Yeri's hand was warm on his shoulder and Ryan fought his way back to a neutral expression. He considered walking the rest of the way to the wall beside Nonee, thought of how he'd look, taking three strides to her one, a child to her adult, and stayed behind the wagon with the rest.

"That was unexpected," he said at last.

The look the trader shot him combined surprise and amusement. "Did you think we all agreed on how to handle this?"

"*This* is between the weapon and the House of Marsan." He didn't appreciate the amusement and let it show in his voice.

They saw no one between the market and the gate. Even the sheep had been moved from that section of grass. Keetin gestured at a scythe abandoned by half a row of dry peas. "They'll be glad when we're gone."

Yeri spread his hands. "And they'll be just as glad when you return."

"So they'll either be very glad then," Scholar Gearing announced dryly from behind them, "or they're not very glad now."

Yeri opened his mouth, visibly reconsidered, and closed it again.

NONEE.NOW

Nonee paused, palm flat against the Broken Door. She turned, found the scholars, and tried to change the odds. "You don't need to go into the Broken Lands. There are records in Gateway."

Kalyealee who-could-be-heir rolled her eyes. "Records written by scholars?"

"No."

"Then they're invalid until we have observations, made by scholars, for purposes of comparison." Scholar Gearing looked smug. Nonee wasn't always good with facial expression, but smug seemed accurate. "We're here to advance the Scholarship of the Broken Lands, and that would be difficult indeed from behind this wall. Wouldn't it?"

Nonee stared at him.

One of the guardians hid a snicker in a cough.

"Knowledge is power," Scholar Gearing declared at last, drawing himself up as straight as his pack allowed. Nonee wondered if he knew the mages had once said the same. "Our scholarship will make Marsanport stronger."

"How?"

His nostrils flared. "The knowledge we return with will add to the bulwark of knowledge that keeps Marsanport safe."

It was a hard-fought battle, but she defeated the urge to ask *how* one more time. Instead she said, "Only if you return alive."

Scholar Gearing's chin rose so high his beard bristled. "Is that a threat?"

"An observation."

"They're here with the Lord Protector's approval," Ryan Heir said quietly. "They're included in the Last Command."

She met his gaze. "But they could remove themselves."

"Yes," Kalyealee who-could-be-heir snapped. "But we won't."

"They're aware of the danger, Nonee."

No, they weren't. She tipped her head back. "Kai! Are we clear?"

The archer leaned out from the top of the wall, glossy black braid falling forward over his shoulder. "Nothing in sight, Nonee. Haven't heard screaming for a while."

"Not for a while," Keetin Norwin-cee murmured. "Great news."

It might be. It might not. She opened the door.

Kalyealee who-could-be-heir, for all she shook with the need to move forward, stayed back until the all-clear, then took her assigned place in the middle of the march without complaining.

Nonee would have liked her better if she'd rushed ahead. Enthusiasm could be excused when calculation couldn't.

LYELEE.NOW

Lyelee could see no reason they had to remain on the pounded dirt path when it ran along the side of a ruined road. It was in significantly worse condition than the road in front of the tenements, but not so bad it couldn't be walked on.

"Bad enough," Nonee argued when she pointed that out. The weapon threw a branch that sank into the pavement. "Anything that is or was alive, it absorbs. More slowly than it used to," she added after a moment. "There was time to pull Ali Tark free."

"That's encouraging," Destros noted.

"He only lost his right foot."

"And that's not."

"How much has it slowed?" Lyelee demanded, kicking a rock onto the road and watching it bounce. "If you've kept track of the rate of decay, we can compare it to any functioning mage-craft we find."

"Compare what?" Ryan asked. "You'll have no rate of decay for your functioning mage-craft."

Trust Ryan to use his brain at the most inconvenient time. "We can track . . ."

"No."

She glared at Nonee. "No?"

"No."

"No time," Ryan expanded, and fell into step at Nonee's side.

If Lyelee wanted to instruct them on how it could be done, and she did, she'd be instructing their backs.

"Do you see the remains of the roofline on that house?" Gearing pointed at a distinctive, swooping overhang.

"Hard to miss," she muttered. The bits of roof/wall still standing rose three stories up out of the tangle of vegetation. Extrapolating from the ruins, the building had once been close to the size of her family's country home, for all it was still within the borders of old Gateway. Living in proximity to the mages had clearly made some people wealthy. Granted, it had most likely also made them dead, but they'd had over a thousand years to enjoy it. When measuring more than a thousand years—and she hated the imprecision of the word *more*—against a single war, however destructive, the result favored mage-craft.

"That roofline—just beyond where it meets the baluster—has the same design aesthetic as the rooflines you see in the older parts of Bondty. We can therefore conclude there were Bondtians in this area before the Mage War." He snorted, a familiar superior sound. "Regardless of what they say."

If the ubiquitous "they" had ever said there were no Bondtians in Gateway before the Mage War, Lyelee hadn't heard them—but then she couldn't be privy to every argument in the Scholar's Hall. She shifted to settle her pack more comfortably on her shoulders, then turned and leaned out to see around the three guardians bringing up the rear of the march. She could still see the wall. They hadn't traveled far.

Then a huge arm pushed her back and an enormous hand lifted Gearing up into the air as the ground under his boot, two small strides from the path, collapsed in on itself.

As Lyelee staggered, Destros steadied her, his hand on her pack keeping her from falling on her ass. "Scholar?"

"I'm fine."

Nonee set Gearing down on the path—more emphatically than Lyelee thought was called for—squatted, and peered into the darkness. Sniffed once at the rising damp, and said, "Cistern. Nothing of value left in it."

"Value?"

"Possessions kept safe from the fires." She straightened, twitched her tunic down. "Clean water."

Gearing sniffed, masking embarrassment with disdain. "I thought Gateway had plenty of water."

"Now. The West River comes out of the Broken Lands. Took a while to clear it." She moved back to the front of the line.

Keetin passed Ryan a silver coin, distracting Lyelee, who'd intended to ask how they'd cleared the river. And when. And what had been in it that had needed to be removed. Ryan grinned when he noticed her watching, flipping the coin off his thumb, up into the air. "You should be happy I bet on you, cousin."

She snorted. "You should share your winnings, then."

"You should all stay on the path." Nonee had already pulled ahead and they scrambled to catch up.

"Ryan!" Lyelee lengthened her stride as far as the weight of the pack allowed. "We need to take notes. We'll need to compare the damage closest to Gateway with the damage further away."

"No one's stopping you," Ryan responded without turning.

"We can't write and walk. We'll stop here, make our observations. Stop again . . ." She squinted against the sunlight reflecting off the road. ". . . there, by the broken pillar."

"Keep walking, Lyelee."

"The Lord Protector . . ."

Nonee cut her off. "The Records in Gateway hold multiple studies of the damages between the wall and the line. Salvage maps. Drawings. Lists of finds."

"And again, not recorded by scholars," Gearing sniffed, hands plucking at the fabric over his thighs as though he were trying to twitch his absent robe into place.

Lyelee couldn't see the weapon's back, only the huge pack. She glared at it anyway.

"You'll show us these records when we return." Gearing sounded as though he were instructing the weapon to have an analysis done by Twosday. A tone that brooked no argument.

"No." Apparently, Nonee was tone deaf.

"No?" A pair of small brown birds flew up out of a tangle of vine at Gearing's volume. "We are scholars!"

"Sa Toolis will show you, if she agrees. She keeps the Records."

"Why weren't we taken to her immediately?" he demanded.

"You decided to investigate the tenements," Keetin reminded him. "You booted out of the Hall so fast, we assumed no one in Gateway had anything to say you wanted to hear."

"Because we weren't taken to the records."

"Which weren't written by scholars."

"That should have been our decision to make!"

"Because you're scholars?"

"Yes!"

Keetin's howl of laughter spooked another three birds up into the air. Two made it to the branches of a slender tree. The third disappeared in a loop of vine. As the bird's bones broke, Lyelee frowned and tried to calculate how much normal vegetative movement had been increased. And how little this was like normal vegetative movement.

"Okay." Keetin swallowed his amusement as everyone but Nonee stared at the feather wafting slowly to the ground. "I understand why you want us to stay on the path."

Nonee's enormous pack rode her shrug up and down. "Bird vine can't hurt you. It might hold you until your struggles bring strangle vine, though. Keep walking."

Once again, she was two or three body-lengths ahead. How was she supposed to protect them from up there?

"Why do you let strangle vines grow so close to the wall?" Lyelee demanded, scrambling to catch up. Her pack shifted, she tipped sideways, and felt Destros grab a strap and haul her upright again. Good. Part of the guardian's protection detail *should* be keeping her on her feet.

"Strangle weed keeps down the number of shattered who get through to the wall."

"Not the shattered that fly." She'd seen Nonee destroy the flying not-a-bird after the healer's burial. She remained annoyed at Captain Yansav, who'd prevented her from investigating the pieces.

"Not all of them."

That appeared to be all Nonee intended to say on the matter.

Lyelee repeated the description of the bird weed to herself three times to ensure she'd remember it when she drew it later. When she glanced over at her mentor, she saw the muscles of his neck between beard and collar were corded. "You'll crack another tooth if you keep that up," she murmured for his ears alone. When flared nostrils were his only response, she added, "They should have taken us to the records."

"I doubt anything the uneducated of Gateway calls a record would be useful," Gearing muttered. "Without scholars, they'll have had no idea of what was important enough to record. There's likely no more than a pearl or two among piles of oyster shells and, while it would have been useful to determine that ourselves, we need to concentrate on the new information we, as trained observers, can add to the Scholarship of the Broken Lands."

He wasn't wrong, but she knew that tone. Ryan had used it often back in their shared childhood when his brothers had denied him something they enjoyed because he was too young or they were being the flaming assholes their situation allowed. *I didn't want it anyway,* said the tone.

All of the vines covering the ruins couldn't be carnivorous or the competition for nourishment would have them attacking the path. She pushed a broad leaf aside with her boot. Some were clearly wild grape. Some were . . .

. . . moving on their own. About as far from both sides of the path as she could throw a rock, leaves rustled. There was no breeze.

"How fast does strangle weed move?" she asked.

Nonee blew out an audible breath. "Fast when it's close enough to strike. Not very fast before then."

"You've cleared it back from the path?"

"Yes."

"Why doesn't it attack you?"

"It does."

But it wasn't able to strangle her. As Nonee's throat was as big around as Lyelee's thigh, that wasn't surprising. No point in creating a weapon that would be taken out by the landscaping. "Were the vines purposefully created by the mages or did they appear after the war?"

"After the war. Still could've been purposefully created," Nonee added after a moment.

Eventually, the rustling stopped and the ruins were covered with brambles and trees rather than vines.

Nonee called a halt.

Ryan's hand went to his sword hilt. Lyelee wondered if he thought he could draw it from his scabbard without cutting himself. "Is something wrong?"

"The old man needs rest."

"I most certainly do not," Gearing protested, sinking onto a lichen-covered rock and swaying slightly. His pack rose up off his shoulders, most of the weight on the rock.

Lyelee realized she'd been hearing him breathing heavily for long enough the sound had faded to background noise.

"I merely need time to acclimatize," he continued. Trembling fingers pushed buttons through loops, and when he finally got his vest open, sweat stained his scholar-blue shirt almost black.

"Drink more." Nonee squatted in front of him.

"If I drink more, I'll have to piss more."

She shrugged. "Easier for you."

Gearing half smiled, left hand clutching the top of his satchel. "True enough."

Like that hadn't been a conversation they'd had all the way from Marsanport to Gateway. The captain and Servan had a carved scoop that took care of the vulnerability that came with dragging a bare ass out of trousers by the side of the road. Lyelee had worn her scholar's robe when she hadn't felt like sharing it. Squatting in the robe was simple and private. Nonee wore a tunic and short trousers. Did an ancient mage-crafted weapon have as much trouble peeing in the bush as any woman? She opened her mouth to ask when Ryan cut her off.

"You should go back," he said flatly, his own pack now leaning against his legs. "The heat, the clothing, and the pack combined are too much for you."

Gearing's lip stuck as he lifted it. He licked his teeth, took another swallow of water, and said, "I am not going back."

"At this point, if he goes, we all go and start again tomorrow." Nonee stood and turned to Harris. "Take three waterskins out of his pack."

"You're already carrying twice as much as the rest of us," Ryan protested.

Lyelee rolled her eyes and let her pack slide off her arms to the ground. "She's an immortal mage-crafted weapon, I think she knows how much she can handle."

"I can take another." Destros lifted his chin under Nonee's scrutiny.

"And still fight?"

"Extra protection over the spine and kidneys. And you'd be surprised at how fast I can drop a pack."

"Yes, then."

Harris glanced at Ryan, who nodded.

"Oh, sure," Lyelee muttered, pulling out her notebook as the redistribution began. "But could we stop to document our observations? No. The Lord Protector will hear how scholarship was valued on this trip," she added, using short, choppy lines to draw what she remembered of the Bondtian roof. More importantly, the Scholar's Hall would receive a detailed narrative. Distance from Marsanport had helped Ryan forget how much he'd need the Scholar's Hall when—or if—he became Lord Protector.

Eventually, the road curved to the left. The path went straight.

With the turn barely behind them, Nonee placed her hand on a pillar of stone a shade lighter than her skin and half again as tall. "This is the farthest point of the old city."

On the one side, the side they'd come from, vines and ruins. On the other side, the side they were about to cross into, grass. Mostly grass. Probably grass. It was green and knee high and Lyelee wasn't a Scholar of Nature.

Keetin whistled through his teeth. "The old city covered some ground."

"The wealthy use a lot of land."

"Less of a prime location once the Mage War started."

She shrugged. "By the time it finished, yes. Gateway wasn't hit until the mages were dead and the mage-craft out of control."

"So controlled mage-craft was never an issue?" Gearing asked thoughtfully.

"Depends on what you mean by issue."

Lyelee let Gearing's voice become a background drone and checked the stone for carvings. Nothing. Not even the worn possibility of a carving. Typical. History seldom considered the needs of scholars. "Did the pillar look the same before Gateway was destroyed?"

"Don't know."

No, why would she? She'd have been at her mage's tower, defending the mage who'd created her. "So you didn't see Gateway until after it had been destroyed? When you came through with Captain Marsan?"

"Yes."

"You took this path?"

"Yes." Lyelee had barely begun ordering her questions when Nonee pointed toward a clump of three broad-canopied, flat-topped trees and said, "Best to spend the heat of the day out of the sun."

Nonee began walking again and Ryan called, "Let's go." Like he was actually in charge and not following where Nonee led.

NONEE.NOW

Nonee thought of the terrain to come. Scholar Gearing had kept up, but it had cost him. Although younger than the prominent bones of his wrists suggested, he'd been worn down, not strengthened by the long trip from Marsanport. He'd get weaker, the farther into the Broken Lands they went, until someone died trying to keep him alive.

Within the protection of the circle, Scholar Gearing dropped his pack on the path and collapsed. He turned his head, drew in a deep breath, and asked, "What is this?"

"Chamomile." Tiny daisy-like flowers rose above short fronds. Arianna had wondered why she'd asked Healer Tanis who kept herbarium for so much of it. "And thyme." Wooly thyme. The leaves had felt like lamb ears when she'd touched them first in wonder.

"Planted by the healer," Scholar Gearing declared, as though he'd solved a puzzle.

"Not by, for. Lie on it or sit on it," she told the rest. "Stay on the path if you're standing. Boots cause too much damage."

"*You* planted it?" Scholar Gearing sounded incredulous. As though she'd told him Arianna's cat had been the gardener. "You?"

"Yes."

"Why?"

"To set this place apart." Nonee checked for incursions and ignored the scholar's questions until he finally fell into a sulky silence.

Kalyealee who-could-be-heir was a different problem. Nonee watched as the novitiate picked a chamomile flower and a sprig of thyme and slid both into her satchel, intending her harvest to be unseen. It was a short step between hiding a flower and hiding things more dangerous. Kalyealee who-could-be-heir believed she couldn't be hurt in the pursuit of knowledge. Part of that was age. Nonee had seen generations come and go and the follies of twenty were consistent. The rest was training.

Scholars. Fleeing the Mage War and its twisted reality, bloody and burned, Captain Marsan had created *". . . scholars to build the foundation of a new society. We will never be at the mercy of mages again!"* She remembered the captain shouting those words. She remembered the captain threading the fear of mages through the tapestry of her people. She remembered what happened to those who'd suggested going back. Or who'd tried to continue the work they'd been doing in Gateway before the Mage War.

"This is what mage-craft creates," the captain had warned as the weapon she'd brought from the Broken Lands tightened her grip until bone shattered.

Nonee remembered everything, her memory part of the mage-craft that had formed her.

She remembered how the scholars had argued when Garrett Heir had taken her from Marsanport. Not because they feared for the city without her protection, because she should be given to them for study. Given the explosion that had leveled a wing of the Scholar's Hall in the first year Garrett's father was Lord Protector, she suspected the scholars weren't so different from mages in the end.

Her time spent with Scholar Gearing and Kalyealee who-could-be-heir hadn't changed that suspicion.

"No need for a guard." She stood behind Captain Yansav's shoulder, impressed by how the captain controlled the reaction she'd been trying to evoke. "Rest while you can."

After one emphatic exhale, Captain Yansav nodded and raised her voice. "Don't fall asleep. We can't take this apparent safety for granted."

Nonee approved.

Across the clearing, Keetin Norwin-cee circled his arms, stretched out his back, and asked, "Is it safe to remove my vest?"

"Have you gotten faster at getting it back on?" the captain asked dryly, before Nonee could reply.

"I have not." He slapped his chest, palms leaving damp marks on the scale. "Sweating under leather and steel it is, then."

"Puts hair on your chest," Destros told him.

Captain Yansav was still smiling when she turned her attention back to Nonee. Her smile didn't last beyond the turn. "How safe is it here?"

"Safe enough." Nonee had made the area within the trees for Arianna. When she could no longer walk this far, Nonee had carried her. "Watch for the wasps. They nest in the grasses beyond the trees and live too short a life to be discouraged."

"Discouraged?" Kalyealee who-could-be-heir frowned.

"Discouraged," Keetin Norwin-cee repeated. "If Nonee kills every-thing dangerous that enters this area, the smarter dangerous things learn they're likely to die here and stay away."

"And the stupid things?" Cali/Servan asked.

"Don't stay away and they die." He grinned. "I think we can handle wasps."

"They attack your eyes," Nonee told him. "Dig in for the liquid."

"Or not."

"But they're small and easy to crush."

"So, good news/bad news?"

"Yes."

Keetin Norwin-cee broke tensions with a skill equal to Arianna's skill in healing more physical hurts. High enough placed to be friend to both members of the Lord Protector's family, he wasn't so high he couldn't joke with the guardians. Smart enough to take orders from Captain Yansav, but able to think for himself. Her first impression had been correct, Ari-anna would like . . . would have liked him. She wondered how well he could use the sword he carried.

"May I light a fire?" Harris had moved quietly to her side, stopping far enough away he wouldn't startle her.

She couldn't be startled. "Why?"

"For tea?"

She didn't feel the heat, but the others did. She could smell it. "Tea?"

"Mint." His gaze slid past her shoulder. Calm. Unchallenging. She'd seen him look at both young lords the same way. He knew where he stood in the hierarchy. He knew where they stood as well. "Helps a cold lunch settle."

Arianna had said the same. "Uses water."

"We need to keep drinking."

Truth. But . . . "Best not. Fire could attract attention and a fight will uproot the plantings."

Harris acknowledged the point and crossed the circle to hand Ryan Heir one of the boiled eggs he held. And a radish.

Of all of them, Harris was not her concern. He'd protect the heir, but not die foolishly for him. He considered her just another way of protecting the heir. Like the guardians. Or perhaps like the guardians' weapons. His way of keeping Ryan Heir alive was matter-of-fact. Arianna would have liked *him* too.

Every now and then, Ryan Heir moved like Captain Yansav. Nonee assumed she'd had a hand in training him. That was good, she acknowledged, settling into a squat. They'd have an advantage when they fought together.

After a moment, he came and sat beside her. "You're studying us," he said, wiping egg off his fingers.

"Yes."

"Why?"

He thought he knew, but she liked that he asked. Liked that he'd noticed.

"There's time now." She chewed and swallowed the hunk of fat packed with dried berries and grains she'd taken from her pack, the summer heat slicking the surface with grease. Later, she'd live off the land the way softer people couldn't.

"It helps you to plan what you'll need to do if you understand what we can do." When she blinked, he grinned, scratching the sparse edges of his beard. "I'm smarter than I look."

"Yes."

He laughed at that and she had to stop herself from smiling. It was good to be understood in turn.

ARIANNA.THEN

Arianna pressed her back against a tree and yelled, "Ignore the head! The neck is the weak point!"

The large woman—Arianna had to find her a name—wrapped one

massive hand around the shattered's shoulders, one around the head, and ripped the head off the body.

Garrett fought well, but not as well as Norik, whose fighting abilities were clearly one of the reasons he'd been brought along. The two younger men—boys really . . .

Arianna smacked a shattered away from them with her staff. The large woman caught it by a hind leg and smashed it into a tree hard enough that blood and guts sprayed a pattern over the rest of the clearing.

The boys fought back to back, supporting each other.

And then it was over. They'd handled themselves well enough, but it was the large woman who'd killed all seven shattered.

"You're very bloodthirsty for a healer." Garrett grinned at her almost mockingly.

"Their skulls are very thick. She might have been able to crush the bone, but I didn't think we had the time."

"I wasn't referring to the warning. I've never met a healer who used their staff as an offensive weapon."

"This isn't Northport . . ."

"Marsanport."

"Right." The name of the city at the other end of the road hadn't been Northport for a very long time. The first of the talents who'd made their way up the Mage Road had told them of the change. And why the change had been made. Arianna wanted Garrett to remember he was heir to a city-state that only existed because his great-great-grandmother had been willing to kill thousands. He needed to be a little less proud of that. "I use the staff because everyone takes a turn to keep the shattered off the walls."

"What were those things before the Mage War?" Malcolm asked, staggering closer, one arm thrown over Petre's shoulder.

Blood matted in Malcolm's eyebrow and dribbled down the side of his face, but it wasn't serious and Arianna knew better than to fuss over a young man who hadn't requested fussing. "I don't know what they were, but I do know that this type of shattered, this pack or another, has attacked the wall half a dozen times since the Hunter's Moon." She used the staff to lift a broad paw high enough to expose short, blunt claws. "It's all teeth all the time with them."

"Yes."

Startled by the growled agreement, they turned together to see the large woman throwing the bodies out into the grasslands, the silence deep enough that each crunch of dried stalks and splat of impact sounded clearly. When she turned and saw them watching, she shook her head and bent to pick up the next piece.

Arianna thought she looked pleased with herself.

"Blunt-force trauma."

"What does that mean?" Malcolm asked, eyes squinted shut.

Arianna peered into the cut that ran along the top of his eyebrow, dragged down the lower edge a bit with her thumb, holding him still with the rest of her hand. "It means some part of the shattered hit you hard enough break through the skin. Possibly the side of a tooth. Not a point or there'd be more damage."

"It bled bucket-loads."

"It's a head wound, of course it bled bucket-loads." She closed the wound, licked her thumb, and smoothed it over the join, wiping it clean and sealing it closed. The damp strip of paper she pressed onto it was more for emotional security than physical. "But if you need to think happy thoughts, a lot of blood means it bled itself clean. Don't open your eyes until I clean them—your lashes have stuck together."

He sighed. "Will it scar?"

"Do you want it to?"

"Uh . . . no?"

She glared up at Garrett, who stood behind Malcolm trying not to laugh. "Then it won't."

"Took the blow through the cuff." Norik turned his palm down to show her a purpling bruise. They all had bruises; it was the puncture centered in this particular bruise Arianna needed to see. "The leather of the sleeve will turn a sword." When Arianna raised a brow, one corner of his mouth twitched up. "A sword less than enthusiastically applied, granted. Still."

"Still," Arianna agreed, dripping an alcohol tincture into the wound.

Norik sucked air through his teeth. "They attacked the hand holding the sword, not the sword."

"They're not stupid." She showed him the round of paper before gently sealing the puncture. "You're not imagining things if you smell honey. You didn't bleed much and it'll help stop infection."

"The shattered aren't stupid?"

She started, and twisted to stare up at Garrett until he raised both hands and backed away. He'd been close enough, he'd breathed the question into her hair. "Are you checking my work?"

"Do I need to?" He folded his arms. "The shattered?"

A quick look around the area showed that everyone was listening. Arianna sat back on her heels and sighed. "These are at least as smart as dogs." They looked a bit like dogs, although the back leg joints bent the wrong way. She didn't like thinking of what they might have been. "Some others have nothing more than animal cunning. Some are . . . aware."

She had no idea of the language Petre spoke, but the string of words was clearly not a prayer.

Bodies disposed of, the large woman swept her gaze around the clearing and dropped into her usual squat, her knees not quite reaching her shoulders, her weight, Arianna realized, resting forward on her folded legs. She was significantly more flexible than anyone with that much muscle should be.

This close, the whites of her eyes weren't actually white but a very pale gray. That would make any number of diagnoses difficult, Arianna noted as she squatted as well, skirt billowing. After a moment, she fell back onto her ass and crossed her legs. "After consideration, I, personally, am going to sit."

The huff of breath might have been amusement.

The ground cover was sparse between the three large trees. Arianna could see wild carrot, and colt's foot and runner grass, all but the grass browned by the season. Six days into Frost Moon, the plants had definitely been touched by cold. Leaning back on her elbows, she stared up into the canopy. About half the large, oval leaves had fallen and the rest were a mix of brown and orange. In the summer, the trees probably left a near perfect circle between them for the sun to come through. She had no idea what type of tree they were, but even if they'd been planted by mages, she was sure they hadn't been created by mage-craft.

They felt sturdy and the space between them felt peaceful.

"Do you have a name?" Arianna listened to the leaves rustling while she waited for an answer.

"No."

"You should have a name."

"Shouldn't you ask her if she wants a name?" Garrett called.

Arianna spent a lot of time fixing twelve-year-olds. She could hear guilt in the taunt. "You're right," she said, and heard Norik smack the Heir of Marsan on the shoulder as she turned back to the large woman. "Do you want a name?"

This time when she waited, she listened to the two men quietly arguing.

"Yes."

"What would you like to be called?"

The large woman blinked twice. Then again. And again. Blink blink pause. Blink blink pause. Her expression . . .

Confusion. Consternation. Arianna couldn't think of any other possibility but fear, and it couldn't be that. "Not sure?"

"Yes. No."

That was definitely relief, and Arianna wondered when the large woman had last been asked her opinion on anything. And if she should slip a laxative into Garrett's dinner. She leaned back on her elbows again. "You know, this could be a nice place if it wasn't for the residue of gore."

After a moment, the large woman said, "Yes."

Then she said, "U Vi Li."

"Uvili?"

"Yes."

"That's a Shurlian word."

Arianna started as Petre squatted beside her. She hadn't heard him approach. "What does it mean?"

He smiled. "Strength."

She laid her hand on a thick, gray wrist. It was cooler to the touch than Arianna was used to, even considering temperatures during the Frost Moon. "You're more than your strength, you know."

"Yes. Uvili."

Across the clearing, Garrett laughed. "Easy to ask, Healer. Harder to listen."

He was annoyingly right.

"Uvili it is," she said.

"Yes."

RYAN.NOW

Ryan ducked instinctively when Nonee grabbed the attacking shattered by the hind leg, swung it off of Keetin, and smashed its head against the side of an enormous boulder. Bone cracked. Brains and blood sprayed out in a glistening arc.

Straddling Keetin's feet, teeth clenched to keep from vomiting, Ryan slammed the edge of his sword into the closest creature's shoulder. It slid off, leaving shoulder and creature undamaged. The shattered lunged before he could regain his balance, and twisting out of the way put him on his knees.

"Go for the eyes!" Captain Yansav's voice rang out above the sounds of the pack.

The eyes were small and piggy. Could lizard-dog things have piggy eyes? That was just one animal too many in the mix. When a crossbow bolt slammed in behind its front legs and it lurched sideways but stayed standing, Ryan jabbed the point of his sword in under the brow ridge and, more by accident than design, shoved the blade into the creature's skull until it hit bone on the opposite side. He'd only just managed to yank the blade free when Nonee roared.

Not only loud, it was . . . wide. Heavy. A warning and a blow at the same time.

As one, the living creatures turned and fled.

She bellowed again, and threw the lizard-dog with the shattered skull. It slammed into the three at the rear of the retreat. One of them stayed down.

Ears ringing, bones vibrating, Ryan dropped back to his knees. "Kee?"

Gasping for breath, cheeks pale under his tan, freckles like flakes of dried blood, Keetin waved a hand until Ryan caught it and hung on. "Knocked the air . . . out of me. Might bruise . . . a bit."

"They were waiting for us."

He looked up as Captain Yansav approached Nonee, cleaning her blade with short, sharp, threatening movements.

Nonee didn't seem threatened. "Yes."

"How did they know where we'd be?"

She patted the boulder, avoiding the splatter. "This marks the Broken Line."

Captain Yansav took another step, and leaned out, eyes narrowed. "It doesn't look any different."

"On this side, the land is stable and the shattered breed true, no more changes. Past the boulder, things change."

"And what side of the line were these creatures from?"

"This side. Arianna thinks . . ." Her fingers closed. Stone crumbled. ". . . *thought* they live underground somewhere between the wall and the line but the den's never been found."

Still holding Keetin's hand, Ryan rose up on his knees and tried to peer past the boulder. He could no more see a difference in the trees and the underbrush than the captain could. *And I bet that's what makes it dangerous.*

"What happened when you . . . yelled?" The captain bent and yanked the crossbow quarrel free from the remaining corpse, as though she hadn't just demoted Nonee's roar to a squabble between partners or noises in playgrounds.

Nonee shrugged. "They were reminded they could die."

Blood dripped off the point of the quarrel. "Reminded that we can defend ourselves?"

"Yes."

"That you were with us."

Not a question.

"Yes."

"They know you . . ." The captain paused to toss the quarrel back to Curtin, who grunted his thanks. ". . . because they attack the walls."

Nonee nodded. "Yes."

"And you don't stay behind the walls."

"Yes."

"They're able to reason."

"Yes."

"Well, isn't that just flaming great," Curtin growled.

Keetin twisted out of his pack and sat up, releasing Ryan's hand to press his own against his chest. "As long as Nonee's willing to scare off the wildlife, we may survive this yet."

"Does it always work?" Ryan helped Keetin up onto his feet, one of them, possibly him, gripping too hard.

"Some run." She shrugged again. "Some don't."

"I knew it couldn't be that easy." Keetin sighed dramatically, and Ryan managed to smack his shoulder as though he hadn't almost died.

"Get that vest off. I need to see . . ."

Captain Yansav stepped in close. "You need to check on your people, my lord."

All your people. Not just Keetin, who'd gone down in front of him and not gotten up again. Ryan blinked and turned. He felt as though he were reconnecting with the greater world—or at least the greater world that ended at the edge of the clearing. The three guardians and Harris continued to surround the two scholars. Lyelee looked indignant, but that could have been because all six still wore their packs, and oiled canvas crowded her on all sides. While he watched, she set both hands against Curtin's pack and shoved, brows drawing down when she had no effect. Scholar Gearing looked as though only the pressure of the packs kept him on his feet. Ryan raised his voice and tried to sound resolute as he asked, "Is anyone hurt?"

"No, sir." Destros gripped an axe in each hand. Blood dripped off both blades. "They ran before they got lucky."

"Good." For now. He turned his attention back to Nonee. "Will they return?"

Nonee lifted the shattered he'd killed by its back leg. "Not tonight."

"Is it safe to camp here?" The plan had been to camp at the line and cross in the morning. If this was the line . . .

His stomach growled, then twisted at the stink of the spilled blood. He'd seen animals butchered. He'd watched Harris gut fish and rabbits and wild turkeys and a deer. It should have smelled the same. It didn't.

"Safe?" Nonee paused, the creature dangling from her hand as though it weighed nothing at all. "Safer than there," she said at last, indicating the land beyond the boulder with the swinging corpse.

He had the feeling that from now on *safer than* would be as good as it got. "All right." He raised his voice again. "Make camp."

"And a fire, my lord?" Harris called.

He glanced at Nonee and squared his shoulders. "If anything's going to attract attention, it'll be the blood. Light a fire."

Nonee stared at him for a moment, then nodded, once. It looked like approval. He felt his cheeks grow hot.

Captain Yansav's expression looked nothing like approval. She huffed out a breath and growled, "Clean your blade."

There were brains on his blade. Brains and blood and a dead giant lizard-dog thing swinging . . .

"What are you doing with that?" Lyelee demanded, pushing her way out between Servan and Curtin. "We need to examine it!"

"You're a Scholar of History." Sucking air through his teeth, Keetin pulled the strap free of the last buckle on his vest. "Remember?"

"And that creature is a historical artifact. Created by a force that defines a moment in history!" She was both too old and too much a scholar to stamp her foot, but her pack hit the ground with a thud.

"You can't exactly question it, Lyelee."

"I can dissect it!"

"Historically?" Keetin asked as Ryan slid the scale vest carefully off his shoulders.

"Don't be an idiot!"

"Easy there, Lye." Keetin staggered back as though the weight of the vest had been the only thing holding him in place. Ryan grabbed his arm before he fell.

"What do you expect to find?" he asked, propping Keetin against the line marker.

"How would I know?" Lyelee demanded. "This creature is completely unique to my experience. The point is, I'm a scholar, and the unknown is what . . ." Her attention flickered to Nonee, who'd almost left the clearing carrying the body. "Leave it right there! Leave it! Ryan!"

Ryan sighed. She assumed Nonee would listen to him because the Lord Protector's Last Command declared it so, not because he was in command. "Examine it at the edge of the camp, but only until you lose the light. Don't bring it or any pieces of it closer to the fire."

Lyelee's eyes narrowed. "Order Nonee to tell me everything she knows about the creatures."

"No."

"No?"

"You want her to tell you something, you ask her. Her choice if she tells you." Leaning closer to Keetin, he could smell the oil the other man rubbed into his beard even though he'd been out of oil for days. Maybe he only thought he could smell it. "Anything broken? Ribs? Collarbone?"

"Hand to my heart, I'm bruised but that's all." Keetin lifted his shirt, exposing a rough-edged purple circle the size of Ryan's palm already rising on his pale skin.

"Ryan!"

Ryan sighed again and stepped away from Keetin to face his cousin. "I'm not ordering Nonee's attention away from keeping us alive."

"A scholar in search of knowledge is more important than . . ." Her eyes widened and she raced across the clearing, dodging around Harris, who'd begun to dig a fire pit. "Nonee! You're dragging my specimen!"

"Yes."

❧

"It's usually thicker. The heat's softened it some."

Ryan glanced over as Curtin smeared the soft cream on Keetin's bruise and laughed at the expression on Keetin's face as he peered down his nose at the way his minimal chest hair clumped together in greasy curls. Then laughed again at Keetin's look of betrayal.

He hadn't expected to laugh tonight.

❧

Leaning back, shoulder pressed against Keetin's, both hands cradling a tin mug of tea, Ryan looked around the fire. The temperature had barely dropped with the sun and the Rose Moon had risen nearly full, so Harris had built the fire for cooking, not for heat and light. They continued feeding it from the pile of deadfall for comfort. On the road, they'd have been asleep by full dark and up before dawn, but the darkness around them had changed.

Tomorrow they'd cross into the Broken Lands. Tonight, the fire was familiar.

From the expressions he could tease out of the shadows, there seemed to be too much thinking going on.

"Nonee." He shifted toward her. "Any chance you can tell us what we're likely to face once we cross the line?"

Nonee opened her mouth. Lyelee cut her off. "I know you've read both chronicles, Ryan. Did you retain none of it?"

The three guardians exchanged a look. Captain Yansav pinned Lyelee with a glare the scholar ignored. Harris jabbed a stick into the fire, sending sparks dancing up into the night. This was the Lyelee they'd left Marsanport with, wrapped in the superiority of her scholarship. Three days out, Ryan had overheard Curtin and Servan talking about leaving her by the side of the road. Gearing, they could ignore. Lyelee had demanded their attention. As the days passed, the eight of them and the road had worn the edge off her pedantic disdain. It seemed to be back.

"Nonee was there." Keetin saluted the weapon with his mug. "If she has something to say, I wouldn't mind hearing it."

Lyelee sucked in a breath, inhaled a bug, and began to cough.

It seemed like a good time for Ryan to have his question answered. "Nonee?"

"It won't be what Garrett Heir described." She blinked and added, "Whatever he described. The land shifts. Changes. It won't be the same twice."

"Then it'll be different on the way out from the way in?"

Nonee looked across the fire at Servan and nodded. "Could be."

"Worse?"

"Could be."

"Wonderful."

After a long moment, Nonee shook her head. "No."

Servan laughed and Ryan realized Nonee had made a joke.

"Will it be less dangerous than in the chronicles?" Destros asked, poking the fire. "Given the time that's passed? Could've worn the edges off things."

"It'll be different." She absently rolled a stone between her fingers. "It may be more dangerous. It may not."

Chin tucked into his chest, Curtin scowled over his folded arms. "If you don't know, what use are you?"

"Curtin."

"Captain?"

"She knows how to survive in the Broken Lands," Ryan said softly. "We don't." Curtin had been the choice of a Court faction that followed Captain Marsan's rules against mage-craft so strictly they'd nearly had a ship rumored to use a wind-worker burned at its mooring. Donal, as heir, had stepped in and ordered the ship away from Marsanport. The faction had then accused the wind-worker of capsizing his brothers' boat in revenge. They'd still been shouting about it when Ryan had arrived at the Citadel after the funerals. Once on the road, Curtin had assured him he would tolerate the weapon for the sake of the Black Flame and the safety of Marsanport. Lyelee had pointed out that the flame was, at the very least, based on mage-craft, and Curtin hadn't spoken to her in anything but tones of icy politeness for almost three days.

When Curtin continued to scowl, Ryan added, "You know we need her."

As Curtin reluctantly nodded, Keetin poked Ryan in the side. "Only because the Court would like you to actually make it to the fuel and come back alive."

"And gain new information about the Broken Lands," Lyelee said, lifting her mug.

"No, that's what the Court wants you to do." Reaching past Ryan, Keetin poked Lyelee, who slapped at his hand. "You're here so we don't have to remember shit."

"I'm here because you couldn't remember literal shit if it got up and started talking to you."

"I think I'd remember that."

"I don't." She drained her mug, cleared her throat, and looked across the fire at Nonee. "If the Broken Lands has changed, do you still know the way to the fuel?"

Everyone, save Gearing, who looked to be asleep hugging his satchel to his chest, and Harris, who was nestling the empty mugs back into the kettle, looked toward Nonee as well. Ryan wanted to assure them that of course she knew the way, but he closed his teeth on the words and waited with the rest for Nonee's response.

"The fuel won't have moved. Some landmarks are fixed in time and place." Nonee closed her grip on the stone, then dusted the crushed remains off her fingers. "And the tower calls."

"Tanika Fleshrender's tower. Where you were created."

She stared at Lyelee for a long moment, but all she said was, "Yes."

There were six mage-towers, according to the Captain's Chronicle. Captain Marsan hadn't named the mages, nor had the Lord Protector, but Ryan knew the scholars had the collected memories of the Five Thousand, and Lyelee had probably found it there. "So the fuel is in Tanila . . ."

"Tanika," Lyelee corrected. "Tanika Fleshrender."

"Seriously, Fleshrender? That's a little on the nose, isn't it?"

"Yes. She named herself. She was proud of what she could do."

"That's a little creepy," Keetin muttered.

Ryan agreed. "So she wasn't born with the name and then decided to live up to it?"

"No." Nonee answered before Lyelee could and repeated, "She named herself."

Harris poked the fire again and Ryan strained to hear what Nonee wasn't saying. Finally, he'd had enough of the lingering silence. "And the fuel is in her tower?"

"Yes."

"Still?"

"Yes."

"How long will it take to get there?"

Nonee shrugged. "Longer than you'll be happy about."

Lyelee bristled. "Because you think Scholar Gearing and I will slow you down."

"Yes. But you won't go back, so . . ." Nonee shrugged again.

Servan snickered.

❦

Ryan had gotten used to a bedroll on the ground, to the sounds of his companions, to the patterns of leaves, black against the night sky, but he couldn't sleep.

His legs and his shoulders ached, but that wasn't it.

He sweated in his vest, but Captain Yansav had *suggested* they keep them on in case they were attacked in the night. Even Keetin wore his over darkening bruises.

He could hear Destros snoring, the little popping sound Servan made as her lips parted with each exhale, and Lyelee murmuring, unable to quit arguing even when asleep. In the distance, a bird cried out wheet, wheet, WOO at random intervals. Anywhere else, he'd doubt the bird would survive the night. Here, it could easily be the size of a horse and luring unsuspecting predators in close.

He missed Slate.

His brain kept replaying death scenes from the Heir's Chronicle, only the dead all had Keetin's face. The Lord Protector'd had a healer with him as well as the weapon, and while Curtin had trained everyone but the scholars in battle aid during their travels, an actual healer might have done more than insist Keetin drink a bitter tea before he slept.

He wondered if the Lord Protector had sent the scholars to learn what Nonee had become.

He had to piss. No, he didn't. His body couldn't possibly hold more liquid than he'd already gotten rid of.

Leather creaking, steel scales whispering against each other, Ryan rolled up onto his feet, picked up the sheathed sword lying on the ground beside him, and crossed to the boulder at the edge of the Broken Lands where Nonee kept watch. Apparently, she wouldn't need to sleep for a few days.

She didn't move as Ryan approached. People were never entirely motionless. She was.

"I was wondering," he said quietly as he stood beside her. "Shouldn't you sleep while we're on this side of the line? Once we cross, aren't you as vulnerable as we are?"

She huffed out what might have been amusement. "No."

"But you *are* vulnerable."

"Yes. Still less than you."

He couldn't argue with that. The distant bird called again and Ryan leaned back against the stone, careful to avoid the stain. "I wish I knew how much longer this is going to take. If the flame burns out . . ."

"The scholars slow you."

"And water is wet."

"Yes." After a moment she added, "Your Lord Protector wants the scholars here."

"He didn't at first. A few people in the Court pushed for it, but he told them to go burn." Ryan smiled at the memory. "It was the most coherent he'd been in ages."

"Coherent?"

"He's old. His mind wanders."

"As long as it returns."

"So far." Ryan reached back and touched stone. "Anyway, Lyelee spent a couple of hours in with him and somehow convinced him to send them along. She told us she'd explained how knowledge needed to be reclaimed, not wasted." He crossed his legs at the ankles and grinned. "The consensus is that he agreed just to get her to shut up."

"No."

It was an emphatic no. Ryan frowned. "Well, yeah, we're not serious about it, but . . ."

"The scholars add danger." She folded her arms, and when he glanced up, she was frowning as well. It folded her face into a terrifying pattern and he had to look away. "His reason for sending them is important enough to risk you and to risk the flame."

Ryan hadn't thought of it that way. "Maybe he needs the support of the Scholar's Hall," he said around a yawn.

Nonee made a noise that wasn't quite neutral. "Scholar Novitiate Kalyealee Marsan-cee will be heir if you die."

A discussion of what would happen if he died. Yeah, that would help him sleep. "Her mother wants her to become Lord Protector and her mother's brother is even more ambitious. But Lyelee doesn't care about politics." He yawned again. "Except intellectually. Personally, I'd rather not die." He'd rather no one died. He'd rather no one *had* died. He'd rather not be here. "Did she learn anything, examining the creature?"

Nonee had stayed with her during the examination. He'd noticed that yes or no questions always received yes or no answers and was surprised to hear, "Maybe."

"Maybe?"

"Hard to know what she learned without knowing what she knows."

It took Ryan a moment to detangle the words, but, in his defense, it was the middle of the night. "I think she went into history because no one's willing to talk about the Mage War and the time before it. The denial drives her crazy." The night seemed darker, and when he blinked, his eyelids took effort to lift. "The family thought she'd be a Scholar of Flesh. Doing research, not dealing with patients. She'd be terrible with patients. When we were kids—she was ten, I was nine—there was this elderly barn cat that had been sick for a while, and she was there when it died. She asked if I wanted to watch her cut it up. I declined the honor and I've been a disappointment to her ever since." Not smart enough. Not driven enough. "If I don't make it back with the fuel before the Flame burns out and she's expanded the Scholarship of the Broken Lands, she might be acclaimed heir." He'd learned from experience it was easier to deny the job when there was no chance of being expected to do it. "If I don't make it back at all, the job's hers."

"It's a test."

He blinked, confused. "Getting the fuel?"

"The Broken Lands."

"No, the Lord Protector said publicly that there's things in the Broken

Lands that only the Heir can deal with. And he should know, right? He's been here. I figured it was a kind of blood magic or something, tied back to Captain Marsan."

Silence.

Snoring. Popping. The bird.

Wheet. Wheet. WOO!

More silence.

"Go to sleep," Nonee said, at last.

GARRETT.THEN

Garrett straightened and turned to face the healer. "I beg your pardon?"

"I said, what happens if you don't make it back? If you die out here . . ."

"You could sound a little less matter-of-fact about that."

Arianna rolled her eyes. "If you die *tragically* out here and no one returns with the fuel for the Black Flame, what happens?"

"For a healer you're awfully quick to kill everyone off. Fine." He raised a hand, although he doubted it would have held her silent had she wanted to continue talking. Over the last couple of days, he'd learned that not much stopped her and respect for his position wasn't on that very short list. She was the first person he could remember spending time with who didn't care that he was the Heir of Marsan. She probably cared more about the weapon. "If I don't return with the fuel, the Black Flame will go out and the people of Marsanport will panic. The panic will fuel riots, Marsanport will burn, and people will die."

"Why?"

"Why what?"

She made a noise that sounded like impatience distilled. "Why will people panic? What does the flame do?"

"Do?" He glanced at Norik, who shrugged and continued running a whetstone along the edge of a dagger. No help at all there. "It represents the power of Marsan."

"How?"

"How does it represent the power of Marsan?" What kind of a question was that? "It's what it does." He could hear another *how* coming as she drew in a breath and hurriedly added, "It burns on the top of the tallest tower in the Citadel, a Black Flame as tall as three tall men . . ."

"Or four medium-sized women," Norik put in.

"You're not helping."

"Your pardon, my lord."

Garrett flashed flames at him, had to explain the gesture to Arianna, and hoped that would be the end of trying to explain things that didn't need explanation because they were *known*.

"Okay. It burns." Arianna crossed her legs, heavy skirt billowing, and poked the fire with a stick. "And?"

"And it represents the power of Marsan." He tossed an apple at each of the boys, one at Norik, and sat before tossing one over to the healer.

She took a bite before saying, "If the flame goes out, nothing changes beyond the flame going out."

"It's an idea."

"More wars have been fought over ideas than over land," Norik added, slicing his apple in half.

"That's depressing."

He shrugged. "A little."

When she turned her attention to her apple, Garrett assumed she'd finally got the point.

"But isn't the power of Marsan here, with you?"

Or not.

"Because we're getting the fuel?" he ventured.

Arianna gave him both eyebrows at full lift, the expression emphatic enough to be visible by firelight. "Because Captain Marsan wouldn't have been able to slaughter a community and turn Northport into Marsanport without *her*." Half-turned toward the weapon, she added, "I don't blame you, by the way. You didn't have a choice." And then back to him. "But why would your father . . ."

"The Lord Protector." He'd always been more the Lord Protector than Garrett's father, and that had better not be sympathy on the healer's face.

"Why would the Lord Protector . . ."

At least he'd redirected her ire toward his father.

". . . allow you to take the power of Marsanport away? If the flame goes out, and the people riot, wouldn't he prefer to have Uvili there to control things?"

"He . . ." Garrett paused, suddenly unable to answer in front of the weapon. Which was ridiculous on a number of levels. To begin with, it didn't care what he said unless he was giving it an order. And it certainly didn't need to be told what his father thought of it. "He kept it chained." Arianna raised a brow, but he didn't correct himself. He couldn't say he kept *her* chained, not even to himself, not and ever look his father in the eye again. "He said it was a monstrous relic of the past. That if we were to support scholarship, why would we cling to the evidence of mage-craft."

"Chained? And Captain Marsan's people allowed that?"

"Captain Marsan's people? The Five Thousand?" Those who'd staggered down the Mage Road bleeding and broken? Those who thanks to the weapon had become the politicians. The land owners. The wealthy merchants. The members of Court and the Scholar's Hall. "No one but her keepers had seen her for years until I stumbled on her. I was . . . eight." Too old for nurses. Not quite old enough to train in the weapons yard. "It was the rainy season and I was bored, so I went exploring in the oldest parts of the Citadel where I wasn't supposed to be. I found her in one of the cellars." He'd followed his nose, followed a smell that wasn't damp and mold but something alive. "I'd just finished reading the Captain's Chronicle, and to waste the weapon like that . . ."

"Wait." Scowling, Arianna raised a hand. "So what you cared about was your father's waste, not her?"

"It's a weapon."

"She's a person."

"I cared about its condition the way I'd care if any weapon were treated with such a complete lack of respect. A sword or an axe . . ."

"Swords and axes don't feel."

"But people feel for them." After a moment, she nodded, granting his point. Garrett took a deep breath. "I argued with my father about it for years. He finally brought it out to repair one of the inner walls . . ."

"So she can build?"

"No. But she . . . IT," he emphasized the word hard enough to remove her smug expression, ". . . can carry stone and place it." He could see Arianna thinking repair work didn't sound like something a weapon would do. "It had to be told how to carry it and where to place it."

Arianna waved that off. "Please. They'd have to tell *you* how and where."

Norik snorted. Garrett was glad the boys were huddled together, paying no attention to a boring conversation; his oldest friend could take liberties they couldn't. "People were terrified. They threw rotten fruit, fish, anything that fit in their hands. Father felt like he'd made his point and locked it back up. Then the flame flickered and the Scholars of the Flame said the fuel had nearly burned out." He threw his apple core into the fire and watched the rising sparks. "Given the potential for rioting and ships arriving from around the Great Lake to attack once we'd been weakened, the Lord Protector ordered me into the Broken Lands to find more fuel. I asked for permission to take the weapon with me, to raise the odds of my survival. He said no at first, but the Court was on my side and eventually he gifted me the word that controls it."

No one knew how the Lord Protectors controlled the weapon, only that they did. Theories ranged from *it swore an oath to serve the line* to *they shared a brain.* Garrett had the latter explained to him by a gleeful child who'd told him someday he'd have to cut out a piece of his brain and share it with the monster. He'd been appalled to discover that apparent adults also believed that nonsense.

Norik and the boys knew the truth. He'd told them on day three, after they'd left the land his father controlled. They deserved to know they were safe.

"There's a single word, a word of power, that controlled each of the weapons. Captain Marsan brought the word with her out of the Mage War and passed it down to her daughter to her daughter to her son to me."

"That's horrible!" Arianna pointed the burning end of the stick at him. "She's not only been enslaved, but you've taken away her self-determination."

"Self-determination?" Garrett stared at her in disbelief. "You give a weapon self-determination and you can't control what it destroys."

"If it's capable of destroying things without you, it's capable of learning what not to destroy. Or . . ." She waved the stick like a torch. ". . . here's a radical thought, learning not to destroy at all."

"It's a weapon!"

Norik grunted, the noise neither agreement nor disagreement but something in between. Both boys stared at him, the fire reflected in their eyes. Across the fire, Arianna gazed at him with . . . pity? Why pity? She was the most irritating person he'd ever met. And he'd spent time with the head of the Scholar's Hall. He didn't look at the weapon.

After a long moment, long enough for the boys to sag back toward sleep, Arianna said, "What about the other words? There were six weapons."

"Captain Marsan only had the one word. According to her chronicle, the five other weapons were destroyed in the war."

She glanced toward the Broken Lands. "Are you sure?"

"Yes." Because he was responsible for the lives he'd brought with him and uncertainty would get them killed.

The night was colder than he was used to, but dry. In Marsanport, the damp would carry a temperature this low under clothing and into flesh. The sky was clearer than he'd ever seen it, the stars so bright they looked almost close enough to touch. He listened to the soft *shook shook* of Norik's whetstone, and beyond it to the wind in the trees, bare branches tapping out messages to each other. Near the ground the air was still, and drawing a breath in through his mouth he thought of a white wine the ships brought from Cridan every fall.

"Do you have younger brothers or sisters?"

It seemed the healer hadn't realized the time for talking had ended. "Two," Garrett told her, already aware she'd just ask again. "A sister three years younger and a brother four years younger than her. Why?"

Arianna used the burnt end of the stick to sketch a symbol on one of the rocks surrounding the fire. "How well does your sister get along with your father? How much does she argue with him? Does she argue that a weapon he clearly considers monstrous isn't?"

"It can be both monstrous and a valued weapon."

"You had clothing made for her."

Garrett frowned. "How . . ."

"She didn't wear those leathers in chains."

"It was the decent . . ."

"The decent thing to do? And yet your father didn't do it."

"She wasn't seen. It didn't matter."

"And if you don't return with the fuel, it won't matter." Arianna looked up from her sketch, her voice a gentle contrast to the steel in her gaze. "The Lord Protector has a child he gets along with better than he does with you. It makes sense that he'd send you for the flame. Not only are you and your arguments gone, but you've taken the monster from the Citadel."

"That's not . . ."

"What happens to her if you die in the Broken Lands and the word that controls her dies with you? Does the Lord Protector believe that with no one commanding her, she just shuts down?"

"Yes, but . . ."

"Who told you there'd be panic and riots?"

"That's not . . ."

"I very much doubt that he expects you to return." Her mouth twisted into something Garrett didn't recognize as a smile. "He certainly didn't expect you to find help."

"The healer makes a lot of sense."

"Norik!"

Norik slid his dagger into its sheath and met his eyes. "Who sends their heir on this kind of one-in-a-million-chance quest? You're a decent fighter, but we both know fighters who can put you on your ass. The Lord Protector doesn't expect the weapon to keep you alive because he doesn't expect anything of it." He grinned. "And he doesn't like me much, either."

"My mother left him for your oldest sister."

"That's hardly my fault."

"No argument."

Although no one had ever suggested Norik had anything to do with his sister's actions, he'd had to walk a fine line between invisible and contrite at Court. Garrett had searched him out for friendship because of the Lord Protector's animosity—a part of Garrett's teenage rebellion he gave thanks for every day. If he survived this, he expected it to be more because of Norik than the weapon.

Both Arianna and Norik waited for his response. He wasn't sure he had one. "So what are you saying? That the Black Flame is an excuse and the Lord Protector has sent me to the Broken Lands to get rid of me?" He didn't like the look they exchanged. "He's my father."

"Then let's give him the benefit of the doubt." Arianna's tone was so matter-of-fact, Garrett felt himself grabbing onto it. "Let's say it's not an execution. It could be the trip is a test."

"A test?"

"You argue with him, so he doubts you. This trip is all about you proving yourself worthy of becoming the Lord Protector."

"By returning with the fuel for the Black Flame," Norik added.

She tossed her stick onto the embers and they all watched it burn. "Sure. That too."

NONEE.NOW

Nonee watched Scholar Gearing rise from his bedroll and stumble to the shallow trench dug at the edge of the camp. She'd lost the argument that placed it behind a broad, dense bush, thick enough to shield the shortest of those using it from the neck down, a triumph of modesty winning over safety. When Gearing squatted, he disappeared completely.

After a few minutes, he stood.

To her surprise, he circled the camp and stopped beside her, his satchel slung across his body, hand clutching the strap, elbow holding it close to his side.

"If I stay on the ground all night, I'm stiff in the morning," he said quietly, answering a question she hadn't asked. "I need to get up and move around a couple of times."

He needed to sleep. No point in saying so, he had to know.

Free hand tugging his shirt, untucked and flapping around his legs like the robe he missed, he asked, "Are there mage-crafted terrors surrounding the camp?"

"Not surrounding."

"But there are mage-crafted terrors out there?"

It depended on what he considered a terror. She gave him the easy answer. "Yes."

They stood in silence for a moment. He watched her. She watched the company sleep. Kalyealee who-could-be-heir's eyes jumped and rolled behind her lids, right hand twitching where it rested on her hip. Destros slept on his back, an axe on either side, broad chest lifting the scale mail with every breath. The guardians slept easily in their vests. The lordlings didn't. They'd all removed their helms. Keetin Norwin-cee shifted in his sleep, forehead creased in pain. Offering comfort, Ryan Heir slept with his hand on the other man's arm. In the old days, they'd have been called shield-mates. She didn't know what they'd be called now, although she knew there'd be a name for it. People liked to name things.

They'd named her unnatural. Monster. Although she supposed they meant the same thing.

"We have records in the archives that say you can see in the dark."

She waited. To give Gearing credit, he caught on faster than many.

"*Can* you see in the dark?"

"Yes."

"How well?"

"Better than most. Not as well as some."

He snorted softly. "That's not the answer you give a scholar. We need definitives. You say, *I see as well as* . . . Or you point to an item and say, *I can see this but not that."* Moving past her, placing his right side against her left, he leaned against the boulder. She wondered if he thought his satchel was safer with his body between it and her. If he thought that a scholar's body was untouchable? Perhaps in Marsanport it was. It seemed that scholars had gained in power since she'd been taken away, power enough to convince Garrett Lord Protector to send Scholar Gearing to a place where even the young and fit were likely to die.

Sending Kalyealee who-could-be-heir was easier to understand.

What part of his name was Gearing, she wondered, the beginning or the end? Most people had more than one. Even she had two, although with Arianna gone, no one would speak the other again.

He had no fear of her. Even Kalyealee who-could-be-heir had a little.

"I know you don't want me here, but I want you to understand that this is the chance of a lifetime." He shifted, looking for comfort against the stone. "I am the first Scholar of the Broken Lands to actually enter the Broken Lands."

"Not yet."

He surprised her by chuckling. "True enough. My novitiate has no idea of how this will change her life. She's barely begun her scholarship and, while she was instrumental in convincing the Lord Protector to support our presence on this journey, she's more interested in reclaiming what was lost than in studying what remains. Brilliant mind, the brightest of the current novitiates in any scholarship, but then, I had the training of her. Her background, as a Marsan, made it hard for her to relinquish power, but I persevered. She has a great many questions for you."

That was obvious. "You don't?"

"I wanted to know how well you see in the dark, you answered me." She felt him shrug, a tiny lift of the shoulder by her elbow. "I've read the papers by scholars who spoke with you during Captain Marsan's lifetime in the earliest days of the Scholar's Hall. I may be the only one who's studied them in generations, and that makes me someone who knows more about you and your kind than anyone still alive." His statement sounded like a warning. "I knew how well you saw in the dark before I asked."

"Why ask?"

"Correlation. To see how truthfully you'd answer my question. Had you given a different answer, I'd begin to doubt you."

"The answers to the early scholars could have been lies." She could tell he hadn't thought of that by his sudden intake of breath and the snorting out of inhaled insects. When he breathed steadily again, she said, "Sleep. Travel gets harder from here."

"I know." He straightened. "I hope you've found this conversation as useful as I have."

She watched until he lay back in his bedroll, satchel on his stomach, both hands resting on the pouch, and wondered what it was he'd wanted her to know.

❧

Three blood bats touched down like whispers against her skin just before dawn. Asleep, she'd have never felt them.

The three of them together almost filled her hand. Blood dripped between her fingers when she closed them, her flesh muffling the sound of crushed bone.

She wondered if Marsanport remembered her. If they remembered how she'd claimed Northport for Captain Marsan and the Five Thousand. Did they celebrate the founding or did they try to forget? She remembered a stone room and chains she could have broken, and suspected the latter. What would they think of her if she went back?

She wouldn't ever go back.

She set out to check the perimeter as Harris woke, blinking at the pale light.

"Any trouble?" he asked, joining her when she returned to the rock. He was still looking past her, not at her, but he could have been speaking to any of the company, and his expression showed only an interest in her answer.

"No."

The corners of his mouth twitched up within the confines of his beard. "Nothing you couldn't handle."

It wasn't a question, so she didn't answer it, unsure if he referred to the shattered or the members of the company. She could feel Curtin's glare from across the camp. Now she had the time to look, the skin of Harris's throat, hands, and around his eyes said he wasn't much younger than Scholar Gearing, although in better shape—back straight, muscles firm, eyes clear. "You're old to be in Ryan Heir's service." Nothing in her voice except light curiosity, as Arianna had taught her.

Harris plucked a leaf from a bush, rolled it between his fingers, sniffed it, and said, "Lord Marsan was new to his role when the Black Flame flickered."

New and unsure. Still unsure. How bad had he been in the beginning? "You bring experience over enthusiasm."

"Almost exactly what they told me." He smiled then, the smile of one old campaigner to another.

He wasn't smiling at her. He was scanning their surroundings for excuses. For reasons not to look directly at her.

That didn't matter.

He was smiling with her. *This is how we're the same,* his smile said. Most people ignored everything but the differences.

"Were you in his brother's service?"

"I was not, thank the flame." Thumbs hooked in his belt, Harris turned his gaze toward the camp. "His brother was an ass. By the time he was born, it was clear the Lord Protector would have no children of his own, so Donal Marsan-cer had always known he would be heir after his mother and behaved accordingly. He treated service like he was entitled to it and he got worse after his mother died. He might have been an entirely adequate Lord Protector at another time, but he wouldn't have made it back with fuel for the flame. Donal Marsan-cer didn't listen to anyone he considered an inferior. He wouldn't have listened to the captain. He wouldn't have listened to you. Would've tried to use you like his ancestors did."

Nonee wondered how that would have made him an adequate Lord Protector, but her experience of politics before Gateway had been as the stick, not the carrot, so she remained silent.

As Curtin stirred and sat up, Harris glanced up at the sky and frowned at a high drift of cloud. "Okay to light a fire?"

She lifted her face to the breeze, separated the scents, and said, "Yes."

"Good. It's always better to start the day with a hot cup of tea."

"Pain-bark in Keetin Norwin-cee's?"

Harris nodded. "Boy's got to be hurting."

They broke their fast with cold eggs and oat cakes. And black tea. How many kinds of tea did Harris carry? Not her business, Nonee decided.

Tea weighed very little and he knew his strength. She ate a cured pig shoulder, lightening her pack by the weight of a small child. She tossed Destros a piece and ducked her head when he thanked her. He was large. Like her. He'd need the meat.

Harris kept the fire small and smokeless. She could leave the camp to him. With so many to watch over, that would help.

". . . and yes, robes mean you may be attacked with your ass out, but try and run with your pants down." Scholar Gearing yanked his trousers into place with one hand, satchel clutched close in the other as he stepped out from behind the bush masking the latrine.

"You won't convince me, Scholar." Curtin followed him. "If I'm attacked with my trousers open, at least I've got a weapon in my hand."

She saw Kalyealee who-could-be-heir mouth the response along with the guardian. Then grin at Ryan.

They shared a history, Ryan Heir and his cousin. It wasn't all bad between them.

That was good.

Garrett Heir had been sent by his father for fuel because his father had feared he was soft. He'd objected to her treatment and had been sent away with her to learn . . .

That she was a weapon, not a person.

That as heir, he was as much a thing as she was.

Garrett Lord Protector had sent both his heir and the scholar who-could-be-heir to the Broken Lands knowing what they'd face.

Arianna said that when something happened three times, it became tradition.

Had said.

RYAN.NOW

Ryan stepped into the Broken Lands with the brain-spattered boulder on his left, and felt nothing at all.

Keetin hummed thoughtfully on his right and said, "I'd expected more."

"I could put an arrow in your ass, my lord."

"Thank you, Servan, but I'll learn to live with my disappointment."

"Still no sign of mage-craft," Lyelee declared over Servan's laugh. She sounded annoyed, as though the Broken Lands were purposefully not living up to her expectations. Scowling, she waved a hand in front of her face. "Am I the only one being bothered by gnats?"

She was.

"Biting?" Nonee peered down at her.

"No. They're not even landing; they're swirling around being very, very irritating."

Keetin grinned. "Looks like they're trying to get your attention, Lye. They heard a scholar was coming in and they want to be studied." He spread his arms. "The Scholarship of Gnats!"

"You need to remember to respect," Lyelee began, spat out a gnat, and coughed out a mangled, "Shut up!"

Ryan heard Nonee sigh and wondered if she thought of them as children. From her perspective, they were ridiculously young and ridiculously fragile.

Ignoring Lyelee's background muttering, he looked around the Broken Lands and saw only trees, bushes, and the footprints Nonee's weight had pressed into the dry summer ground. First past the boulder, she'd turned to watch them enter. He should have sent her ahead to ensure their safety, but he hadn't needed to. She'd gone on her own. "It looks the same," he said when her eyes locked on his. "It doesn't look dangerous and that makes it more dangerous." His thought from the night before spoken aloud. But that wasn't quite it. "Makes us less likely to be careful."

"Yes."

"Does it make it more dangerous than giant lizard-dogs?" Keetin wondered, moving up beside Ryan and breaking a dead branch off a bush.

"Weren't giants," Nonee huffed.

Keetin jabbed the branch into the bush like a sword. "Well, not from your perspective."

Overnight, his bruises had darkened into purple and green blotches the size of Ryan's palm, heat rising off the puffy, discolored skin. Curtin had applied more cream, but the weight of clothing, the weight of the scale vest, the pull of his pack had to be painful against his chest, and he was hiding that pain behind a frenetic mood.

Tapping the branch against the edge of his helm, Keetin frowned. "So if it looks dangerous it's dangerous, and if it doesn't look dangerous, it's dangerous. What about Lyelee's gnats?"

"They aren't my gnats," Lyelee snapped.

Nonee stepped closer, swept her hand past Lyelee's face, and peered at her palm. Lyelee flailed, grabbed at Servan's arm, and nearly took the archer down with her. Ryan bit back a laugh.

"These are harmless." Nonee wiped her palm on her tunic.

"Which implies there are gnats in this general area that aren't harmless." Keetin glanced around, as though expecting someone other than Nonee to have an answer. "How do we tell the difference?"

"Check to see how badly you're bleeding," Ryan told him.

Keetin laughed. Ryan met his gaze and waited until the laughter stopped. Keetin's brows drew in. "You're serious?"

"I think I'm getting the hang of this place."

"Yes," Nonee said. Under the rumble, Ryan thought he heard approval. Before he could decide if he was perceptive or desperate, the captain called him forward.

She'd stopped beside a slender tree with striated gray bark and dark leaves. Looking up, he could see pale fuzz covering the underside of the leaves. Looking down, he saw bare ground within the shadow of the canopy. Looking out, he saw they stood very near the edge of a large clearing.

The grasses around the trees where they'd made camp had been summer dried and going to seed. Here, red and purple and yellow blooms split the meadow into swaths of color. Clumps of dark stems topped with creamy foxtail heads rose Ryan's height above the grass. The buzz of bees and other insects seemed slower, deeper. The whole thing was beautiful. Different. Wrong.

Captain Yansav pointed toward the dark line of evergreens. "The land begins to rise once we gain those trees. I don't trust this open area."

He wasn't sure what he was supposed to say. He could see that the land rose. He'd seen it from the wall. He could see how exposed they'd be crossing the grassland. He knew the captain had a reason for stating the obvious, he just didn't know what it was. If she wanted information about what they might face, about what might take advantage of that exposure, she needed to ask Nonee, not him.

Or *he* needed to ask Nonee? Because he was in command. Not the captain. Not the weapon. Him.

Ryan honestly couldn't see what difference it would make in this instance. Hand on the hilt of his sword, he turned . . .

. . . and came face to chest with worn leather. He managed to contain most of his reaction and Nonee caught him before he could fall backward, setting him gently to one side where he could watch the rest of the party move to join them. Gearing careened from tree to tree. Lyelee crashed through the underbrush, grinding out a monologue on the historic importance of paths not quite under her breath. Keetin was a little quieter, Servan and Curtin quieter still, and, for all his size, Destros maneuvered his bulk through the trees as though he'd practiced walking quickly and quietly through the woods while wearing scale armor and carrying a full pack. Nonee had made no noise at all.

Given their physical differences, the captain and the weapon wore much the same expression of stoic endurance over disbelief. Did they disbelieve the same things? Ryan wondered. And did stealth even matter in the Broken Lands?

"We'll be exposed crossing the meadow." Maybe it was large enough to be a meadow. Maybe it wasn't. Ryan kept talking before Lyelee could correct his terminology. "Is there another way?"

"No." Nonee's arm looked very similar to the trunk of the tree beside her, and that meant the tree looked as though it were made of stone. She pointed toward the evergreens. "If anything happens, run for the largest tree."

Unmistakable, the largest evergreen towered above the tree line, a serrated green spear stabbing the sky.

"Anything?" Gearing sagged, already breathing heavily. "Not very definitive. Do you expect something to happen?"

"Always." She waved a hand at the open ground. "Cross in the same order you used on yesterday's path. Don't wander off, it makes it harder to find the body."

As expected, all three guardians laughed. Curtin barely smiled, but it amounted to the same thing given his feelings about Nonee. A moon ago, Ryan would have assumed they'd thought the weapon was kidding, but he'd discovered on the road that living by the sword—or the axe or the bow—encouraged a dark sense of humor. "Okay," he said as they shuffled into march order, felt his checks heat as Captain Yansav glanced over at him, and fought the blush down. "We're in pairs, so each pair decides who keeps an eye on the ground and who watches the sky."

"We're responsible for each other's safety now?" Lyelee threw up her hands. "Why then did we bring guardians?"

"Isn't she supposed to add, *no offense?*" Servan murmured at the edge of hearing.

"What precisely do we watch for, sir?" Captain Yansav spoke over the archer.

"Precisely?" Ryan turned toward her.

The captain raised a brow.

All Ryan knew was that the thought of being so exposed lifted the hair off the back of his neck. "Nonee?"

"Looking down, watch for lines pushed through the grass from below." She swept her right arm in front of her, sketching sinuous curves in spite of heavy muscle.

"Snakes?"

"Snakes," she confirmed.

"Poisonous?" Destros asked.

"Large. Looking up, watch for heat shimmers lying horizontal in the sky."

"Horizontal heat shimmers?" Ryan tried to imagine what danger a horizontal heat shimmer would be to them and failed.

"D'lan Gee . . ."

"One of the mages," Lyelee interrupted. "They reworked air. More specifically, weather. The mage-craft they released in the war was responsible for the fog and the storm in the Heir's Chronicle."

"Sixty-three years ago," Ryan reminded her. "The shimmer, Nonee?"

"If the shimmer touches you, you burn."

"Like, sun-burn?" Keetin asked.

"Like pile of ash."

"All right, then . . ."

Captain Yansav stepped forward, scanning the sky. "How do we fight it?"

"You get out of the way."

"That's not . . ."

"But you have to see it, first." Nonee shrugged. "Almost everything else will announce its attack. The Broken Lands aren't subtle."

Lyelee snorted dismissively. "Oh yes, that meadow looks so dangerous. A bright sun in a clear blue sky, the wildflowers, the butterflies . . ."

Just beyond the underbrush, at the edge of the meadow, a pale purple flower wrapped its petals around a small yellow butterfly. A moment later it expelled the wings, broken and blackened, one at a time.

Captain Yansav's grunted disapproval of carnivorous flowers broke the silence. Ryan turned to Nonee, who shrugged again and said, "Could have escaped from a mage's garden."

He shook his head, glaring at Keetin, who'd collapsed against him, laughing. "Why would they grow a flower that eats butterflies?!"

"Because they could." Lyelee sounded intrigued now, annoyance discarded. "Why wouldn't they explore the extent of their power?"

Shoving Keetin's head off his shoulder, he turned to face his cousin. *Exploring the extent of their power* was one of the accepted causes of the Mage War. "You sound like you approve."

"I sound like I *understand*." Her emphasis on the final word suggested only an idiot wouldn't get the difference.

He wasn't sure he did.

❧

Halfway across the meadow, Nonee froze.

Ryan stopped scanning the grass to either side of the path and pulled Keetin to a stop.

The rock directly in their path was as high as Nonee's shoulder, shaped roughly like an egg that had been frozen as the chick began to push its way out. Above the bulges, just under the egg's upper curve, was the suggestion of a face. Although not as tall as the foxtail plants, the rock rose well above the top of the grasses. They should have been able to see it from the tree line. They hadn't.

Nonee took half a step back.

"I dreamed of this last night." Lyelee stepped out of line, striding forward until Captain Yansav's arm stopped her progress. She ducked under it and snapped, "What do you think you're doing?"

"Keeping you alive, Scholar."

"It's a *rock*."

"A rock you dreamed of." The captain would have to do more than block Lyelee's way to stop her again. Ryan saw her consider it.

"What did you dream?" Nonee shifted her weight from foot to foot.

Lyelee folded her arms. Her chin rose. "Scholars have definitively proven that images thrown up by the unconscious mind have no importance in the waking world."

"What did you dream?" Nonee repeated.

"Answer her, Lyelee." When she turned toward him, Ryan shook his head, denying the effect her scowl had on him. "Nonee's asking, and that makes it safety, not scholarship."

"I don't . . ."

"Answer her."

"Fine," she snapped. "I saw the rock, this rock or as near as makes no statistical difference, surrounded by fog, and I heard voices."

Nonee's nostrils flared. "What did the voices say?"

"Nothing I understood, although . . ." Her expression shifted into the aggressive consideration Ryan defined as scholarship. ". . . one of the languages had a slight similarity to Shurlian."

"Nahgo Sahn was from Shurlia. He was the last of the mages to join the procession."

"He was from the Cavid Kingdom," Lyelee corrected. "A loose confederation of tribes that held Shurlia's position at the south end of the Great Lake. It wasn't Shurlia at the time of the mage's procession. I am a Scholar of *History*," she added when Nonee stared at her.

After a long moment, Nonee swept a gaze over the rest of the company, no longer strung out in marching order. "Did anyone else dream of voices?"

No one spoke.

The lizard-dogs in Ryan's dreams hadn't spoken; their mouths had been too full of bloody flesh.

"Hey, I dreamed of . . ."

Ryan poked Keetin in the arm. "No."

He grinned, eyes crinkling at the corners. "You don't know . . ."

"Yes, I do."

"I dreamed of birds." Servan shrugged when all eyes turned to her. "It sounded like they were talking. Couldn't figure out what they were saying, but they sounded lonely."

"How do birds sound lonely?" Destros wondered.

"Dream," Servan reminded him. "Dreams don't make sense."

"Bird calls aren't voices," Lyelee snapped. Ryan assumed she was annoyed they were discussing Servan's dream, not hers. "Even the gray parrots from Shurlia only mimic speech."

Nonee turned toward Servan, physically dismissing Lyelee's observation. Ryan bit back a grin at his cousin's expression. "If it happens again . . ."

"I'll let you know." Servan nodded.

Lyelee took a step closer to Nonee and folded her arms. "Now that you've dealt with Guardian Servan-cee's talking birds, either move out of my way so I can examine this rock or explain why I can't."

"Why *we* can't," Gearing interjected.

Ryan glanced back at the older scholar and saw he'd slipped out of his pack and had sagged against Destros. The big guardian caught his eye, raised a hand, and signaled an *all clear*. Ryan assumed the sign meant he shouldn't worry about the old man having collapsed from heat stroke.

Nonee shifted her weight from foot to foot. Again. Ryan dropped his hand to his sword hilt. The guardians had noticed her unease as well. Servan had an arrow on the string.

"This wasn't here," she said. "And then it was. It's never been seen before. It's too . . ." She spread her arms as words failed her. ". . . too *big* to be this close to the line."

Even Ryan could tell that *big* wasn't the word she'd wanted. "It's here because of us. We've been noticed?"

"Yes."

"We should destroy it, my lord."

When Ryan turned to look, Curtin's hand was on his sword hilt. "Why?"

"Why?" Curtin glared past him at the rock. "It's mage-craft!"

"We're in the Broken Lands." Lyelee rolled her eyes. "Mage-craft isn't exactly an unexpected phenomenon. Here we have the sudden appearance of a rock that looks like it has a face. Nonee has a face that looks like it's made of rock. Is there a connection? Is it Nonee the Broken Lands have noticed? Does it matter? The temperature is rising as we contemplate the possibilities, the sun draws moisture from our bodies, and had we not paused for a pointless discussion, I'd have finished my measurements by now."

Sweat rolled down Ryan's back. Had the face grown more distinct?

"We should have seen it from the edge of the meadow," Curtin growled. "We didn't. You didn't, Scholar. Where did it come from?"

"Mage-craft," Lyelee said, mockingly.

Nonee sighed. Her entire upper body rose and fell on the exhale. "People lived around the mages, people who came with them. People who came after them. People who were here before they arrived."

Lyelee circled the standing stone. "The Captain's Chronicle states that the land was uninhabited when the mages arrived."

Ryan had no memory of that particular entry.

Nonee shook her head but kept talking as though Lyelee hadn't spoken. "They couldn't all be saved. Some were too injured, some were too far away."

"Only five thousand of all the people in Gateway and the Mage Lands walked the Mage Road with the captain," Gearing said softly.

"Five thousand by the end," Nonee corrected.

Gearing waved that off. "No one knows the number of the dead, so we use the number of those who survived to reach the Great Lake. Five thousand and thirty-one to be exact, not counting Captain Marsan and you. *The Five Thousand* is symbolic convenience, not accuracy."

They all knew that, had been taught it as children, but Nonee knew the number of the dead. Ryan was as certain of that as he'd ever been about anything.

She nodded toward the rock. "Some who remained were claimed by mage-craft."

"Wait." Although Ryan spoke to Nonee, not to his cousin, Lyelee paused, the foot she'd raised settling back on the ground. "When you say claimed by mage-craft, are you saying that's an actual face? That a mage took a person and stuffed them into a rock?"

The features had become more distinct.

Nonee studied the rock for a moment. "Might not have been deliberate."

That didn't help. Ryan was inclined to think that from the point of view of the person in the rock there'd be no great difference between it happening accidentally or deliberately. "Do you know who they are?"

"They've been dead for over a hundred and seventy years." Lyelee wiped the sweat from her forehead with the palm of her hand. "The correct question would be, *did* you know who they were."

The eyes on the face in the rock didn't move.

Did they?

Shadows shifted across the surface, defining brows, cheekbones, lips.

The mouth was half open.

Had it been open before?

Ryan shook his head, unsure of what he denied. "It looks as though it's trying to speak."

"As though *they're* trying to speak." Nonee's voice held layers. "They're not a thing."

Someone snorted. Ryan thought it was Curtin. Or he thought Curtin was the most likely to dismiss Nonee's correction. A correction by a mage-crafted weapon who'd been a thing in Marsanport for over a hundred years. "They," he repeated, for Nonee's sake.

It was a rock now.

It had to be a rock now.

A shadow rippled down the stone. Top to bottom. In bright sunlight. In a treeless meadow. Where had the shadow come from?

Lyelee's shadow fell across the face.

It didn't react, although Ryan half expected it to. "Lyelee, leave them be."

"Don't you want to know why *this* is what appeared when the Broken Lands noticed us?"

He did. "Do you have a way of finding that out?"

"I won't know that without a full examination of the rock." She leaned in, close enough her breath had to be lapping against the stone. "Taking into account of what Nonee knows about the rock."

"How long will it take?"

"I won't know that until I finish."

He wanted to know, but . . . "We need to keep moving."

Lyelee half-turned to glare at him, opened her mouth, snapped it closed, and stepped back from the rock so quickly she stumbled, the weight of her pack driving her to one knee.

The mouth on the face in the stone was closed. It had been open before. Ryan was sure it had been open before.

"What did it say?" he demanded, holding out a hand to help her up.

Eyes rolling, Lyelee pulled free of his grip the moment she was standing. "It's a rock."

The sweat that ran in warm, wet lines down his neck and under his collar had little to do with the heat. "What did it . . ."

"They," Nonee growled.

Ryan closed his eyes for a moment before continuing. "What did they say?"

Lyelee waved at gnats he couldn't see. "It didn't . . ."

"What did they say, Novitiate?" Gearing stepped forward, staggered, and waved off Destros's offered hand. "According to the only living being who'd know, this is a mage-crafted casualty of the Mage War."

Ryan was a little surprised the look Lyelee shot her mentor didn't knock him back off his feet.

"Free me." Her lip curled. "The rock said, *Free me.*"

They were still alive within the stone. Or they were the stone. But still alive. And had been for a hundred and seventy-six years. Ryan felt his stomach twist. He swallowed bile. And again. Behind him, someone spat, less successful at keeping their breakfast down. "Nonee, can we help?"

"No."

Lyelee turned back toward the stone, one finger tapping against her lower lip, expression speculative. "If a record of the specific mage-craft remains, then it might be undone."

Nonee blinked. "Are you here for the fuel or to try and undo the damage of the Mage War?"

"We haven't time to do both." Ryan was unable to look away in case the mouth opened again. How could they walk away and leave such horror to continue? "The flame can't go out."

"Why not?" Head cocked, she added, "Do you worship the flame?"

"I don't . . ."

"Your people."

"No. We don't."

She shrugged. "You swear by it."

"No. No, we do not!"

Keetin coughed out something close to a laugh. "We flaming well do, Ryan."

Ryan pivoted to face him. "It's not the same kind of swearing."

"But it is swearing." He raised his hand and flicked flame.

"It's not. We . . . we don't . . . There isn't . . ."

"We may not have time to undo the damage of the Mage War," Lyelee interrupted the protest Ryan couldn't find the words for, "but I am a scholar, and given access to the mage's records, I . . ."

"We," Gearing interjected.

". . . we can save this person."

"Which mage's records?" When neither scholar answered immediately, Nonee added, "There were six of them. And their records were in languages you couldn't understand."

"We're scholars," Lyelee began, came up against the perfectly blank expression on Nonee's face, and stopped. "Fine. But you take the responsibility for leaving them here."

"Yes."

She waved a hand at the rock. "Like this."

The mouth had opened again.

Ryan glared at his cousin. Her attention remained on the rock. The words were right, but the emotion behind them wasn't sadness or anger or disgust, it was frustration at not getting what she wanted. He'd heard it often enough when they were young. "Leave it, Lyelee."

"Why? Because you . . ."

"Captain!" Curtin's call cut him off. "Ripple in the grass like the weapon told us to watch for. Moving this way fast."

"Go!" Nonee stomped her feet, and Ryan felt the impact through the soles of his boots. "Now!"

Captain Yansav pulled her sword. "Servan! Take point!"

"Taking point, Cap!" Servan ran past, light on her feet in spite of the pack.

"Destros, Curtin, the scholars!"

Both men snapped out, "Scholars, Captain!" as they began to move.

Curtin fell in behind Gearing, who struggled to lift his pack. "Leave it, Scholar!" Gearing didn't hesitate, he released the straps and began to run. Curtin scooped it up; even double laden, he had no trouble maintaining the scholar's pace.

Lyelee remained by the stone. Destros grabbed her by the pack and lifted pack and scholar both into the air, ignoring Lyelee's protests. They weren't moving fast, but they were moving.

"My lord, run!"

Ryan couldn't see the ripple. "Captain, Nonee . . ."

"If she needs help she'll ask for it!"

Nonee stomped again.

Keetin pulled his sword and ran with it out.

Ryan followed, sword sheathed.

Servan waited, arrow on the string, at the edge of the meadow.

In under the trees, Ryan slid out of his pack, tossed his helm on it, and went back for Gearing, dropping his shoulder and heaving him up over his back, barely breaking stride. From the color of Curtin's face and the way he sucked air through his teeth, he was willing to bet the skinny old scholar was lighter than his pack. He'd probably stuffed it with books when no one was watching.

"That," Gearing snarled as Ryan set him on his feet, "was unnecessarily undignified."

"So's dying."

"You don't know . . ."

The ground trembled under a triple stomp—BOOM BA BOOM!

Ryan turned and stepped aside as Destros and Lyelee passed, her feet on the ground, but the big axeman taking the weight of the pack she still wore. Captain Yansav backed down the path of crushed grasses, sword in one hand, long dagger in the other.

BOOM BA BOOM

Nonee turned to the left.

A flash of light rose up out of the grass.

And kept rising.

No. Not light. It had substance, although it was hard for Ryan to focus on it.

He felt Keetin's breath by his ear. "I flaming hate snakes."

That was a snake?

BOOM BA BA BOOM

How could the sound of bare feet against dry earth get louder?

The beam of light . . . no, the *snake* swayed. Toward Nonee and back. In and out. The wedge-shaped head wore a blinding crown of reflected sunlight.

"I've got a shot, Cap."

"Let the weapon deal with it, Servan."

BOOM BA BA BOOM

The snake collapsed back into the grass.

BOOM BA BOOM

They were too far away and at the wrong angle to see it leave, but Ryan assumed Nonee had watched and waited until the ripple was a safe distance away before she turned and jogged toward them. "Crystal snake," she said, as she reached the trees.

"Actual crystal?" Lyelee demanded, pushing forward.

"No."

"And it was more afraid of you than you were of it," Keetin declared. "That's what they always say about snakes," he added when Nonee turned to face him. "That they're more afraid of you than you are of them."

Nonee thought about it for a moment, then said, "No."

Ryan had no idea what she'd just denied. "You didn't kill it." When she merely blinked, he added, "Why didn't you kill it?"

"No need."

"It was a giant crystal snake," Curtin snarled.

"Yes." She nodded at Servan's bow. "Wouldn't have worked."

"Good to know." Servan slid the arrow back into her quiver. "Me, I'm glad you didn't kill it. It was beautiful."

With Curtin muttering under his breath in the background, Nonee looked at the packs, at the panting scholars, and said, "We stop at the fixed point. This way."

Ryan frowned as he shrugged into his pack. The snake had been beautiful, but by leaving it alive Nonee had left open the chance they'd be attacked by it again. He didn't want to sound like Curtin, but shouldn't the lingering mage-craft they encountered be destroyed if possible? Regardless of what it looked like? And what about the rock? Did it mean anything more than that they'd been noticed? Was it a warning?

Stupid. It was a person in a rock. Of course it was a warning.

But that meant the Broken Lands . . . thought. Had a consciousness of some sort. On purpose or by accident? And did it matter?

Of course it mattered.

He just couldn't see how.

"You're making the face again." Keetin reached over and rapped on his helm.

"What face?"

"The one you wore the first week at the Citadel when you didn't have a flaming clue what was going on and weighed every decision like it was life or death." When he glared at Keetin, unimpressed, Keetin laughed. "I didn't say it wasn't apt, under the circumstances."

"You say too much," the captain murmured as she passed them.

Ryan resisted Keetin's laughter as long as he could, but ended up laughing with him. Even Lyelee snickered, although, given Lyelee, she was probably laughing at, not with.

The fixed point wasn't far from the edge of the meadow. The tallest tree in an evergreen forest of giants, it had deeply grooved bark, drooping branches that began far above his head, and needles nearly as long as his forearm. Ryan estimated it would take three or four Nonees linked hand to hand to circle it. Trees didn't grow that big naturally.

Nonee patted the trunk like it was an old friend. For all he knew, it might have been. "You should be safe here for a short time."

"While you do what?" Lyelee demanded, dropping her pack.

"Find the second fixed point." Nonee lifted her head. "There was a river."

Ryan couldn't hear moving water. Her nostrils flared; he sniffed as well. He couldn't smell it either. "The river's a fixed point?"

"No. The cave behind the waterfall is a fixed point."

Trapped between the forest and the waterfall had been how the Lord Protector referred to it in the Heir's Chronicle. Ryan felt a chill run down the center of his back, although it was nearly as hot under the trees as it had been in the meadow. "Wouldn't it be faster if we all searched?"

"No." The captain and Nonee answered together and exchanged a look that made Ryan feel nine instead of nearly twenty.

"Stay close to the tree." Nonee waved a hand at the high branches, the lack of underbrush, and the thick layer of dead needles that gave the immediate area a parklike setting. "The lines of sight are good, nothing should be able to sneak up on you, but be careful."

"Of what?" the captain asked. "Specifically."

"Specifically," Nonee repeated, "everything."

Captain Yansav crossed her arms. "What happens if we're attacked while you're gone?"

She shrugged. "You fight."

"We fight," the captain repeated after a long moment. She turned to give orders to the guardians as Nonee disappeared behind the biggest tree.

※

"Anything following?"

Arrow on the string, standing sideways to the grassland, the bulk of her body tucked into the shadow of a tree, Servan kept her eyes on the meadow. "Not that I can see, my lord."

Ryan could see the line of crushed and broken grasses their boots had left and, in the distance, the pale gray of the stone painted with golden highlights by the brilliant afternoon sun. "What *can* you see?" Servan's ability to see farther than the rest of them had been proven multiple times on the road.

"The face is on this side of the stone now."

She sounded as though she were commenting on the view from the Citadel wall. *The market is very crowded today. The bakery has a new striped awning. The face is on this side of the stone now.* Ryan could see the stone, but not the face. His vision was nowhere near as good as Servan's. He was fine with that. He swallowed, and then again. "You're taking it well," he managed at last. "Not just this, but . . . all of this."

"It's not what I expected," Servan said slowly. "I expected chaos and that we'd have to fight for every step. And wonder," she added after a pause. "I expected wonder and broken pieces of history that would astound us."

He snorted. "You and my cousin both."

The corners of her mouth twitched up. "Yes, sir." A deep breath. A nod toward the stone. "So far, it's just sad and horrible."

NONEE.NOW

Nonee should have been able to hear the river from the first fixed point. She had before. She'd led them to the river, following her ears, then followed Garrett Heir as he led them along it to the waterfall. She'd come this way seven years ago and the river had still been flowing between banks crowded with willow. The tiny fish that swarmed onto the land to hunt had been new, but the river had been where she remembered it.

Not only had the river disappeared, but the land had changed. The evergreens remained, the land still rose toward the distant mountains, but once away from the first fixed point, cliffs of pinkish gray rock began to divide the land into layers. An almost perfect circle of rock rose higher than her head like a pillar crowned with trees.

The cave had been behind a waterfall.

Without the river, without the waterfall, it could be in any of a hundred pinkish-gray rock faces.

All she could do was move at her best speed toward where memory told her it had been.

From rock to sand to bleached soil. Past low, needled bushes heavy with waxy blue berries, and past squat, twisted trunks that had once stood as tall and straight as those next to the meadow, she ran up a slope so steeply angled she had to grab what seemed solid, and when nothing did, drive her fingers into the ground.

The land looked as though something large had moved beneath it and thrown it aside like a child too hot under a heavy blanket.

Something might have. As long as it stayed beneath, she could ignore it.

A slice of sky warned her to slow, and she stopped well back from the edge of the cliff.

Dry and rocky land spread out from the bottom of the nearly vertical rock face until it reached a double line of willows stretching off to the north.

Still no river, but she thought the willows marked where it had been. The rise and fall of the land had made it hard to judge distance.

In Gateway, Healer Tanis grew willows for the pain-relieving properties of their bark. Nonee closed her eyes and remembered Arianna laughing as she stripped young, flexible branches. Remembered Arianna reaching up and rubbing a soft gray bud against her cheek.

"We call them cat's paws," Arianna said.

Cats wouldn't come near her.

She had no time for this. She opened her eyes.

This far into summer, there'd be no buds.

She leapt off the edge. She'd have to find another way down for the company.

An ivory-colored dust cloud rose around her when she landed.

"Who," said the bones, *"disturbs my rest?"*

She counted six teeth and a few small bones that remained whole.

She waited.

"Oh," said the bones, *"it's you."*

Mage-craft sank into bone. She crushed a tooth between thumb and forefinger as her only response.

The space between the willows where the river had once run had become a path of smooth red dirt scattered with polished rocks.

Nonee pushed through the trees. Slender branches wrapped around her throat. She grabbed the trunk of the attacking tree and yanked it from the ground. Long lines of roots cracked like braided bull-hide against her skin. With both ends writhing, Nonee changed her grip and threw the tree high into the sky. Before it began to come down, she moved onto the open ground that marked the river's old course, and ran.

When roots broke the ground, she pounded them flat.

It took longer than she liked to arrive at the end of the line of willows, at the clearing, the cliff, and the cave.

The cave hadn't changed. It still looked like an open mouth.

All that remained of the waterfall and the pond was a tiny pool of clear water tucked off to one side. Nearly hidden within the angle of a broken rock, it wasn't large enough to hold even Kalyealee who-could-be-heir's hand, and she was the smallest of the company. Physically.

ARIANNA.THEN

Arianna watched closely as Norik slipped out from behind the waterfall and eased along the narrow ledge of damp, slippery rock. It would be so easy for him to fall, to slip unseen below the water.

He didn't. He leapt to drier ground, stubbing his torch out in the dirt. "Cave's empty and it's deep. There's a crack in the back wall, but it's too small for anything bigger than a bug to use."

"Are we camping in it?" Arianna asked, hands tucked into the folds of her skirt. "With a fire going, it'll be warmer than the open air."

"Damper behind the waterfall," Garrett pointed out.

"Not exactly dry out here," Norik grunted.

Arianna smiled as he shook a drop of water off his boot, as fastidious as a cat. He had a point. The cliff was at least four full stories high, and the water sprayed a fair distance out from the rock.

"We'll stay back by the trees." Garrett waved a hand as though they might have forgotten where the trees were. "Too easy to be trapped in a cave."

"We're making camp now?" From the edge of the grassland to the waterfall; they hadn't been walking for that long. Arianna assumed that if she could keep walking, they all could.

"We've got firewood and water." Garrett checked the sky. "We won't find a better place before dark."

The lower curve of the sun hadn't quite touched the horizon. The sun set noticeably earlier every night, and they still had part of the Frost and all of the Snow Moon to get through before it turned.

"Malcolm, Petre . . ."

The snap in Garrett's voice jerked them away from the edge of the pond.

". . . pick a spot where the trees block the wind and check that the ground's dry."

Petre grinned and scratched at the edge of his scruffy beard. Arianna wondered if he realized how young it made him look. Of course he didn't. "But we were so looking forward to camping in mud, my lord."

"Really?" Garrett grinned back at him. "Well, that can be arranged."

Watching the relationship between the two younger men and the heir had raised Garrett in Arianna's esteem. They respected him, they obeyed him, and that seemed to be all he required. She wouldn't say they were friends, exactly, but they were closer than his rank suggested they would be.

Uvili was slowly sweeping her gaze from waterfall to pond to forest edge and back again. She looked like she expected trouble, but to be fair, she always looked like she expected trouble.

Leaving her pack leaning against Malcolm's, Arianna walked to the edge of the pond. Three ducks of a type she'd never seen before swam by the far shore. They were about equally black and white, a high tuft of feathers rising from the top of their heads. The water itself was startlingly clear, clear enough she thought she could see duck feet paddling below the surface. Looking down past the toes of her boots, she could see dark caverns in among the tumbled boulders that covered the pond's bottom and wondered if they held fish. And if the fish could be safely eaten.

"Looks cold."

She grinned up at Norik as she tucked her skirt between her legs and squatted, using her staff for balance. "Cold or not, I still wouldn't mind a scrub."

"I'd rather wallow in my dirt than freeze my nuts off. And we'd best fill the waterskins before you dive in."

"Of course." She stretched out a hand and hesitated, fingertips just above the surface. It did look cold.

"Healer!"

≈

"I'm fine," Petre muttered as Arianna turned his hand in hers, examining the rising lines of blisters. "It's just itchy."

"Don't scratch it." Still holding his hand, she squinted down at the forest edge. "Is that the plant?" The three red leaves cupped up around the stem were familiar.

"Yeah. I shifted it to get a piece of dead wood behind it."

"That's all this is, then, a reaction to the blast."

"Blast?" The fingers of his other hand flexed, scratching the air.

"It's what we call that plant. Most people blister when they touch it." She frowned as new blisters rose while she watched, the fluid inside straining at the tight dome of translucent skin. "You're clearly among the few who overre-act." Leaning out to see around him, she pointed with her free hand. "Mal-colm, could you get me that plant over by the triangular rock?"

"This?" He poked it with the toe of his boot. "It's frost-killed."

"The leaves, yes. The stem should still have some juice." Arianna recap-tured Petre's fingers as he pulled free. "Don't touch yourself with that hand."

Malcolm snorted with laughter as he gave her the gem weed, and the two older men grinned.

"I meant your face, but yes, that too." While stripping off the dead leaves and crushing the stems between her hands, she told them the story of Lari-anne, who'd spent three days sitting in cold water last summer. "Her bonded insisted on her wearing mittens in bed until almost the end of the season." She spat onto the pieces of plant, then rolled them between her palms until the heat forced the last of the soft tissue out of the stems. Had it been summer, she'd have separated the fiber from the gel, but she didn't want to waste what little there was. "This will keep the blisters from spreading until we can find more weed." She patted the green paste onto Petre's heated skin and wrapped a piece of fabric around his wrist to keep the cuff of his jacket from abrading the blisters.

Petre sighed. "That helps."

"Good. Malcolm?"

"I can't find any more, Healer," he called from within the trees. "I mean, there's a couple of really dead things that might've been gem weed once, but nothing alive."

"Malcolm!" Garrett barked out the young man's name and Arianna flinched at the sudden sound. "You've gone far enough."

"I can still see you, sir."

"Good. Now get your ass back here."

"Yes, sir."

About to ask Garrett if he'd heard something or was merely indulging in a little justified paranoia, Arianna was distracted by Petre flexing his blistered hand so vigorously bits of the paste flaked off. "Stop that. And don't scratch. You'll be in worse shape if you break the blisters."

"But it itches."

He sounded so much like her seven-year-old nephew, she had to turn away to hide her smile. Young men didn't appreciate reminders of how close their childhood lingered.

"Distract yourself by collecting firewood," Garrett told him, staring back along the way they'd come. He'd sent Uvili twenty strides downriver, but didn't seem reassured that she was on guard. "We're going to need to keep the fire going all night."

Arianna opened her mouth to tell him fire might not help, that these were the Broken Lands and for all they knew fire would attract the shattered, but she closed it again without speaking. They'd find out soon enough and she'd rather find out with a fire than without one.

Norik stared across the pond at the trio of ducks, dark shapes against the water in the last of the light, and put an arrow on the string. "Do you have an objection to fresh meat, Healer?"

"Why would I?"

"I would have thought healers were against causing pain."

"Then don't cause pain." When he turned toward her, she smiled. "As I understand it, you're a good shot. If the duck is alive one moment and dead the next, what pain there is will be fleeting. I'm curious about how you're going to retrieve the body, though."

He glanced at the ducks, then back at her. "You had said you wanted to bathe."

"I have an objection to being your bird dog," she laughed. "And I think . . ."

With a sudden flapping of wings and spraying of water, all three ducks took flight. They crossed in front of the waterfall in a tight wedge and followed the curve of the pond, screaming, "No, no, no, no, no!"

Arianna saw Uvili turn her head to watch them pass. Saw her half raise one arm, then let it fall back to her side. Had she been going to stop them? Greet them?

"I'm not terribly familiar with ducks," Norik said, quietly, as though he were commenting on nothing stranger than the weather. "Do they usually . . ."

"No. They don't."

He slipped the arrow back in his quiver. "Well, that's disturbing."

"It itches!" Petre shook his blistered hand then scrambled to his feet. "I'm going to put it in the water. The cold might help."

"Go with him." Garrett threw two empty waterskins at Malcolm. "Fill these and make sure he doesn't fall in."

"Yes, sir."

"Don't push him in, either."

"Yes, sir." His second agreement was more resigned than enthusiastic.

"Is that likely to happen?" Arianna asked as Petre and Malcolm moved out of the circle of light toward the pond.

"Always smart to cover all possibilities," Garrett told her, shifting the pan of sausages on the fire. "I guarantee he thought of it."

"Really?"

Garrett shrugged. "I would have at his age."

"You did," Norik pointed out.

Arianna shook her head. "You two have the . . ."

Petre screamed.

If Arianna hadn't been watching Uvili, she wouldn't have seen her move. One moment, she squatted on the other side of the fire, the next she was at the pond, both young men in her arms.

The water at the edge of the pond roiled. Arianna thought she might have seen a dark shape dive back below the surface, but then she only had eyes for the blood pouring from the end of Petre's arm. "Clamp it off!"

"No, no, no, no!" Malcolm reached across Uvili to grab at his friend's shoulder.

Uvili dropped him and closed her free hand around Petre's wrist.

"Norik!" Garrett was on his feet, sword in his hand.

Norik stared down the arrow pointed into the water. "I don't see anything."

"Get away from the edge!"

"I can't shoot it from . . ."

"Now!"

Digging into her pack, Arianna yanked out the sack of powdered witch hazel and her operating kit, then covered the ground to Petre's side in an undignified scramble.

He was unconscious. Arianna glanced at the massive arm resting across his collarbone, decided it was a mercy if Uvili'd choked him out, and said, "Lift the stump so I can see it." Daylight would have been best, but moonlight would have to do.

"Stump?" Garrett demanded.

Petre's arm ended halfway between elbow and wrist. Or, where his wrist had been. The bite had clean edges, with no sign of teeth. Very little blood oozed out through Uvili's grip.

Arianna had hoped for a flap of skin. "Uvili, can you keep the pressure on? And hold the arm perfectly still?"

"Yes."

Even with Uvili's help, her hands were red by the time she'd tied off the major blood vessels. Pulling a slender knife from the kit one-handed, she flicked off the sheath and hit Garrett in the ankle.

He turned far enough to see her without losing sight of the pond. "What are you doing?"

Knife in her hand, Arianna leaned in close. "Best to deal with this while he's out."

"Not what I asked!"

"I need skin to cover the stump. Unless you have some to offer, shut up." She worked quickly, cutting away the flesh that had been in contact with the shattered's . . . teeth, for all it looked as though a blade had been used. She was vaguely conscious of Garrett comforting Malcolm, and of Norik watching the water as she switched to her saw. The metal had been scavenged from the ruins outside the wall. The notches on the blade were tiny, and very sharp. It had taken Koe Ramsin, the blacksmith, six attempts to match her specifications.

"That's not big enough . . ."

"Shut up."

Cutting the ends of the bones back so they were slightly shorter than the trimmed muscle gave her almost enough room.

"Garrett, bring me the bandages from the front pouch in my pack." The curved needle slipped easily through the flap of Petre's skin, and with a finger under the waxed thread to keep it up above the bloody flesh, she carefully pulled the edges together. She couldn't, wouldn't cut back enough for full coverage, but only a double finger-width of open wound remained when she finished. Her left hand cupped over the seam, she used her right to scoop witch hazel out of the bag, tumbled it off her fingers into her palm, and realized she needed another hand. "Garrett, there's a glass jar in my kit, long and narrow with three raised dots . . ."

He dropped to one knee beside her. She didn't hear rummaging. That was good. "Got it."

"Three drops on the powder in my hand."

"Wouldn't a bowl . . ."

"Skin contact helps. Three drops!" She felt each drop hit. When reddish brown foam threatened to spill out between her fingers, she coated the torn flesh with the paste. "The bandages . . ."

"By your left knee."

As she placed a quilted pad over the end of the stump, Uvili moved her hand up Petre's arm, giving her room for the binding. "Only a weapon, my ass," she muttered, wrapping the pad in place. Sitting back on her heels, she checked her work, then cupped the stump gently between both hands. Breathing slowly, she emptied her mind of blood and torn muscle and crushed bone and pain. Two days passed between heartbeats. Two days might be enough, but just to be safe she pushed through one more, straddling the line between what Petre needed and what she could give. There'd be no warm bed and hot meal waiting for her, so turning herself into an exhausted pile of mush wasn't an option.

The three days of healing had given his body a chance to move on from the trauma. Things felt . . . not good, but almost there. "Okay," she said, opening her eyes and allowing her hands to drop down onto her lap. "Let's see if it holds."

Slowly, the large gray hand loosened its grip on Petre's arm.

Arianna held her breath. Took a breath. "Carry him to the fire. I need to ready a painkiller for when he wakes."

"Yes." Uvili rose, Petre cradled in her arms as though he weighed nothing at all.

Bloody cloth and bits of excised flesh went into a bundle thrust into Garrett's hands. "Burn this."

He was back by the time she had her blades wrapped to be cleaned later and her kit tucked away. When she tried to rise, he tucked strong hands under her arms and helped her to her feet, his mouth so close to her cheek that she felt as much as heard him say, "Malcolm, lay out Petre's bedroll."

"Sir." Malcolm's voice sounded thick, although he'd stopped crying.

Her lower legs numb, Arianna took a step and nearly fell.

Garrett steadied her. "I've never seen a Scholar of Flesh work so quickly."

"Then you've seen Scholars of Flesh lose patients," she snapped, took a deep breath, and murmured, "Sorry." She opened her eyes to see him watching her with what looked like concern. He nodded like he understood how she felt. He couldn't, but for no logical reason at all it helped that he thought he did.

Arianna chewed cold sausage, tugged her quilted jacket closer around her body, and listened to Norik comfort Malcolm. Still unconscious, Petre's pulse was strong, his breathing shallow but regular. Given the minimal bruising rising above the stump, Uvili had impressive control over her strength.

And a kind heart. She'd settled the boy on the far side of the fire, away from the pond.

"So . . ." Garrett leaned toward her as he poked at the fire with a branch, nudging the metal cup of willow-bark tea safely out of the way. ". . . I understand the cutting and sewing, I've seen Scholars of Flesh do similar. What was going on there at the end?"

She swallowed the mouthful of meat.

"Because something was definitely going on," he added, volume carefully below the crackle and hiss of the fire. "I could *feel* it."

He could feel it. He didn't sound happy about it.

Captain Marsan had come out of the Broken Lands. From what little Arianna understood about Marsanport's hierarchy, the rest of Garrett's family line would have been made up of Gateway's refugees. What was his blood telling him?

She considered lying to him. He'd be happier if she did.

She didn't. "I'm a healer."

"And?"

"And I'm a healer. I gave him three days of healing." She took another bite of sausage and watched his grip tighten on the branch.

Sparks flew as Garrett poked the embers. "It was mage-craft."

"No."

"No?" His upper lip curled. "Then what the flame was it?"

"A talent."

"You gave him three days of healing. I'm not seeing the difference," he growled.

"Talents do one thing. Only one thing. We have a lot of them in Gateway because quite a few talents accompanied the mages and very few of them went with Captain Marsan. It occasionally skips a generation or two," she allowed, "but if it's in the bloodline, it stays in the bloodline."

Wills hadn't been the only abused talent Gateway had taken in; the world at the end of the road wasn't kind to those it saw as different. Tregor had arrived only three years ago. He'd traveled impossibly far, by land and sea, following the stories of the mages' journeys. He'd arrived exhausted and starving, with an open, weeping wound in his side. The infection had begun shutting down organs, and in spite of everything Arianna and the other healers had tried, he'd died eight days later. They'd never found out what he could do.

"Talents do one thing?"

"Yes."

"You heal."

"I heal," she agreed.

"And skin contact helps?" Jabbing the branch at a half-burned piece of wood, he shook his head, as if trying to shake the thought loose. "How does it help?"

"I can't explain it."

"Because it's bullshit!"

"Garrett . . ."

"So if talents do one thing, what do mages do?"

"Mages do all the things."

He looked up and stared at her for a long moment, firelight flickering in his eyes. "All the things?" he repeated.

"Specifically, they can make *all the things* do what they want." She kept her voice matter-of-fact, pulling lessons from her childhood. "Rearranging reality breaks them in the end, and those who manage to put the pieces back together never quite get it right. A single broken mage can be dealt with by their extended community . . ."

"Like a rabid dog."

"Like a rabid dog," Arianna agreed. "But when they decide there's safety in numbers, gather from different lands, and form their own community, then they define that community. They have the last word, no questions, no debate, and . . ." She waved a hand toward the edge of the firelight.

"Thousands died."

"Yes. Because eventually, if they wanted to challenge themselves, they had to challenge other mages. At least that's one of the theories about what caused the Mage War." She rolled up onto her feet as Petre moaned, and by the time she'd taken the mug from the fire, Garrett had Petre's head on his lap, Norik and Malcolm standing around him.

"Drink," he said quietly, raising the boy's head without being told as Arianna held the mug to Petre's lips.

Petre opened his eyes. Closed them. Opened them again. He tried to push the mug away. His brows drew in; he blinked at the stump, then let the arm fall. Although Arianna caught his elbow before the stump hit the ground, Petre paled from the pain of even that much contact. "Drink a little more," she told him. "It'll help."

"No." He rolled his head away from her. "It's horrible."

She smiled. If he was with them enough to complain about the taste, he'd stay.

GARRETT.THEN

Garrett watched Arianna, the healer, with a talent that had to be a type of mage-craft, cradling Petre's head in her lap and needed to move, needed to fight back, needed to do *something*. He stood, waved a hand toward the weapon standing in the darkness between the pond and the fire, acknowledged Norik's plea to be careful, and went to join her.

Thousands died. But not Petre. Because Arianna had a talent.

It wasn't mage-craft.

He doubted the Scholar's Hall would recognize the difference.

Standing back of the weapon's right shoulder, out of her way should she need to fight, he asked, "Do you know what that was?"

After a long moment, she growled, "That?"

"In the pond." How many *thats* were out there? "Do you know what attacked Petre?"

"No."

"But the mages had water creatures?"

"Yes."

"Or beasts the war could have shattered into water creatures."

"Yes."

"We'll never be able to anticipate an attack. I'm beginning to realize this isn't going to be a fair fight."

She snorted, sounding so much like his father's chamberlain, he almost smiled.

Without the weapon—only with them because of his father's contempt—they wouldn't have stood a chance. Hand on his sword hilt, Garrett wondered if a little less dependence on the weapon and a few more crossbow quarrels might have been a better idea. Shoot first, identify the body later.

"Do you know what's out there?" he asked.

"No." She stood, weight braced over thick legs, ready.

Garrett squinted as he turned toward the fire. The flames burned a hot yellow-orange, the triangular framework of dead wood throwing little smoke. As he approached, he realized branches about as big around as the healer's wrist now surrounded the fire pit like spokes and, as he watched, Malcolm circled the blaze, using the side of his boot to shove each branch a little further into the coals.

"Torches, sir. For light, or for weapons. I've got a bunch more piled by for when these burn down." Malcolm wiped one palm against his thigh, switched his sword to that hand, and wiped the other. "I should take one of them and go get more. There's a lot of dead wood close and we'll need enough to last until dawn. We can't run out. I need to . . ."

"Stay."

Malcolm paused, half-turned. His head dropped forward.

"You saved his life." Garrett gripped the boy's shoulder. "You couldn't have prevented what happened."

"I could have . . ."

"No."

"But . . ."

"No." Reaching out, he wrapped a hand around Malcolm's wrist and pulled his sword arm in against his side before the despondent swinging of the boy's blade did actual damage. And then, because it couldn't be said enough to a twenty-year-old who'd just seen his best friend lose a hand, he repeated, "You saved his life."

"Ari saved his life."

"Which I couldn't have done had Petre gone into the pond."

They turned together to face the healer. One of her square-fingered, capable hands rested on Petre's forehead, the other clutched a mug tightly enough Garrett could see the shadows the moon made between the raised lines of tendons fanned out over the back of her hand. Shifting his gaze to her face, he saw more shadows under her eyes. Both might have been a trick of the firelight, but he didn't think so. She nodded toward the mug propped at the edge of the fire. "Malcolm, I need you to make sure this tonic stays warm, not hot. Petre will need to drink every time he wakes."

"But you . . ."

"I need to clean my equipment. I need you to watch the tonic."

He wet his lips and nodded. "I can do that."

"I know."

Malcolm settled by the fire, Petre's head carefully moved from Arianna's lap to his. Garrett dropped to one knee by his side. The cloth wrapped around the end of Petre's arm gleamed gold in the firelight, with no dark stain to mark where blood had leaked through the padding. His chest rose and fell, his chin nestled into the folds of the scarf his brother had wrapped around his neck the day they'd left, and above the edge of his scruffy beard, his cheekbones looked sharp enough to cut meat. He'd lost weight. Lost what little boyhood fat he'd had left when they set out.

His eyes flicked back and forth behind closed lids. Garrett suspected he knew what Petre dreamed of; knew that when he closed his eyes, he'd dream the same.

"Skin contact helps," he said, and moved Malcolm's hand to cup Petre's cheek.

When he looked up, Arianna was smiling at him, so he went around the fire and joined her. They sat in silence until the water in the pot in front of her began to boil.

"Wouldn't that be easier in daylight?" he asked as she slid a slender knife blade into the water.

"Yes, but . . ."

"But you want to reduce the amount of fresh blood smeared around the camp," he offered when the silence lengthened.

"That too."

Her hand shook as she removed the knife and dipped in a curved needle, the dark thread nearly invisible in the dark. He was—not glad but something like glad, to see her affected by what had happened. In his experience, Scholars of Flesh saw injuries as an opportunity to gain new knowledge of wounds.

"Is the pain greater when I press this?" Scholar Ha had asked, dealing with one of Garrett's training-yard injuries. Comfort wasn't a part of their scholarship.

It seemed healers, however tainted by mage-craft, had emotional reactions.

Unless it was the effort of healing that caused her hand to shake.

What cost for what she'd done?

What cost for the use of her *talent*? For her? For Petre?

She tucked the needle into her kit and sighed. "We should go back to Gateway. For Petre's sake."

For Petre's sake, he would. Go back, see him safe, start out again a little more aware of what they'd face. "We can't." He gestured to where the weapon stood, having shifted to face the woods, to face the way they'd come. Before he could explain, a discordant braid of howling explained for him. "They're between us and the line, and they'll be able to take us out one at a time if we're on the move. As either Norik or I will have to carry Petre, we'll be two fighters down. We need them to attack on our choice of ground to give her . . ." He nodded toward the large absence of light that defined the weapon's position. ". . . the best chance to beat them."

Arianna dipped a piece of cloth into the boiling water, waved it in the air for a moment, then began to clean her saw. "I wouldn't have chosen this piece of ground."

"Granted." He smiled, although it felt more like a grimace on his face. "But on the bright side, any shattered that go into the water won't be getting out again."

"True. And most shattered are animal enough to be careful of fire," she added thoughtfully. "If we build a circle around Petre, it'll help keep him safe if it comes to a fight."

"When."

"Fair enough."

"He'll want to fight," Malcolm called.

"He can't . . ."

Malcolm stiffened indignantly. "He's right-handed."

Garrett caught Arianna's eye and bit back inappropriate laughter as she said, "Well, that's different, then."

"Garrett!"

Norik's warning jerked him around to face the pond. He thought the scraping and pounding was the weapon running toward them until a broad-mouthed, glistening face jabbed into the light—a giant frog crossed with a Shurlian crocodile, with lumpy glistening skin, black eyes on the top of its head, and far too many teeth.

Arianna threw the pot of boiling water in its eyes.

It hissed and reared back, then the weapon's shoulder sank into the pale pouch of skin under the bony ridge of its lower jaw. Claws at the end of enormous webbed feet dug into the ground, but she forced it back toward the water.

Garrett grabbed a burning branch and leapt to his feet. Sword in his right hand, torch in his left, he stumbled over ridges of dirt as he charged forward. The hiss of an arrow sounded strangely loud over the noise of the waterfall, but he heard no impact. Norik cursed.

Then he heard a splash. The silvered water roiled around a single dark shape, weapon and shattered wrapped too tightly together to see them as separate creatures.

Surging. Thrashing. Roaring.

Sinking.

Then quiet.

Ripples lapped against the shore.

Malcolm joined him with another torch, slipped on the wet rock, and caught himself with only the toe of his boot in the water. He leapt back and stood panting.

Garrett could see only the reflected light of the two torches on the smooth surface of the pond, night having settled back onto the water. There was no indication of the battle happening below. Or had the shattered already won and settled to the bottom to feed?

"How long can she hold her breath?" Malcolm whispered.

"I don't know."

Norik joined them, an arrow on the string. "Hide's too tough to pierce."

"Whose hide?"

"The shattered was a big target, even in the dark." A curve of teeth, white in the depth of his beard. "I'm pretty sure I missed the weapon."

Garrett glanced back at the fire to see Arianna standing over Petre, staff in her hands. He could hear the crackle and hiss of fire devouring the branch he held. Malcolm's breathing. His own blood pounding in his ears.

The roar of the waterfall.

Water lapped against the rocks. Harder. Up over the toes of his boots.

"Get back!"

Water poured down the hairless dome of the weapon's head, and a darker line of liquid ran down her upper arm to pool the crease of her elbow.

"Is it dead?"

She swallowed, and drew in a deep breath. "Yes."

"Was it alone?" Garrett demanded.

"No." She held up two fingers.

"Is the other one dead?"

"No."

"Then what . . ."

To Garrett's surprise, she cut him off. "Not hungry."

"The second is eating the first one?" Norik asked. "The one you killed?"

She turned then, to look directly at the archer. "Yes."

Norik coughed out a surprised laugh and Garrett assumed it was at how much that yes had sounded patiently patronizing. "So we're safe here for the night?"

A single howl answered. Long, lingering, and much closer.

"No."

"Timing," Norik sighed, "is everything."

"So I've heard." Garrett started back toward the fire. "We need to establish a defensive position. We'll move into the cave." At the fire, he saw Arianna had Petre up on his feet, swaying but standing. "Can he walk?"

"Slowly." She shifted to take more of Petre's weight. "If we go into the cave, we could be trapped."

"We could be slaughtered outside the cave. If she doesn't have to keep us safe, she'll have less trouble dealing with them." He turned and beckoned the weapon closer.

"Uvili!" Arianna twitched toward her. "You're injured."

"Yes."

Garrett stepped between them. "Check it later."

The next howl sounded like it came from the edge of the firelight. From the weapon's lack of reaction, Garrett assumed it hadn't.

"Arianna, get Petre to the cave."

"My pack . . ."

"I've got it." Garrett swung his own onto his shoulders. "Malcolm, take Petre's."

"Then how can I fight?" Malcolm protested.

"You won't. She will. Sheathe your sword before you hurt someone . . ." He took his own advice. ". . . and go."

"Yes, sir."

The next howl came from multiple throats.

Unencumbered by an extra pack, Norik grabbed an armload of branches.

The weapon growled. Garrett understood the sentiment; faster would be better, but they were held to Petre's slow shuffle along the rock ledge toward the water.

The howling came closer and changed, the sound lifting the hair on the back of Garrett's neck. He swiped his forearm over his face, wiping away sweat. *They want us to break and run so they can pick us off as we panic.*

Arianna followed Petre up the narrow path, bracing him against the rock with her staff, her voice a prod to keep him moving.

Shadows leapt in the flickering firelight that illuminated the cliff.

No. Not shadows . . .

Behind him, the weapon roared, the sound vibrating blood and bone. Garrett would have pissed himself had he water to spare.

She spread her arms, leaning forward into the sound. He had the word. He controlled her. He'd never been afraid of her, not having first seen her slumped in chains waiting patiently to be used. When she turned, he realized she'd stopped roaring, although the sound seemed to continue, moving back along their trail until it faded into the distance.

She turned toward him before he got his mouth closed and looked pointedly over his shoulder at the cave.

***

There was room for them all and a few more besides, the sound of the waterfall strangely muted by the surrounding rock.

Wider than the rest of them, the weapon had gotten wetter. At some point, some point Garrett had missed, she'd retrieved her flat, leather hat.

"Never heard her roar before." Norik leaned close, his pack and the branches already placed out of the way, bow back in his hand. "You think it was a warning?"

"No. A threat." The wall to Garrett's left curved out and was almost smooth, like the inside of a bubble. The wall to his right was covered in . . .

"Mushrooms." Malcolm held one in his hand and Garrett could smell the rot they grew in. "Are they safe to eat?"

"No." Arianna settled Petre in the depth of the left curve. He whimpered as she lowered him to the ground. "Malcolm, get the bedrolls spread, then tuck up behind him. He needs to stay warm. Anything wet needs to come off."

When Malcolm glanced his way, Garrett nodded.

"Off all of you," she said, glancing around, squinting toward the torchlight. "It's too late in the season to spend the night in wet clothes. Put on whatever you've got that's dry. Wrap yourself in a bedroll if that's the only option."

"Once we're sure we're safe," Garrett added.

She sighed and muttered, "Fine."

He swore as the flame reached the end of the branch and tossed it out past the flowing water. The smoke . . .

. . . curled against the roof of the cave, a pale, sinuous gray line against the dark rock. At the rear wall, it slipped into a crack about a finger-width wide that grew to nearly a handspan where it touched the floor. He wondered what size bugs Norik had seen if he considered the triangular opening only wide enough for bugs. "If the shattered attack the cave, they'll have to do it one at a time." One at a time, they couldn't get past the weapon. Which, he supposed, made them as safe as they'd been since leaving Gateway.

"I'm more concerned with the shattered in the pond," Norik admitted. "And whether or not it'll finish its snack and invite itself in."

"No."

Together, they turned toward the wall of mushrooms to find the weapon chewing on a large, fleshy disk nearly the same shade as her face.

She'd offered the information, not answered a question. Garrett tried to remember if it was the first time. "You're saying the shattered in the pond won't come into the cave?"

"Not hungry." She stopped chewing before she answered. Not manners, no matter what the healer might suggest. Speaking while chewing could waste food, and flame only knew how often she'd been fed before he'd found her in the depths of the Citadel. "Not in before."

"It wasn't in the pond before?"

"We could see the bottom," Norik reminded him. "And it looked empty."

"No."

Norik huffed out a laugh. "Fair enough. We didn't see it . . . them, that doesn't mean they weren't there."

"No. Not here before."

Garrett frowned. "So they haven't come into the cave before?"

When she nodded, Malcolm called out, "How does she know? She's never been here before."

"Best guess, it would have destroyed the mushrooms." Norik gestured with an arrow. "If the second shattered's as big as the first, it's too big to avoid them."

"You said they weren't safe to eat," Malcolm grumbled as he draped his wet jacket over a rock before wrapping a blanket around his shoulders.

Garrett remembered being Malcolm's age, how he had always been hungry. The boy's appetite aside, if the mushrooms were edible, it would help stretch their supplies.

"They're not safe for *us* to eat." Arianna tossed Garrett the pot she'd taken the time to secure in the midst of an attack. "Give it a good rinse in the waterfall, then start a fire so I can brew more willow bark. For Petre," she added before he could remind her he wasn't under her command. "We're short a mug." Helping Malcolm settle behind his friend, she nodded toward the weapon. "And Uvili can eat what she wants."

"Well, yeah." Malcolm draped his arm and half his blanket over Petre's side. "Who's going to stop her?"

The weapon glanced over at Garrett as if to say, *you could*. He could. He had the word. He could command her to stop eating for no other reason than to prove his power over her. He wondered if his father had gone to her cell to prove his power. Or if he'd proven his power by ignoring her completely.

A sword or an axe wouldn't have cared. Had she? Did she?

When he did nothing at all, she moved to the back of the cave, shrugged out of her pack, and leaned it against the wall.

Garrett frowned. It looked more like a wall than the back of a cave, the stone smooth and rising straight from floor to ceiling. The odds of that happening naturally were low. "Is this a mage-room?"

"No."

"Mage-room?" Norik snorted.

"No one asked you." Garrett raised his voice. "Is it safe?"

Leaning forward, she sniffed the crack in the wall.

"Well?"

She moved her pack until it covered the widest gap. "Now."

"Now?"

The look she shot him reminded him uncomfortably of his grandmother. "Now." Gathering up an armload of mushrooms, she squatted at the edge of the damp, stared out at the falling water, and began to eat.

"Okay, then." Turning to check on Petre, Garrett wondered why Arianna was smiling. "Is he . . ." He let the question trail off. Of course the boy wasn't all right. He'd had his hand bitten off, then been hustled into a cave ahead of a pack of attacking lizard-dogs.

"He's doing okay, all things considered." She said it as much to Malcolm as to him, and Garrett saw her grip Malcolm's shoulder as she stood. She dropped a handful of dried bark into the pot of water he'd settled into the small fire, pulled out another packet of something, and crossed to the weapon. "I'm so sorry, I should have looked at your arm ages ago."

The weapon looked past her at Garrett. She looked . . . confused.

"Caring for one injury," Arianna continued, taking the weapon's hand

and turning her toward the weak light thrown by the fire, "is not an excuse to forget that other injuries need your attention."

And Garrett remembered black blood running down the weapon's arm. He'd seen it, and almost immediately forgotten it. The trip through the waterfall had washed the blood away, but he could just make out a dark puncture in her upper arm. "Your skin turns blades."

"Tooth."

"The thing in the pond bit you?"

"Yes." She frowned. "No."

"It drove a tooth into you? It wasn't actually a bite."

She sighed and seemed pleased he understood. "Yes."

"Mage-crafted creatures can hurt you?"

"Yes."

"That's a complication," Norik murmured.

It could be.

She'd looked down at the healer, wiping a cloth over the wound, then back at him. If she'd had eyebrows, they'd have been drawn in. As it was, her brow had folded down to nearly touch the top of her nose. The rest of her body was rigid, immobile.

Garrett realized she had no idea what was happening.

She seen—burn it, she'd helped—Arianna care for Petre, but was unable to recognize that care when applied to herself. Had no one ever cared for her? Her keepers in the Citadel had thrown food at her and thrown buckets of water over her. He'd taken her away from that, but he'd assumed she was indestructible and treated her accordingly.

He'd always believed that in this, at least, he was a better man than his father. Maybe he wasn't. Maybe he should try to be.

LYELEE.NOW

"Lyelee! Nonee said to stay close."

Lyelee stopped, turned, and glared at Keetin, who'd stripped off vest and shirt, exposing the deep purple bruising across his chest. When it became apparent her expression wasn't enough to gain a response, she snapped, "Close is not an empirical term. Close enough to be seen? Close enough to be heard?"

"Close enough you don't get eaten."

"Eaten by what?" With a wide, sweeping gesture, she indicated the lack of underbrush between the trees, the ground carpeted in fallen needles, and the quiet that made their surroundings feel more like a library than a forest. "We're the only living creatures in the immediate area."

"Exactly. There should be birds and insects."

"How do you know?"

"There's always birds and insects."

She folded her arms. "Define *always* relative to the Broken Lands."

"Unless you've made visits you haven't informed us of, Lord Norwincee . . ." Gearing emerged from behind the designated tree. ". . . you can have no idea of what *always* means in this specific area."

Keetin smiled—although Lyelee had no idea what he was smiling *about*—and raised both hands. "I surrender before your superior reasoning."

"As you're intended to," Gearing muttered, settling into a cradle made by a loop of exposed root. "Take measurements, Novitiate."

She almost told him to take his own flaming measurements, to act like a Scholar of the Broken Lands. Why was he even here if he wasn't going to add to their scholarship?

"Lyelee," Ryan called before she could leave. "Superior reasoning aside, be careful. Something's watching."

"What? And from where?"

He shook his head. "Can't you feel it?"

"Feel it?" She swiped the sweat off her forehead with her palm. "Ryan, you don't believe you can feel anything. You're denying every word as it comes out of your mouth."

"I'm not . . ."

"Yes, you are." Lyelee shook her head, exaggerating the movement, and dropped her voice to imitate her cousin's. *"Can't you feel it."*

"I don't . . ."

"You believe that because we're in the Broken Lands something should be watching. However, unless you have solid, factual information about why I'm in danger, I'm going to use this rare opportunity where we're neither moving nor being hindered by an ancient weapon to gain independent knowledge of the Broken Lands." She swept her gaze over Keetin, her mentor, and Captain Yansav, who'd just returned from checking on Servan. "Unless anyone else has more to offer than a feeling?"

Captain Yansav frowned. "Put your vest back on."

She thought of pointing out that Keetin was half naked, but even the thought made her sound like a petulant twelve-year-old. Teeth gritted, she returned to her pack and shrugged into the vest, yanking off a dangling thread from the shredded armhole as the weight settled on her shoulders. "Anything else?"

"If you're attacked . . ." The captain raised a hand, cutting off Lyelee's protest. ". . . by a currently unknown enemy, it will take longer for us to reach you the farther away you go."

Fact, not feelings. Lyelee appreciated a statement of fact delivered as though she were an adult, and a scholar, and capable of making her own decisions. "Thank you, Captain. I'll keep that in mind."

Considering the defenses Captain Yansav had set up—Servan at the meadow, in case, Lyelee assumed, the snake or the stone should follow them, Curtin and Destros off to either side but close enough she could see their backs through the trees—the captain believed it unlikely anything would come at them from the direction the weapon had taken. Or she believed the weapon would stop anything intent on attack before it reached them. Or she was watching that direction herself.

"You're not going with her, Scholar Gearing?" The captain shifted until she could see them both.

"Trees." Eyes closed, Gearing pressed his satchel against his stomach under folded arms. "I have no interest in trees."

And what if I found a ruin? Lyelee asked herself, walking away. Easy answer. She'd be considerate and not wake him. She wasn't particularly interested in trees either, but Gearing had forgotten where they were. What if the trees weren't trees? The stone hadn't been a stone. Or not entirely a stone.

"Free me."

Who was to say what these trees had once been? If the weapon stayed away long enough, she could collect enough unique information to—if not answer—at least ask any number of new questions.

With limited time, the last thing Lyelee needed was the distraction of an idiot audience, so she moved far enough from the weapon's fixed point to keep it from being an issue. Two trees past where Destros stood axe in hand, she pulled a triangular piece of thin wood from her satchel. Holding it by the ninety-degree corner, she squinted along the longest edge and moved back until she could put the tree at the triangle's far point. Continuing to move back until the point and the top of the tree lined up exactly, she scuffed a mark in the forest floor, put the triangle away, and pulled out her measuring chord.

Take measurements, Novitiate.

Of course she was going to take measurements. And samples. What else was she going to do with a tree? Question it?

"Did you need a hand, Scholar?"

Heart in her throat, she whirled around, but it was only Harris, no doubt away from the fixed point to perform a helpful and servant-like activity. "No. I do not." When he continued to watch her with polite interest, she assumed he needed instruction. "The distance to the tree, plus the distance between my eye and the ground, gives us the approximate height of the tree." Scholarship included sharing knowledge with the less informed. Not all knowledge; the Scholar's Hall kept what they considered dangerous, or inflammatory, or unnecessary knowledge to themselves. "Once we have the height of one tree, we can make comparisons, determine a localized average, and use that information to develop theories about the area."

Harris squinted at the top of the tree. "That seems more like forestry than history."

"Trees live a very long time."

He nodded, although he clearly hadn't had the education to understand. "Of course, Scholar."

If she could take the tree down, she could read history from the rings. If she could take down the tree the weapon referred to as a fixed point, she could see evidence of the Mage War. She could see at least some of how the land had been broken. There was a chance she could see beyond the war, to the mages themselves. She could find evidence of mage-craft within the wood. She could . . .

"Scholar?"

The possibilities slipped away. "What, Harris?"

"You seemed distracted."

"I was thinking," she snapped. "You should try it."

The short-sightedness of non-scholars was a common complaint around the Scholar's Hall and she *would not* allow it to keep her from knowledge. She made precision measurements as she returned to the tree.

Still no birds. Or insects. She wouldn't give Keetin the satisfaction of hearing her admit he was right, but it was . . . unusual. If she breathed in through her mouth she could taste the silence on her tongue. Silence had a flavor. She'd never realized that before. It had put the others on edge; it showed in their posture, in the constant small contained movements, in *their* silence.

Nor would she admit to Ryan that the further she moved from the fixed point, the more she felt as though she too were being watched. Not by anything so mundane as a man who mended clothing and made tea, but by something infinitely large and at the same time, impossibly small.

She'd bring a Scholar of Philosophy with her the next time she came. They'd enjoy analyzing the dichotomy. And they'd be ecstatic delving deep into the meaning of her dreams.

She hadn't only dreamed about the rock and its captive. She'd dreamed and woke and dreamed and woke half a dozen times through the night. Unfortunately, only two of the dreams had remained at sunrise; she remembered the rock and she remembered being up high, hand holding a branch, and hearing a child's voice singing out a child's rhyme. *"Plant the dragon's tooth to grow a dragon, one hand deep in mage-worked dirt, trap a death to free a life, three drops of blood to make it work."* The voice had used the trade tongue that connected the city-states and countries around the Great Lake—not a language likely to be used by any child in Gateway—and she didn't need to be a Scholar of Literature to recognize that the poetry was appalling. Neither of which was the point. She'd dreamed of the rock and the rock had appeared . . .

She circled the chosen tree, maintaining a consistent, practiced stride length, and recorded this number as well.

On the far side, out of sight of even Destros, she secured her satchel and jumped for the lowest branch, toes of her boots pushing off protrusions in the trunk. For some things, trousers were easier than robes. High enough she could cling with one hand and reach up with the other for the next branch, she pulled herself into the tree and found space to stand. Shoulder against the trunk, she rubbed the fingers of her right hand against her left palm. She couldn't see the sap oozing from fractures in the bark, but the evidence said it was there all the same. Still, sticky hands were better than slick hands, she allowed, as sweat dribbled down the crease of her spine. The temperature in the tree felt slightly higher than the temperature on the ground. Not because hot air rose, but as though the tree itself were warm.

Another branch up. Then another. The branches extended out from the trunk, almost like a spiral staircase—Lyelee could see design in the ease of the climb. When she finally paused—far enough from the ground she doubted she'd survive a sudden return—a flicker of movement at the edge of her vision caught her attention.

Stepping around to the other side of the tree, boots carefully tugged from the clinging bark and just as carefully placed again, she found a snake about as big around as her baby finger and nearly three times as long with the front two-thirds of its body engulfed in an amber sphere of resin. It thrashed wildly in a desperate attempt to free itself. Lyelee pressed the tip of a finger against the sphere and realized it was still fluid enough to surrender its captive should she catch hold of the tail and gently tug.

She watched until the snake stopped struggling, until the slender throat no longer fluttered, fighting for breath. Until the golden eyes dulled. Saw the resin darken, solidifying in minutes instead of years. Prying the nodule off the tree, she held it on the blade of her knife.

"Lyelee!" Keetin stared up from the ground, one hand shading his eyes. "What are you doing up there?"

"Gaining knowledge." She shifted to block his view of her hand and the snake's dangling body.

"Knowledge of what?"

"Of how the Broken Lands work." With no desire to become a sample herself, she checked for resin before leaning against the tree and pulling a piece of waxed cloth from her satchel, cupping it in her palm as she coiled the snake into it.

"I thought the point was that the Broken Lands didn't work."

"Scholarship doesn't understand how they work. It's not the same thing." The small bundle fit perfectly into the space at the end of her notebooks. "What do you want?"

"Nonee's back."

NONEE.NOW

Nonee pointed at the puddle. "There."

"That was the pond?" Kalyealee who-could-be-heir frowned at the puddle, unimpressed. "That?"

"Yes."

"This is where Petre D'Certif-cee lost his hand?"

"No." Nonee pointed to where the red rocks became gray and the red dirt became brown. The change marked the edge of the absent pond. "*That* is where he lost his hand."

The scholar swept a narrow-eyed gaze over the immediate area, as though she were searching for evidence to support Garrett Heir's chronicle. Or perhaps she searched for Petre's hand. Had it not been chewed and swallowed then eaten again as part of the defeated shattered's stomach contents, she might have found it. These were the Broken Lands and Nonee had seen stranger things.

Ryan Heir stepped up beside her, rubbing at the welt a willow root had left on his cheek. "Do we have to go through the cave?"

"Yes." She wondered what the Heir's Chronicle had said about the passage. Garrett Heir hadn't said much at the time, and all Arianna had ever said, both then and years later, was that it had been too personal to share. They'd shared a life, a home, laughter, sorrow, but never that. Nonee had walked into darkness and out again, had seen nothing, had heard nothing, had walked surrounded by the smell of the tank. She hadn't told Arianna because she hadn't wanted her to understand what that meant.

"It's still light." Ryan Heir squinted at the sky. "We should keep moving."

Nonee glanced at the pink and orange bleeding up from the horizon. Arianna had loved sunsets. Not sunrises—she'd sleep until noon given half a chance—but if she could, she'd pause a moment to watch the sunset. Nonee had seen the day end more times than she could count. To be fair, she'd seen it begin almost the same number of times even if Arianna hadn't.

Wouldn't.

Not ever again.

"There isn't . . ." She hissed a breath in through her teeth and began again. "There isn't enough remaining light to reach the other side."

He scowled at the sunset much as his cousin had scowled at the puddle. "Then we should make camp here while we can see. Better the flame we know."

"Yes."

"At least we don't need to worry about creatures coming out of the water."

Nonee followed the direction of his gaze. It was possible the entire volume of the pond had become the little bit of water they could see.

She'd seen things made impossibly small and still remain what they'd been.

The shattered could still be in there.

The cave would be safer.

Against her advice, they made camp on the red dirt in the middle of where memory put the pond.

"Better sight lines," Captain Yansav told her.

"Not from below," she said.

❦

"Are you going to sleep?"

Squatting, Nonee could look Ryan Heir in the eye without bending her head. "Yes."

"But . . ."

"Nothing hunts along our trail, nothing howls in the wood. Later . . ." She shrugged. They didn't need her to see that they were fed, to dig a latrine, or to secure the perimeter. Between them, Captain Yansav and Harris had that in hand.

"You're resting now, in case we're attacked later. Good. Sort of good. Not the attacked later part." He rocked back on his heels, half turned, and said, "I love mushrooms. Harris could fry them up with the rest of that chunky bacon. You're certain *we* can't eat them?"

"Yes." Her stomach was full. They'd tasted like the past.

"All right, then." He flashed her a grin that heightened his resemblance to Garrett Heir. "We'll try to keep the noise down."

He was making a joke, because, so far, there'd only been bruises. "Good," she said. "Noise attracts predators."

When she woke, it was fully dark, although the moon hadn't yet risen to dim the stars. The Archer stood guard by the blazing arc of the Road and the curve of the Star Pond lapped against the Dancing Child. The mages had other names for the stars. So had Garrett Heir. Nonee liked the names Arianna used.

Far enough from the fire that he saw her straighten, Harris raised a mug. She nodded and crossed to his side.

She drained it. He refilled it with what remained in the pot. She recognized the flavor. "Chamomile."

"Mostly," he agreed. He nodded toward the fire, where the three guardians were gathered around the captain. Keetin, Ryan Heir, and Kalyealee who-could-be-heir were talking together, probably arguing, and Gearing Scholar was already asleep. "They're nervy tonight, so they all had some. You were napping."

"Then they were safe."

He snorted. "That's what Lord Marsan told them."

"They don't always listen."

"Not always." After a moment, he added, "More than they did when we started."

"Good."

"It helps that you obey him."

She heard both amusement and a warning in his voice and smiled at the warning behind what little coverage the mug allowed. That he would warn her, knowing what she was, was a gift.

Destros paced slowly around the camp to stand beside her. His dark eyes were clear, his scarred hands steady on the handle of the big axe. The relaxed tension in his movements told her he was ready to fight, but would be just as happy not to. Arianna had said relaxed tension was a contradiction. Nonee had said she hadn't met enough fighters. Close now, Destros smelled of sweat and leather and steel. He was so much larger than the rest, she'd started to think of him as near to her in size. This close, she couldn't ignore that he wasn't.

After a moment breathing in through his nose and out his mouth, he said, "Quiet night."

"Yes."

"Unusual?"

"Luck."

He grunted out half a laugh. "I'll take it."

They stood close enough she could feel the heat of his body. She thought of leaning closer still, but didn't. Knew better. Had been taught the lesson by other large men. If she didn't move, he might not move away. They stood together watching the camp.

From the amount of movement, no one but Gearing was sleeping much. They'd thrash, they'd settle, they'd thrash again. It reminded her of ripples across the water of the pond.

"The Broken Lands aren't restful." She wanted her words to prod him into speech. She didn't want to talk, but she'd like to listen.

"No, they aren't." He caught a laugh before it could draw the others even further from sleep and after a moment said, "I spent some time on the Great Lake taking out pirates; it feels like that."

"You were a sailor?" The ships that hadn't made it out of Northport harbor in time had been broken. The sailors had drowned.

"Flame, no. Too big to live shipboard." Leaning the axe against his leg, Destros scratched through the thick, dark hair under his chin. It sounded dry. "The Lord Protector sends out guardians when he's serious about clearing the thieving shit-heels off the water. I was one of the flaming stupid lot who jumped between ships after grappling and bashed in pirate heads. Seems that's a specialized skill sailors don't have. But if you don't go after the pirates . . ." He glanced at her, then quickly away. ". . . they think they own the lake. Sometimes, they make nice with each other and go hunting the ships hunting them. This . . ." The axe, back in his hand, cut an arc through the air. "This is like that. Like watching the night, knowing the murdering scum-suckers were out there and never knowing if this was one of those times that half a dozen ships were waiting for you in the fog."

Nonee considered the similarities. "It's not knowing," she concluded at last.

"That it is."

The usual noises rose from the camp. The surrounding night was unnaturally quiet. Kalyealee who-could-be-heir threw one of the smooth, red rocks at Keetin Norwin-cee, presumably to stop him snoring, and Ryan growled at them both to go to sleep for the flame's sake.

"Less chance of drowning in the Broken Lands," Nonee said as Destros began to walk away.

"That's comforting." After a moment, he turned and frowned. "Less chance?"

She shrugged.

❧

Curtin had second watch. She didn't expect his company.

He paid more attention to her than to guarding the camp. It didn't matter. She'd deal with anything that approached. Captain Yansav hadn't told her why she'd split the night into four watches, though Nonee suspected she wanted to give the guardians something to focus on besides the rats the Broken Lands had set loose in their brains.

Not actual rats.

Not yet.

Gearing got up, used the latrine, went back to sleep.

Curtin kept staring.

His mouth moved as he talked himself into whatever it was he felt he had to do.

A heat shimmer blotted the stars. She'd never seen one pass at night, but then she'd never been across the line when it was so warm. The heat had barely eased after sunset. She watched it until it disappeared in the distance, grateful it had stayed high, hating that there were things in the Broken Lands she couldn't fight.

The evergreens had pushed out a line of advance almost to where the edge of the pond had been, larger than they should have been able to grow in the length of time she'd been gone. The breeze that rustled leaves moaned when it passed through their needles. The light of the moon shone through the leaves, but not through the evergreens.

Briseis Galanos had crafted with plants. Nonee had never met her but Tanika Fleshrender had spoken of the other mage as tiny and clever. The evergreens could be hers. The willows could be as well.

Curtin walked toward her, his movements jerky as though he were fighting a compulsion. He stopped when he finally stood close enough he could speak without waking anyone who might have found sleep. He hated her, not the others.

"If I were to run you through, would you die?"

Not a question she'd expected, but not unexpected either. "No."

"You can't die?"

"Your sword won't go through. Or in," she added after a moment.

His nostrils flared with force of his inhale. "You were created by magecraft," he snarled. "Only pain and suffering comes from mage-craft."

That was the song of Captain Marsan and the Five Thousand. Sing it often enough and everyone grew up knowing the words.

"You're not a person," he continued, "no more than the shattered are wolves or birds or vines. My family had a relic, brought with them during the March of Pain. When my ancestor refused to give it to the scholars, you killed her. Crushed her head to pulp between your hands."

Captain Marsan, the Lord Protector, had commanded it.

Some of those who commanded her feared mage-craft would sweep them up again, destroy the new life they'd built on the ruins of Northport. Those who showed sympathy to mage-craft were rooted out and destroyed to the cry of *never again*. Fear defined what sympathy meant.

She obeyed the one who held the word.

She didn't think she was a person then, no matter what Arianna said.

"When the Lord Protector's father brought you out to show the people, so they knew you were still *protecting* them . . ."

A symbol, like the Black Flame. Then back to chains and darkness.

". . . my grandmother threw a brick at your head. You should have been destroyed."

She remembered the brick and the fierce woman who'd thrown it. She remembered stomping her feet and roaring to keep the Lord Protector's attention. To keep from having to obey. She remembered everything but what she chose to forget.

"You're dangerous."

"So are you." It was something Arianna had said often in the beginning.

"She's dangerous!"

"So are you!"

"I'm a guardian. I don't kill the innocent."

"Doesn't that depend on what orders you're given?" She glanced at Ryan Heir.

Curtin looked over as well and his brows drew in. "He wouldn't . . ."

He might. Experience had taught her that orders depended on circumstances. And circumstances changed.

"Everything changes," Arianna told her. *"That's one of the few things we can depend on. Change is constant."*

"The children . . ." Curtin shook his head. "They like you. They climb on you. They know you won't let them fall. They *trust* you. You're not . . ."

Not what he expected. "History and reality have less in common than most imagine."

"What?"

She shrugged. "Words from a book."

"You *read*?"

"Slowly." She held out her hands, each larger than his head. "Books are so small. Scrolls so delicate."

He made the noise she'd heard children make when they faced betrayal, when they learned that what they believed wasn't always what was.

His mouth worked for a moment, then he spat, "Mage-craft corrupts everything close to it."

Did close to it mean near to it or like it? she wondered as he circled around to where he'd been and turned his back on her. Or did it matter?

The breeze moaned. She didn't trust the trees.

LYELEE.NOW

Lyelee knew that ponds disappeared all the time. Climates changed, rivers shifted, but the imprint of the pond always remained. She frowned up at the cave, exposed by the absence of the waterfall. This pond had been dug deep enough into rock by falling water that it could hold at least two large, aggressive shattered, and sixty-three years wasn't long enough for it to have become a flat area of reddish earth supporting a few patches of low-growing succulents and a statistically significant number of smooth red stones.

She held the dragon's tooth carefully cupped within the curve of her fingers to keep it from being seen.

The child had been told to plant the tooth to grow a dragon.

It could be—probably was—a bit of whimsy, an older brother amusing a younger. Lyelee assumed they did that. She had no brothers and Ryan's had never been amusing. But mage-craft had existed. Nonee existed. Without further investigation, who could say dragons didn't grow from teeth?

And then there was the rhyme.

Perhaps she'd worked out the rest of the faded childish scrawl without realizing it and sleep had removed enough distractions for the words to rise to the forefront of her mind.

Perhaps not.

Given the unnatural appearance of the pond, it had to have recently been filled in by mage-craft—where *recently* referred to a time within the last sixty-three years. The location received sunlight for most of the day and the puddle—currently an arm's length away from the toes of her boots—would supply water: the light and water necessary for the growth of seeds. If the tooth was a dragon seed . . .

Lyelee dropped to one knee and began to dig. The dirt shifted easily. Unnaturally easily. There were none of the ubiquitous red stones in the hole.

one hand deep in mage-worked dirt

One hand deep was not a quantitative measurement.

trap a death to free a life

She curled the snake around the circumference of the hole and tucked the tooth into the center of the circle.

three drops of blood to make it work

Work and dirt did not rhyme. Sloppy. She pricked her finger with the needle she'd taken from Harris's sewing kit, let three drops fall onto the tooth, and hurriedly filled in the hole, feeling slightly foolish.

Illogically, the ground was flat once all the dirt had been returned, as though she'd added nothing to its volume.

"I wouldn't put your hand in the water."

She stood, brushed red dirt off her knee, and turned to face Keetin. "The water's clear and there isn't enough to fill the kettle."

"Pond had to go somewhere and there's no point in tempting the shattered by waving a tasty bit of meat in their metaphorical direction."

"Metaphorical? Big word."

He grinned. "I know a few."

Past his shoulder, she could see Ryan waving a scale-mail vest. "Ryan wants you."

"Yes, he does. Because I was voted the best ass in the Citadel three years in a row."

"He wants you to put on your armor."

Keetin glanced back at the camp. Ryan waved more pointedly. "So it appears." Lyelee wondered if Keetin knew he had his hand pressed against his chest again. "Which does not change the observation about my ass," he pointed out as he turned. "You coming?"

"Why not." How long did a dragon take to sprout? When they returned this way, would she be able to definitively conclude that planting the tooth in this particular mage-craft-soaked location either did, or did not, produce a dragon? Would it need another hundred years? How long would she be in the grave before it emerged?

"I had no idea you entered donkeys into competitions," she said as she fell into step beside him.

His laugh drew the attention of everyone in the camp, and he spent the next few moments repeating her juvenile play on words.

No one asked her why she was at the pond.

Lyelee frowned up at the evergreens. Had they moved closer?

RYAN.NOW

Ryan held his torch to a crack between the slabs that blocked most of the passage at the back of the cave and peered through.

"What do you see?" Keetin called from the mouth of the cave. He didn't like enclosed spaces and had declared he'd come no further in until he had to.

"I see rock."

"Not exactly helpful."

"Thank you for that insight, Lord Norwin-cee." Ryan stepped back, wiped his sweaty palm against his thigh, and shifted the torch to his other hand. "If we have to clear this, then we'd best get on with it."

He was surprised by how smokeless the torch had turned out to be. He'd expected them to use lanterns, but dead wood was easy to come by and lanterns meant oil and oil weighed a lot more than the torch-wraps Gateway had provided. Most of the smoke the torch gave off drifted through cracks in the barrier, leading the way.

"Ryan?"

When Ryan turned, Keetin had actually taken a step into the cave. "What?"

"Weren't we going to get on with clearing the rocks?" He stepped back out into the sunlight as Ryan joined him. "Where *we* means Nonee, of course."

Nonee waited below the cave for Ryan to give the order. Everyone was waiting for him to give the order. "All right. Let's go, then. Nonee, if you would."

No one offered to help. He expected they all realized clearing the barrier would go faster if they stayed out of her way. After all, according to the chronicle, she'd built it.

"You going to be okay?" he asked, following Keetin down to the missing pond.

"I wasn't the one staring at nothing for half the morning."

It hadn't been that long. Ryan handed the torch to Destros, and hurried to catch up so he could help Keetin into his vest. "I'm not the one who got slammed by a lizard-dog."

"For the five thousandth time, Ryan, it's a bruise." Keetin rolled his shoulders, settling the weight. "I've gotten worse in the practice yard."

"You're lying."

"Of course I am. Let it go."

"We'll need to pause after completing the passage so I can record the effects," Lyelee announced, not quite pushing between them. "The details will be useful to the Scholar's Hall even if you don't include them in your chronicle."

Keetin rolled his eyes. Ryan didn't—but it was close. "Let's get through the passage first."

And there was her *your best will never be good enough* expression. "You need to learn to plan ahead if you're going to be Lord Protector."

"I'm planning to confine all scholars to the Hall," he muttered to Keetin.

Lyelee snorted. "I can hear you."

By the time Nonee finished, the shifted slabs of rock filled most of the cave, leaving only a narrow path down the center. Ryan wondered if she'd eaten the few remaining mushrooms before blocking access. Calluses on his fingertips caught on a rough edge of rock, lighter, even after sixty-three years, than the rock around it. Broken by Nonee's fists to allow his great-uncle access. Rebuilt into a barricade after their return with the fuel, but whether to keep things in or out he had no idea. And wasn't going to ask.

The reopened passage stretched out into the distance, far enough he couldn't see an end. Long enough that in his chronicle, he'd call it a tunnel and leave *his* heir better prepared—no matter how short a time they'd borne the title. Wider than Nonee, higher than Nonee and her pack, the walls were the expected rough rock, but the floor had been polished smooth. Reflections of torchlight danced across the surface. Reflections were not supposed to move like that. "Did the mages make this?"

Nonee snorted. "Not on purpose."

Sword in one hand, torch in the other, Captain Yansav fell into place beside him. She'd insisted on the lead position, arguing an enclosed area wouldn't confine her skills like it would Nonee's. Given Nonee's rock-breaking ability, Ryan doubted her assessment, but they didn't have time for an extended argument about ancient weapons and modern beliefs about their use.

The torch-wraps burned too clean and too bright to be the strips of oil-soaked cloth they appeared. Watching the light banish shadows to crevasses and distance, Ryan admitted that should he discover the wraps were entirely mage-crafted, he wouldn't get rid of them. Today torch-wraps, tomorrow feed the hungry with food pulled from the air, the day after turn an infant into an immortal weapon. He could see the progression. He could also see and breathe in the passageway, and that didn't seem like such a bad thing.

"I don't like this," Curtin muttered.

"Burn it, Curtin, you cry mage-craft every time we run into shit you don't understand."

It seemed Servan had Curtin well in hand.

"Are we there yet?" Keetin whined.

Lyelee actually giggled. Tensions eased.

It was cooler underground. Scholar Gearing perked up like a goose after the rain and joined Lyelee counting steps, the numbers a quiet background murmur correcting another missing specific that could mean absolutely nothing by the time Ryan's heir made the trip.

Nonee twisted to ease her pack through a tight section. Then again. Then Ryan's left shoulder scraped the rock. Then both shoulders.

"Hey, Nonee!" Keetin's voice was just a little too loud. A little too cheerful. "It never gets too narrow for you to get through, right?"

"It didn't."

"Wonderful."

A hundred and eleven steps later, the passage widened and curved, the arc tight enough to significantly shorten the line of sight.

"Dead end," Captain Yansav called back.

"No it isn't," Nonee amended as they gathered. She slapped her hand against a diagonal crack in the right wall slightly wider than the length of Ryan's forearm.

"Through there?"

"Yes."

"Lead on, then." Ryan spread his hands when Captain Yansav turned to glare. "If Nonee can still get through, we all can. If she can't, we have to find another way."

"You broke the other rock." Keetin had his teeth clenched. "Break this rock."

"Can't. Might cause a cave-in." The matter-of-fact rumble of Nonee's voice sounded almost kind.

"Anyone with eyes could see that," Lyelee sneered.

Ryan was almost positive Nonee did nothing but move toward the crack, but Lyelee backed up so quickly her pack bounced off Destros's chest.

Stuffing her right side into the gap, leaning back against the angle, Nonee shuffled sideways into the darkness, dragging her pack. Ignoring the captain's clear, albeit silent desire to have him move away, Ryan gripped the edge and leaned in. He could hear leather scraping, quiet grunting, multiple small cracks, the fall of loose stone, and profanity in a language he didn't know. Then he remembered the temple in Gateway and realized it might be prayer. Would prayer in this place also be profanity?

"What do we do if she gets stuck?" Servan wondered.

"We render you down for fat and grease the rock." As everyone turned toward him, Destros spread his hands below an expression of affronted innocence, barely visible between helmet and beard. "What? It's not like we need all three of us."

"The fuel is more important than individuals," Curtin added, solemn tone at odds with his grin.

"We also need someone who can hit what they aim at," Servan pointed out. "And you've both got more fat on you besides."

Curtin tapped his chest. "It's not fat, it's fluffy muscle."

"More like fluffy . . ."

"Enough." Captain Yansav raised a hand to keep them quiet and turned to Ryan. "What do you hear?"

"Nothing." Not even breathing. He should have been able to hear breathing . . .

"Through," Nonee called, voice distorted. "Go two by two. Carry a pack between you."

"Packs off." Captain Yansav lowered hers to the floor of the cave. "Guardians will be making multiple trips."

"Because we're stronger," Destros said, catching Scholar Gearing's pack before impact.

"Because I said so."

"That too."

"Nonee!" Keetin shuffled closer to the crack. "Are you coming back?"

"No. She barely made it through," Ryan told him before Nonee could respond. "Since you're here, Keetin, you lead the way."

Keetin glared at him like he'd been betrayed by Ryan or the passage or life in general. "First so I don't back out?" he murmured.

"First so you don't have time to work yourself into a panic," Ryan replied, mouth almost touching Keetin's ear, and added at a normal volume, "Watch your head."

Keetin and Destros with a pack between them.

Lyelee and Scholar Gearing without a pack.

This was going to take a while.

When it was finally Ryan's turn, he paused, right leg in the crack, and thought, *This is impossible.* There was no way an adult could work their way through such a minimal space. The mage must have included a compression factor in Nonee's creation. Then he tilted his hips, found the angle, and slipped in. With Servan holding the other side of his pack, he shuffled sideways, breathing shallowly, body curved, shoulders back. He kept his eyes closed, not wanting to see if there were faces in the rock and wishing he hadn't remembered there might be. His vest whispered warnings against alternate sides of the passage. Against both sides at the same time. He sucked in his stomach. It didn't help. His left shoulder screamed from supporting the weight of his pack at an awkward angle, and his left hand began to cramp around the pack's leather strapping. He forgot to count his steps and felt as though he'd shuffled forever. Finally, his reaching right hand waved in air and he opened his eyes to torchlight.

"It's a good thing tits squash," Servan muttered, releasing his pack and flexing her hand the moment she was clear.

"Under armor?" he asked, shoving his helm back into place.

She glanced down at the scoring across the metal scales. "You'd be surprised."

Keetin, Nonee, and the Scholars made only a single trip. Ryan wanted to believe familiarity would breed calm if not contempt or comfort. It didn't. The chamber on the other side of the crack had room for all of them to sit comfortably, so they took a moment to breathe when they were done.

"What was that?" Head cocked, Curtin's hand went to his sword. He frowned. "Sounded like . . . a soft . . . plop?"

Ryan backed up as a pale brown spider, as big around as an old-fashioned copper coin, dropped from the ceiling, paused for a moment, then scuttled out of the light. He raised his torch. There were a lot more up there, the pattern of their movement a multi-legged version of the kaleidoscope he'd had as a boy.

"The torches are warming the air." Lyelee crouched and made an unsuccessful grab at one of the spiders. "It's waking them up."

"It's midsummer, why are they asleep?"

"Busy spring?"

Another two spiders dropped. Nonee carefully brushed one off her shoulder.

"My lord." The captain's voice had picked up an edge and her shoulders had risen. "Lower your torch."

"But . . ."

"Now!"

❧

Ryan lost track of time. They burned through the original torch wraps. Lit new ones. He wanted to ask Nonee if they'd have enough, but if the passage had changed she wouldn't know and it wouldn't be worth Lyelee disdainfully declaring him insecure.

Having become used to rock pressing close around him, he stumbled as he stepped out into an enormous cavern, the far walls only barely visible in the torchlight. Captain Yansav had her torch raised and her head tipped back. Assuming an absence of spiders, he looked up.

The ceiling was at least three Nonees high. White cones pointed down into the cavern, their surface rippled as though they weren't entirely solid.

"What are they?"

"Rock." Scholar Gearing sat on a stump of the same white rock, the point lying some distance away. "Built up over time by dripping water. There's caves by Midport with similar formations."

"But there's no water."

"Now."

"There's nothing to see here," Lyelee said, arms folded. She nodded toward the shadows. "We travel straight across, according to the chronicle. We're on the correct path and we're nearly through. Let's keep moving."

Keetin smiled, although his teeth were clenched. "She makes an excellent point," he ground out. "Nonee?"

"That way." She pointed.

Lyelee sighed. "Straight across. Like I said."

This passage out of the cavern looked identical to the passage they'd taken out of the cave. Not just the same, Ryan realized, touching a familiar pattern in the rock, but identical. "Nonee, have we gotten turned around?"

"No."

Then the torches went out. One minute lit, the next not.

"According to the Heir's Chronicle, we'll face ourselves in the darkness." Lyelee sounded intrigued.

Keetin didn't. "We all know that, Lye. You know what we don't know? The details, making the chronicle significantly unhelpful. The next Heir of Marsan gets the expanded version; do you hear me, Ryan? Your chronicle is going to have all the details. I'll write it myself if I have to."

"Like that'll happen," Lyelee muttered.

Ryan stepped sideways until his shoulder touched Keetin's. Keetin leaned into the warmth. "You were there, Nonee. What can you tell us?"

Lyelee sighed, her disdain distinctive in the dark. "Of us all," she quoted, "only the weapon remained unaffected."

It took Ryan a moment to identify the soft click/hiss as Servan pulling an arrow from her quiver. He wasn't the only one to recognize the sound.

"Put it away, Servan."

"If I'm going to face myself, Captain, I'd rather do it armed."

"And I'd rather you not shoot the heir. Put it away."

The longer they stood here in the dark, the edgier everyone would get. Ryan took a deep breath and wet his lips. "Nonee?"

She shifted position, bare feet scuffing against the floor, the sound distinctive amid the boots. "Move in single file, keep your right hand on the rock. In time, you'll reach the other side."

"How much time?"

"It varied."

"How," Ryan began, and stopped himself. "Never mind. We should tie ourselves together. Didn't the Heir's Chronicle mention tying themselves together?"

"Yes. The rope was severed."

"Severed?" Heads and hands were severed.

"Between Garrett Heir and Arianna. Between Norik and . . ."

"I get it." Ryan cut her off. "Severed. By what?"

"Don't know."

"According to the chronicle, no one felt the cut." Lyelee tapped a fingernail against the rock. "They were just suddenly separated."

Ryan didn't remember that. Although he remembered the total lack of useful detail Keetin had already mentioned. *We went into the passage. We came out of the passage. We faced ourselves in the darkness and only the weapon was unaffected.* "Well, let's not waste the rope, then. We might need it later. Lyelee, is there . . ."

"Can we discuss this outside?" Keetin interrupted, his voice brittle. "With sky and grass and trees and a lot less rock? Let's get this over with, because I doubt it'll get any better the longer we wait."

A fair assumption, Ryan acknowledged silently. "Nonee, wait until we pass and take the final position."

"Sir." Curtin cleared his throat. "It might be better to have the large heavy object at the front in case one of us stumbles in the dark and the weapon's unable to stop before stepping on us."

Curtin didn't want Nonee behind him, but that said, he wasn't wrong. "Lead the way then, Nonee. Unless you have an objection, Captain?"

"Better we bump into her than the other way around."

"That's what I said," Curtin grumbled.

"Curtin?"

"Nothing, Captain."

Ryan stretched out his right hand until he felt rock. It felt warm where before it had been cool. Stretching out his left, he snagged Keetin's wrist. "It's me," he said softly when Keetin flinched at his touch. He'd barely gotten Keetin's hand pressed against the wall when Destros bounced off them, cursed, apologized, untangled his pack with Captain Yansav . . .

"That's not your left, Destros!"

"Sorry, Captain."

"This," Lyelee announced, "is where a mage-light would come in handy. What?" she demanded of the silence that followed. "It would."

"It wouldn't," Curtin growled.

"And who's to say a mage-light wouldn't have gone out as well?" Ryan asked. "Is everyone touching the wall with their right hand?"

Gearing sniffed. It was a surprisingly distinctive sound. "It's possible you, or any of us, are not touching the right wall. We could have gotten turned around in the darkness and are now facing the wrong way."

Teeth clenched, Ryan let the reaction die down before saying, "Thank you for that observation, Scholar Gearing. Captain, Nonee is in front of you. Is that correct?"

"It is."

"Destros, who's in front of you?"

"Captain Yansav, sir."

"And behind you?"

"You, my lord."

He ran down the line, one by one.

"You're wasting time, Ryan." Lyelee's eye roll was almost audible. "If anyone is still facing the wrong way, they deserve to be lost . . ."

"Enough!"

The silence sounded startled. Keetin huffed out a wordless approval of the reaction, adding, "The sooner we're secure, the sooner we can move!"

Finally, Servan declared no one stood behind her.

Ryan doubted it had taken as long as it had felt, but it must've taken forever for Keetin. It was hard to judge time in such complete darkness. "Good. We're either all facing the right way, or all facing the wrong way. Let's start moving and find out."

"No matter what happens," Nonee said quietly, "don't take your right hand off the wall."

After a moment, the darkness filled with the sound of nine people trying to control their breathing.

"Okay." Ryan pressed his palm against the side of the passage. "Let's go."

He found it easier to shuffle forward with his eyes open, even though he could see no more with them open than with them closed. It was easier to keep his balance. He shuffled. He dragged his hand along the rock. He could smell the Lake . . .

"So you're the heir now. If you felt the smallest amount of responsibility for the people you're supposed to protect, you'd drop out of the succession and give the job to Reyalia."

The voice came out of the darkness behind him. "Keetin?"

"Do I sound like that useless tit? All lies and smiles, that one. Followed us around the Citadel like a stray puppy. Figures you'd take up with someone who'd tell you only what you want to hear."

He stumbled. Flailed his left hand to keep from falling. Only the fingertips of his right touched rock. He took a half step, then a full one, took a breath and pressed his palm back against the wall. "Donal?"

"Cousin Reyalia may be only twelve, but she'd be a better heir and, in time, a better Lord Protector. I know you, Ryan, I've known you since the day you were born, weak and squalling, ready to pack it in before you even got going."

This was the darkness. Not his brother. His brother was dead.

"Spent your whole life ready to pack it in," Corryn snorted from his left, then raised his voice to a whine. "It's too big, I can't climb it. You're going too fast, slow down. I don't want to. I'm afraid."

His *brothers* were dead. He'd seen their bodies when they came out of the water. He closed his eyes.

"I don't feel well. I'm too small. It hurts. The water's too cold. I can't," Josan whimpered to his right.

That was wrong. The wall was to his right. He could feel it under his hand. Couldn't he?

"Lord Protectors don't make excuses," Donal sneered. "They make decisions. You've never made a decision in your life. Hiding behind Father when we tried to teach you what we knew."

Teach . . . he just barely caught the word behind his teeth.

Ryan heard Corryn spit. Heard it leave his mouth, heard it hit the ground. "You're only the heir because you were next. Not because of who you are or what you can do. An accident of birth."

"Like your birth was an accident," Josan laughed. "After twelve years, did you think they wanted you?"

"You were sick more than the three of us put together. Weeping and wailing so people would pay attention to you." Disdain dripped from Corryn's voice.

Donal snorted from deep in his nose. Familiar. "Well, congratulations, people will pay attention to you now. They'll see your every flaw, just like we did. And it won't take them long to realize you don't measure up."

"Not to the position."

"Not to us."

They weren't there. Ryan kept walking. Kept breathing. Kept silent. He wanted to call out, to make sure the others were still with him here in the dark, but he knew what his brothers would say. That he'd never been able to stand on his own and he never would be.

"Josan never expected to be Lord Protector, not with Corryn and me in line before him, and yet he trained for it."

"That's because, unlike some, I knew my responsibility to my family and to my country."

"He trained while you picked your nose and hid from shadows. Grow up, Ryan." Donal had snapped those words at him when their mother had died and he'd been caught crying. He'd been six to Corryn and Josan's nineteen, Donal's twenty-one.

"I'm in the Broken Lands!" Ryan's voice echoed off the rock, although he didn't remember shouting.

"And how did you get here?" Donal asked, then answered his own question. "With a wagon and supplies and Harris to wipe your ass. You're supposed to command the weapon, not endanger Marsanport while waiting for it to pretend to grieve. To pretend to be a person."

"She is a person!" They could speak ill of him, he was used to it, but they'd never met Nonee, they had no idea. Less idea even than he'd had before reaching Gateway. They'd never been able to see the best in those outside their narrow, entitled worldview.

"How would you know what the weapon is?" Josan sneered. "You're barely a person yourself. Lyelee's known you were weak since you were kids and you couldn't kill that cat."

"You don't know she killed . . ."

"You don't know she," Corryn mocked. "Everyone else knew."

"If you knew," Ryan demanded, "why didn't you stop her?"

"She asked you to help. Why didn't you?"

"Scholar Gearing is appalled by your ignorance." Memory showed him Donal flicking long, callused fingers up into the air to mark each point. "Norwin-cee's a suck-up. Captain Yansav thinks of herself as your babysitter. Curtin, Servan, and Destros have been taking bets as to which of them you'll get killed first . . ."

"I killed a lizard-dog!" He could hold his own. He'd learned late, but he'd practiced every day on the road. With the captain. With the guardians. With Keetin.

"Good thing it shoved its eye onto your sword point."

Josan laughed. "Maybe it was suicidal."

"Shut up."

"Burn it, Ryan. You've never been able to take a joke."

With nothing to grip, nothing to anchor himself on, he pressed his right hand against the rock until skin peeled off and pain drowned out his brother's voices.

"My lord?"

A hand against his wrist. Warmth against chilled skin.

"Open your eyes, my lord. You're out."

If he was out, shouldn't he be able to see light through his eyelids?

"This way, carefully now."

The calm, matter-of-fact tone smoothed the ragged edges his brothers had cut into his mind. Smoothed. Soothed . . . "I don't need a babysitter!" He opened his eyes to see Captain Yansav gazing calmly at him. A brow rose, but that was all the attention she paid to his outburst. Past her, Destros stood outside a cave opening, an axe in each hand, shoulders squared. Gulping for air, Ryan held up his right hand and watched the blood drip off fingers scraped raw.

"My lord!"

He blinked. Focused. The captain's hair was damp, sweat running down the sides of her face. "What happened to your helm?"

"I threw it at an Imperial Princess."

"You took your hand off the wall?"

"I used my left."

"Did it hit her?"

"Hard to say, since she wasn't actually there."

That made sense. "I didn't punch my dead brothers."

"Good for you." She tugged him forward. "Outside. Or we're going to run out of room. Let your hand bleed for a bit to clear out whatever it might have picked up."

Ryan glanced at Destros as he passed, but the big man only looked thoughtful. Biting back jealousy, he dropped his pack beside a flat-topped, moss-covered stone and sat. His ass ended up on the moss, that counted as *sat* however much like collapse it looked.

He heard voices and a moment later Keetin left the cave, eyes red and blood in his beard below the mess his teeth had made of his lower lip.

Following close behind him, Lyelee looked scornful. "Was that it? So much buildup," she added, stomping past Ryan's mossy rock, "for such a non-event."

Ryan thought about tripping her. "Shut up."

She jabbed a finger toward him. "No one tells a scholar to shut up."

"I just did." He swatted her finger away with his bloody hand and ignored her muttering.

Scholar Gearing staggered out next, nose bleeding. He took two steps, then the weight of his pack drove him to his knees.

"I've got it, sir." Destros hauled the pack off Gearing's back then helped him to his feet, the attempt made more difficult by the double-handed, white-knuckled grip Gearing had on his satchel.

Harris emerged looking ten years older, his voice a rough, painful-sounding rasp. His right hand, like Ryan's, dripped blood.

"Wait . . ." Keetin coughed, spat into the moss, and tried again. "Harris was in front of the Scholars. How did they get past him?"

Ryan handed him a waterskin. "Not the most pressing question I have about that place."

"Fair enough."

Servan staggered out and to one side, dropped to her knees, locked her elbows to hold the weight of her pack, and vomited, nearly face-planting from the force of the dry heaves that wracked her body. "Made a mess inside," she explained, sitting back on her heels, the pack riding up on her shoulders. "Twice. Missed my boots though, so, yay. Heat's going to make it unpleasant going back through . . ."

"It'll be different on the way back." Nonee looked like herself. Like an ancient, mage-crafted weapon unaffected by the darkness. Ryan could understand why people hated her.

"You can't know that," Gearing gasped, chest still heaving.

Nonee frowned, then nodded. She crossed the small clearing outside the cave to the beginning of a path that led up the . . .

. . . mountain.

Ryan tipped his head back. The path led up a mountain, although on the other side of the passage they'd barely been in the foothills. It had been worn deep into the reddish soil between moss-covered trees and stones. Dust motes danced in the beams of sunlight that split the canopy on their way to the ground. To either side of the path, the light gilded the greens and the browns and pooled in hollows.

"Like a temple," Captain Yansav said from the mouth of the cave.

Nonee nodded. "Yes."

Everyone looked to the captain.

"We have temples in Shurlia," she sighed. "The gods are everywhere but Marsan."

"We have knowledge in Marsan," Gearing corrected sharply. "Rather than belief in the unproven."

"The scholars have knowledge. People have faith in the scholars." Captain Yansav spread her hands. "Faith is faith. I assume we're taking that path?"

How many people would it take to wear a path that deep into the ground? Ryan wondered. And where had they come from? More importantly, where were they now?

"It's the only path," Nonee said. "It was stairs before."

"You thinking ambush, Cap?" Servan tossed the captain a waterskin.

"I am. That's the problem when there's only one path, they'll know exactly where we are."

"Who are *they*?" Lyelee rolled her eyes.

"All things considered, Scholar, I'm not ruling anyone out." She took a drink and tossed the waterskin back to Servan. "What's taking Curtin so long?"

Ryan glanced at the sky. They'd gone into the cave in early morning, and left it in mid-afternoon. His stomach growled. "Might as well eat while we wait. Harris."

"Sir." Harris pulled his pack around. The clanking of the pans tied to the outside sounded muted. "Hot or cold?"

The silence grew heavier. The air thicker. It felt like . . . anticipation.

"Cold," Ryan told him.

Servan flipped a branch over with the toe of her boot. "There's plenty of dead wood."

"I don't think we should burn it."

"I agree." Lyelee pulled out a cloth-wrapped packet of dried cherries. "Given the number of different fungi I can see from here, there's no knowing what you'd unleash. Until you unleashed it." She tossed a cherry into her mouth, chewed and swallowed. "And then it would be too late."

That was also a good reason, Ryan acknowledged silently.

By the time they finished eating, they had to admit Curtin wasn't coming out on his own.

"Stay where you are, my lord." Captain Yansav waved Ryan down as he stood. "Nonee. You weren't affected and none of us can go through that again." Ryan glanced at Destros, who frowned. "You need to go in and get him."

Nonee sighed, turned to face the cave, and said, "Yes."

"Cap, if he's in a bad way, he won't go with her." Servan spread her hands. "We all know how he's got a stick up his ass about mage-craft."

"Stick up his ass indeed," Gearing growled. "Mage-craft is based on dangerous assumptions and nearly killed the Five Thousand!"

The captain raised a hand. "Not now, Scholar. Do you want to go back in there, Servan?"

"I . . . I don't . . ." She took a deep breath and expelled it all at once. "No, Captain."

The afternoon was nearly over and Ryan was dangerously close to tying Lyelee to a tree in order to keep her from wandering off by the time Nonee emerged carrying Curtin's body over her shoulder. One hand braced his hip, the other held his pack, and Captain Yansav's helmet hung from her belt.

"Burn it all," Servan swore.

No one was surprised, Ryan realized. They'd known. They'd been mourning him while they waited.

"Was he dead when you found him?" Lyelee asked, sliding her notebook back into her satchel and rising.

"Lyelee!"

"It's a valid question." The captain stepped around Ryan. "You'd best answer it, Nonee."

"Not only dead, but cold." Squatting, Nonee let the body slide off her shoulder onto the ground. "Dead for some time."

Lyelee dropped to one knee and pushed two fingers into Curtin's throat under the edge of his beard. "No pulse. And even considering the lower temperature in the cave, he's colder than most corpses."

"How many corpses have you been that close to?" Keetin asked.

"Over the last eight years? Five hundred and sixty-three. The Scholars of the Flesh allow me to observe." She leaned in until she was almost nose to nose with Curtin. "The Scholars of Philosophy have a theory that if a person dies with their eyes open the last thing they saw is recorded on the back of their eyes. I wish I had a strong light and sizing glasses with me."

Before Ryan could speak, Nonee's hand slipped in under Lyelee's face and closed Curtin's eyes. "The mages thought the same."

"A point in their favor." Lyelee straightened. "I wonder, if I removed the eyeballs, could I check them later?"

Ryan heard someone growl—it might have been him—and snapped, "No!"

"No? Grant us your wisdom, then, Heir of Marsan. How long do eyeballs take to decay?"

He had to swallow before he could answer, but all he managed was a strangled, "Lyelee."

"Fine." Rocking back on her heels, she stood. "It's not as though I have a way to store them safely."

"Yeah, that's the problem," Keetin muttered. "Not that you're a ghoul and Curtin's dead. Nonee, what do you think killed him?"

"He took his hand off the wall." She stood as well, making the clearing seem significantly smaller, although it was the same size it had been when she left.

"Mage-craft, then." Gearing clutched his satchel, pressing it against his stomach. "No one died in the passage when the Lord Protector was heir."

When the Lord Protector was heir . . .

"So it's my fault?" Ryan snarled.

"I didn't say . . ."

"You might as well have, Scholar."

"And now we all know what you faced in the darkness." Lyelee pressed a hand against his chest and moved him back a step. Was it the same hand she'd used to touch Curtin? "Speaking as family," she continued, "your brothers were entitled assholes. Speaking as a scholar, they didn't know half of what they thought they did. More importantly, they're dead. Stop letting them run your life."

They all knew what he'd faced? Ryan glanced around the clearing. Of course they all knew. They'd all known his brothers at the Citadel. Had heard his brothers talking about him.

"Those in service at the Citadel weren't fond of your brothers." Heads turned toward Harris, who faced Ryan with the same matter-of-fact expression he wore to face a cooking fire. "They considered most people beneath their notice."

Ryan found an unconvincing laugh. "So not just me."

"No, my lord."

"Nonee, why do you think the Lord Protector's crew got through with no fatalities?" Keetin asked. "What?" he asked when attention turned to him. "She was there."

"Yeah, she was." Ryan bounced his shoulder off Keetin's, grateful for the abrupt change of subject. "Nonee?"

"When Garrett Heir and his people met the darkness, their minds were on the loss of Petre's hand." She glanced down at Curtin. "That may have protected them from being lost in their own fears."

It sounded good, Ryan acknowledged. Not that it mattered to Curtin. "We haven't time to give him to the fire." And they'd already decided a fire would be a bad idea. "We bury him."

"We haven't time for that either," Lyelee argued. "Leave him. The land will take him."

"Yes," Nonee said.

Ryan heard a world of warning in that single word. Where would the land take him? And what would it do with him when he got there? "He's a friend and comrade, Lyelee, not something we just throw away. We bury him."

While Nonee dug the grave, they divided the contents of Curtin's pack, barely finishing before bedrock made the hole as deep as it was going to get. Destros laid the empty pack into the hole first, then Nonee placed the body on top of it, crossing Curtin's hands over his chest, exposing scraped and bruised knuckles. They left his sword in the sheath attached to his belt, but kept his daggers and his crossbow.

"Really the Lord Protector's crossbow," Destros muttered. "We signed them out of the armory."

"Yeah," Servan half laughed. "Gotta bring it back. We don't want to get him into trouble."

When Ryan took up a handful of dirt, Nonee stopped him.

"Purkin-flower distillate." She held up a flask. "To keep the shadows out." When Ryan, remembering the flowers around the bier, nodded, she dribbled a line of liquid down the length of the body.

"The Chronicles of the Five Thousand say some of the mages dabbled in necromancy," Gearing said.

"Where?" Keetin demanded.

With everyone's attention on Gearing, Ryan studied his cousin's expression. It looked . . . mocking.

"In the addendum," Gearing said at last. "There's a number of disjointed reports not copied into the text of the chronicles." He tightened his grip on the satchel.

"Necromancy. Wonderful." Keetin turned back to Nonee. "Got enough of that purkin-flower distillate for all of us?" Keetin asked.

"No." Nonee picked up a handful of dirt. "Vaylin Curtin-cee spoke to me of how he hated mage-craft and all that came of it, but he'd begun to recognize his hatred had been built on sandy ground." She tossed the dirt into the grave, small stones chiming against his scale.

Ryan stepped forward and opened his hand. He'd been holding it so tightly, the dirt fell in a solid clump. He'd gotten Curtin killed. Failed him. "Vaylin Curtin-cee . . ." He swallowed. Started again. "Curtin told me that I might make a decent swordsman if I stopped closing my eyes when I thrust."

"I've told you the same thing," Keetin murmured, and grunted when Ryan's elbow made contact. "Curtin laid a fine harmony line under the March of Five Thousand. I'll miss singing with him."

"He liked my biscuits."

"He was unexpectedly well read."

"He was a considerate lover." Looking a little surprised by the emotion in her voice, Lyelee dropped her dirt, brushed off her hand, and touched Servan's offered fist with her own.

"He did this thing with his tongue . . ."

"Servan."

"Yeah, Cap?"

"I don't think he'd want to be remembered . . . Actually, never mind. Yes, he would." Captain Yansav closed her eyes while her dirt fell, her lips tracing silent words. When the patter against the scale stopped, she opened them and said, "There was no question he would have made captain someday."

"He owed me twenty anchors. Two month's pay." Destros dropped his handful of dirt and rubbed the back of his hand over his eyes. He swallowed, his throat clicking. "Guess he had the last laugh about those three eights."

ARIANNA.THEN

Arianna glanced over to where Malcolm held a waterskin up to Petre's mouth, all but forcing him to drink. "He's doing surprisingly well, all things considered. If he gets enough liquid into him and we don't get attacked by anything particularly horrible until he's got some strength back, there's no reason he won't be able to ride home with you."

Garrett dropped to sit beside her, nodding toward the two boys. "Isn't that one of the skins with the beer in it?"

She shrugged. "Beer's essentially liquid bread. Petre needs to regain his strength and the alcohol will help dull the pain." Nostrils that flared with each short, hard breath told of a greater pain than he'd admit to. "All things considered, we should be thankful it was a clean bite."

"All things considered," Garrett growled, "I'm not going to be thankful the creature's teeth were sharp."

"Fair enough."

Leaning back against a moss-covered rock, Arianna tucked her feet under her skirts for warmth. They'd come out of the passage in back of the cave a lot higher in the mountains and the air was both drier and colder. The trees surrounding them had dropped their leaves, leaving every branch bare. Strangely, the moss that made up the only undergrowth remained a vibrant green. It covered the ground, went halfway up the trunks of the trees, and extended out over the stairs in a resilient carpet. Only Uvili's footprints were visible on the long length of shallow, stone stairs they'd already climbed, her weight crushing the moss beyond recovery.

Garrett winced as he stretched out his left leg, the knee cracking. "I didn't want to get caught on these stairs in the dark."

With two or three hours of light left, no one had wanted to camp in the clearing outside the cave, not with the great black hole in the rock looming over them absorbing any light that fell into it. They'd climbed without stopping, but the sun was setting and they hadn't reached the top. Petre's injury hadn't slowed them—he'd made the climb in Uvili's arms—there were just so many stairs. Arianna's knees and hips ached from climbing, her shoulders and back ached from the weight of the pack, and if Uvili was right and they had as many more stairs still to climb, she was fairly certain she'd agree with Garrett about the mages being evil incarnate by the time they were done.

"Could be worse," she said. "This landing's big enough to spend the night on as long as we're willing to sleep close. You should have come in the summer," she added when Garrett scowled. "The evenings go on forever."

"So do these stairs," he muttered, getting to his feet. "Norik! We're making camp, gather wood for a fire."

"No." Uvili shifted until she became a barrier Norik had to conquer.

Arianna saw Garrett stiffen, knew he was about to order her out of Norik's way, and called, "Why not?"

"Fire bad."

"Fire warm," Garrett snapped. "And there's plenty of dead wood around."

She shifted again as Norik attempted to go around her. "Bad."

"The wood's bad?" he asked.

"No."

"There's not much room, granted, but we're on stone. We won't burn the forest down." Norik sounded calm. Reasonable. As though he were talking to a small child. Or a dog. Arianna hoped it was the former; she liked the archer.

Uvili shook her head. "Fire bad."

"You can't reason with her, Norik. She doesn't understand." Garrett blew out a deep breath and ran his hands back through his hair. "I'm going to have to give her a direct order."

"Wait." Arianna stood and moved past Garrett into Uvili's line of sight. "If we light a fire, will we put ourselves in danger?"

"Yes."

"How?"

"That's too complicated for her to . . ." Garrett's protest trailed off as Uvili squatted and yanked up a handful of moss.

The green seemed to bleed into the gray of her palm. "Fire." A breath, and the moss flew all over the landing.

"Fire will spread the moss?" Norik shook his head. "You may not have noticed, but the moss is already covering everything."

"Yes." She shook her head and frowned. "No."

"Fire will spread the moss," Arianna repeated. She twisted the thumb of her left mitten as she thought, knowing she had very little time before Garrett gave a command that couldn't be disobeyed. "Fire will . . . Spores. Fire will release the moss's spores!"

"Yes!" Uvili's expression held pleasure and relief equally mixed.

"Except," Arianna said reluctantly, "that's not how moss works. Moss needs moisture to release spores."

"No." She pulled up another handful. Arianna usually saw that expression on the mothers of small children. "Fire."

"This moss needs fire?"

"Yes." Her sigh added a distinct *finally.*

"Moss spores don't harm people," Garrett declared.

"How much do you know about moss?" Arianna demanded, turning to face him. "I'm not saying you don't, I'm sure the study of plants and their uses is essential to the Heir of Marsan. However . . ." She cut him off before he could respond. ". . . this time, you're right, but that's luck, not knowledge. However, this is mage-crafted moss. So it's very likely that someone who was herself mage-crafted might have more information about the dangers inherent in burning it than any of us would." Some of the moss-covered mounds back between the trees took on ominous possibilities. They'd seen no sign of wildlife. "Just to be clear," she asked, turning again, "the moss isn't dangerous unless it's burnt?"

"Yes."

"Fine, no fire then." Garrett emphasized his declaration with raised hands, like an acolyte in the temple. "We'll sleep cold. I'm sure it'll do your patient no harm at all, Healer."

Arianna answered his glare with a smile, a little impressed that he'd trusted Uvili's word. However reluctantly. "A little cold will do him less harm than having his lungs filled with spores." She prodded the moss with the toe of her boot, watching it compress and spring back. "At least it's soft."

❧

Arianna jerked out of a light doze when Petre moaned. His forehead was cool, but the moonlight showed his eyes moving behind his lids. A nightmare then, not pain. If a shattered had leapt out of the water and bitten her hand off, the experience would return to twist her dreams for the rest of her life.

Leaning in until her lips were just above the boy's ear, she murmured, "Happy memories, Petre. Sunshine, and warmth, and hot food, and soft beds.

Friends and family. A brown dog with a smiley face and a curly tail to lick your fingers when you sneak it food from the table."

The tight line of his brows relaxed.

Pain management was a part of healing, and while it didn't take as much from her as helping flesh and bone to knit together, her heart was racing and she knew she wouldn't be able to sleep for a while. She slid carefully out from Petre's side and smiled as Norik shuffled closer without waking.

Moss muffling her footsteps, she crossed the landing. Uvili shifted in what looked like welcome.

"So, more stairs tomorrow." Which wasn't her brightest observation since the stairs clearly continued until they curved out of sight.

"Up," Uvili agreed, sounding no more thrilled by it than Arianna.

"How far?"

"Up." She sighed, then repeated, "Up."

Arianna laid her hands on arms bigger around than her legs and pushed up gently, fully aware that she'd have a greater chance of raising the wall around Gateway. "Lift your shoulders, then lower them again. Up then down. It means you don't know. There's nuance too, but we'll go into that later."

Massive shoulders rose. Stayed up. Fell.

"That's it."

They stood together for a while, facing the rising stairs.

"This isn't a criticism," Arianna said, trying not to see the shadows of deer and foxes and grouse in the unending moss, "but how do you know we're going the right way?"

"Home."

It took her a moment to tease out the probable meaning. "You can find your way home? To the tower where you were created? And that's where Captain Marsan got the fuel?"

"Yes. Yes. Yes." She looked pleased with herself and Arianna realized she'd answered all three questions. She was recovering the ability to communicate at an incredible speed.

Resilience must have been mage-crafted in.

"So you know exactly where we're going?"

Her sigh was deep enough to move the bare branches of the nearest trees. "No."

"Ah. There's a number of ways to get to your home, and you won't know the route we're going to take until we're on it."

"How did you get all that from a single word?" Garrett asked behind her.

Arianna managed to keep her reaction down to a sudden widening of the eyes that only Uvili saw. "I'm just that smart."

"Yes."

LYELEE.NOW

Lyelee slid her notebook into her satchel and reluctantly turned her back on the building at the end of the red dirt path. Deaf to reason, Nonee had told her to stay at the edge of the clearing. That if Lyelee followed her into the building, she'd be carried back to the others. That every time she followed, she'd be carried back. Until the day had been entirely wasted.

"Your choice," Nonee had said, turned, and walked toward the building.

So Lyelee had stayed where she was. Made her sketches at an inconvenient distance. And finally, simmering with frustration, she joined Ryan at the top of the path. "We'd have moved on by now if Gearing had let Nonee carry him."

Ryan grunted an agreement. "At least he let her carry his pack."

"She carried his pack *and* Keetin's. It's a safe conclusion that Nonee could have carried both packs and Gearing, and still beat the rest of us to the top. Or the middle," she amended, since the mountain continued to rise behind them. "He's not even that old."

"Keetin?"

"Don't be an idiot."

"I guess it's all catching up to him."

Lyelee couldn't compare Gearing's current shape—visible in shirt and trousers—to his former—hidden under his robe—but his hands had grown coarser, his knuckles had swollen, and it was possible his eyes had sunk further back into his skull. Glancing down the path, she saw the top of Keetin's head come into view, the top of Gearing's visible a step later when they'd made up the difference in their heights. "His timing leaves something to be desired. If he'd admitted to exhaustion before we left Gateway, we could have left him behind."

"I tried to leave him behind."

"You tried to leave us both behind."

"And for the sake of scholarship, I didn't."

"The Scholarship of the Broken Lands would have been safe with me." Lyelee folded her arms. "And moving significantly faster."

"So why not learn about something while we wait? Something besides the building," he added hurriedly, as though she'd immediately run off if given his permission. As though Nonee hadn't taken command from the captain, bypassing him entirely.

"I'm too irritated by the time we're wasting." She could see Destros now. He'd volunteered to walk behind Keetin and Gearing, guarding their backs. Keeping to that tottering pace would have driven her mad.

Clutching Keetin's elbow, Gearing leaned into the younger man, swaying slightly with every step, the path here near the end of the climb only just wide enough for the two of them side by side. The nine . . . no, eight of them had spent the early part of the morning climbing single file at the scholar's wobbly pace until Captain Yansav had agreed to split the party.

To be fair to Gearing, Lyelee admitted he wasn't the only one short on sleep. Unwilling to camp by Curtin's grave while contemplating necromancy, they'd climbed until they lost the light, then wrapped up and lain in a line along the path, cradled in the depression made by those who'd come before. Although according to the Heir's Chronicle, those who'd come before had climbed stairs.

The Heir's Chronicle had noted no fires could be lit while surrounded by the moss, as spores were produced by the heat. Lyelee hadn't had a chance to test the chronicle's accuracy, but she'd managed to get a good handful of moss into a sample bag while Nonee and the rest were distracted by the partially covered, crumbling bones of a deer.

In the interest of not disturbing their surroundings, the latrine had been dug in a section of the path they'd already traveled. The chronicles hadn't mentioned what the Lord Protector's party had done. Maybe Nonee had held them out over the moss.

A flying insect landed on Lyelee's arm. She slapped it, squashed it flat, and flicked the body away, leaving a smear of bright red blood behind.

"So." Ryan rocked back on his heels. "You had sex with Curtin?"

She rolled her eyes. "What are you, twelve? And what's said at the grave remains at the grave. Yes, I had sex with Curtin. And Servan, if you need to know that before she dies. Although I'm a scholar, so in point of fact, they had sex with me."

"On the road?"

"To the side of the road, if you must know."

"How did I not . . ."

"You're not very observant."

"And yet you wanted to throw him away."

"It wasn't Curtin. Curtin died and left his meat sack behind."

"Lyelee . . ."

"Ryan."

"Do you have knowledge of the Broken Lands you're not sharing?"

She sighed. It had taken him long enough to get to the point. "Of course I do. I'm a Scholar of the Broken Lands. I've combed every possible detail out of the archives, and the details I'm not sharing have no relevance to what we've experienced so far. When they become relevant, I'll share them. Until then, muddying the journey with unnecessary information seems counterproductive."

"Who decides when that information is necessary?"

Lyelee rolled her eyes. His father had done Ryan no favors keeping him home in the country after his mother's death. He should have spent part of every year in the city, learning how the world worked. It would have made him a better heir and a less irritating person. "I decide. Or were you not paying attention when I reminded you that I'm a Scholar of the Broken Lands?"

"Just a little bit farther," Keetin caroled before Ryan could respond. "We're almost there."

"Don't talk to me like I'm a child, Lord Norwin-cee," Gearing snapped.

"Wouldn't think of it. I was talking to you like you were a decrepit old man."

Gearing twisted and glared up at him. Keetin stared placidly back. After a moment, to Lyelee's surprise, her mentor burst into laughter.

"How," he asked, when he'd regained his breath, "did I spend a full moon's passage on the road with you and yet never noticed you were such an asshole?"

"You were distracted by more scholarly topics?"

"That must be it."

They separated as they reached level ground, both breathing heavily, both dripping with sweat. She suspected Keetin, his chest looking as though it had been covered in splotches of black currant jam, had appreciated the slower pace as much as Gearing. Destros nodded to Ryan and again to her, then walked over to Captain Yansav, the spring in his step denying that he'd spent the better part of the morning climbing a mountain.

"What took you so long?" Ryan asked, handing Keetin a pouch of dried cherries.

Keetin flicked flame at him.

"I lost count," Gearing said quietly, lowering himself to sit on a fallen tree. "How far did we climb?"

"Too far," Lyelee told him.

"Accurate. Although not useful."

"Five thousand, three hundred and twenty-eight steps, from where we slept last night."

"Too far indeed." Tucking his satchel between his feet, he shrugged out of his vest and wiped sweat off his face with his shirt-tail. "Where's the weapon?"

"In the building, scouting." Or hiding items of interest. Lyelee wouldn't put it past her. "I made a sketch, but there's no way of knowing if it's the same building referenced in the Heir's Chronicle, given the lack of detail in the historical text."

At the head of the path, we entered a building and exited in time by way of a green and yellow door.

Although that was an entry the Scholar's Hall hadn't condensed in later editions of the chronicle, it was minimally helpful at best. Never mind how much knowledge they'd lost to time, how much had they specifically lost by the absence of a scholar in the Lord Protector's company?

Servan had taken position at the top of the path, bow in hand—in case of pursuit, Lyelee assumed. As they'd seen nothing alive since entering the cave by the nonexistent waterfall, what, she wondered, did Captain Yansav think might be pursuing? Curtin? Did she worry that Nonee's herbal remedy would be unable to prevent necromancy inherent in the soil?

Actually . . .

How long could the dead walk in this heat without rotting apart?

The path remained empty, no corpse appearing to answer her question.

Gearing had drifted off during the brief time her thoughts were elsewhere. Did he dream? Lyelee wondered. Did he dream as she had on the path of the possibilities of mage-craft unconstrained by fear and prejudices? Of lost knowledge not only found but used again, this time by scholars trained to know the difference between facts and fictions? Did it matter?

A line of drool glistened in his beard.

No, it didn't matter.

His snoring drove her toward the building. Round, two stories high with a flat roof; it looked like a short tower. Whitewash had flaked off about two-thirds of the bricks. Although Lyelee had never studied the disintegration rate of whitewash, she suspected that in one hundred and sixty-three years more should have disappeared. Mage-craft benefiting the building trade—not one of the recorded memories of the Five Thousand had mentioned *that*.

Stepping out into the clearing, barely past the point Nonee had indicated she not cross, Lyelee leaned closer. It looked as though the large rectangular window directly over the door still contained glass, but that had to be a trick of the light. She could see the front edges of small square frames protruding from opposite sides of the curve and assumed they delineated small, square windows. The ornate, pale doorframe took up a third of the center front although the door itself was barely the width of Nonee's shoulders, the rest of the space filled in with a decorative metal grill.

Was decoration its primary or secondary function?

The toes of her boots kicked through the grass.

It was hard to tell at this distance, but the ornamentation on the doorframe looked very much like the ornamentation over the door at the warren in Gateway.

Six, seven, eight steps closer.

Definitely the same symbols. A historical tie that merited investigation.

Notebook in hand, she moved close enough to capture the details.

A flash of wings appeared at the edge of her vision. On the left. Then on the right. As she lifted her head, a bird passed so close to her face she felt it push the air out of its way. Now they had her attention, two of the birds rose, disappeared against the sky, and reappeared as they dove toward her. A third shrieked a challenge.

She touched her fingers to the bright line of pain across her cheek and brought them away stained red.

Unable to look away, she watched the third bird fly directly at her.

Then a gray hand snatched the bird out of the sky and threw it to knock down another. Both bodies slammed into a tree and dropped broken to the ground. Challenges rang out from hidden birds in the surrounding forest, but none took to the air.

They were larger on the ground than they'd seemed while moving. Gull-sized. Perhaps even larger, taking the amount they'd been crushed into consideration.

"Told you not to go close to the building." Nonee dusted feathers off her hands, raised her voice, and added, "The next fixed point is inside."

"You didn't mention birds," Lyelee muttered. "Are we all likely to be attacked as we approach?"

"No."

"Because now they know you're with us?"

She stared at the birds for a long moment before she said, "Yes."

"Did you find the exit mentioned in the chronicle?" Gearing called, rising to his feet.

"Yes."

But Lyelee was close enough to see her face. "What aren't you saying?"

Nonee tipped her head to meet her eyes. "Did Garrett Heir write of a green and yellow door?"

"He did."

"Same door." Her massive shoulders rose and fell. "Might not be the same exit."

"Why didn't you check?"

"No point. The exit changes every time the door opens."

"Was that an intentional function of the original mage-craft?"

"Does it matter?"

"Answer the question."

Nonee smiled.

Lyelee took an involuntary step back . . . directly into Ryan's path.

He grabbed her arms and spun her to face him. "Lyelee, are you . . . You're bleeding."

"It's nothing." The blood had already begun to grow sticky and the sharp pain of the initial cut had dulled to a throb.

"It's nothing now," Keetin put in from behind Ryan's left shoulder. "But if that gets infected, we'll have to amputate your head."

"You're really not funny," Lyelee muttered, teeth together to keep her cheek still.

He grinned. "I'm a little funny."

Nonee rejoined them, holding her pack in one hand and a clay pot in another. She thrust the pot toward Lyelee. "Use this."

Lyelee worked the cork out and sniffed the contents. The thick cream smelled faintly of honey. "What is it?"

"To prevent infection and the loss of your head."

"See, Nonee thinks I'm funny."

"That's not what I asked," Lyelee said, ignoring Keetin's observation. "You told me what it's for. I asked what it was."

"It's a tisane in whipped oil. Arianna made it. Use it or have your face fall off," she added when Lyelee opened her mouth again. "Don't care either way."

❧

Lyelee stayed on Nonee's heels as they climbed the spiral stairs twisting through the center of the building.

Two stories. Three stories.

"Is this a mage's tower?"

"No." Nonee took the steps three at a time, only her toes and half the ball of her foot finding room on the steps. "Mage-crafted. To give all six mages equal access to Gateway."

"That's why the destination changes every time you open the door?"

"Yes."

"And the mages could control that destination, but you can't?"

"Yes."

Lyelee thought about the ground they'd covered. "It's not exactly close to Gateway."

"Closer before the war."

Had the Mage War moved the tower? No, it was simpler than that. They were in the Broken Lands. The land itself had moved.

Four stories. Five.

Lyelee saved her breath for the climb. For placing her feet carefully in the center of the deep dip worn into each step.

Six stories.

"You'll be able to bounce a dagger off my ass when we reach the top of these things." Servan's voice drifted up the central space. "Hey, Nonee! The stairs do end, right?"

"Yes."

"When?"

"Not yet."

"Oh joy."

"Enough." Captain Yansav's voice filled the stairwell. "More attention on your surroundings. Destros?"

"We're good, Captain."

He was carrying Gearing. Nonee carried both their packs.

Seven.

Eight.

A door?

The wooden door—surrounded by the same pale stone as surrounded the exterior door—had been placed in the exterior wall, flattening a section of the curve. They were six floors above the perceived external height of the tower, so where did the door lead? Could a door be built in a wall that didn't actually exist? That, Lyelee decided, was another question for the Scholars of Philosophy. "There's no way to open it."

Nonee pointed to deep gouges in the pale stone.

There was a description of the gouges in the Heir's Chronicle. "That's where . . ."

"Yes."

Nonee was still alive. Was the creature? Lyelee knocked twice. Waited. And was about to knock again when a double boom shook the door. She didn't remember stepping back, but her pack seemed to be pressed against the opposite wall.

"Did you lose a finger?" Keetin asked, crowding up a step.

"No!"

"Pity." He grinned, face dripping sweat. "I didn't think it would take me this long to collect that bet."

"Lyelee, you're blocking the stairs. If we stop, we'll never get moving again."

She leaned out around Keetin and flicked fire at Ryan. As she straightened, her foot slid off the worn edge of the step.

Keetin caught her. "Careful, Lye. Don't knock us back to the bottom, Servan's ass won't be up to another climb."

"You're an ass!" Servan's voice drifted up the stairwell.

Nine. Ten. Eleven floors.

Though the stairs had been narrow enough they'd had to climb in single file, they ended in a circular platform large enough for all nine . . . eight of them, an ancient weapon, and their packs. A green and yellow door—the same design as the unpainted door three floors below—broke the curve of the stone wall.

"Might have been nice if the Lord Protector had prepped us for the stairs," Keetin panted, leaning back so the wall could take the weight of his pack.

Nonee shrugged. "He didn't climb this high."

"But it's the same door?"

"The door is the fixed point."

Lyelee pivoted on the spot. "Where's the light coming from?"

Nonee pointed up.

A ball of light filled the space where a rosette should have joined the ribs of the tower's roof. "That single mage-light has been illuminating the entire stairwell since the mage-war?" Lyelee didn't wait for a response. It hadn't really been a question. "Think of what the Scholar's Hall could do with it."

"Apparently, we could light stairwells." Gearing ignored Servan's snicker. "How long will it shine?"

"Forever." Nonee frowned at the light and shrugged again. "Or not." She tucked a finger into the door's metal ring, and turned the latch.

The open door framed white . . . Fog? Mist?

Ryan shook his head. "No. We're not stepping into fog."

"Not fog." Nonee glanced through the door. "Not a danger fog," she amended. "This is the only way to the fuel."

"It can't be the only way."

Nonee waited.

He sighed. "This is the only way?"

"Yes." Nonee raised her left foot. Paused. "Follow quickly so you don't get lost."

And was gone.

❧

Lyelee hated vomiting. She'd known people who didn't mind it, who reversed the digestive process, wiped their mouths, and got on with their lives, but she wasn't one of them. With nothing left to expel, her stomach convulsed, the last of the yellow-green bile dripping from her nose. Breathing in was a struggle. Breathing out brought another convulsion. Then coughing. Her elbows threatened to collapse and she didn't care that the puddle of vomit had begun to soak through the knees of her trousers.

"Up you come, Scholar." Her weight dangled against the straps of her pack, then she was more or less upright, fighting to get her feet under her. Destros maintained his hold until she was steady, then stepped back. He looked exactly like he had on the other side of the door—sweaty and large.

"That didn't . . ."

"Affect me? No."

She wiped her nose on the lower edge of her tunic. "That's really annoying."

"I can see how it would be." He smiled and walked over to where Gearing lay like a turtle on its back, his pack holding him to the floor while he struggled weakly against it.

"Curtin wouldn't have enjoyed that," Servan muttered and spat into a corner.

"Did anyone?" Lyelee snarled. At least she hadn't been the only one to vomit. In Servan's corner, three chunky puddles stained the . . .

. . . worn parquet floor.

The room was large, and rectangular, with the remains of ornate moldings on walls and ceiling. The ceiling had been painted a pale cream, the walls a pale blue, and gilding flaked off the moldings. Darker patches showed where pictures had hung, and darker streaks where water had seeped in. They stood clustered together in one narrow end, facing double doors in the other. Three tall, arched windows divided a wall to the right. It looked like a perfectly normal ballroom. Except for the excessive ornamentation and the dirt, it could have been in the Citadel. On the wall behind them . . .

"There's no door." Lyelee reached out, but couldn't bring herself to touch the wall.

"There never is," Nonee said from the center of the room.

"Then how do we get back?"

"The trick is knowing where the door should be."

"Scholars of Philosophy," Lyelee muttered under her breath, then took the waterskin Servan offered and rinsed out her mouth. "Stay away from the corner where the floor's dark," she said after she spat. "The wood's rotten."

"How do you know that?" Keetin asked.

She smiled at him. "Scholar." Darny's mother; but that was none of Keetin's business.

They were on an upper floor. The window glass was so filthy she could make out only vertical blurs that might be trees and a lower, flat blur that could be a wall.

"This does explain why there wasn't a city at the other side of the Broken Lands," Gearing said, suddenly beside her.

Lyelee tried unsuccessfully to clean a circle of glass with her thumb. "Until we get to the other side of the Broken Lands, that's only a theory."

"You're not going to the other side of the Broken Lands," Ryan said as he passed.

"Also a theory," Lyelee told him, turning away from the windows.

The double doors opened into a broad hall overlooking the magnificent sweep of a white and gilded staircase descending to a large lobby.

"What are these?" Ryan pried a pale brown half-circle off the railing with the blade of his knife.

Nonee leaned in and frowned. "Fungus."

"Like in the cave."

She shook her head. "No."

"Edible?"

"No."

"That was a very definitive no," Lyelee said, moving closer. "You've seen these before?"

"Yes. Crafted by Briseis Galanos during the war."

"Like the moss?"

"Yes."

"There's a lot more of it on the lower level." Ryan tossed the fungus over the railing. "We're going down there, aren't we?"

"Yes."

The stairs were clear until the lowest three steps, where fungus had covered the edges—leaving only a small amount of open tread. It rose up the wall almost to Lyelee's hips. When she pressed a fingertip into it, expecting to break through the surface, it dimpled. When she removed her finger, the dimple slowly filled in.

The lobby floor felt soft under her left foot, but it had held Nonee, so she forced her right foot down and walked away from the stairs, stepping around patches of fungus on the wide, painted boards.

"This way." Nonee led them to the right.

The further they walked from the stairs, the thicker the fungus became, and the patches on the floor became a stubby forest of waist-high growth they had to wind around.

"If we knock one over," Ryan began.

"Don't!" Nonee barked. "And don't look up!"

A piece the size of a wagon wheel dropped off the ceiling onto Gearing's head, the sides drooping . . . no, wrapping around his jaw and moving toward his mouth.

If he'd been looking up, it would have dropped *into* his mouth. Lyelee tucked her chin in—far enough for safety, not so far it kept her from tracking the process of the fungus on Gearing's head. It was clearly a different species than the bulgy columns growing out of the floor and moved surprisingly fast considering what it was.

Ryan jabbed his fingers under the closest edge and ripped it away.

"That was . . . That was . . ." White showing all around his eyes, Gearing swallowed. "That was . . ."

"Decide what it was when we're out of here, Scholar." Ryan pushed him forward. "Keep moving!"

Another piece dropped, hit Nonee's shoulder, and slid to the floor. One fell in front of Destros and he smacked it out of the air with the side of his axe.

Lyelee reached into her satchel for her sample sticks, but before she could get them out, Ryan grabbed her arm. She jerked loose, stumbled, and thrust her entire hand into a bulgy column. The broken edges pressed against her wrist and, as she watched, began to thin and stretch up her arm—not so much independent movement as accelerated plant growth. The interior felt cooler than the air, the lower temperature pleasant against over-heated skin. She could still move her fingers, although it was becoming difficult to determine where they ended and the engulfing fungus began. Frowning, she tried to pull her hand free, and failed.

"Lyelee?"

"There may be a numbing agent involved."

"Of course there is." Keetin held her wrist, while Ryan ripped the fungus away. Ragged chunks flew in all directions, bouncing off the walls, the floor, her body. "Burn it, Lyelee, open your hand!"

Reluctantly, she forced her fingers to uncurl and the piece she'd been clutching fell to the floor.

"I don't see any damage." Ryan flexed each finger, both men concentrating so hard on one hand that they missed her slipping the piece she'd caught with the other into her pocket. "Any pain?"

"No." It felt like the dirt under her fingernails had been pushed down into the quick, but that was more pressure than pain.

"If you could get moving, my lords!" Servan's arrow hit the center of yet another circular piece sliding down the wall. The piece split around the arrow and rejoined below it.

"At least they're easy to outrun," Ryan muttered as he grabbed Lyelee's left arm. He pushed her toward Keetin, and the two of them dragged her forward.

"I don't need your help!"

"You're getting it anyway."

At the end of the hall, Nonee stood by an open door, ready, Lyelee assumed, to slap attacking fungus out of the air as each of them passed.

Destros, Gearing, and Captain Yansav had come to a stop just inside the new room, almost but not quite blocking the way. Harris stood off to one side, throat working under his beard. The room was hexagonal; the walls were floor-to-ceiling windows made of huge sheets of impossibly flat glass that tinted the light a pale green and the dancing dust a glittering gold. The glass in the scholars' solar had cost a small fortune. This must have cost a large one. The visible parts of the floor were patterned tiles, deep green vines still vibrant around the edges of each square. The glass doors at the far end of the room opened into an overgrown garden.

But all that became irrelevant next to the pillars of fungus, some as tall as . . .

People.

"These were people." Now she'd said it, Lyelee could see the soft definition of heads and arms and legs, legs that spread out at the floor into a broad, fluted base. "Is this the result if you can't break free of the fungus?"

Nonee traced a path through them without making contact. "Yes."

"Did they stand there and let it happen?" Servan asked. When Lyelee turned toward her, she was wiping the tip of an arrow off against her thigh. "Face it, that stuff in the hall wasn't exactly fast."

"It's been there for years," Keetin said as he began to circle the outside of the room. "Maybe it slowed down as it got older, like so many things do."

Gearing huffed out an indignant breath of air, but before he could protest, Harris's quiet voice silenced the room again.

"This was a child."

"It has less definition than the larger pillars," Lyelee noted, joining him. "Because it had less substance? Because its structure was incomplete and therefore less rigid?"

"They're not an it, Scholar." Harris inclined his head toward the child fungus and continued toward the door.

With all eyes avoiding the dead child, Lyelee broke off a small, protruding piece and slid it into her satchel, not wanting to combine and possibly contaminate it with the sample in her pocket. "So we're leaving? Without exploring the building? Just walking away from any knowledge it could hold?"

"Knowing about this," Ryan replied, "about fungus people, that's knowledge enough for me."

"And if we're walking away from information that could benefit Marsan?"

"Then we are. Nothing that causes this kind of suffering would be worth the cost."

"You don't know that they suffered. And you can't put a price on knowledge you don't yet have." She glanced around the room, but not even Gearing met her gaze. Surprisingly, Nonee did.

Head cocked, the weapon spent what felt like half a day searching her face and finally said, "Ryan Heir is in command."

"Of you." She stood motionless until Nonee looked away. Had she found what she'd been looking for? What *had* she been looking for?

Ryan sighed loudly enough to draw all attention to him. "Feel free to stay behind and search the place, Scholars, but we won't wait for you. The Black Flame has flickered and we have fuel to retrieve."

Heads nodded. Lyelee sighed back at him. "I know why you're here."

"Why we're here." His chin, covered in multiple lengths of his ridiculous beard, lifted and his eyes narrowed. "Outside. Now."

"Sir!" Captain Yansav smacked her fist against her chest—a Shurlian salute she hadn't made since the first days on the road. Lyelee hoped its reappearance was sarcasm, but suspected it wasn't. "Servan, on point. Let us know what you see. Destros, watch her back."

"Captain."

"On it, Cap."

It would make more sense to send Nonee. They had no more idea of what they'd face out that door than they did any previous door, but Lyelee knew the captain was making a point. Supporting the illusion that Ryan was in charge was clearly more important than safety.

Although they started moving first, the guardians barely managed to stay ahead of the rest of the group. It seemed no one wanted to stay and find out how this had happened.

"There are other rooms," Lyelee began, and stopped when it was clear no one was listening.

"I don't get how anyone could stand still and let this happen." Servan had reached the open semicircle of floor just inside the exit. "If the fungus in the hall was the cause . . ."

"If you were on your own, and the same number dropped on you as dropped on us in the hall . . ." Beside her, Destros shook his head. "The stuff was heading for Scholar Gearing's mouth when Lord Marsan grabbed it. Maybe if it gets inside this happens."

Lyelee remembered how it felt as if her fingers had merged into the fungus. "The numbing factor, once absorbed, slows the victim and assists the colonizing factor in entering the body. Notice the relaxed slump of the shoulders, a posture that supports the theory."

The guardians at the door turned with everyone else to stare.

"No sympathy for the dead?" Ryan asked.

"Sympathy seems a little pointless when they've been dead for so long. I'd prefer to understand what killed them."

"That's not . . ." He closed his eyes for a moment and when he opened them said, "Let's go."

Even Gearing shuffled into motion—then stumbled, and tipped sideways as he recovered, arms flailing.

The closest fungus toppled and shattered, breaking apart with a soft *poof, poof.*

"Run!" Nonee scooped up Gearing, and raced for the door. "Don't breathe in the spores!"

Breathing in the spores would certainly give the fungus access to a warm, moist interior . . .

How long would it take? Did the infected remain aware?

The featureless faces all seemed to be watching her.

She ran.

Harris caught her arm as she tripped over the threshold, hauling her upright and propelling her further away from the building as Ryan and Keetin each grabbed one of the huge glass doors and pushed them shut.

"The glass should be broken," Gearing noted.

The captain's brows met under the edge of her helm. "That's what you take from this, Scholar?"

"It's a valid observation, given the time they've remained unbroken. We can record this as further evidence of beneficial mage-craft."

"No such thing," Ryan declared, rolling a stone planter in front of the doors. "It's unbroken glass around a room of people turned to fungus."

"The second point doesn't cancel out the first," Gearing told him.

"Are you expecting them to charge out after us?" Lyelee asked, gesturing at the planter.

Ryan smiled tightly. "It's what you don't expect in the Broken Lands that can kill you."

"We can inscribe that on your chronicle."

"You can inscribe that on your . . ."

"We should put in some distance." Keetin moved between them. "Spores are small and I doubt those doors are airtight."

"Spores are small," Gearing muttered beside her. "When we return I need to have a word with the Master of the Teaching Scholars."

"Make them small words," Lyelee agreed.

A stone path led straight from the glass doors to a gate in the surrounding stone wall, the garden a tangled thicket crowding up against either side, huge pink flowers blooming among finger-length thorns—a bird skull impaled on one, a rotting squirrel on another.

"Burn it!" Destros yanked his pack free of the branches and three sets of desiccated wings dropped to the ground.

Small white mushrooms gleamed in the leaf litter.

"Harris, your hand." Lyelee nodded toward a line of blood down one finger as he freed the corner of her pack from the thorns.

"Damage I did going through the darkness, Scholar." He showed her his knuckles. "Keep cracking the scabs when I use my hand, that's all."

"Good. In case these thorns are poisonous," she added, when he raised a brow. All things considered, it seemed like a logical assumption. "Better it's an old wound than a new one."

"Yes, Scholar. Your cheek is bleeding as well. It might be better not to touch it until you wash your hands."

She paused, one hand, the hand she'd thrust into the fungus, half raised. "Good point."

The gate was locked or the latch had rusted shut. Ryan, with a complete disregard for preservation, told Nonee to knock it down. While she waited, Lyelee glanced around the garden. With luck, there'd be a strangle vine or something similar she could sample. If she could get a leaf node, there was a chance she could . . .

The tall, pale, vaguely egg-shaped rock tucked into a corner of the garden looked familiar. The same broad, shallow dent in the upper curve. Lyelee squinted. The same hint of a face?

She took a step off the path only to be hauled back by her pack.

"Come on, Scholar." Destros tugged her toward the gate. "We're leaving."

"Unhand me! I need to . . ."

"Not be a fungus."

"Not be treated like a package!" When he released her, she took two steps back, but couldn't see the rock. Had she ever seen the rock? Of course she had. It had moved into the meadow; it could move out of the garden. For variable definitions of the word *move*, given that it was a rock.

"Scholar."

Free me. It had sounded surprisingly calm about it.

"Scholar!"

"Fine." Lyelee pushed past the big guardian and out the gate.

The gate led out onto the inner edge of a huge, flat plateau that ended in a curved cliff. Below the cliff was a very large lake. As they all took a moment to catch their breath, Lyelee realized the sun wasn't where she expected it to be. "How far have we traveled?"

Nonee shrugged. "No way of knowing."

"There is always a way of knowing. How can you live in such willful ignorance?"

Nonee shrugged again.

Keetin snorted. "She does okay."

"You'd know," Lyelee muttered, thumbs stuffed under her pack straps to hold her hands in place. Her cheek itched and she could feel a line of blood crossing her jaw. It would feel so good to throw herself into the lake, wash away the greasy patina of grime and the stupidity she was forced to travel with. A small patch of fog rested on the water. Her gaze skipped past it—nothing good came of fog in the Broken Lands—and she focused on the distant headland. "Is that a building?"

"Yes."

Given the distance, it had to be enormous. "Is that where we're going?"

"Yes."

"It looks like it grew out of the water." Servan had her helm in her hand, face lifted into the breeze. "Or grew down into the water."

"Like fungus?" Destros asked.

"Too soon," Servan muttered under Nonee's emphatic denial.

"Right." Ryan adjusted his pack and stepped forward. "Just a bit farther before we rest. Scholar Gearing . . . ?"

"I can go a little longer," Gearing sighed. "If we stay away from stairs."

"What the scholar said." Servan held out her fist and waited until Gearing finally tapped it.

Spread out—Lyelee didn't know about the others, but she needed a little distance after nearly a day and a half of walking in single file—they crossed the plateau toward the cliff edge.

"I wonder what's keeping the ground cover so short?" The breeze carried Destros's voice to her.

"Carnivorous sheep?" Keetin suggested.

"Why would you even say something like that, my lord?"

"Carnivorous sheep wouldn't be eating the grass," Lyelee sighed. "That's explicit in the word *carnivorous*."

About halfway to the cliff, Lyelee turned to look back and realized the building they'd just exited continued out onto a promontory similar to the one across the bay. Behind the garden wall, behind the conservatory, the tree-covered land gained elevation until it curved out into the water. She could see multiple walls stacked in strange angles, some still rising to a jumble of curved roofs. Trees grew through the ruins, and the apparent size of those trees at such a distance gave her some idea of the ruins' scale. "Nonee, is that a mage-tower?"

"Yes."

Clutching the straps of her pack, she hurried to catch up, grabbing Nonee's arm to slow her when she came alongside. "Are you telling me that we were in a mage-tower?"

"No." Nonee stopped and turned. "In the farthest building from the tower. There's an entire village between that building and the tower."

"The tower is up there under the trees?"

"In the trees."

"Mages couldn't have transported directly from the small tower to the mage-towers," Gearing said, joining them. "If the mages didn't get along, that kind of access would be a security problem." He huffed out a breathy, self-conscious chuckle. "And I think we can safely say they didn't get along."

"Given the fungus," Servan added, "I think we can safely say there was also a security problem."

"The point is," Lyelee interjected before anyone else could join in, "we're walking away from a mage-tower. Walking away and ignoring information that could open the past!"

Everyone turned to stare. She might have been shouting by the end.

Nonee's massive shoulders rose and fell. "There's no fuel there."

"I did say you could stay, Lyelee," Ryan called.

She flicked fire at him and ignored Gearing's disapproving grumble at the vulgarity. "We're walking away from history!"

"And toward history." Nonee nodded across the bay, at the distant jumble of light and shadow. "It wasn't a pleasant history."

Lyelee rolled her eyes. "Pleasant, unpleasant; that's not relevant."

"Learning about that past . . ."

"Studying the past. Scholars study, others learn from us."

Nonee cocked her head and Lyelee could almost feel the weight of her gaze. "Yes," she said at last, sounding sad about being corrected, as though Lyelee had declared Arianna's teaching of language insufficient.

Which wasn't Lyelee's problem. She rubbed at the cut on her cheek, grown tight and painful in the sunlight, and stared wide-eyed down at the red on her fingers. She hadn't washed the fungus off her hands.

NONEE.NOW

Nonee could hear the wistfulness in Ryan Heir's voice, knew he wanted to make camp here on the plateau where there'd be no eyes in the surrounding shadows. "It's too open up here," she told him. "If a wind comes off the water at night, you'll be blown into the swamp."

"*The* swamp? The swamp from the Heir's Chronicle?"

"Possibly."

"Possibly? How many swamps are there on the way to the fuel?"

"No way to know." She shrugged. "Things change."

"Of course they do." Gaze locked on the horizon, he sighed. "Let me guess, there's still a few unleashed mage-winds blowing around and if a wind comes off the water at night it'll be an attack."

"Possibly."

He ignored her weak attempt at humor and sighed again. "And there's no knowing what kind of an attack it'll be until after it happens."

"Yes." Most of the winds had weakened and disappeared when the mages lost control, but the plateau was exposed and most didn't mean all. The fog patch out on the lake had drifted toward the far shore. With luck, it'd stay there.

"That shimmer . . . ?"

"Just heat. Natural."

Ryan Heir visibly gathered himself and turned. Sometimes Nonee forgot how young he was, then he'd move in such a way as to remind her. "We'll eat up here then, in the open. Rest for a while. There'll be plenty of light remaining to head for . . . Where?"

Nonee waved toward the faint indication of a road, barely visible through the grass. It ran past the far side of the garden wall, led down off the plateau toward the bay, and ultimately to the other tower. Boe Mah Sing and Tanika Fleshrender had been friends. Or as close as mages came. When the Mage War began—although not yet a war—they'd been on the same side. That hadn't lasted. "The road will flatten and widen when it turns halfway down the cliff. There's a place that's sheltered and defensible."

"Halfway?" His brows drew in. "We can't make it to the bottom before dark?"

"No."

He glanced back at the curve of the garden wall, then out over the water, then at her. Then he nodded. "Halfway it is." Leaving the edge of the cliff, he called out instructions to rest and eat. Not quite giving orders, although intending to be obeyed. Garrett Heir had used the same tone.

Raising her head, Nonee could see birds circling over the ruins of the closer tower. She wondered if their ancestors had gotten to pick Boe Mah Sing's bones clean. It would have been the least he'd owed them.

"Here." She handed the corked pot to Harris. "For your knuckles."

"This is what you gave the scholar novitiate? After the bird?"

"Yes. Arianna makes . . ." She paused and swallowed the word. ". . . made it to prevent infection."

Harris's expression held sympathy. "Did you help?"

"Not with this." She spread her hands. "Too big for the delicate work."

Working the cork free, he drew in a deep breath. "It smells like honey."

"Arianna made plenty that smells like honey. She says . . . said good-tasting medicine would actually be used." The familiar scent, the familiar glisten of the cream over abraded skin deepened the ache.

"Arianna sounds like she was very wise." Pushing the cork back into place, he returned the jar. "I'll remember her name. The dead live on if their names are remembered," he added. And frowned. "Not necro . . . necromatically." He touched his chest. "Here."

"Yes." The jar looked like a child's toy in her hand.

Harris cleared his throat, dropped his attention to his pack, and pulled out a string of summer sausage. "We'll need water in the next day or two."

It smelled like the sausage Arianna took in trade when Ingin Soral the butcher needed the pain in her shoulder eased. "There'll be plenty of water soon."

He huffed out a quiet laugh. "Why doesn't that sound like a good thing?"

Nonee allowed the corners of her mouth to rise into the hint of a smile. "Because you've been paying attention."

❦

"Isn't it inconvenient for a weapon to help heal wounds when your purpose is to cause them?"

Nonee stared at Kalyealee who-could-be-heir for a long moment. In the Broken Lands, she was a weapon, no matter how much more than a weapon she'd been as a part of Arianna's life. She held out her hand for the jar.

"I want to take this back to the Scholar's Hall and have it analyzed."

"No."

Kalyealee who-could-be-heir set the jar on Nonee's palm as though she'd always intended to return it. "If we're going to waste time . . ."

With no immediate threat and clear sight lines, even the guardians had relaxed. Curtin's name brought fond laughter as they shared memories of him. That was good. Harris had handed out portions of food then sat a little to one side to eat his own share. Keetin Norwin-cee had made a number of suggestive statements about sausages until Ryan Heir had thrown the last radish at him. Scholar Gearing had eaten and gone to sleep, head on his pack, hands clutched around his satchel, face turned toward the sun.

". . . tell me about Tanika Fleshrender's tower. It doesn't look like a tower," Kalyealee who-could-be-heir pointed out dismissively. "A tower is a narrow structure taller than its surroundings. Even from here, that is an architectural horror story."

"Yes."

Kalyealee who-could-be-heir waited.

Nonee waited longer.

"Oh, for . . ." Kalyealee who-could-be-heir rolled her eyes. "What's it like on the inside?"

"Larger. Constantly changing between fixed points."

"Like the Broken Lands in miniature."

"Yes." Nonee turned to stare across the lake at the headland. She'd never thought of it that way. "The village is on the far side." As Kalyealee who-could-be-heir opened her mouth, she added, "All the towers had villages. Servants, subjects."

Experiments.

Nonee remembered the tank, and the blood, and those who died birthing monsters.

"Will we be taking this mage road straight to Tanika Fleshrender's tower?" Ryan Heir asked once camp had been set up and Harris had lit a small fire, using twists of dried grasses for fuel.

"Yes." Nonee settled into a squat, the memories closer than they'd ever been. She pressed her palm against the road, still warm from the heat of the day.

The roads had been built long before Tanika Fleshrender built her, but the mages liked to talk about themselves and Tanika Fleshrender enjoyed company. On her terms. They told stories of how back in the before days, they'd gathered together, personal animosity buried under the unstoppable power of six mages cooperating, and traveled to find a place where they'd have the freedom to be themselves. When they'd landed at the north end of the Great Lake and headed toward an empty land—empty but for a few scattered, primitive settlements, easily dealt with—they'd needed a way to be both connected and separated from the world. The Mage Road had unfolded beneath their feet as they walked. Or as their litter bearers had walked. One mage, Nonee assumed it was Dybrin Amsputov, had ridden a giant lizard.

Kalyealee who-could-be-heir folded her arms. "So, no more portals."

"One more. But you'd have to spring the trap."

"The trap?" Ryan Heir shook his head. "Of course there's a trap."

"Traps." She straightened and remembered ships crossing the lake and docking at the pier. She remembered the last ship and how the sailors had screamed. "The harbor at the bottom of hill was neutral ground, but when the road begins to rise again, there's traps."

"But only one portal." Ryan Heir sounded weary of the whole thing.

Nonee almost smiled. "Yes."

Kalyealee who-could-be-heir folded her arms and glared. "There's no mention of traps in the Heir's Chronicle."

"Because Garrett Heir didn't come this way, and he faced other . . ."

"Problems?" Scholar Gearing offered.

She wondered what Garrett Heir had written in his Heir's Chronicle. "Yes."

GARRETT.THEN

Garrett felt the ground give below his foot, stepped back, and watched the indent fill with brackish water. "It's getting wetter."

"It's about to be a swamp." Arianna stabbed the ground ahead of her with her staff. "I'm sorry," she continued when Garrett turned to glare, "weren't we stating the obvious?"

He heard Petre manage a breathy laugh so he forgave the comment, stepped onto a slightly higher bit of ground, and said, "At least the water levels are low."

"Sir?"

He shifted far enough to see Malcolm frowning, head cocked. The younger man could hear a frog fart in a storm, according to Norik. "What is it, Malcolm?"

"There's something moving out there. Something big."

"Out there?"

Malcolm waved his arm, a huge, sweeping movement that didn't narrow down the direction. "In the swamp."

Garrett raised a hand, and when the sounds of his companions dropped to quiet breathing and the occasional sniff, he tried to hear something more than the breeze rattling seed pods and the distant complaints of crows. He thought . . . He might have heard . . . "Was it moving in the water?"

"Yes, sir."

Reptiles large enough to take down cattle lived in the delta where the southern end of the Great Lake feathered before emptying into the sea. Crocodiles. Ganapods. Bilong lizards. While scholars might insist they were too far north for reptiles that large, the scholars were in Marsanport and they were in the Broken Lands and all bets were off. "I suggest we try to stay out of the water."

"It's about to be a swamp," Arianna said again; pointedly, as though he hadn't noticed.

He shot her an insincere, Court smile. "Then we try hard. Sing out if you hear it again, Malcolm."

"Yes, sir."

"By the Snow Moon, this high in the mountains, the water would be frozen solid. Maybe not the deepest parts, but the rest." Arianna jerked her staff out of the mud and flicked a dark lump off the end before Garrett could identify it. There might have been tentacles. "If you'd left home just half a moon later, the walking would be so much easier." She sighed, and added a step later, "At least there's no bugs."

From a distance it looked as if the trees standing with their roots submerged had answered the season and dropped their leaves. Up close, it was obvious they were dead.

"Lots of firewood," Norik noted, breaking off a branch and smacking it into punky pieces against the trunk. "Or not." He dusted off his palms. "Bigger problem might be finding a dry spot to build a fire."

There was dry ground not far behind them and nothing but dead trees, muddy hummocks, and water ahead. Garrett moved closer to the weapon, who stared out at the swamp, brow furrowed, and touched her lightly on the arm to get her attention. "We have to go through?"

She sighed. "Yes."

"There's no way around?"

Her focus remained on the swamp.

"If there was, I'm sure Uvili would have taken it." Arianna sounded certain. Garrett envied that just a little.

If the portal had sent them here, perhaps they were meant to be here. Perhaps, but he doubted it. Mage-craft was not to be trusted. "Did you hear what Malcolm heard?" he asked the weapon.

She shrugged.

"You heard something?"

"Yes."

"Something large?"

"Yes."

"Do you know what it was?"

She shrugged again.

Arianna snickered.

And that answered the question of who'd taught the weapon the dismissive gesture. Not that Garrett had had much doubt. "All right." It wasn't, but they couldn't stand around waiting for the Frost Moon. "Lead on. And remember we're not as waterproof as you."

"We're exactly as waterproof as she is," Arianna protested. "Skin is skin."

"Hers turns blades."

"She's barefoot."

"Wet boots are going to be just as cold and she won't feel it."

"Are you sure? Have you asked her?"

The weapon turned pointedly toward them.

If she'd had eyebrows, Garrett knew they'd be up. "Right. We're coming." Into the swamp.

"When you stir it up, it smells like something died," Petre muttered.

And there was that.

"Hold!"

The weapon stopped and turned to stare back at him, her expression edging on impatience. Garrett wondered if Arianna had taught her that as well. "There's something off to the right . . ."

Moving slowly, testing his footing with a branch, he pushed his way through a line of dead, hip-high bushes and saw a woman walking chest-deep in the center of an open channel. No . . . not walking, not with moss growing on her head and shoulders. "It's a statue."

"No." The weapon stood just behind him.

"No?"

"Person."

"It's a statue of a person."

"No."

He saw a breeze stir the end of a weed dangling from the statue's extended arm. Except there was no breeze. "Is it moving?"

"Slow." She frowned and glanced over at the healer, the entire company having gathered around them.

"Moving slowly?" Arianna asked.

The weapon shook her head. "Time."

"Time is moving slowly?"

"Yes."

"Mage-craft!" Malcolm surged forward to get a better look, sword tangling in the dead bushes.

Garrett had realized early on that Arianna granted both boys more leeway than either Norik or himself, but she snapped at Malcolm to be careful and clutched the weapon's arm. "She's alive?"

"Yes."

"Can we save her?"

"No."

"Is it one of the mages?" Petre asked, leaning against Norik's side, injured arm bound to his chest.

"No."

The water in the center of the channel shimmered in the weak light coming through the cloud cover. It looked as though oil had been spilled and had never dissipated, clinging instead around the walking woman.

"We can't just leave her," Arianna protested.

"We can't do anything for her." He paused. Sighed. And surrendered. "Uvili, can we help her?"

"No." She led the way north, along the channel.

They crossed on a crumbling stone bridge, the weapon carrying their packs across one at a time to keep the shifting weight from affecting their balance. Then she carried Petre across while they all ignored his protests. The surrounding water was murky, not oily, but Garrett considered the time taken well spent.

✍

"We need to find a place to camp," Arianna declared, stopping suddenly.

Garrett glanced up. Bands of orange streaked the sky just above the horizon. "We still have light enough to find our footing."

"Now, but we won't soon. This isn't the sort of place . . ." Her gesture took in the water, the hummocks of dead grass, the low bushes. The ripples. ". . . we can settle into after dark. And Petre needs to rest."

"I wanted to make more distance."

"Yes, well, Petre wants his hand back and I want one of the scavengers to find me a second pearl earring. You don't always get what you want. I can see higher ground off that way."

He sighted along her outstretched arm. "Could be nothing more than a clump of taller trees."

Arianna ignored him and picked her way forward until she could put a hand on the weapon's wrist, using her staff to point to where the clump of trees was silhouetted against the sky. When the weapon turned to him, Garrett nodded. He hated to admit it, but the healer was right. Petre needed to rest. A few moments later, when the weapon beckoned them forward, he was glad to go.

The trees grew on a rough circle of higher ground nearly as large as the training corral at the Citadel. All seven grew in the same quarter of the island, surrounded by thorn bushes. It wouldn't be worth the bloodshed to put them to the axe. Dead bracken, flattened into multiple circles in multiple sizes, covered the rest of the ground. Two boulders, one round, one plinth-like, nestled in the broadest arc of the eastern curve.

When they found dry ground under the sod lifted for the fire pit, even the weapon looked relieved.

✍

"I miss Kanalik," Garrett sighed, his back against his pack, his hands wrapped around a mug of tea. "You never realize how much you've come to depend on a horse until he's not there."

"He hates water," Norik said flatly. "You couldn't ride him in this."

"I know. But he was warm."

The temperature dropped further as the dark deepened and it soon became obvious they'd have to spend the night wrapped around each other. His feet painfully cold, even in dry socks, Garrett almost envied Petre, who'd be tucked between Malcolm on one side and Arianna on the other.

"The better to keep an eye on his breathing," she explained softly, waiting beside him as the boys got comfortable.

"Do you stay this close to all your patients?" He didn't mean anything by it, but he knew it was a mistake the moment the words left his mouth.

Her eyes narrowed. "The ones who lose a hand and have to sleep in a swamp, yes."

As she strode away, Norik raised his brows and shook his head. "Is this you flirting?" he asked. "Because you burn it, if it is."

"I'm not flirting."

"Good."

"You're sleeping on the other side of her."

"Color me surprised."

❧

Garrett half expected to wake to frost, but it was almost warm, even after he untangled himself from the pile of bodies. He stretched, pissed into the channel that ran past the southeast curve of the island—the water was already unsuitable for drinking so why not—froze for a moment, then tucked himself away as if he hadn't seen movement from the corner of one eye. Not the something Malcolm had heard but perhaps the evidence of its passage. He walked over to where the weapon stood by the taller rock.

Her chin was up, her nostrils flared, and muscles twitched and danced under her skin, evidence of the internal battle she fought to keep herself still. She reminded him of a bird dog with a scent, held in place by her master's command.

"I got a glimpse," he said softly, placing her body in the way of anyone watching from the swamp. Provided they'd remained where he'd seen them. Thought he'd seen them. "What's out there?"

Frowning, she shook her head.

"You don't know?"

She shrugged.

He shifted enough to see past the weapon's bulk, but hopefully not enough to be obvious. He could see thorn bushes and bracken swaying, a broken branch dangling from a tree, and lingering shadows, deeper and darker than they should have been. Either something large and silent had passed or a random and independent breeze, mage-crafted for no good reason, hid in the swamp.

"Morning, sir."

"Malcolm."

He smiled as Malcolm staggered to the edge of dry land and fumbled with his trousers, turning aside to give what privacy he could. He turned again as the weapon surged past him, and swore as she hooked a massive arm around Malcolm's waist, pulling him back to solid land. The edge of the island crumbled, clots of dirt splashing into the channel.

Ripples stretched the oily sheen in multiple directions.

The oily sheen was new.

"Where the flame did that come from?"

"War."

"I meant just now."

She made a contemplative noise and said, "Swamp."

Malcolm snickered.

Garrett let it go. Testing his footing, he leaned over and looked into the water. He stroked a hand over his beard. His reflection did the same.

Then his beard and hair grew gray. His cheeks hollowed. His eyes sank in. His skin pleated. He lost two teeth on the left side. His ears jutted out from the sides of his head, earrings emphasizing how long and dangling his lobes had become.

The weapon's hand broke his line of sight and she pushed him gently but inexorably back until he stood by Malcolm's side, breathing as though he'd been running, not standing still. "What was that?"

"Time."

"Like the mage-crafted time that slowed the walking woman?"

"Yes." She waved an arm. "All here."

"All over the swamp?"

"Yes."

"Are you saying there's patches of time out of joint all over the swamp?" Arianna asked.

He hadn't heard Arianna join them.

"Yes."

"And if we fall into one?" He fought the urge to move to the center of the island and stay there. The woman in the water had been slowed. His reflection had aged at high speed.

The weapon shrugged.

Arianna smiled proudly.

The sky was a solid sheet of muddy gray.

"I think it's going to rain."

Garrett glanced over at Petre, carefully stepping from one hummock to another as they left the island. "What makes you say that?"

"My wrist hurts." Garrett blinked and Petre laughed, soft and breathy. "Get it, my lord? Like a wound that tells the weather."

"That'll be useful." Not as useful as a hand, but he was pleased Petre could joke about it. Despair killed as surely as blood loss, if not as quickly. Not that he approved of the message. His boots were already wet and they'd barely set out.

"Garrett."

He raised a hand to hold the others in place before he moved as quickly as possible up to Norik's side.

"Look there."

It looked like a footprint. A large footprint filled with water, surrounded by water. Then the water rose a bit further, and it was gone.

"Look familiar to you?" Norik nodded toward the weapon. "You think she was wandering around out here last night?"

If he squinted, he thought he could still see the imprint of individual toes. "She was on watch. If she thought something was heading in, she might have headed out to cut it off."

"You going to ask her?"

"No."

Norik made a noncommittal sound. "Why not?"

"We need to trust her to do her job."

"She can't disobey you."

"I know." His father wouldn't have trusted her.

But if she hadn't left the island, what then?

The air grew damper. Then the dampness separated into individual drops. Cold water dribbled down the back of his neck, sending a line of ice under the layers intended to keep him warm and dry.

"Next time," he grumbled, shifting his shoulders under the weight of his pack, "we do this in the summer."

Norik snorted. "Next time, it won't be our . . ."

Garrett froze as a howl cut off the end of Norik's response. He'd have liked to call it a distant noise, but it was uncomfortably close. "More lizard-dogs?" he asked, lowering his foot into the water as quietly as possible.

The weapon stood so still he wondered, just for a moment, if she'd been caught in mage-craft. Then her shoulders sagged and she said, "No."

No. He'd known it hadn't been lizard-dogs. Rather than braided cries announcing the strength of a hunting pack, this had been a single, deeper voice, undulating up and down the scale like one of the singers his father had brought in from Southport.

"It sounded . . ." Arianna paused, frowned, and shook her head.

"You recognize it?"

"No."

For all their voices were nothing alike, the healer's denial sounded remarkably like the weapon's.

He counted his heartbeat while they waited for the howl to sound again. At ninety he said, "Let's go. We might as well be a moving target."

He might have heard splashing in the distance. It might have been nothing.

When they stopped at midday, Petre's face had grayed, his eyes had sunk into purple shadows, and flecks of dried blood darkened the curve of his lower lip where his teeth had closed on soft flesh.

Garrett leaned close and pitched his voice for Norik's ears alone. "She could carry him."

"The healer? She's stronger than she looks, but . . ."

"The weapon, you ass."

Norik snorted. "She'd have to drop him if we're attacked. Still . . ." He chewed and swallowed a piece of jerky. ". . . lying at her feet's probably the safest place in the swamp."

"Unless she steps on him."

"There's that."

"The two of them could stay here."

"Petre and the weapon?"

"We could pick them up on the way back," Garrett continued, ignoring the question. Norik flaming well knew who he was talking about. "The weapon could find them again."

"Or find their corpses, if whatever's out there howling finds them first."

"Could be a frog. Some frogs have huge voices."

Both Norik's brows went up. "And feet?"

Garrett ignored that too. "Petre needs rest and warmth. He won't get that if we go on, or go back."

"So the weapon carries him?"

They turned together to watch the weapon chew something she'd pulled out of the mud.

Garrett sighed. "Looks like that's the best we can do."

<hr>

"No." Petre's chin rose. "I lost a hand, not a foot. I can walk."

"Now," Garrett agreed. "But the going will be easier once we're on dry land, so the weapon . . . so Uvili will carry you out of the swamp and you'll walk when every step doesn't take the effort of a half day's march."

"And if we're attacked?"

"You think she can't deal with anything that's stupid enough to attack the strongest member of the party first?"

Petre glanced over at the weapon, who blinked at him. Garrett didn't find that particularly comforting, but Petre's shoulders came down as he visibly relaxed. "I guess she'll have time to put me down."

<hr>

They could see the land ahead rising, but darkness fell before they reached the edge of the swamp. Garrett had decided to keep going, regardless of the potential pitfalls—literally pitfalls, the world had dropped away under his feet that afternoon and only Norik's quick reaction had kept him from sinking into the suddenly loose mud—but agreed to stop when they found another island, smaller than the one they'd spent their first night on, but just as dry.

Petre looked a lot better.

"He fell asleep," Arianna told him, as Petre hurried away from the weapon, his cheeks dark.

It took Garrett a moment to recognize the expression on the weapon's face. She didn't know what she'd done to drive Petre away. As Malcolm offered to hold Petre's dick and got a punch in the arm from his friend's remaining fist, Garrett crossed to her side. "He's embarrassed." When she turned to face him, he nodded toward Petre. "He doesn't want you to think he's weak. It might be best if you stay away from him for a while until he gets over himself."

She frowned, then she nodded and moved as far in the opposite direction as the island allowed.

It allowed enough distance that when the edge collapsed under Petre's feet as the other island's had under Malcolm's, she wasn't close enough. She managed to grab hold of the worn hem of his jacket.

The ragged edge tore.

Petre twisted as he hit the water, his hair suddenly gray, then gone— showing scalp then skull. He was a rotting corpse by the time he was fully submerged.

"No!" Arianna's hand held the weapon in place the way his hadn't. "He's dead and we don't know what the mage-craft will do to you!"

Malcolm sobbed, wrapped in Norik's arms.

Garrett could see the gleam of bone under the water's oily surface. He couldn't stop thinking of how Petre's beard hadn't yet grown together under his chin, the bare skin exposed by his defiance when he argued against being carried. He wanted to scoop out the bones and take them home, but he couldn't.

The loss of a hand wouldn't have been enough to stop Petre from riding back to Marsanport with them.

He hated himself for realizing they could move faster now.

RYAN.NOW

Ryan would have had them on the road at dawn, but, as irritated as he was by the delays, he didn't want to kill Scholar Gearing, so they waited until the sun was a handspan above the horizon before waking the old man. Exhaustion had granted him a better night than the rest of them. Ryan had dreamed of the Black Flame engulfing Marsanport, Keetin had muttered about stones piled on his chest, and Lyelee had been smiling both in her sleep and after she woke, a sharp bared-teeth expression that made the hair lift on the back of Ryan's neck.

"Is that the swamp where Petre D'Certif-cee died?" When Nonee turned, frowning, Lyelee rolled her eyes. "According to the chronicle, he died in a swamp in sight of dry land that led to the mage-tower and the fuel." She waved toward the fetid water, tufts of coarse grasses, and dead trees that stretched off on the left of the road. "Swamp." And then toward the headland. "Mage-tower that holds the fuel."

"Yes." Nonee's fists opened and closed by her sides. "And no. This is probably the swamp. But a different part of the swamp."

"It was *possibly* the swamp on top of the plateau," Ryan reminded her.

She shrugged. "It smells the same."

"The type of mage-craft that killed him appeared at the previous campsite as well," Lyelee said before Ryan could argue that *all* swamps smelled the same. "Do you think it was drawn to intruders in its territory?"

Nonee exhaled a long breath. "Yes."

Ryan frowned. The chronicle reported that Petre had been killed by lingering mage-craft that had appeared like an oil slick on the water. It said nothing about any mage-craft appearing at the previous camp. But Nonee confirmed it had happened. Where had Lyelee learned about it?

"So the mage-craft," Lyelee continued, "and according to the chronicle, this was pure mage-craft not a creature, has agency?"

"No."

"Then the land itself has agency?"

Nonee stared into the swamp for a moment. "Maybe."

"Maybe," Lyelee repeated, rolling her eyes. "I'll need to conduct a few tests, and see if . . ."

"You didn't think to tell us that before?" Ryan interrupted. "That maybe the Broken Lands would be actively not only passively trying to kill us?"

Lyelee sputtered but Nonee swung around to face him. "Does it matter?

You knew the land kills, knew it would kill at least some of your company, and you came anyway."

"I had to!"

"Did you?"

"If the Black Flame goes out, Marsanport will fall!"

"Why?"

"Because . . ." Because that was what he'd been taught. What they'd all been taught. He jabbed a finger in Nonee's direction. "Stop asking me questions I can't answer!"

"Let's pick up the pace." Keetin raised his voice and Ryan wondered if the swamp was listening. "The sooner we get the fuel, the sooner we're out of here, and the happier I'll be."

※

As the road reached its lowest point, it became a barricade between the swamp on one side and a harbor on the other. A lane nearly filled in with boulders and dead, broken trees led to a low building.

The Lord Protector had taken shelter from a storm in a building down a lane just past a bridge.

The road continued toward a stone bridge that arced over the channel where the swamp spilled into the harbor.

"Nonee, is that," Ryan began.

"Yes."

"We'll stay well away, then."

"Good."

"Wait just one minute!" Gearing protested, indignation giving him strength. "We need to search for surviving evidence in order to expand our knowledge of . . ."

"No."

"You don't tell me no." Gearing folded his arms and scowled. "If we can confirm . . ." A roar out of the swamp cut him off. He staggered back, as though the sound had applied an actual physical force.

All three guardians had their weapons up and ready before Ryan managed to fumble his sword free.

A boulder arced out of the swamp and smashed onto the road. The road held, the boulder shattered. He thought he heard bells chiming and then realized it was the sound of stone fragments hitting scale armor.

"Back up the road!" Captain Yansav pointed with her sword as though she thought they might have forgotten what *back up the road* meant. Heart pounding, Ryan wasn't entirely certain he hadn't.

"We should go forward!" Lyelee protested.

Before Ryan could grab Lyelee's arm, a second boulder landed nearer the bridge. Lyelee stumbled back, arms windmilling, and would have fallen had Keetin not caught her.

She shook free of his hold. "We have to get over the bridge before it's destroyed!"

What would Donal do?

"I'd get over the bridge before it's destroyed, not run away with my head up my ass."

"Ryan!"

A hand grabbed his shoulder. He managed to focus on Keetin's face. "I heard . . ."

A dripping log hit the road, the wet pieces slamming against Nonee's legs.

Who'd load a siege engine with a log?

"Captain! There!" Servan fired.

Ryan thought he saw a large animal moving through the underbrush, but the trunks of dead trees broke the movement into segments and he couldn't identify what it was. Given the size and the speed, it should have made more noise.

Nonee charged forward. Ryan knew she was fast; he hadn't realized how fast.

Something in the swamp roared again and an enormous skull sailed over Nonee's head, shattering against the road, spraying teeth. Destros's shin guard rang. He swore and lurched sideways.

"Back!" Ryan shoved Lyelee into motion. Caught a fold of Keetin's sleeve and yanked. "Everyone back! Destros?"

"I'm good, my lord." He stumbled once, twice, then he found his balance, turned and moved backward up the road, axes ready.

Over the sound of feet pounding against the Mage Road, of armor jangling, of his blood surging in his ears and his breath catching in his throat, Ryan could hear trees breaking. And then he stopped caring about what was happening in the swamp because he needed all his energy to run uphill. Wearing a pack. And a scale vest. And holding a sword with only the oppressive heat to fight. "The Broken Lands has too many flaming hills!"

"Could be worse," Keetin gasped. "Could be stairs!"

They'd barely made it a quarter of the way back to where they'd camped the night before when Gearing fell and lay panting, unable to rise.

"Captain!"

Captain Yansav paused, took in Gearing and then Lyelee, who'd taken the chance to stop and had bent forward, forearms braced against her thighs. Ryan's legs trembled and sweat poured off his face. Keetin's face had darkened under his tan and turned a deep red. Ryan followed the captain's gaze as she swept it over the ridge of rock now rising between the swamp and the road.

It was quiet in the swamp. No sound of whatever had attacked them. No sound of Nonee.

Still holding her weapon, the captain dropped to one knee and pressed her free hand to Gearing's throat.

Servan frowned down on the scholar. "Is he dead?"

"Does he look dead?"

"Kind of does, yeah."

"He needs to be out of the sun." She looked up at Ryan.

Did Gearing need to be out of the sun more than the rest of them needed to not be crushed by falling boulders? The closest shade was back by where the skull had hit the road. Back down the road they'd just run up. But the swamp was silent. Of course, it had been silent before the first boulder had been flung. He had no idea what Nonee was doing.

What would Donal do?

"I'd let the scholar die. Of course, I wouldn't have been stupid enough to bring a scholar along."

"I'd maybe bring Lyelee," Corryn laughed. *"She can take care of herself."*

Josan snorted. *"And everyone else. She'd be a better Lord Protector than you would, slug."*

"Shut up!"

"Ryan?"

He shook off Keetin's hand. "Just working things out." It wasn't much of an explanation, but it would have to do. "Let's get the scholar into the shade."

Captain Yansav sheathed her sword. "Servan, get his pack off him."

"On it, Cap."

Ryan followed with the pack as the two guardians carried Gearing back down the hill. It wasn't significantly easier than going up. His knees threatened to buckle with every step.

When they reached the living tree at the end of the lane, Harris headed on toward the lake. Although Gearing's pack weighed half what his did, Ryan was happy to drop it, then his own, then his helm, then himself. Lyelee and Keetin had already sprawled on the sun-dried grass. "How is he?"

Captain Yansav dribbled water between the old man's lips. "Between heat, exertion, and age, not good."

"Captain?"

Ryan turned his head just far enough to see Harris holding a pot, water dripping off the bottom.

"How cold?" the captain asked.

"Not cold enough to do damage. Cold enough to help."

She beckoned him closer, then held out a hand. "I'm already down here and he's not likely to forgive you."

To forgive a retainer, Ryan realized.

"Not likely to forgive you either," Harris pointed out, handing over the pot.

"Yes, but I don't give a flaming shit." She shuffled back, turned Gearing's head to the side, and poured the water over it.

The scholar twitched, coughed, clutched at his satchel, and began to mumble an impressive stream of profanity.

Ryan wondered if Lyelee was taking notes.

❧

"You want to tell me what that was about?"

"Which *that*?" Ryan plucked sweat-damp linen away from his arm and didn't meet the captain's eyes.

"You shouted for someone to shut up when no one was talking."

He'd hoped she'd missed that while tending to Gearing. "It was just . . ."

He couldn't tell her he'd heard his dead brothers as clearly as he was hearing her. It wasn't in his head. Well, it was in his head, but he wasn't imagining it.

"You don't have that much imagination. And if you don't want to know what I'd do, don't ask."

"My lord? Ryan?"

"I was just trying to work things out. Uphill. Downhill. The scholar. Boulders." He managed half a grin. "Sometimes it gets loud in my head."

"I can imagine." She gripped his forearm and squeezed. "You made the right decision."

Had he?

"Probably not."

Ryan stared into the swamp. Nonee had been gone long enough for the sun to have moved beyond its zenith. Should they move on without her?

"I would, but then I'm not a useless tit without it around."

"Her," Ryan murmured.

"Lord Marsan." Breathing heavily, Gearing sagged forward as though he still wore his pack. "Who were you speaking to?"

"Myself." He felt his ears heat. "Should you be up and around?"

"Perhaps not, but I wondered, watching you standing here, why you haven't used The Word to command the weapon to return."

"What are you talking about?" Nonee's pack lay abandoned where she'd dropped it.

"The Word that controls her. The Word passed down from Captain Marsan to each of the Lord Protectors who came after."

Corryn snickered. *"He thinks you're an idiot."*

"I don't have a word."

Gearing's hand closed on his arm, his palm hot even through the fabric. "Then how do you control the weapon?"

"I don't *control* her, she's . . ."

"She's a mage-crafted weapon." Gearing's grip tightened. "If you don't control her . . ."

"I invoked the Last Command as I was instructed by the Lord Protector." He yanked his arm free. "Now explain yourself. What word?"

Gearing licked his lips and backed away. "Scholars surrender their sources only to a peer review."

"Not this time. You brought it up. What word?" Out of sight in the swamp, dry wood cracked. Ryan, who'd broken his arm when Josan had pushed him out of a tree for climbing too slowly, flinched.

Lips pursed, Gearing met his gaze, frowned, and finally sighed. "The mage who created the weapons, Tanika Fleshrender—ridiculous name—controlled each of them with a Word. She had a different Word for each weapon," he expanded before Ryan could ask. "The Word was woven into the mage-craft that created them. They can't refuse it."

How did he make capital letters so obvious? Ryan wondered. More importantly . . . "How do you know this?"

"I am a Schol . . ." Gearing's eyes widened at Ryan's expression and he took another step back, hands clutching his satchel. "Our archives contain notes and memoirs from the Five Thousand that were rejected for inclusion into the Captain's Chronicle by the scholars of the day."

Rejected. Ryan rolled the word over and didn't like what he found under it. Really didn't like having his suspicions confirmed. "The scholars deliberately left information out of the chronicles? Decided what should and shouldn't be known?"

Gearing waved it off. "If you publish every little detail, you bury what's actually important in trivia."

"Trivia?" He opened his mouth, closed it again, and finally found his voice. "I don't think the word that controls the weapon is trivial."

"If certain people knew the weapon could be controlled so easily, they'd want the Word. They'd be a danger to the Lord Protector."

Had Donal known the word?

Donal remained silent.

Of course he had.

"Do you know Nonee's word, Scholar?"

Drawing himself up, indignation adding height, Gearing glared down the length of his nose. "I do."

"Use it." Ryan jerked a hand toward the swamp. He wanted to demand that Gearing turn over the word so he could use it himself, but by the time Gearing finished whining about how scholars didn't just turn over information, the sun would be down. He unclenched his teeth and added, "Call Nonee back, Scholar Gearing. Marsanport needs the Black Flame, we need the fuel, and we need Nonee to get it."

"Now, Lord Marsan?"

"Yes, now!"

Gearing preened. Scholars enjoyed showing off the extent of their knowledge. Particularly knowledge they wouldn't share.

The word didn't come from either of the languages Ryan knew. Short and staccato, the sound drew a cold line down his back.

There was still no sign of Nonee.

Gearing opened his mouth again. Ryan stopped him. "Either she didn't hear you, or it didn't work. Either way, that's enough." He was a little surprised Gearing didn't argue, merely stared at him for a long moment, nodded once, then turned away.

A half-dozen birds cried out as they circled over a point deep in the swamp; insects buzzed around Ryan's head. Lyelee coughed, the sound close behind him. He turned to see her and Keetin standing together.

Keetin shifted, boot soles scuffing against the road. "She'll be back."

Heart pounding, afraid of being abandoned before they had the fuel, left to wander in the Broken Lands until they all joined Curtin in the final fire while Marsanport fell before the descendants of those they'd driven away, Ryan had to swallow before he could speak. "You don't know that."

"She has to follow the Last Command, right? If she's still out there, she's stopping something that could prevent you from getting to the fuel." He spread his hands. "When she's done that, she'll be back."

He wished he had Keetin's certainty.

"Unless she's destroyed," Lyelee said thoughtfully. "There's always a chance that she's been lured into the swamp by whatever destroyed the other five weapons. In which case, precedent suggests her odds of survival are low."

Keetin sighed. "You're not helping."

"I'm providing a plausible alternative." She stalked back across the road to join Gearing, a certain stiffness in her spine suggesting she hadn't known about the word either and she wasn't happy.

"She'll be back," Keetin repeated. "Nonee," he added before Ryan could respond. "We can't get rid of Lyelee."

He glanced over at his cousin in time to see her break off her flow of indignant words in order to cough into her elbow, still short of breath from the sprint to safety. "Gearing just told me that the scholars left parts out of the chronicles."

"The boring parts?"

"What?"

Keetin snickered. "You know why no one goes to the bathroom in books? Because it makes the pages stick together. And," he added, "no one wants to read the boring parts. I barely managed to get through what they didn't leave out."

"Sure, but what gives them the right to decide?"

"They're scholars."

"What gives scholars the right?"

"I dare you to ask Lyelee that."

"I don't . . ."

Keetin clucked softly.

"What are your orders, my lord?"

Ryan took a deep breath and wondered if Captain Yansav knew she'd saved him from an awkward conversation or if she'd merely grown tired of waiting for Nonee to return. He took a deep breath and looked around. It was a beautiful summer day, not as hot nor as humid as it had been, with a pleasant breeze blowing in off the lake. The water gleamed silvered blue. The headland rising up behind them held people-shaped fungus. The headland ahead of them no doubt held new horrors. The swamp . . . well, he could ignore the swamp until Nonee returned. Unless she never returned. Unless something else came out of the swamp.

"*Idiot,*" Donal muttered.

"We wait here," he said before the twins could add further commentary. "If Nonee's not back by dusk, we'll return to last night's campsite. It's a more defensible position," he added when the captain raised a brow. "In the morning, we return here, and we wait another day. If she's hasn't returned by then, we'll reassess."

"We know where we're going," Lyelee began and Ryan realized everyone but Gearing had gathered around while he was talking. "We can . . ."

"We wait. Unless you have a strategic objection, Captain."

"I don't, my lord." Ryan relaxed into her approval as she continued speaking. "Servan, eyes on the swamp. I want to know if you see so much as a water bug moving around in there."

"They breed big bugs in these parts, Cap?" Servan asked as she moved past her, bow in her left hand, quiver over her right shoulder. Face turned away from the captain, she winked at Ryan.

"Let's hope not. Everyone, stay aware of your surroundings, don't wander away. Destros, get Nonee's pack off the road. You're the only one of us with a flaming hope of carrying it."

Which was when Ryan remembered. "Destros, you were wounded!"

The big axeman laughed and stomped toward him, exaggerating the movement of the injured leg. "Not a wound, sir, just a nick at the edge of the guard. Bleeding's stopped."

"Considering what caused it," Ryan began, and had no idea of where to go from there.

"Not to worry, I'll have Harris take a look. Nonee gave him some of Healer Arianna's bits and bobs for his kit."

"Good to know." While Curtin had spoken to the healers in Gateway, the dead guardian had been too anti-mage-craft to accept anything from Nonee lest it be contaminated by her touch. He missed Curtin, the stubborn, flaming ass.

"Lake water?" Ryan asked as Harris knelt by Destros's leg, holding a full cup of water in one hand, a rag and a small pouch in the other.

"No, sir. From the skins."

"The lake looks clean."

"A burning sight cleaner than the Great Lake," Destros agreed, tossing his shin guard aside and shoving his pant leg up above the knee.

"Wouldn't use that either," Harris told him, gripping the larger man's ankle to hold him still. "This close to the swamp, flame knows what's in that water."

"And it's a lake in the Broken Lands," Destros pointed out. "Might end up with flippers."

Gearing roused sputtering from his near nap. "You threw it in my face!"

Harris snorted. "Flippers kill slower than heat stroke, Scholar." With the dried blood scrubbed away and the hole in Destros's calf oozing a line of fresh blood, he poured half the water over it.

They didn't have a lot of water left. Nonee'd said it wouldn't be a problem, that she'd see the skins refilled by the end of the day, but Nonee had run off into the swamp. "I should have insisted on details," he muttered. He needed to talk to her the moment she returned. If . . . no, when she returned.

"Is he dabbling in mage-craft, my lord?"

"He, Captain?"

She nodded toward the scholars, but kept her face carefully turned away. "Scholar Gearing. I heard him try to control the weapon with mage-craft."

"He told me he had a word that's been used by Lord Protectors for generations."

"That's how you defend scholarship?" Donal sneered. *"The scholarship that allows Marsan to dominate the Great Lake? The scholarship Captain Marsan erected as a bulwark against mage-craft? He told you he had a* word?"

The captain's eyes narrowed. "Then you should have had that word."

"It didn't work."

Her expression said that wasn't the point as clearly as if she'd said it out loud. "You need to find out what else he knows. Search his satchel."

"Search . . . ?" Ryan's voice hadn't cracked for years, but the thought of Gearing's reaction broke it. He might have thought the same thing, but he would never have said it out loud. And they wouldn't find the bits of the chronicles edited out in Gearing's satchel. "We can't. He's a scholar!"

"And you're the Heir of Marsan."

"Scholars are beyond politics. Their allegiance is to knowledge alone." That was the first lesson every child of Marsan learned. With smaller words, Ryan admitted, but Captain Yansav had come to Marsan as an adult.

She shook her head. "Scholars are people, my lord, and people have been known to acquire knowledge without finding wisdom."

<hr />

"What are you doing?" Ryan demanded. Keetin was standing on one of the destroyed wharf's thick stone support posts, six posts out from shore, stripped down to shirt and trousers. No vest, no helm, no boots.

"I'm trying to get a look at where we're heading," Keetin called back, a hand up to block the sun. "I checked for fog first."

"Yeah, that's what I'm worried about. Get in here!"

"Not yet. I can see a small building at the water level. Can't see the way down to it, but there must be stairs. Unless you get there by mage-craft."

"Or a boat." The sun was warm on Ryan's face, a breeze off the water keeping it from growing uncomfortably hot. He could hear the low mur-

mur of voices behind him, the hum of insects broken by the louder buzz
of a fat bee moving between the bell-shaped purple blossoms dusted over
the bushes that grew up from between the stones. "I wonder if this water's
drinkable. We're running low."

"Not a chance, we're too close to the swamp." Keetin bent forward,
hands cupped around his eyes to block the sun. "It's pretty murky even
out here. I can't see the bottom."

The water that slapped against the rock a handspan from the toes of
Ryan's boots was clear enough for him to see individual colored stones
rolled smooth by waves. To see the shadow of a leaf bobbing on the surface. He'd have assumed it would be murkier closer to shore, but currents
could have shifted the swamp further out.

"If we can't drink it," Keetin called, "we could always swim in it.
Wash away some of the stink."

The water slapped the shore hard enough to splash up over Ryan's
boots.

A greenish-brown curve appeared against the pale stone of a post and
sank again.

"Keetin! Get back to shore!"

To his credit, Keetin didn't argue.

One post. Two. Four to . . .

The first tentacle was as big around as Ryan's arm. The second, a little
larger. The third wrapped around Keetin's legs.

Ryan had his sword in his hand when he hit the water. Was waist deep
when he felt something slide against his hip. Both hands on the hilt, he
stabbed down. The point of his blade sank into something. The sword
jerked out of his hand; he lost his footing and flailed forward, dragged by
the loop around his right ankle.

Keetin hit the water, screaming.

Then Destros was there, axe slamming down, sheets of water rising
like wings on either side of the blade.

Released, Ryan stumbled and nearly fell.

Keetin's head broke the surface. Then he was gone again.

Three arrows slammed into the loop of glistening flesh arcing up out
of the water.

Keetin reappeared.

Ryan felt a band tighten around his arm. Saw Destros go down, nearly
taking the captain with him.

Water closed over his head.

He got his feet under him and pushed up. Got high enough, Captain Yansav hacked the thinner tentacle off his arm. Fell back into shallower water as the lake bed shook.

Water fell up.

Rock vibrated under his ass.

Nonee charged past him.

She held a tentacle in each hand by the time she reached the third post. Had disappeared entirely under water by the sixth.

Destros hauled him up onto his feet and the captain herded them back to the shore.

By the time Ryan turned, wet boots slipping on wet rock, Keetin's head was out of the water again. He'd been dragged far beyond the end of the wharf in an impossibly short time. His shoulders, arms, and hips emerged, a large gray hand holding him upright. When Nonee's head appeared, water sluicing off the curve of skin, he slid down until he sat on her shoulder.

"Is it dead?" Captain Yansav shouted.

"No." Nonee tossed aside the length of flopping flesh she held in her left hand. "Too big." She spat. It sounded like a solid hitting the water. "It pulled back to the center of the lake."

"What is it?" Lyelee demanded, eyeing the severed tentacle as it sank.

"Mage-crafted," Nonee said shortly, as though that was enough. She dropped to one knee as she hit dry land and Destros helped Ryan pull Keetin off her to the ground, where he rolled onto his knees, arched his back, sucked in air and propelled it out again with a wet painful cough that sounded as though he'd spit his lungs into the spreading puddle beneath him.

Ryan remembered his brothers, silent, limp, and bloated as they were carried out onto the dock.

Keetin kept coughing.

Alive. As long as he was coughing, Ryan reminded himself, he was alive.

Lyelee jabbed a finger into Nonee's shoulder. "Where were you?"

"Keeping you from being crushed by missiles thrown from the swamp."

Ryan could read the need to argue on Lyelee's face. He wanted to yell, to demand to know why she'd left them unprotected. Had she'd known about the creature in the lake? He bit down on the words and said, "Did you get them?"

"Them?"

"The people working the siege engine."

She frowned, but before she could speak, Keetin sat back on his heels and Ryan dropped down by his side, rubbing his back. "Are you okay?"

He managed a terse, "I'm great." Coughed again, six or seven rough barks, and gasped, "What was that?"

"Nonee says it's mage-crafted."

"No shit." Keetin spat and took a cautious breath. Another. Then jerked forward, coughing again.

"Can it come out?" Servan asked, arrow on the string pointed toward the water. "Onto land?"

Nonee stood and skimmed water off her leathers with the edges of her hands. "No."

"Good."

"But its arms can."

Ryan glared up at her. "You knew it was there."

"Yes." Nonee met his gaze.

"You should have warned us!"

"How?" Keetin gasped. Coughed. "She was . . ." Coughed. ". . . chasing an enemy . . ." Coughed. ". . . through the swamp."

She still should have warned them, not run off and left them in ignorance. Keetin had nearly died.

"Ow!" Keetin jerked his arm out of Ryan's grip. "What was . . . that for?"

"You nearly died!"

"Why were you in the water?" Nonee asked, folding her arms.

"I wasn't in the . . . water until that . . . thing grabbed me." Tendons on his throat stood out as he struggled not to cough. "I was on a . . . post. Looking at the mage . . . tower."

"Don't do that again."

He flicked flame at her. "No shit."

"All right, enough!" Captain Yansav snapped. "If that thing can reach out of the water, let's all move away from the water."

"Wait," Ryan commanded before anyone could move. "Nonee's here now and Keetin isn't ready . . ."

"I'm fine." He coughed again, drier but more painful sounding.

Nonee stared at Destros's pant leg, the spreading red diluted to a pale pink. "You're bleeding."

Destros glanced down and shrugged. "It's nothing. Happened before I charged in to save the day."

Her eyes narrowed. "You went into the water with a fresh wound?"

"Yeah, but . . ."

To Ryan's surprise, Nonee dropped to her knees and wrapped a hand around Destros's ankle. "It needs to be purged."

"Purged?" He tried to step back, but it was clear to everyone watching he was going nowhere. "That's . . ."

She shoved the wet fabric up his leg, closed her mouth over the wound, and her cheeks hollowed.

Harris shoved his shoulder into the larger man's armpit and kept Destros standing.

The guardian had barely begun to swear when she rocked back onto her heels and spat blood into her palm.

The black speck in the red had multiple, threadlike legs. One hand still on Keetin's back, Ryan leaned over Nonee's shoulder for a closer look.

Destros blinked at her. "You sucked a baby tentacle monster out of my leg?"

"Yes. Fresh blood attracts them." It cracked audibly when she crushed it between her thumbnails.

Lyelee, sample box in hand, jerked at the sound. "That creature had historical significance!"

Nonee scraped the residue off on a rock. "Yes."

"You're destroying the historical record! Wiping out unique evidence of the Mage War! From now on . . ." She jabbed the box toward Nonee's face. ". . . scholarship will take control of all such finds!"

"No."

"The Lord Protector . . ."

"Knows the dangers of the Broken Lands better than you do."

"He approved the petition for scholarship," Lyelee snarled. "He sent us here!"

Nonee stood and cocked her head, her expression carefully blank. "Yes."

Chest heaving, Lyelee glared up at her, but before she could speak— because if Ryan had noticed the multiple layers of Nonee's answer, Lyelee must have—Destros broke the silence. "So, Nonee, just the *one* monster in my leg?"

Nonee's posture softened as she turned toward him. "No."

"No?" Destros shot a narrow-eyed glare at the dribble of blood running down his calf. "And the others . . . ?"

"Gone." She looked as close to embarrassed as her features allowed and ducked her head, looking almost shy. "Eaten."

"They won't . . . ?" He waved a hand toward her stomach.

"No."

"Okay, then."

He was taking the idea of multiple tiny tentacled monsters inhabiting his body better than Ryan would have. Than Ryan was. His skin crawled at the thought.

As Harris took Destros to one side, Arianna's paste pot in his hand, Nonee swept her gaze over the other three in dripping clothes. "Strip."

"Strip?"

"They need wounds. Eyes, mouths, noses . . ."

Captain Yansav blew her nose, snot and water splatting against a flat rock.

". . . don't give them access," Nonee continued. "But the smallest wound will."

"We need to move away from the water. Now." Captain Yansav's voice was steel.

"If you've been . . ." Nonee frowned. ". . . infected, there's limited time to save you."

"Strip," Ryan barked, ignoring the captain's reaction.

"Yeah, stripping." Coughing, Keetin struggled to get his shirt over his head. Ryan moved in to help. The bruising on his torso had turned green around the edges, the center of the impact still deep purple. His fingers trembled as he unbuttoned his trousers, but he sounded almost normal as he said, "I'd like to remind you all that the water was cold."

He managed a grin when Servan whistled.

"Ryan Heir."

"I know, but . . ."

Bruises were already rising around Keetin's waist, his thighs, and one arm. There were no breaks in the skin.

"Now."

He dragged his eyes off Keetin and stripped.

Captain Yansav's skin was whole.

Nonee took his hands in hers and scowled at the tears around his fingernails. "Not deep enough," she said after what seemed like days, and released him.

Ryan fought to keep his hands at his sides. "So I can get dressed?"

"Yes."

After the intimacies of the road, they'd seen each other in every state of undress, but this, this was being put on display, and that had always ended in his being found wanting.

"Only because you're a waste of space."

"The water was *quite* cold, my lord," Harris murmured, scooping Ryan's wet clothes up off the ground.

The heavily emphasized, insincere sincerity pulled him out of the impending spiral, and Ryan grinned as he dragged wet linen up over his thighs. "In case I haven't made it clear, I'm glad you're with us, Harris."

"You'd have starved without me, sir."

Ryan's grin broadened. "You're welcome." As his head emerged through the neck of his shirt, he saw the captain thrust Keetin's vest at him, scales rustling.

"This works better if you wear it, my lord."

"I'd have sunk to the . . . bottom, Captain." He took the vest, then let it drop as he coughed.

Captain Yansav stared at him for a long moment, nodded, pivoted on one heel, and snapped, "What happened in the swamp?"

"Got away," Nonee growled.

"Away? Right." The captain swept a gaze around the company and settled her helm on wet hair. "We move off this road and into a defensible position on higher ground now!"

Arrow still on the string, still pointing out into the lake, Servan shook her head. "We're not going to make the top of headland before dark, Cap."

The captain's nostrils flared. "So you suggest we linger between the enemy in the swamp and the enemy in the lake?"

"Uh, no, Cap."

When he lifted it onto his shoulders, Ryan's pack was lightest it had been, a reminder that the water was almost gone. Sunlight danced mockingly across the surface of the lake. Wisps of fog clung along the far shore.

Nonee crossed the stone bridge first. If it could hold her, it could hold them all. At the same time. While dancing.

"You call that clumsy shuffle you do dancing?"

"It isn't how well the pig dances . . ."

". . . but that it dances at all."

Ryan barricaded his response behind clenched teeth. His brothers had had a dancing master. He'd been too young at the time and the master hadn't been rehired for him.

The captain kept them moving as quickly as possible; their pace, as always, set by Gearing. Ryan wasn't sure if it was the rest, the creature in the lake, the attack from the swamp, or the combination of all three, but the scholar made good time on the flat and barely slowed as he stepped onto the bridge.

Ryan glanced over the edge as he reached the apex of the arc. The weeds growing through the surface of the water swayed in the currents. Or maybe not in the currents. "Nonee, does the creature extend tentacles into the swamp?"

She paused on the other side of the bridge to look back at him. "Probably. There's nothing left alive in the lake."

"Why hasn't it taken over the swamp?"

"Lingering mage-craft." She shrugged. "Competition."

"Wonderful," Keetin murmured beside him before beginning to cough again, fist pressed against his chest, trying to force the last of the lake out of his lungs. He went to spit into the water, thought better of it, and spat on the stone instead.

"My lord Marsan! Lord Norwin-cee!"

They were the last two on the bridge and the captain wasn't happy. Ryan gave Keetin a shove toward the road and fell into step beside him, trying not to wince at his hacking cough.

Nonee believed the . . . infection needed a wound.

Lungs had to be at least as warm and damp as the inside of Destros's leg.

Just beyond the bridge, the road had been shattered.

"This was done some time ago," Lyelee noted.

"Does it matter?" Ryan asked wearily.

Lyelee glared at him. "Apparently not."

The hole had filled with water. Not rainwater, not in high summer, so either the lake or the swamp had found a way in. The gap was too large to jump, even without packs.

Ryan scratched at the beard growing back in under his chin. "If Nonee stands in the center, we can step onto her shoulder, then across."

Nonee dropped one of the decorative stone pillars that had anchored a corner of the bridge into the gap.

"Or that," Harris said quietly.

All four pillars and a bit of parapet made an uneven path that rose barely a handspan above the surface of the water.

Gearing slipped as he crossed, windmilling his arms and sounding like a startled duck. With Harris's help, he regained his balance and kept walking, loudly declaring he needed no assistance and that they should all remember he wasn't more than a year or two older than Harris and hardly as decrepit as they all liked to believe.

"The Lord Protector's party lost their slowest member in the swamp," Keetin murmured by Ryan's ear.

"And?"

"Maybe I should seize the moment."

"You can't push him in."

"But . . ."

"No."

~⚬~

On the far side of the harbor, the road rose in a gentle curve up to the headland. The further they climbed above the swamp and the lake, the less Ryan stared at his hands, wanting to claw off his skin and rip out any multi-limbed creatures making a home in his flesh. Destros didn't seem bothered by the idea that he'd actually had said creatures living inside him, more concerned with mournful observations of how his leathers had stiffened as they dried while Servan ignored his complaints and told impossible stories about seafood. Keetin kept coughing, but Ryan convinced himself that each cough sounded drier than the one before. Although she still held her sword, the rigid line of Captain Yansav's back had relaxed. Giant not-squid and flung skulls joined the list of things that hadn't cracked Harris's quiet competence. And although the two Scholars grumbled, the rise and fall of their arguments had become the background to Ryan's life.

Things were almost back to normal.

For certain values of normal.

A little up ahead, Harris got Nonee's attention and pointed toward an obviously artificial plateau by the side of the road. The plateau looked perfect, large enough to hold them all, small enough they wouldn't feel exposed. A lichen-covered slab of rock nearly as tall as Nonee held up the fall of the hill, the summer-browned grass was too short to hide large predators, and the three trees just off the road offered a welcome patch of shade.

It looked like it had been designed for picnicking in happier times.

Or for welcome visitors to wait in comfort while the traps up ahead were disarmed.

Legs burning, sweat running down his sides, stomach pressed against his backbone, Ryan was all for stopping to eat, but Nonee shook her head and indicted they should keep going. He could see the wisdom in getting as far away from the water as possible, but it wouldn't be long before Gearing would have to rest, giving them no choice about the location.

Not wanting to bellow his protest, Ryan lengthened his stride until he'd nearly caught up, and snapped his mouth closed when he realized all three trees grew from trunks that looked like elongated bodies, feet stretching toward the ground, backs impossibly twisted, mouths open too wide.

Except this was the Broken Lands.

If they looked like elongated bodies . . .

And one of them was—had been—a child.

Branches reached toward the road as they passed. Leaves whispered. No one listened to Lyelee insisting they should stop, and she muttered under her breath about wasted opportunity until they reached a similar plateau further up the road.

This rock was shorter, the grass a little longer, and there were no trees close enough to whisper.

Another night, they'd have eaten, rested, then walked on until dusk, using the hours of summer sunlight that remained, but it was clear to Ryan that Gearing was done. The older scholar barely managed to eat a piece of jerky and a handful of raw peas before falling asleep. Keetin dozed, a mug of Harris's mint tea clasped loosely between his hands. Satchel across her lap, Lyelee curled her left arm around the paper resting on it, protecting the notes she scribbled with her right from prying eyes.

Ryan could feel a demand to see her work rise in his throat, pushed out by the growing suspicion that the Scholar's Hall edited the truths they taught. Before he could begin another futile argument about the privilege of scholarship, he joined Nonee at the edge of the camp.

Back toward the harbor, the lake shone silver-blue, deceptively peaceful, the fog still hugging the far shore. On the other side of the road, the swamp stretched off until it disappeared into a low-lying mist.

"What you chased in the swamp," he said at last, "was it someone like you?" When she glanced over at him, he shrugged. He'd put the pieces together while he climbed. "Big and gray and not an elephant."

Her mouth twitched. "Not an elephant," she agreed.

"Someone like you."

"Yes."

He reached down, pulled the seed head off a stalk of grass, and stripped it between his fingers. "Did you see it in the swamp the last time, when Petre died?"

"No. He didn't come close enough."

He. Not it. She. Not it.

"But you knew he was there?"

"Not knew; suspected."

"Did you tell the Lord Protector or was it omitted from his chronicle?"

"Omitted?"

"Left out." When she frowned, Ryan realized she hadn't been asking what the word meant. "It seems to have happened once or twice." He glanced back at the two scholars, fully aware that Nonee hadn't actually answered his question. He dusted grass seeds off his hands. "The Captain's Chronicle says the other five weapons were destroyed. That only you survived."

"The Captain was wrong."

About a few things, Ryan thought, but before he could pull a question from the hundreds trying to form, Nonee's gaze jerked to the sky and she held up a hand for silence.

The black specks, the crows circling over the far headland, seemed closer, but still too far away to cause concern.

Then Nonee crouched.

Leapt up.

Grabbed . . . a piece of the sky.

The ground under his feet trembled when she landed.

Her fingers had closed around the throat of a large, gray bird; talons reached to rip and tear, wings slammed against her, the beak opened and closed even after she ripped the head from the body.

"I didn't see it!" Ryan scrambled away from death throes that gouged furrows into the ground.

Nonee kicked the bird over onto its back, exposing a mix of blue and white and pale gray feathers. A stroke of her foot and the mixture changed. Another stroke, it changed again. "You can't see the hunters from below," she said.

"Mage-craft," Lyelee declared, leaning around Destros, pencil still clutched in her hand.

Only Ryan could see Nonee roll her eyes. "Boe Mah Sing created them to feed his flocks. Crows are carrion feeders. The hunters created carrion so his crows could feed."

"How . . . responsible of him."

"Eventually," she said, staring off at the distant flock of crows.

Ryan decided not to ask her what she meant; it would likely be worse than he imagined. "How many of them are there?"

"Only Boe Mah Sing knew." She shrugged. "Time for lots of eggs since then."

"Are there more up there now?" Captain Yansav held her sword again, although what use it would be against an essentially invisible bird, Ryan had no idea.

"At least she has it out," Donal scoffed.

"Better Ryan doesn't pull his . . ."

". . . so he doesn't cut his own feet off." The twins snickered together.

"Nonee!"

Nonee turned her head as the captain snapped her name and Ryan realized she'd been staring at him, head cocked, during his brothers' commentary.

"Are there more?" Captain Yansav repeated.

"They were solitary hunters." Nonee shrugged again. "They've had time to change. There's been inter . . ."

"Interbreeding to create the birds that attacked me! That's what you meant by *unexpected*. Not that they attacked, that they existed." Dropping to her knees, Lyelee flicked the feather pattern with her pencil, while reaching for the head with her other hand. "There is a visible similarity in the shape of the skull and the breadth of the chest. What birds did Boe Mah Sing use to create them?"

"Only he knew."

"Raptor claws and wings, but that beak . . ." She held up the head—it was larger than Ryan's clenched fist—and stabbed the long straight beak into the ground. "No raptor ever had a beak like this. There's spurs on the wing joints and the flight feathers . . . Ow!" The hunter's head hit the ground and rolled. "Those are sharp!" Glaring at the wing's edge, she put her bloody finger in her mouth.

Leaning past her, Captain Yansav used her sword to sweep the breast feathers back and forth. Then she squinted up into the sky. Then she turned to Nonee. "You can see them."

"Yes. When they come close enough."

"Can you teach Servan to see them?"

Nonee studied the archer for a moment, but finally shook her head. "She'd need mage-crafted eyes."

Servan took a step back and held up both hands. "That's a big burning no."

"No one survives to craft them," Nonee reassured her. Servan didn't look reassured.

"So our survival depends on a mage-crafted weapon." Gearing stumbled a little as he joined them around the body of the bird. His eyes were bloodshot and it didn't look as though his nap had done him much good. "Except that I spoke her word and she didn't obey. Captain Marsan's notes explicitly stated that none of the weapons could disobey."

"I don't remember that in the chronicle," Destros murmured.

"That's not the point!" Gearing snapped.

It was a point that needed making, but before Ryan could say so, Lyelee rocked back on her heels and stood, slipping three breast feathers into her satchel. Later, Ryan told himself. He'd deal with that later. "Did you pronounce it correctly?" she asked.

Nonee answered before the older scholar could. "Close enough."

Gearing folded his arms. Ryan noticed his wrist bones had grown even more prominent. "So you heard me?"

"Yes." She made it sound like *obviously*.

"Then why didn't you obey?"

"You don't have to answer," Ryan told her.

"If she hadn't run off," Lyelee snapped, "we'd have known about the squid . . ."

"It's not a squid!" Gearing interrupted.

"She's standing right here." Ryan shifted so he stood between the scholars and the weapon. "Talk to her instead of about her."

"She doesn't need your protection." Lyelee rolled her eyes.

"And yet, she has it." He felt the air currents shift as Nonee adjusted her bulk behind him.

Gearing stepped closer. "I demand she answer!"

"She doesn't . . ."

"It's okay." Her hand rested cool and heavy on Ryan's shoulder, the sound of her exhale too impatient to be a sigh. "It's not speaking the word, it's holding the word, and only one person can hold the word at a time. Tanika Fleshrender gave the word to Captain Marsan just before the end. Garrett Heir gave the word to Arianna before he left."

"Which is my point!" Gearing waved the piece of paper he pulled from his satchel. "The healer is dead. I hold the word now."

"Not how it works." Her tone slid into warning.

Ryan frowned. His great-uncle had given the word to Arianna. Nonee had been with the healer when she lay dying. "Arianna gave you the word before she died."

"You weren't there," Gearing scoffed. "You're guessing."

"Ryan Heir is right."

"Even a broken clock is right twice a day."

Ignoring his brother, Ryan turned under the weight of Nonee's hand. "You hold your own word."

"Yes."

"But you obey the Last Command." Captain Yansav still hadn't sheathed her sword, the point resting against the dead bird's breast.

"Yes. The Last Command was given by Garrett Heir while he held the word."

"Years ago," Lyelee said. "And you're still bound by it?"

"Yes."

"Why?"

Nonee shrugged.

"No," Gearing snapped. "That is not a secret you get to keep. Not when our survival rests in your hands."

"She keeps what secrets she needs to." Ryan drew himself up straight, as much as his aching back protested the attempt, turned back toward the bulk of the company, and met Gearing's eyes. "How much more relevant information are *you* concealing, Scholar?"

In the silence that followed, Ryan could hear Harris poking at the fire, Keetin's congested breathing, and, although he was probably imagining it, the distant calls of Boe Mah Sing's crows.

Gearing raised a hand and stroked his beard, slowly, deliberately, as though he were cutting down a novitiate who'd dared to question what was known. "You have no authority over scholarship, Lord Marsan." He turned on one heel and strode back toward the fire. It would've been impressive on the stone floors of the Scholar's Hall. On a hill covered in summer-dead grasses, it was both wobbly and pretentious.

Lyelee paused, eyes narrowed, and before following said, "If you're imagining you sound like the Lord Protector—you don't."

Ryan heard a soft, disapproving huff of breath from behind him, although he wasn't entirely certain who or what Nonee disapproved of.

NONEE.NOW

Nonee's hand engulfed the mug of tea Harris gave her and the two of them looked down at the body of the bird.

"Can we eat it?" Harris asked.

"No."

He gave a noncommittal hum and her heart lurched, reminded of Arianna, who made . . . used to make a similar sound as she thought things over. "Can you eat it?"

"Yes." She didn't have to, but she could. Should. Take it away once darkness fell so they couldn't see her devour meat, bones, and viscera. So they couldn't see how different . . .

"I could send the boys for more wood and I could cook it for you." Harris prodded the bird gently with the toe of one boot. "If I cooked it whole, it wouldn't be ready until morning, but you'll have to eat then too."

"Thank you." He couldn't look at her, but he still tried to erase what differences he could. "But no."

RYAN.NOW

Ryan threw up an arm over his eyes to block the light and gave serious thought to stuffing dirt into his ears to block the high-pitched, three-part whoop rising above the calls of less annoying birds. After a moment, he sighed and rolled up onto his feet, fist shoved into his mouth to block a jaw-cracking yawn.

He hadn't slept well. He'd dreamed of water closing over his head. Of Keetin torn apart by tentacles, torn into pieces so small they became red/black currents in the water that twisted away from his reaching hands. He woke, more than once, to Keetin coughing.

He'd been awake when Lyelee had risen to circle the camp before lying down again. It looked like she was talking to herself, lips moving, hands waving, but the only sound she made was a soft, dry cough that made Keetin's wet bark sound worse in comparison.

He'd seen Gearing rise twice to piss then drop back to sleep immediately after as though his world remained empty of monsters. He should've let Keetin push him into the water.

And speaking of water, the waterskins were gone.

"Nonee's taken them to the lake," Harris told him, voice low so as not to wake the others. "To fill them."

Ryan stared at Harris for a long moment before he found his voice. "To the lake?"

"Yes, sir."

"The lake with the giant tentacled creature that tried to kill Keetin and reproduced inside Destros's leg?"

"Yes, sir."

"That can't be safe."

Harris bent forward to blow on a nest of small sticks laid over last night's coals. When they caught he said, "I believe Nonee's in no danger."

Then Nonee was back. One moment she wasn't there, the next she was, festooned with most of the company's waterskins, a handspan at the bottom of her leather tunic dark and wet. "Nonee. You've got . . ." He waved a hand at the bulging skins. "We can't drink that."

"Why not?" Lyelee argued. Ryan hadn't noticed her join them. "The water *was* remarkably clear. I made a note of that at the time. If the creature's offspring can be filtered out . . ."

"Filtered out?"

"The Great Lake drowned your brothers and yet continues to provide Marsanport with water," she pointed out. "It's a little late to get fussy."

The muscles of his back tightened. "Fussy?"

She sighed. "When your conversation devolves to echoing words and phrases, you give the impression of stunned stupidity. If you don't drop that particular vocal mannerism before we return home, the Court will eat you for breakfast. And speaking of breakfast . . ." She turned to Harris, who'd been building the fire into a hot, all but smokeless blaze. ". . . oat-cakes again?"

"They pack light, Scholar. There'll be tea if we have water."

Lyelee folded her arms and raised a brow in Nonee's direction.

"All the water went first into this skin . . ." Nonee lifted the larger, ornate skin she'd carried from Gateway. ". . . then was poured through a piece of silk into the others."

"Silk filters mage-crafted squid babies?" Keetin asked.

Ryan jumped.

"Your situational awareness needs work," Captain Yansav said on his other side.

"And it's not a squid," Gearing added.

Destros shook his head. "I don't think I'm comfortable drinking squid-baby water."

Servan mumbled agreement.

Seemed like everyone was up.

"It's not a squid!" Gearing repeated.

Nonee glanced at Ryan. He sighed. Lyelee was right. The water had looked clear and clean, and under normal circumstances he'd have had no trouble drinking it. But these weren't normal circumstances, even if he refused to say *squid babies* aloud. "Nonee, is the water safe to drink?"

"Yes."

"Because of a piece of silk?"

"No." She shook the larger waterskin hard enough Ryan heard something thud against the inside. "Because of a purification stone."

"A purification stone?"

Lyelee snorted dismissively. "You're doing it again."

"Lyelee." Keetin made her name a warning.

"He won't learn if I don't point it out to him."

The problem was, however smug and sanctimonious she sounded, she wasn't wrong. Ryan raised a hand to stop Keetin's next words and Gearing jumped in.

"It's mage-craft!"

Given how little her facial features moved, Ryan was impressed at how clearly Nonee expressed a silent doubt in Gearing's intelligence as she said, "Yes."

"How does it work?" the older scholar demanded. "How did you manage to keep it functional after all this time?"

Ryan remembered the fountain. How the water had suddenly cleared after the third woman arrived. "It's not from before the Mage War, is it?"

She nodded at him, a single dip of her head. "No."

"There are mages in Gateway." Lyelee's eyes widened and she repeated the statement with considerably more enthusiasm. "There are *mages* in Gateway!"

"No."

"You just said . . ."

"Not mages, talents. People who can do one thing. Purify water. Scoop light into lamps. Start fires."

"Yeah, that never ends badly," Servan muttered.

"Heal," Nonee continued. "Truth tell."

Ryan frowned, several entries in the Heir's Chronicle suddenly making more sense. "Arianna . . . She was a talent."

"Yes."

"Did the Lord Protector know?"

"Yes."

The Lord Protector knew mage-craft lingered in Gateway. And he also knew that sooner or later another Heir of Marsan would be retrieving more fuel from the Broken Lands. Would first retrieve the weapon from Gateway. Where mage-craft lingered.

"Why," Ryan demanded, turning to face Gearing, "was that information left out of the chronicle?"

"We were never given *that* information!"

But they had been given other information they'd left out. Once he had the fuel, left the Broken Lands, and was back in Marsanport, he'd deal with the Scholar's Hall. "Harris. Get the tea made. We don't have time to linger."

"Sir." Harris reached out and Nonee tossed him a waterskin.

"Mage-crafted water!" Gearing shouted, sketching indignation in the air with both hands. "You want us to trust mage-crafted water!"

Ryan glanced around. The two scholars looked excited, both sets of nostrils flared as though they were on the scent of something new. Which, he supposed, they were. Captain Yansav scowled out over her folded arms, but she could be scowling at anything. Keetin and the two remaining guardians watched and waited. Harris was making tea.

He couldn't order them to trust the water.

"You couldn't order a fish to swim."

He hooked a waterskin off Nonee's arm, and took a drink. Swallowed, shrugged, and said, "No one's going to force the water down your throat."

His teeth may have been clenched against the possibility of mage-crafted squid babies, but he didn't think anyone noticed.

"My lord." Harris handed Ryan an oatcake, then asked Nonee if she wanted breakfast, as though they hadn't just been talking about mage-craft still being practiced in among the ruins of what mage-craft had destroyed.

She smiled, obviously trying to keep her face from falling into terrifying lines and not entirely succeeding. "Thank you, no." A jerk of her head down toward the lake. "Ate already."

Keetin sank down cross-legged by the fire and held out a hand. "I could eat."

The tea made with the new water tasted of days on the road and nights around a fire just like it always did.

Destros squinted into his mug through the rising steam. "Be a different morning were Curtin still with us. Lots more shouting."

"Just thinking that," Servan agreed.

"Can't actually say I care much for the thought of talent-crafting, though. Not when mage-craft set the Five Thousand on the road, broken and bleeding. Still, there's dealing with mage-craft and dying of thirst, and I know which I'd prefer." The big guardian tipped his head, tightened his grip on the mug, and tossed back the contents.

His eyes widened, whites showing all around, and he spat the tea out onto the grass. "Hot! Hot! Hot! Sweet burning flame that's hot!"

"Idiot," Servan muttered, swiping at the splatters on her legs.

Ryan laughed with the others, wondering how many talents it took to create a mage and how many mages it took to start a war.

They'd made good time with half the climb to the headland behind them when Nonee raised a hand. Ryan moved to the front of the line. "What is it?"

"Trap." She stepped off the path, picked up a rock the size of his torso, planted her feet, and threw it two, maybe three body-lengths ahead. Darkness rose around it. When the darkness disappeared, the rock remained.

"What was that supposed to prove?" Lyelee had come to stand at Ryan's side, breathing heavily, with a white-knuckled grip on the straps of her pack.

"Tanika Fleshrender used the traps to gather raw material. She didn't want rock."

Lyelee nodded. "The darkness indicates the position of the portal."

"Yes."

"Can we use it?"

"Can we what?" Ryan demanded.

"It's a portal, Ryan." Lyelee's voice edged on patronizing. "You've been through one already. Think of the time we'd save. You can't possibly enjoy climbing this endless hill."

Nonee folded her arms. "The trip is survivable. The destination . . . That depends."

"Depends?" Ryan didn't like the sound of that.

"On the condition of the workroom."

"The mage has been dead for years, long past caring if her workroom is in no condition for company." Lyelee stepped forward.

Nonee grabbed her pack and held her in place. "She liked her raw materials willing to do anything to make the pain stop."

Ryan steadied his cousin as she jerked free of Nonee's grip, both of them aware that Nonee had allowed it. "No shortcuts," he told her.

"What happens if we move off the road?" Captain Yansav's tone said she knew *something* would happen.

Nonee scooped up two smaller stones and threw them into the distant grass. This time, the darkness rose like snakes twisting in the air, hunting for prey, sinking back into the ground rather than dissipating.

"Not portals?" asked the captain.

"Not portals," Nonee agreed. "Death."

"So." Captain Yansav drummed her fingers on the pommel of her sword. "An approaching party would see the first of their number disappear from the road. They'd leave the road, and die."

"One way to discourage visitors," Keetin muttered, flicking the seed head off a brittle grass stalk.

"Okay." Ryan took half a dozen strides down the hill, ignored Gearing demanding to know where he was going, and returned with his head no clearer. "How did you get past this the last time?"

"By going in the other direction. She had no problem with people leaving after she was done with them."

"And if she wasn't done with them?"

"They didn't leave."

"Right. Okay. You came out of the swamp in the village. Which way?"

Nonee pointed toward the forest.

"You could knock out a path and we could get in through the village. Avoid the traps entirely."

Keetin raised both hands. "Oh no. I remember the part about the village. Gave me nightmares."

"The village has nothing to do with us," Gearing declared pompously. "The mage-tower is right there; why add unnecessary delay?"

"Delay beats dying," Destros responded solemnly. "It'll take a lot longer to get back with the fuel if we're all dead."

He didn't mention that they'd already lost Curtin, but then he didn't need to. It wasn't something that Ryan would ever forget.

"There must be a way past." Lyelee glared at the place the darkness had disappeared, as though she thought she could intimidate ancient mage-craft. "Tanika Fleshrender couldn't have captured or destroyed everyone who approached this door. Nonee, you said she was friends of a sort with Boe Mah Sing; how did he reach the door?"

"He sent someone in his livery through the portal."

"Well, then . . ."

Ryan cut Lyelee off. "To die?"

"Eventually. If she was willing to see him, she disabled the traps." Nonee threw another rock.

Ryan watched the darkness rise and fall. "He'd send someone else through to check, wouldn't he?"

"Yes."

"Wouldn't want to work for that asshole," Servan muttered.

Destros snorted. "Not that a mage who named herself Fleshrender was a sweetheart."

"Those assholes," Servan agreed.

"You have a limited time to get the fuel, Ryan." Lyelee folded her arms. "Make a decision."

Gearing mirrored her position. "One that avoids delays."

Ryan doubted either Lyelee or Gearing gave a flaming rat's ass about the fuel they'd been sent to find. They wanted into the mage-tower, sooner rather than later. "Nonee . . ."

The earth trembled underfoot.

Nonee met the charge of the huge gray creature head on. The impact drove her off the path. Her feet gouged trenches through the grass, coming to a stop perilously close to where the darkness rose.

"It looks like Nonee!" Keetin yelled.

Large. Gray. Hairless.

"Not entirely." Servan shifted, trying to line up a shot.

The attacker was naked and physically male, although the indicators were as minimal as Nonee's.

"Can't see why you'd have trouble saying it's a small dick." Josan snickered. *"You must think it every time you look down."*

The second weapon fought like a beast, all strength and fury. Nonee chose her counterattacks. Exploited weaknesses. *He'd* been living wild since the Mage War. *She'd* been with Captain Marsan, with Garrett as Heir . . .

. . . and between captain and heir, she'd been chained in the Citadel.

What had that taught her except that his great-grandfather was an asshole? Ryan wondered.

Keetin grabbed his arm and yanked him back as Nonee slammed into the ground close enough to cover them both with dirt. He spat out a mouthful of grit, heard Lyelee cough, heard a bowstring sing, and saw an arrow shatter against a muddy, bare shoulder.

They slammed together again and crashed down the hill like a landslide, earth rumbling beneath them.

Everyone scattered.

Battering each other with rocks and trees and fists, they fought their way back up the hill.

Everyone scattered again.

On one knee, driven off the road almost to the edge of the cliff, Ryan braced his hands against the ground as the weight of his pack pushed him forward. He couldn't see Lyelee, but he could hear both her and Keetin yelling. Probably at each other. Harris had an arm around Gearing's waist and was essentially carrying the scholar to relative safety.

On his back, plowing a furrow through summer grass and sun-dried dirt, the attacker crashed through the closest trees, lurched to his feet, grabbed a broken tree as big around as his torso, and threw it. Nonee leapt the trunk and charged toward him.

He threw another three trees before she reached him.

Grabbed him.

Threw him.

Threw herself after him.

He roared. It was the first sound either of them had made. Feet braced against her belly, he flung her off and scrambled toward the rock Nonee had thrown at the portal.

Harris pushed Gearing out of the way, then jumped back as a gray arm dripping dark blood swung past him, an elbow the size of a ham clipping his shoulder.

Fighting the weight of his pack, Ryan surged up onto his feet.

Harris staggered. Two steps. Three.

Darkness rose.

Lying where Harris had flung him, Gearing clutched a piece of paper and shrieked out a list of words.

At the fifth word, the attacker froze.

Nonee's fists smashed into his face, his chest, his stomach, driving him back.

Darkness flared again.

Half the hill collapsed in on itself.

ARIANNA.THEN

It looked to Arianna as though someone had drawn a line between the swamp and the ruins of the village. On the one side, the swamp. On the other, the village. They didn't so much meet as stop where the other began.

The village had been destroyed. Walls had been melted, twisted, and flattened. Walls still standing bore the marks of fire and . . . Arianna squinted toward the gouges. Fire and claws? There'd been dragons before the war. It looked as though there'd been dragons *in* the war.

No plants had begun to reclaim the space. She could see no green, only black and gray.

Uvili squatted beside her, bare legs streaked with slime. She'd carried significantly less of the filthy water out of the swamp than her companions. The shortest of the group, Arianna had waded through water up to her breasts and now her skirts hung heavy and stinking.

She glanced over at the three men mourning Petre now they had the time, arms around each other, foreheads together. She mourned the boy herself, knew she'd see him stripped to bone, sinking into the mud every time she closed her eyes, but she had the living to worry about. Petre was beyond her care.

"We need to light a fire," she called. "We need to get dry."

"No." Garrett pulled back, gave Malcolm and Norik's shoulders a final squeeze, and turned to face her. "Fire will give our position away."

Arianna glanced at the gouges again and remained silent.

Uvili stood and pointed up the hill at an uneven roofline just visible past the broken buildings. "There."

"That's where we're going?" Garrett asked her.

"Yes."

"Then we move quickly, warm up while we're moving, and get dry once we're inside."

"Petre," Malcolm began, and shook his head. Petre would never leave the swamp.

Garrett gripped his shoulder. "I'll take point. Norik, the rear. Malcolm, stay with Arianna. We move as fast as we can. You . . ." He looked at Uvili and shook his head. "Do what you can."

While Garrett hadn't blamed Uvili for Petre's death, Arianna suspected he'd been shaken by her inability to save him. The Heir of Marsan had gone into the Broken Lands with the last great mage-crafted weapon. Surely that had meant he was the next thing to invincible.

He might still be; he had the word. Petre, though . . .

They hadn't gone far before Arianna began to catch glimpses of a high iron fence. In a gap left by the destruction, she saw a double gate large enough for two Uvilis to enter side by side. Beyond the gate, leafless trees. Beyond the trees, a building. Filling the entire limited horizon, it was too large to be a house, and too house-like to be a tower. Although, if their destination was a mage-tower and this was their destination, then it was a tower regard-less of appearance.

Not that external appearances mattered much in the Broken Lands.

She stumbled on a piece of broken masonry and, as Malcolm caught her, reminded herself to watch her step. How embarrassing to survive the swamp only to trip and take herself down. Petre would laugh. She wiped at tears with the back of her mitten and couldn't remember ever being so tired.

When the road curved, the building disappeared. Keeping Malcolm well within the reach of her staff, she stepped around a pile of shattered tile and moved a little closer to Uvili's side. "So, the building at the top of the hill, it's where you were born?"

"Made."

"Born. You may have been changed by mage-craft, but you began the way every child began."

Uvili snorted, but didn't argue.

"Garrett." Norik turned the single word into a warning.

"I hear it."

Arianna didn't hear . . .

And then she did.

Shuffling.

It sounded like her mother crossing to the stove, half awake, her loose slippers scuffing against the floor.

It sounded like a patient walking away from their sickbed, weak but healthy.

It was neither.

"Those people . . ." Malcolm's voice, rough from grieving, shook. "Those people are dead."

Those people were skin and bones. Mostly bones. Strips of dried flesh hung from gray-green arms and faces. Their eye-sockets were empty holes, missing the soft tissue so tempting to scavengers. The jaws that should have fallen off moved up and down, yellowed teeth clattering together.

Half a dozen of them shuffled out to fill the narrow path between two collapsed buildings, blocking the route up the hill.

Garrett pulled his sword. "What foul mage-craft is this?"

"Seriously?" Arianna searched her pockets for her flint and steel. Not in her jacket. She switched her staff to her other hand. Maybe her skirt pocket . . . "I should think the kind of foul mage-craft is obvious. It's the kind that raises the dead." Her fingers closed around the waxed box. "Also, swords won't work. Nor arrows," she added as a shaft shattered ribs on the way through, and clattered against stone behind the still-lurching body. "The pieces will remain animated and dangerous. When the dead walk in Gateway, we use fire."

"What?"

"Fire."

"The dead walk in Gateway?"

"Not so much since we started using fire. Probably helped that there were a limited number of intact bodies in the ruins." She was cold and wet and in no mood to pander to Garrett's ignorance. The seals on the box had held against the swamp and her tinder was dry. She needed something to burn, but all she could see was broken stone.

Garrett stepped back, arms spread as though he intended to protect her with his body. "We don't have time to light a fire!"

"Is this as fast as they can move?" Norik demanded, moving up on her other side.

"I have no idea." Tinderbox in her left hand, staff tucked into the curve of her elbow, Arianna reached back over her shoulder with her right, working her fingers in under the top flap of her pack. She hooked a linen pad, stuffed into her pack in case they were in the Broken Lands for longer than the nine days she had remaining.

The tip of Malcolm's sword rang against a cracked cobblestone. "They'll chase us back into the swamp. I can't . . ."

"Malcolm." Garrett used what Arianna had begun to think of as his Lord Protector voice. Firm, but kind.

Malcolm swallowed audibly and raised his sword. "Yes, sir. I'm okay."

They all ignored how the blade trembled.

One moment Uvili was at her side, the next she held one of the dead at shoulder and hip, ripped it apart, and bashed the halves together. Crushed bone fell in a circle around her like dirty snow. The hip bones became curved weapons to smash the next body apart. Bending under reaching arms, she grabbed both skeletal legs in one big hand and used the body like a club to knock the last three dead off their feet. As the dead she held tried to fold back toward her, she smashed it into a pile of stone. An arm flew past her and all three of the remaining fingers scored dark lines across her thigh.

Garrett tensed to leap forward. Arianna grabbed his jacket and snapped, "She's bleeding! What do you think they'd do to you?"

"I can't just watch . . ."

"Try." Arianna slapped his arm with the pad. "Stay out of her way."

His brow furrowed. "Why are you holding a . . . Skull!"

Teeth clattering, the skull rolled toward them, bounced off an angled cobblestone, and gained enough height that it headed straight for Garrett's knees.

Norik swung his bow and smacked it hard enough to send it the rest of the way down the hill. Arianna heard a distant splash.

"Two points." Norik managed most of a grin at her expression. "You don't play games in Gateway?"

"We do, but . . ."

"My lord!" Malcolm pointed, his whole arm shaking. "She's cleared the way!"

Uvili stood surrounded by bone. She glanced back at them and said, "Run."

"I can light . . ."

"Run!"

Arianna's legs were lead and her wet skirts made it feel as though she had a child wrapped around each ankle, but she ran. Malcolm stayed by her side.

The dead shambled out of broken doorways and climbed down fallen roofs, moving like lizards over the few remaining tiles. They came from behind as well as from in front, and there wasn't always time for Uvili to break them into small enough pieces.

Garrett's sword swept down and took off a piece of Arianna's skirt when a hand clutched the hem and began to claw its way up toward her. A moment later, she slapped her staff through a pile of leg bones as they began to reform. Blood trickled down her cheek and she could taste iron in every labored breath.

Then Garrett was at the gate. A bruising grip on her arm flung her forward and through. She stumbled, fell into Malcolm, and they held each other up, watching Uvili stomp one last ribcage flat before joining them. As she passed through the gate, she brushed bone dust off her hands and relaxed.

There were no more dead. Either they were all in pieces or the fence marked the edge of their territory. Arianna hoped for the former and would settle for the latter.

Malcolm's left ear was bleeding, the hair around it a matted mess. She shoved the pad into Malcolm's hand, then slid out of her pack, kneeling beside it to pull out her kit.

"Arianna?" He waved the linen rectangle.

"Press it against your ear." No need to set it on fire now.

"You have a cut on your face."

"I know."

"Will Petre . . . ?"

"Walk? No." She had no idea. But she was good at sounding like she knew what she was talking about.

His fingers white around the hilt of his sword, Garrett stepped away from Norik. "Was that . . ." He wet his lips and began again. "Were they there to defend the mage-tower or were they created by the Mage War?"

Uvili shrugged and spread her arms. Dark blood dripped from wounds already beginning to close.

NONEE.NOW

Nonee had uncovered Destros and Ryan Heir when she threw off her blanket of dirt and rock, and the two men helped her uncover the others. Kalyealee who-could-be-heir had two broken fingers. She spat dirt and complained. Keetin Norwin-cee helped to dig as he coughed, lips and teeth streaked with mud. Gearing had ridden the collapse halfway back down the hill and Captain Yansav, her legs still buried, sent Destros to retrieve him.

"Carry him if you have to," the captain grunted, fingers scrabbling at the soil.

Nonee wanted Destros to remain, but no one asked her.

She realized she might not want him there for his ability to lift rock and let him go. He wouldn't understand she wanted comfort.

Servan bled from a bone-deep cut over one eye, but cared more that her bow was in three pieces. Sensible. Her skull remained solid. Bleeding could be stopped. Cuts healed. They couldn't repair the bow.

"No." Nonee stopped Ryan Heir from shifting one of the rocks that pinned the captain. "See how it supports the rest?"

He stared at the puzzle they'd uncovered. "It's stopping that big rock from crushing her legs?"

"Yes."

"Then by all means, my lord, leave it where it is." Captain Yansav frowned, arms bent up at awkward angles to keep them out of the way. "I can move my right foot. There's a space there, if that helps."

"Yes." Feet braced beyond the rocks in question, Nonee squatted. "This will hurt."

The captain snorted. "Of course it will. Do it."

Bodies were flexible, rocks were not. Not even for her. Knuckles brushing against Captain Yansav's armor, Nonee worked her hand between the scales and the rock, compressing the captain's chest until her whole arm was between them and she could ease the rock away.

"Daughter of a deceased goat!"

Nonee remembered Shurlian curses. Captain Marsan had used the same one.

"Ryan Heir, Destros, Servan . . . take hold of the captain." She waited until the men had a grip high on both arms, Servan's hands tucked into the captain's armpits. "On three, pull. One. Two." Her arm a spear, she thrust it deep as she lifted, the weight of the largest rock pressed against her forearm. "Three."

They lifted her upright as soon as she was clear, but the captain's left knee couldn't hold her weight. She dropped back to the ground. "It's not broken," she growled. "If I bind it, it'll be fine."

Servan knelt by her side. "Cap, your sword . . ."

"Buried." With two fingers, the captain pressed the triangular fold of skin back into place on Servan's forehead while smacking the archer away from her boot with the other hand. "My lord, if you could bind this before she bleeds to death."

"Harris . . ." Ryan Heir shook his head and scrambled for Harris's pack, dragging it out of a loose pile of dirt, digging through it for the rolls of cloth. He froze, the cloth half out of the pack. "Harris was wearing this."

"And his clothing," Nonee agreed. "The trap takes only bodies."

"Servan's still bleeding," the captain ground out through clenched teeth. "Nonee, can you find my sword down there?" Her skin glistened and her nostrils flared.

"Only dirt and rocks. No sword. Nothing metal." Nonee flexed her arm, rocks grinding together as she shifted them. She couldn't fling the rocks, there were too many people around, so she yanked her arm free as they fell. A jagged edge gouged a trench into her flesh without breaking the skin. Her elbow ached, but the ache wouldn't last long, so she ignored it.

Ryan Heir pressed a folded cloth to Servan's forehead and secured it in place in spite of trembling fingers. "Harris . . ."

"Is in the workroom." She straightened carefully, weight equal over both feet. Once a hill had fallen, it would fall again.

"We have to get to him."

Him. Harris. He'd been kind. "Yes."

"It smells up here," Kalyealee who-could-be-heir called from the safety of the undisturbed part of the hill. "It smells like rotten chicken guts."

"Specifically chicken?" Keetin Norwin-cee asked, binding her broken fingers to the whole finger beside them.

She pushed at his shoulder with her other hand. "Shut up." Tear tracks cut a line through the dirt on her face, but she hadn't made a sound when Keetin Norwin-cee straightened the broken bones. Nonee was reluctantly impressed. Arianna said . . . had said that injuries of fingers and toes caused pain out of proportion to their size.

As Nonee climbed up onto solid ground, she picked up a small boulder and threw it at the portal. And then threw another into the grass.

No darkness rose at either trap.

"They're not working?" Keetin Norwin-cee asked, spat, ran his tongue over his teeth, and spat again.

"They've not reset." She smelled rot. The life anchoring the portal to the path had been released in the landslide, although the body remained. It would be close to the surface, but not, she hoped, exposed. She remembered what it had looked like when it was buried.

Ryan Heir dropped Harris's pack and straightened, wincing as the weight of his own pack shifted. "I can't wait for Destros and Gearing to get back here. Nonee, can you carry me and run?"

"Yes."

"I fail to see why she needs you." Kalyealee who-could-be-heir stepped between them.

Ryan Heir pushed past her, rocking her back on her heels. "The locks of the tower do not yield to the weapon. The Heir's Chronicle? Maybe you should have studied it."

Kalyealee who-could-be-heir flashed fire with her unbound hand. Nonee liked the gesture. It saved a great many words. "And why don't they yield? Because the mage who made her didn't trust her."

"Mages don't trust," Nonee said flatly. "Not their creations. Not each other. Only themselves."

"And trusting in yourself, in your ability, is such a terrible thing." Kalyealee who-could-be-heir tossed her head.

"Only themselves," Nonee repeated.

"I heard you the first time."

Had she? Nonee wondered.

Keetin Norwin-cee waved a hand toward her. "No offense, Nonee, but I kind of understand why they wouldn't trust you. If they'd done to me what they did to you, I'd want to get some of my own back."

"If they'd made you indestructible? Essentially immortal?" Kalyealee who-could-be-heir jabbed her bound fingers toward Keetin Norwin-cee. "This prejudice, this skewing of history to see mage-craft only as destructive, is why expanding the Scholarship of the Broken Lands is so important!"

Ryan Heir's chin rose. "Enough!"

"Agreed." Captain Yansav sank to the ground and used both hands to shift her injured leg. "Nonee, take Servan. You'll need someone who . . ."

Nonee reached out and caught Servan just before she hit the ground.

"Just dizzy," she muttered as Nonee lowered her the last little distance. "I'm okay."

Nonee met the captain's gaze. "Head wound."

The captain sighed. "Yes."

Keetin Norwin-cee coughed, wet and ragged. The captain could barely walk. Destros had not yet returned, held to either Scholar Gearing's pace or the scholar's weight.

"Enough wasting time," Ryan Heir declared. "I'm going in after Harris!"

"No." Kalyealee who-could-be-heir folded her arms. "You're not going in alone. You could destroy irreplaceable scholarship."

"Or it could destroy him," Servan muttered, fingers poking at the cloth wrapped around her head.

Nonee sighed and tucked Ryan Heir under one arm. Blades couldn't pierce her skin; she was safe from his fingernails.

"Both of them?" the captain asked over protests, as Nonee tucked Kalyealee who-could-be-heir against her other side.

Nonee met the captain's gaze again. "She could be heir."

After a moment, the captain nodded.

RYAN.NOW

Ryan clenched his teeth to keep them from taking a piece of his tongue and tried not to puke. Traveling by ancient mage-crafted weapon was fast, but that was all it had to recommend it.

Nonee didn't slow, she stopped, and he opened his eyes as the ground came up to meet him. A few minutes on his hands and knees seemed like an excellent idea. An hour or two seemed like a better one, but he didn't have the time, and before his stomach had fully settled, he sat back on his heels.

The building he faced was enormous. He was too close to see the whole thing, but it looked like it had been made of six or seven large buildings shoved together, with nine or ten smaller buildings randomly attached. The walls were clad in wooden shingles, the roofs were slate, and although no two windows were the same size, they were all surrounded by the same carved wooden framing. A surprising number of the small glass panes were intact. A second look and he could see that the rambling, haphazard nature of the structure camouflaged extensive damage. The building had taken several solid hits during the Mage War. Weathered beams jutting up like wooden teeth showed where an entire floor had been ripped off the northwest corner.

"Is it structurally sound?" Lyelee wheezed, on Nonee's other side.

"Some of it," Nonee told her.

Gripping Nonee's wrist, Ryan hauled himself onto his feet and stumbled toward the large, arched door. He scrubbed at his beard, and, still not entirely sure he wasn't going to throw up, asked, "What do we do to get inside?"

The door had no visible hinges or latch.

Nonee tapped the wood just right of dead center. "Press here."

Ryan pushed his palm against an area as unmarked as the rest of the door. He felt more than heard a double click as a piece of wood rose and slid to the right, exposing a small, square hole.

"There's an iron loop in the hole. Pull it."

"In my opinion . . ." Lyelee moved to Ryan's other side. ". . . sticking your hand in that hole would be unwise."

"Do you have a better idea?" He wiped sweaty palms against his thighs.

"We take a moment to study . . ."

"Harris doesn't have a moment." He shoved his left hand into the hole.

"Idiot," Donal scoffed. *"You could have broken a window and gone in that way."*

"At least he used his non-dominant hand."

"He doesn't have a dominant hand. He doesn't have a dominant anything."

The sides of the hole pulled at his sleeve and scraped against his forearm as a fingertip touched metal. Teeth clenched, he shoved harder until he could hook a finger in the loop and pull.

The door swung inward, pulling his finger from the loop and the wood from around his arm.

Lyelee pushed past him, into the building. He leapt forward on her heels. As Nonee cleared the threshold behind him, the door slammed shut, plunging them into darkness.

For a moment.

"The mage-lights still work," Lyelee announced, breaking the silence.

Ryan glanced up and saw half a dozen balls of white light floating between the beams, just barely illuminating the long, looping lines carved into the dark wood, most of their light directed downward. The room had six wood-paneled walls, five doors, and a hearth. Four of the doors were single slabs of carved wood, the fifth was a wide double door with ornate steel handles. On each side of the double door was a tall window constructed from single sheets of impossibly large and impossibly clear glass.

Nonee grabbed both handles and opened the door. Sunlight poured in. Outside was blue sky and sun-bleached grass. At the edge of the overgrown garden, Ryan could see where the road up the hill became a path.

"Mage-craft," Lyelee announced.

"No flaming shit," he muttered, then raised his voice. "Nonee, Harris!"

Nonee ducked through the door to the right of the hearth, mage-lights flashing on when her foot touched the floor. Running full out, Ryan could just keep up. He could hear Lyelee complaining behind him, but he kept his attention on Nonee, half afraid he'd lose her if he looked away.

As they slowed to descend a delicate spiral staircase that shouldn't have been able to hold Nonee's bulk but somehow did, the wall moved under his braced hand. Rocking back, he curled his fingers away from a writhing figure with too many arms that seemed to be trying, and failing, to break free of the wood. "Nonee . . ."

"They bite," she said, squeezing around the final turn. "And they don't let go."

"Great. Lyelee!" He held both hands carefully away from the wall as he continued to descend. "Don't touch the carvings! They're dangerous."

"Mage-tower," Lyelee yelled back. "Of course they're dangerous. If you'd paid attention to . . ."

Nonee reached the lower level and sped up, pounding footsteps drowning out Lyelee's voice.

Ryan followed her around a corner and another and another, and considered asking if the lack of doors meant there were no actual rooms in the mage-tower except for the workroom.

Finally, they entered a hall so long the door at the other end seemed no more than knee high.

"The workroom," Nonee said, rocking to a stop.

Harris was on the other side of that door.

Gasping for breath, air burning in his throat, he pushed past her and had gone half a dozen steps when he realized distance had nothing to do with the size of the door. Another few steps, and he had to bend or brain himself on the lowering ceiling. A few more, and he had to crouch.

"Ryan!"

"Stay back, Lyelee! I've got this."

LYELEE.NOW

Lyelee watched Ryan drop from a crouch onto his hands and knees. "Does he think the ceiling is coming closer?" The carvings along both sides of the hall watched him pass. Were they activated by proximity?

Nonee shifted. "If Ryan Heir keeps moving forward, he won't be harmed."

Lyelee pulled pencil and notebook from her satchel. She could note the rough placement of the carvings now and add detail when she got closer. "And if he stops moving forward?"

"Then he could be harmed."

"How?"

Nonee shrugged, jostling Lyelee's arm and sending the pencil skittering across the page. "Tanika Fleshrender played with expectations."

"Expectations? If he worries about being hurt, the odds of him being hurt are higher?"

"Yes." Nonee looked down at her, brow creased, as though she were surprised Lyelee had drawn the correct conclusion.

"Scholar," Lyelee muttered, returning to her sketch. Nonee had no idea of what scholars were capable of. But then, so few did.

RYAN.NOW

Ryan rose up on his elbows to pull himself forward and his shoulders brushed against the sides of the hall. His back pressed against the ceiling. "There had to be easier ways to protect the workroom," he grumbled.

"It's a test," Donal told him. *"And you're failing it."*

The damp cloth over his elbows provided traction against the polished wooden floor. He rammed the toes of his boots against the wall beneath the lowest carvings, and pushed himself forward. Almost . . .

Then he cracked his head on the ceiling. The walls moved in closer. Rocking from side to side to free himself, he jammed himself in tighter.

His breath misted against the floor and he wasted a moment wondering who'd been polishing the wood for the last hundred and sixty-three years. He should go back. Send Lyelee in. She was smaller. She'd be able to wriggle close enough to reach the door.

"Send Lyelee in? She doesn't listen to you."

"No one listens to him."

"Why should they?"

He couldn't move forward. He couldn't move back . . .

Heart pounding, he reminded himself he wasn't trapped because he wasn't alone. "Nonee?"

Nonee didn't answer.

"You call this a rescue, little brother?"

"Harris'll be dead by the time you get there."

"Good thing he's no one important."

He couldn't breathe.

He remembered how the carving had writhed. Remembered the carvings lining the hall.

He jerked back, shuddering. Then he twisted and jerked forward again as what felt like a serrated sliver of hot iron was driven into his calf.

Gasping, his shoulders curled in, and he jerked like a fish gaffed to the bottom of the boat. He could hear his brothers laughing at him.

"Did he get a splinter in his precious little leg? Is he going to cry about it?"

"Shut up, Donal!" In a minute, Nonee would see he wasn't moving, grab his feet and drag him out. He wasn't stuck here. He wasn't . . .

He squinted. With the mage-lights warping the shadows it was hard to tell how close he was to the door, but it looked closer than it had a moment ago. Shaking sweat out of his eyes, he stretched out his right arm. Almost. Tucked his left shoulder back. Muscles and joints along his right side protesting, his fingertip touched wood.

Just. A. Little. Further.

His lungs burned.

His left leg felt as though it were on fire.

He couldn't smell smoke. He wondered if that mattered.

He poked the center of the door and a panel opened. Forced a finger into the hole. Hooked it over the loop. Pulled.

And found himself lying on the floor in front of a full-sized door in a large, well-lit hall.

Gasping, tasting blood, he flopped over onto his back to see Nonee approach, knife in hand. The pain in his leg stole his question.

On her knees beside him, she was all he could see. Had she always been so enormous? Had he shrunk with the . . .

"Burn it!" Ryan lurched up, as though the piece of his flesh she held on the point of her knife had been tied to his shoulders, the pain pulling him . . .

He frowned. It hurt. But it hurt like someone had dug a fish hook from his leg, not like ripping the entire leg off was the only way to stop the pain.

"You're bleeding all over the floor." Lyelee stood on his other side, looking down, head cocked.

Balanced on the blade of Nonee's knife was a tiny face covered in blood with a chunk of . . . of his leg protruding through the spaces between triangular teeth. More disturbing, it wasn't a head. Just a face with distended cheeks. Only Nonee's hand on his leg kept him from squirming away.

"Oh, a little face! I'm so scared!"

"It came from here." Lyelee pointed at the blank bit of polished wood within a row of similar faces. "Fortunately for you, you were only in range of the lowest level. The upper carvings are much larger and would have presumably done more damage. Although I'm not sure how; they don't have mouths."

"On their faces," Nonee said.

"Ah." She moved closer to the carving in question. Close enough, Ryan enjoyed the thought of it taking a piece out of her.

And was just as glad when it didn't. He wouldn't wish that pain on anyone.

Nonee pressed her thumbnail against the blade to crack the face like a tick, then dragged his left pant leg out of his boot and ripped off the fabric below the bite, using it to pack and wrap the wound. Sweat plastered his clothes to his body and later there'd be nightmares, but the door was open—he'd opened the door—and Harris was on the other side. The moment Nonee tied off the dressing, he held out a hand. "Help me up."

He staggered as he put his left leg down, pain shooting up hip high, but he gritted his teeth and pivoted around his right. "Let's go. Nonee, any traps?"

"Any *more* traps," Lyelee corrected.

"No."

The door opened into a rectangle of darkness. Total, absolute darkness.

"That's the workroom?" Lyelee seemed unconvinced.

"Yes." Shoulders angled to fit, Nonee stepped over the threshold and disappeared.

Another burning portal.

Harris, Ryan reminded himself, and followed. Between one painful step and the next he found himself in a room nearly the size of the Citadel's largest audience chamber. The nearest tables were empty, but the shelves and cabinets against the walls held thousands of glass bottles and beakers: some empty, some full of colored liquid, some he didn't want to study too closely. The mage-lights, hidden in among the bales and bundles hanging from the high ceiling, were significantly brighter than those in the rest of the tower. There were no windows.

Abandoned for so many years, it should have smelled of dust and ancient herbs.

It smelled of blood and shit.

"Harris!" Ryan charged forward and ran into Nonee's arm.

"Careful," she told him.

They found Harris by the far wall, hanging naked from a metal frame. Blood dripped off his heels into a shallow basin. Nothing visibly supported his weight.

His breath slid between lips chewed bloody. His eyes were closed.

Ryan gave thanks for small mercies.

There was a drain in the bottom of the basin.

"Is he dead?" Lyelee called.

"No," Ryan began.

Nonee cut him off. "Yes."

"He's still breathing!" Ryan meant to command, but, even to his own ears, he sounded more like a demanding child. "Get him down! Now!"

She sighed, but tucked her fingers in under Harris's armpits, her thumbs stretching across his chest. To Ryan's surprise, she didn't lift him, she pulled him toward her, away from the frame.

Away from the thousands of slender spikes driven into Harris's back— into the back of his neck, shoulders, arms, buttocks, legs . . . Spikes long enough that they'd gone through muscle and into the organs those muscles protected. In places, they had to have gone into bone.

Ryan swallowed. And again. Refused to vomit.

Hanging from Nonee's hands, Harris spasmed. Muscles twisted under his skin, arms and legs flopped without the strength to flail. Blood flow increased for a moment, spattering against the slate floor beside the basin, then tapered off.

Nonee shifted her grip and eased Harris down on the closest table, stepping aside and leaving room for Ryan to come closer. He took a step. Braced himself on the edge of the table. Took one more.

He couldn't hear Harris breathing. Had moving him killed him?

"Failed again, little brother."

He leaned in until Harris's blood-encrusted beard brushed his cheek, his ear almost touching the older man's lips, his right palm just left of center on Harris's chest. Beneath the wiry curls, the skin felt cool and damp.

Beneath the skin, beneath the bone, Harris's heart thumped weakly. Once. Then again.

Beneath Ryan's ear, Harris sucked in tiny sips of air then gasped them out again.

"He's not dead!" He looked to Nonee.

"Not yet."

Ryan had seen his share of bodies, even before they'd brought his brothers ashore, but he'd never seen anyone die.

"The Scholars of Flesh believe the brain continues to be aware until the end," Lyelee announced.

Aware of the punctures. Aware of the blood dripping into the basin. Aware . . .

"Don't touch him." Ryan pushed her reaching hand away.

She tossed her head. "When his heart stops, his blood will stop moving, and his brain will starve, but until then, his brain is functional." She frowned. "There've been attempts to maintain the brain artificially after the body dies, but with no success. The brain starves too quickly. That said, given the length of those spikes, he should have died instantly. If mage-craft is keeping him alive, mage-craft could heal him."

"Lyelee."

"Except mage-craft has been deliberately forgotten, the history erased . . ."

"Lyelee!"

They should have moved faster. Should have sent Nonee crashing through the tower, through the doors, through the traps. Harris should have stayed in Marsanport, lived to be old.

"I'm sorry," he whispered.

He received no absolution. Only fast, shallow breathing that sounded as though a thousand spikes had lodged in Harris's throat. Breathing that sounded as though Harris had screamed until he couldn't scream any longer.

Muscles twisted inside the clammy sheath of skin. The breathing stopped.

Then began again.

Ryan stepped back and only Nonee's grip kept him off the floor as pain shot through his left leg, lines of fire burning down into his foot, up into his hip.

On the table, Harris whined.

Ryan recognized the sound. He'd been making that sound in the hall outside the workroom. "He's in pain. Pain like from the bite on my leg. Does each hole . . . the holes where the spikes went in . . . does each hole hurt like the bite?"

"Yes." Her hand was a cool support against his side.

He blinked. Tears ran down his cheeks into his beard. "If your Arianna was here . . ."

"No." Nonee's lips twisted. "Not even then. Only mage-craft can counter mage-craft."

He heard Lyelee sniff derisively. "And we've deliberately forgotten the good with the bad."

"How much longer until . . ." Ryan wet his lips. "Until it kills him?"

Nonee released him without answering.

He glanced over at the frame. At the spikes. At the basin. At the drain. Those caught in the trap were intended to survive until they bled out, mage-craft keeping the body alive in spite of the damage. "She chose pain," he realized. "She could have chosen to make it painless, but she chose pain."

"Yes. She studied pain. Used it in her makings."

"She . . ." Ryan shook his head and couldn't finish. Nonee was a strong, solid presence at his side. A mage-crafted weapon. His to command. "Can you end it? End his pain?"

"Yes."

How much of *her* pain had Tanika Fleshrender studied?

"You know what I'd do, but you haven't the balls for it."

He took a deep breath, drawing air that tasted of blood past his teeth as he held Harris's right hand in both of his. This wasn't a killing, it was a kindness. "End it."

When he'd broken his arm, it had sounded like a dry branch snapping. He'd never seen a hanging, but his brothers had laughed about how clearly the crack had sounded. Harris's neck broke with the same layered sound a turkey's neck made in the cook's hands. Ryan waited until Harris's heart stopped beating, until the body sagged against the table, death releasing it from the rigidity of pain, then he turned away.

"I couldn't . . ." Ryan began and trailed off. Uncertain. His hands were bloody. He wiped his eyes on the back of his wrist. "I'll find something to wrap the body in."

"Those cabinets." Nonee pointed across the room. "Be careful."

He was embarrassingly grateful to move away. The cabinets held cloth, but nothing large enough to wrap around Harris's body. "What about this?" He grabbed the edge of a canvas tarp and dragged it off the top of a deep metal tank.

And nearly gagged.

Blood and shit and viscera.

Too much blood to be Harris's: crimson currents running through thick, dark liquid. Too much bone. Too much. "Is this the other . . . ?"

"Yes."

"You didn't look."

"She doesn't need to." Lyelee leaned in over the other side of the tank, hand cupped over her mouth and nose to block the smell. "The male weapon went through the portal, so he had to be in here somewhere. He's been broken down into raw material to be reused."

Nonee met Ryan's gaze. "Tanika Fleshrender made seventeen weapons, not six. The failures went into the tank. The mothers went into the tank."

"That's . . ." Ryan couldn't find the words.

As usual, Lyelee had no problem. "Harris's blood dripped into the basin, then the basin drained into the tank. Fresh blood must have been a necessary part of the crafting. This is fascinating."

Ryan saw no point in demanding she respect the loss of the man who'd taken care of her, of them all, since they left Marsanport. *Harris is dead, she'd say. Why would he care? We should respect his life by learning from his death.*

She wouldn't be entirely wrong. She was never entirely wrong.

Some days, Ryan hated that about her.

He wrestled the canvas over to the table where Nonee waited. There was surprisingly little blood under Harris's body. Had they taken even a few moments more, would he have died on the rack? Had the pain wiped out all thought of rescue? Ryan hoped it had. Hoped that Harris hadn't been able to wonder why they were taking so long to find him.

Almost hoped he'd been in too much pain to give into despair.

Almost.

"He should have expected you to be late. You're not exactly dependable. I wonder if he screamed your name?" Donal sounded amused.

Ryan shifted his weight onto his left leg and used the pain to drive his brother back to the grave. When he finished wrapping Harris's body, he turned to find Nonee staring at the tank, hands curled into fists, shoulders raised. "Nonee?"

"That's where she spent some of her truncated childhood. The contents, infused with mage-craft, caused her to grow faster as well as larger and stronger." Now standing by a set of shelves, Lyelee used her finger to mark her place in the book she carried. "According to this, Harris's blood is a base to be used as . . ."

"How can you read that?" Ryan snapped, anger easier to feel than grief and guilt. "There's no way the mages used a language you know."

Lyelee rolled her eyes. "If you'll recall, the mages came from different countries and created the trade language used around the lake. This language is clearly one of the roots of that language. I can do a loose translation based on context, but once back in the Scholar's Hall, with access to the archive and samples of the six original languages, I'll . . ."

"You'll leave the book here."

"I will not." She glared across the room at him. "This is a scholarship matter and you have no . . ."

"Leave it," Ryan repeated. His part in Harris's death added weight to his voice.

"You can't . . ."

"Leave it."

Lips pressed into a thin line, Lyelee placed the book on the nearest table.

LYELEE.NOW

Lyelee emerged from the portal into the hall to hear Ryan ask if the fuel was in the workroom. Idiot. Anyone with an ability to reason would have asked while they were in the workroom.

Nonee shifted her burden. A drop of blood rolled off the canvas, hit the floor, and disappeared. "No."

"If the fuel was in the workroom, she'd have said." Lyelee crouched and touched the polished boards where the blood had landed. Completely dry. "Does blood go to the tank from everywhere in the tower?"

"No. Not from everywhere."

Ryan took a deep breath, let it out slowly, and said, "Nonee, I may need help on the stairs. Lyelee, close the door."

"Do the places that transport blood have functions tied to the workroom?" she asked as she straightened. "Or do . . ."

Ryan cut her off. "Close the flaming door, Lyelee!"

Because of course she'd instantly obey a barked command from a boy who'd been given authority by chance. The desire to avoid a tedious argument was not acquiescence. If the trap that had dropped Ryan to his belly was negated by opening the door, then as long as the door remained open, the trap should remain negated. She forced a bit of cork she'd taken from the workroom into the lock, preventing the latch from engaging.

And closed the door.

ARIANNA.THEN

Arianna watched her fingertips leave white imprints in the swollen skin above Norik's hip and shook her head. "It's definitely infected." Reaching into her kit, she pulled out a packet of dried red clover. "Malcolm!" When he turned, she tossed it to him. "Take the pot off the fire and stir half of this into the water."

"Weeds in water," Norik protested mournfully. "I don't get honey?"

"You get honey on the wound after I clean it."

"I don't get a spoonful if I'm good?" He winked down at her.

She grinned. "Good at what?"

"Your choice." He shifted, pushing his hip forward, trying to get a better look, and she smacked his leg.

"Hold still."

"It's a scratch."

"And it's infected." She leaned forward, hand braced against his thigh, nose nearly touching his skin, and drew in a deep breath. Under the sweat and salt and wool and damp and all the days of travel caught between his skin and his clothing, Arianna could just barely smell the slightly sweet scent of wrong. "You've got three layers on," she said, sitting back on her heels, frowning at the bulk of jacket, vest, and shirt held up out of her way. "And all of them are intact. What happened?"

Norik shrugged. "No idea. Heat of the battle. I stretched or rolled or zigged when I should have zagged. Cut on my upper arm is worse."

"The cut on your arm is deeper and it bled enough to wash the poisons out." She leaned in again, only this time she exhaled, her breath filling the space between them with warmth. When she leaned out, the swelling followed her. She caught the pus in a cloth, and wiped the wound clean. Leaned in again . . .

"Am I interrupting?"

Garrett didn't sound happy. Arianna exhaled once more before she glanced over at him. He didn't look happy either, scowling at her or at Norik or at them both. He was obviously not pleased about her using skills he considered a hair's breadth from mage-craft on his best friend. She glanced up to see Norik grinning broadly, his expression the complete opposite of Garrett's.

"I'm being healed," he said cheerfully.

"You've been healed," Arianna corrected, standing and shaking out her skirts. Arms folded, she frowned. "Is anyone else hiding pain or swelling?"

"I wasn't hiding it," Norik protested.

She could hear him tugging his clothing back into place behind her. She kept her gaze on the other two. "Well?"

Over by the fire, Malcolm touched the bandage on his jaw. "You saw to all mine, Healer."

"And you, Garrett?"

Still scowling, he opened his mouth, but a crash from further inside the building cut him off. "I need to check the weapon," he growled when he could be heard.

"That doesn't prevent you from . . ." Arianna began.

Torch in hand, he disappeared through the double doors on the far side of the room. As Norik moved to follow she grabbed his sleeve. "I'm not done with you."

"I need to . . ."

"You need to not die because the infection got into your blood. He's with Uvili. He'll be fine." He'd been fine when he went off on his own to check the surrounding rooms. If he'd found something dangerous, he should have said. "Unless whatever crawled up his butt dies," she muttered, crossing to the hearth.

Malcolm tossed a grin over his shoulder as he put more wood on the fire. They'd found a tumbled pile in an adjoining storeroom, plenty to last through the night. "Really, Ari? You don't know what's wrong with him?" Norik cleared his throat and Malcolm's grin disappeared. "I don't either," he added hurriedly.

As they were clearly keeping secrets, and she wasn't twelve, it seemed more productive to turn her attention to the tea. She checked the color, poured the liquid off the layer of blossoms and leaves settled in the bottom of the pot into two of the tin mugs warming by the embers, handed one to Malcolm and the other to Norik. "Drink."

"What is it?"

"Red clover, to purify your blood." On her way to the pump, she dumped the wet foliage into a dented basin under one of the two huge tables. Half underground, with stone walls and a heavy beamed ceiling, most of the kitchen had survived the attack that collapsed the rear of the mage-tower. Although one corner had buckled, taking half of the north wall down, the other three walls—and more importantly the ceiling—were solid. To her delight, the pump by the deep, stone sink still worked and, after a moment or two, the water had run clear.

Snow would have been easier to purify than any surface water they might find in the Broken Lands, but a deep well was better still. And almost as cold.

"And what of you, Healer?" Norik asked. "You were in the thick of it with the rest of us. Any swelling or pain where a bit of bone or debris punctured the skin?"

Arianna grinned at his pompous, imitation-healer tone. "I don't get infections."

"Because you're a healer and trained to be on top of things." Malcolm rolled his eyes, the expression as close as he could come to telling the older man he'd asked a stupid question.

"And because you're . . ." Perched on the edge of the cracked butcher's block, Norik spread his hands. "What was it? A talent? And you heal your own body?"

"Can you be killed?" Garrett demanded from the doorway.

She rolled her eyes much as Malcolm had earlier. "Of course I can. I don't heal instantly, it just gives me an edge."

"And you don't get infections," Norik added.

"And I don't get infections."

Garrett snorted.

Arianna leaned toward him. "Do you have a problem with . . ."

"What's up with the weapon?" Norik cut her off.

"Couldn't get a door open; they're all like the door we came in, the latch is too small for her hand. She took the wall down instead." Garrett crossed to the hearth and threw his torch on the fire. "How many talents are there in Gateway, Healer?"

She backed away from the spray of sparks. "I don't know."

He stepped toward her. "Try again."

"All right." She met him halfway. Of course she knew. What kind of healer would she be if she didn't? "It's none of your business."

"I am the Heir of Marsan!"

"So what?" The light of the fire extended just far enough that she could see Norik and Malcolm exchange a speaking glance safely behind Garrett's back. "Marsan is nothing to us. Admittedly," she spat, not bothering to hide her irritation, "life would be easier if Marsanport allowed traders access to the road. But we manage quite well, thank you. We don't need you, but we helped you regardless. And . . ." She stomped hard on the protest he was about to make. ". . . try to remember I—a talent—volunteered to come with you because you had no idea what you'd be facing in the Broken Lands."

"And you do?"

"I know more than you."

"Did you know about the mage-craft that killed Petre? Or the monster before that? Or the walking dead? Or did you decide not to tell us?"

She heard Norik suck in a breath behind her. She recognized displacement of grief. She knew Garrett wasn't actually angry at her. It didn't matter. "You are such an ass!"

If talent was the mage-craft he thought it was, he'd *be* an ass.

Nostrils flared, he was breathing heavily enough she could feel the air moving between them. He opened his mouth, teeth flashing in the dark of his beard, then he snapped them together with an audible click, grabbed another of the prepared torches, and thrust it into the fire. "I'm going to check on the weapon," he growled when it was lit.

"No." Uvili spread her hands. "Done."

Arianna hadn't seen her come into the kitchen, nor from his reaction had Garrett.

"Then I'm going to check on the path you've cleared." It sounded as though his teeth had fused together. "Malcolm, bring the rest of the wood in. I don't want to navigate that storeroom in the middle of the night."

"My lord, that's . . ." Malcolm broke off as Norik shook his head in silent warning. "Yes, sir."

"Norik, check the perimeter. Make sure the door will hold if the dead cross the garden. Now!" he added.

Alone in the kitchen with Uvili, Arianna sighed.

"Hurt. Dead boy," she added when Arianna looked up at her.

"He's hurting because of Petre's death, and that's making him more irritating than usual?"

"Yes. And . . ."

"And?"

Uvili shook her head, then nodded toward the hearth. "Tea?" she said.

NONEE.NOW

Nonee watched Captain Yansav limp over to Harris's body, brace herself on her good leg, bend, and flip the canvas off his face.

"What happened?"

"Nonee killed him."

"Lyelee!" Keetin sounded more weary than angry, but he did sound angry.

"She killed him to end an allegedly agonizing and inevitable dying," Kalyealee who-could-be-heir explained. "But that doesn't change the fact that Nonee killed him."

Ryan Heir sagged against the wall and shook his head. "I gave the order."

Kalyealee who-could-be-heir shook hers back at him, the motion exaggerated. "And Nonee killed him."

The captain looked up from the body and met Nonee's gaze. "Did you?"

"Yes." She'd have done it without the order, but Ryan Heir had been willing to carry the burden. Not the first burden his inheritance had handed him, but the heaviest so far. Not the last burden his inheritance would hand him, but she'd begun to believe he had the necessary strength.

Captain Yansav covered Harris's face and stepped back, turned until she fully faced Ryan Heir, and said, "A hard decision, my lord."

The captain couldn't tell him he'd done well or that she was proud of him, not with Harris's body lying on the ground between them, but Nonee hoped Ryan Heir heard it anyway.

He pushed off the wall. "We need to bury him before we lose the light. Nonee . . ."

"Yes."

The people of Marsanport had no attachment to bodies. She'd seen it when they buried Curtin. She saw when they buried Harris. No one mentioned, then or now, that they wished they could bring the body back to his family. No one was concerned that they would leave him behind. It was housekeeping. She approved. The Broken Lands were unforgiving of sentiment.

She waited at the side of the grave with the purkin-flower distillate.

Destros squared his shoulders. "Given the amount of tea he made since we left home, he had to have been carrying a bale when we set out. Harris was stronger than he looked."

"I can confirm that." Servan grinned. So did Destros. They both ignored the lines of moisture on their cheeks. Then they touched fists. Based on the interaction over Curtin's grave, Nonee assumed Harris had had sex with them both. Then she wondered if Destros only had sex with men. Without lifting her head, she noted how the light from the setting sun lingered on the breadth of his shoulders and acknowledged it didn't actually matter.

"Bales of tea would've been in the wagon," Scholar Gearing pointed out, rubbing at the sweat on his neck. "And I assure you they weren't. But Harris's rabbit stew, with wild garlic and chive," he continued, smiling, "that deserved a place in the history books."

"And those trout." Captain Yansav kissed her fingertips. "Crispy on the outside, never burned."

A chorus of agreement rang out.

Keetin Norwin-cee dropped a handful of dirt into the grave. "Harris mended my breeches, on horseback, without impaling himself on the needle."

"Impressive hand-to-eye coordination," the captain agreed.

"I wasn't wearing them at the time, Captain."

"Slightly less impressive, then."

Everyone smiled, if only for a moment.

From the angle of Captain Yansav's hips, most of her weight rested on her right leg. Nonee hoped her left knee would heal enough to hold her before they started back. Keetin Norwin-cee had found the captain's sword while they waited for Scholar Gearing and Destros, but if she couldn't stand, it wouldn't be much use. They were already down two fighters, the bite on Ryan Heir's calf would hobble him for days, and getting out of the Broken Lands was harder than getting in.

Ryan Heir cleared his throat, once, twice, and finally managed, "Harris never resented taking care of us."

"Why would he?" Kalyealee who-could-be-heir asked, arms folded, fingers of her unbound hand tapping against skin. Impatient. For what?

"Because we're adults," Ryan Heir snapped. "We should be able to take care of ourselves."

"It was his job."

Nonee saw Ryan Heir swallow, but he met Kalyealee who-could-be-heir's narrowed eyes with a strong and steady gaze. "Plenty of people resent the work they have to do."

"Then they should do something else. Although," she admitted, "Harris didn't know much besides taking care of people and he didn't want to learn."

"He didn't want to listen to you lecture."

"That's what I said."

But Kalyealee who-could-be-heir was looking only at her cousin. Nonee could see the faces she couldn't and none of them agreed with her. "He was kind," she said. He'd never managed to look directly at her, but he'd never treated her as other. He'd offered her tea. Made sure she'd eaten. Asked how she'd slept. Acknowledged they were both servants of the Lord Protector.

"You never cleaned a fish for him." Servan broke the silence, both grinning and crying again. "He was a pushy pain in the ass. Took pride in it, too."

"Kind," Nonee repeated. "Not nice. Kind is better." She poured the distillate over the body. "The trap's release has kept predators away, but the sun is almost down. They'll grow brave again."

Ryan Heir nodded. "Let's finish giving Harris Arentin's body to the earth and get inside."

Harris Arentin. He had two names. Although they used his own name, not his family name, Ryan Heir had known it.

Kalyealee who-could-be-heir, who claimed to value knowledge above all else, hadn't known it.

RYAN.NOW

Ryan looked down at the stone stairs, at the slight dip in the middle of each step, at the darkness that claimed the space beyond the spill of light from the six-sided room, and assumed there'd be light once he stepped over the threshold. "I go down the stairs, I grab the fuel, and I climb back up the stairs. Sounds easy enough."

"You forgot *face the eldritch horror*," Keetin said behind him. "And that you can't put your full weight on your left leg. If you make it down—and that's a solid *if*—you'll have to hop back up."

"Hopping beats waiting around until someone else dies."

"And I'd rather you weren't the one dying." Keetin's hand was a warm weight on his shoulder. "Wait until morning. Rest."

"I'll rest after I have the fuel. If I get it now, we can start home at first light."

"And if you weren't likely to plummet down a hundred stairs, breaking your fool neck, I'd back your play, but remember, if you die we'll have to send Lyelee down and no one wants her as Lord Protector."

"Except her mother, her uncle, and about half the Court." Not to mention his dead brothers. He shifted his weight to his left leg and lifted his right. The pain was . . .

Shifting his weight back to his right leg, Ryan waited for the bands of pain clamped around his chest to release and took a deep breath.

"Ryan?"

"On the other hand," he panted, "if I wait until morning, we can leave immediately after I return."

~

"This room," Nonee said, "is safe until the fuel enters it."

Ryan sighed, sliding down the wall until he could sit on the floor, left leg stretched out in front of him. "Good enough. We'll stay here tonight, then. The doors open inward. Prop a pack on each and we'll have advance warning if any . . . thing tries to get in."

Captain Yansav straightened and squared her shoulders. "Nonee, you'll be on guard overnight?"

"Yes."

Arms folded, Lyelee swept a disapproving gaze around the room. "According to the Heir's Chronicle, there's water in the kitchens."

"There *was* water in the kitchens," Ryan reminded her. She wanted to explore. He didn't exactly blame her, but it wasn't going to happen. "And we have water."

"The kitchen has a working hearth," she continued, ignoring him. "Or are we to live on dried fish and berries because Harris isn't here to make the tea?"

"A tea would be lovely." Gearing glanced around, looking hopeful.

Ryan wanted to tell Lyelee she was right, no Harris, no tea, but he sat silent while Nonee checked and pronounced the hearth in the six-sided room usable. He sat silent while Servan slipped out into the gathering dusk to break dead branches off the closest tree. And sat silent while Destros pulled pots and pans from Harris's pack.

The others found the tea comforting. Ryan found it a reminder of how he'd failed.

"You should be used to that by now."

※

"So what do you think these shelves are for?" Servan pointed an arrow at one of the alcoves cut into each side of the gray, stone mantle over the hearth. It was fully dark outside, but the mage-lights were still on.

"Candles?" Ryan guessed. They all needed to sleep, but no one could.

"Homunculi."

Ryan wasn't the only one startled as Nonee dropped the word into the room.

"Ho what now?" Servan prodded after a minute.

"Homunculi are small, artificial persons." Gearing sat up, clutching his satchel, showing more energy than Ryan had seen from him in days. "The Archives had a book, purported to have been written by Parcelcese the Tryronian—much copied of course, the original would be long since dust—brought to Marsanport by one of the Five Thousand from perhaps this very place. The book states homunculi can be made by confining the essence of man in a horse's womb until it is putrefied and begins to move on its own."

Servan made a face and twirled the arrow around her fingers. "That's more than anyone needs to know, Scholar. Disgusting above and beyond is one of the reasons mage-craft is banned."

"No, it isn't!" Gearing's eyes gleamed above the semicircles of shadow that had become part of his face. He looked almost feverish, shifting his weight from side to side. "How many times do I have to tell you, Guardian, that knowledge isn't mage-craft until it's applied!"

"So if you know it, and don't apply it?"

"It's scholarship."

"*Can* you know it and not apply it?"

Gearing slapped his palm down on the floor. "Don't be ridiculous!"

Squatting in front of the exit, Nonee cleared her throat. "The captain said the knowledge of mage-craft would never take root in Marsanport."

"The captain has no business speaking of . . ." Bushy brows drawn in, Gearing glanced over at Captain Yansav then back at Nonee. "You refer to Captain Marsan."

"Yes."

He made a dismissive sound so vehemently the gray hair curling down over his upper lip puffed out. "And you expect me to believe you remember her words, her exact words, after all this time?"

Nonee shrugged. "You believe what you believe."

His chin rose, beard waggling. "Knowledge is not about belief!"

She shrugged again. "Mage-craft can be."

"Mage-craft has measurable results," he snorted, flopping back down onto his bedroll and closing his eyes so emphatically Ryan half expected to hear the lids slam. "Belief has nothing to do with it."

Keetin leaned close, breath warm against Ryan's ear. "What's up with him?"

"He's jealous," Ryan told him. "Lyelee went into the workroom. He didn't." He raised his voice. "Nonee, are these homunu-things likely to show up in the night?"

Nonee's hands closed into fists. "No."

He turned away from her smile, hair lifting off the back of his neck.

"The Heir's Chronicle says the heir has to go after the fuel alone," Captain Yansav said thoughtfully. "That the fuel can only be retrieved by one of Captain Marsan's blood."

Nonee snorted.

Ryan leaned forward. "That's not true?"

"Tanika Fleshrender allowed only one person on the stairs at a time."

"For safety." The captain nodded. "So she'd never face more than one enemy at a time."

"Yes. You enter." Nonee pointed at Ryan, who swallowed and nearly choked on it. "The door closes behind you. No one else can enter until you leave. But it doesn't have to be you."

Ryan thought of the reaction in Marsanport if he returned with fuel Servan or Destros or Keetin or even Lyelee had retrieved.

"*Derision,*" Donal scoffed.

"No one would be surprised."

"On the bright side, you didn't want to be heir."

"No," he said. "It has to be me. It's in the job description." He swept what he hoped looked like a smile around the room. "The heir returns with the fuel."

Nonee stared at him for a long moment and shrugged.

The mage-lights went out.

"Sleep now," Nonee said in the darkness.

Ryan shuffled down until he lay flat on the floor, closed his eyes, and watched Harris die against the inside of his lids.

When Gearing began to snore, it was almost comforting.

He didn't know how much sleep the others got, but he woke half a hundred times, barely dozing in between. He didn't only dream of Harris. Once, it had been Curtin on the spikes. The final time he woke, he saw Nonee silhouetted in the open exit, eyes locked on the dawn. She made a soft huff of acknowledgment when he joined her. He should have a thousand questions to ask her but he could only think of one.

"What if I fail?"

"Then you fail. And your part in the story is done." After a moment she added, "Given what Marsanport believes will happen when . . . if the flame goes out, best not fail." She shifted just enough to bump their sides together, then caught him as he bounced against the doorframe. "You're stronger than you think."

"Yeah. Thanks." He rubbed his shoulder. "You too."

"Yes."

They sat in silence, listening to the others thrash and whimper.

❧

"Get in. Get the fuel. Get out." Captain Yansav handed him the daypack.

Ryan frowned at the weight. "What's in this thing?"

Keetin spread his hands. "Water, dried sausage, oat cakes—crumbling, but still good—bandages, the jar of Arianna's ointment, and the piece of silk the Scholars of the Flame gave you to wrap around the fuel."

"I won't be gone . . ."

"You don't know how long you'll be gone." Keetin frowned, dirt emphasizing the creases in his forehead. "You don't know how long it'll take to get down the stairs. You don't know what exactly you have to do to retrieve the fuel, because for some inexplicable reason, this is where the chronicles get coy. And you don't know what's involved in fighting an eldritch horror or even what one is."

"Fight a what?" Nonee demanded.

"*Eldritch* means strange and sinister," Gearing told her. "Derived from a word used by the Nort, moving up the Great Lake from Southport, which is, of course, as far as Nort traders have ever come. *I retrieved the fuel and fought an eldritch horror.*" He closed both hands around his satchel strap. "I see nothing inexplicable in the Lord Protector refusing to terrify later searchers for the fuel."

"You know what's terrifying?" Keetin demanded. "A complete lack of useful information."

"We don't need to depend on the chronicles, Nonee was there," Ryan reminded Gearing, taking what he admitted was a petty pleasure in the scholar's disgruntled expression. "What did the Lord Protector say he fought, Nonee?"

"Tentacles."

"Tentacles?" Ryan cleared his throat. "Like in the lake?"

"Yes. It's the same lake," she added.

"Same creature?"

"It's all one creature. Don't let it get hold of you and you'll be fine."

"Fine?"

"It's easy to cut through. No bones." She cocked her head. "Why isn't that in your chronicle?"

"Good question." Ryan shot the two scholars a promissory glance. "I'll ask the Lord Protector that when we return."

Gearing stepped back, but Lyelee snorted. "And he'll tell you that the carrots are always underdone and no one cooks them properly for old people. He didn't remember who you were half the time; he's not going to remember why he came to a decision a lifetime ago."

She wasn't wrong, but Ryan didn't think she needed to look so flaming smug about it. Tentacles. The kind that had left bands of bruising around Keetin's body. The kind that would have drowned him had Nonee not returned in time. What would happen if he died fighting?

"If you die, the door will open to another's hand. Your body will be sent to the workroom."

How long would they wait until they sent Lyelee down after him? Keetin and Servan were of the Five Thousand; would they be sent down next? Would Marsanport accept Calintris Servan-cee as heir if she retrieved the fuel?

"Ryan?" Keetin touched his arm, hand warm through his sleeve.

Focus. "Get the fuel and become Lord Protector." He almost managed a laugh. "I'm amazed there aren't a steady stream of ambitious young nobles trying for it."

"Twenty-eight days on the road, the Broken Lands, and an eldritch horror," Keetin reminded him.

"That might discourage them."

"But you're here."

"I'm hard to discourage."

"Would you just go!" Lyelee snapped.

Doing the opposite would be petty and pointless, Ryan acknowledged silently . . .

. . . and opened the door.

GARRETT.THEN

Garrett couldn't hit them, they moved too quickly. Small and dun-colored, they'd attacked the weapon the moment she'd stepped into the six-sided room, a sudden, vicious assault as if they'd known that once she was down they could pick off the rest of the party at their leisure.

There were two.

Only two.

The weapon was fast, but they were faster. She smacked one away from her face and yanked the other off her shoulder, black blood oozing from the hole it left behind.

Arrows couldn't pierce her flesh.

These things could.

The first scrambled around to her back, too far down for her to reach. The second moved from arm to arm, up and down, back and forth. On her back, the blur became a tiny man-shape that spat out a mouthful of leather and closed its teeth on the flesh beneath.

Garrett shoved his blade between the weapon and the creature and threw his weight against it. The creature's body rose but remained attached at tooth and claw.

Norik's arrow passed so close, he heard the air part around it. The steel head slammed through the creature and ripped it free, carrying it to the wall and pinning it to the dark wood.

It wasn't dead. It pulled itself up the arrow.

A second pinned it again.

A third.

Garrett didn't see the weapon catch the other creature, but he heard the body pop between her hands and saw dun-colored dust fall to the floor.

The creature pinned to the wall had been slowed by the fletching on the third arrow. Before it could free itself, the weapon shoved her fingers behind it, yanked it free, and crushed it.

Then she swiped her foot through the dun-colored dust on the floor, scattering it.

"Can they reform?" He was breathing hard, although he couldn't say he'd actually been in the fight.

She shrugged.

"Uvili! You're bleeding!" Arianna surged forward.

Turning toward the door, Garrett saw Norik pushed aside and realized the entire attack had taken place before Arianna had time to step into the room.

❦

The weapon sighed. "Heal. Waste."

"She doesn't want you wasting your supplies on her." Garrett spread his hands as Arianna raised a brow at his translation. "She's saying she'll heal."

"We all heal in time and this time, because I have time, I'm treating *this* wound regardless of what you say."

"Regardless of what she says?" Garrett caught a strand of chestnut hair between finger and thumb, and looped it back behind Arianna's ear, out of her way. "You can't say she's a person then deny her self-knowledge."

Another blood-soaked piece of cloth hit the floor. "Self-knowledge seldom includes an accurate assessment of blood loss."

Garrett recognized the expression Uvili turned toward him and shook his head. "I gave it my best shot. You argue with her if you feel that strongly about it."

"That's a lot of stairs." Gripping one side of the doorframe, Garrett leaned out, tried and failed to see to the bottom.

"Yes."

"And the fuel is all the way down at the bottom?"

"Yes."

He pushed himself back into the six-sided room. "Not all the mage-lights are working."

"No." She frowned. "Maybe."

"They might start working as we pass?"

"Yes."

"If they go out, we'll just keep one hand on the wall. It's not like we can miss a turn," Norik said as Malcolm stepped up to the threshold.

Uvili stopped him. "Heir."

"He's right there." Malcolm pointed.

She shook her head. "One. Heir."

"I lead the way? All right." Garrett stepped over the threshold, down two steps, and turned . . .

. . . to see Arianna checking Norik's hip again. Checking a potentially disabling wound before Norik started down the stairs. Garrett clamped his teeth shut on the words that threatened to spill out. He already owed her an apology of sorts for his reaction in the kitchen. When she raised her head and smiled at the other man, he wondered if it would take getting wounded for her to look at him like that. And if it did, wouldn't it mean that she was only looking at Norik like that because he was wounded? And did he want her to look at him because he was wounded? Or because . . .

He took a deep breath. Not the time. When they were all . . . He pushed his fist against his chest, remembering they wouldn't all be leaving the Broken Lands. When the four of them were safely back in Gateway, he'd speak to her.

As though pulled by the weight of his regard, Arianna turned . . .

. . . and the door closed.

"Burn it!" He grabbed the handle and yanked.

The door opened.

"One!" Uvili told him, and closed the door again.

RYAN.NOW

Ryan jerked forward when the door slammed shut behind him, but because no one knew his heart had leapt into his throat and that it took three tries for him to swallow it down, it didn't count. Head cocked, he listened for whispering but heard only silence.

Anticipatory silence.

"It's stairs," he reminded himself. "Just stairs."

Except for the tentacles waiting at the bottom.

Except for the step that collapsed underfoot. Stumbling, arms windmilling, his right hand slapped against the paneling, his nails dug in under the ornate molding, and three steps down from the broken tread, teetering on the edge of a fall that would probably kill him with no help from horrors, eldritch or otherwise, he found his balance.

Except for the landing where the stairs turned to the right, past a tall, arched window in the outside wall that looked impossibly into the mage's workroom where Harris hung impaled, mouth open. Eyes open. Staring at the window in silent accusation. Ryan jerked back and swallowed twice to keep from vomiting.

He wondered what the Lord Protector had seen.

Maybe the Lord Protector had been smart enough not to look.

He glanced back the way he'd come, half expecting to see Captain Yansav heading toward him, Nonee having overcome the mage-craft on the door.

The stairs were empty.

But they were still only stairs.

Except for the section where the mage-lights had stopped working. He took one step in the light, and the next in a darkness so complete, so impenetrable, he could feel it press against his skin. He was no scholar, but even he knew that wasn't how light worked.

With no other option, he kept his left hand on the wall. He didn't realize he was holding his breath until he felt himself sway, then he sucked in a frantic lungful of air, coughed, and hurried away from the sound lest it draw . . . something. The bite in his calf burned, flames licking down as far as his ankle, up as high as his hip.

Wood became stone underfoot.

Stone became air . . .

Muscles twisted and knotted as Ryan jerked his foot back. Heart pounding, he lowered himself carefully to one knee, left hand still on the wall, right patting the air.

Patting only air.

How many steps were missing?

His sword hissed as it left the scabbard.

He thought he heard something hiss back at it.

Told himself he was imagining things.

When he reached out with his sword, the point of the blade tapped against stone, and it sounded as though the stairs continued just beyond the reach of his fingers. He could jump the break easily were he able to see it.

But he couldn't see it.

The fuel was at the bottom of the stairs and they couldn't leave the Broken Lands until he had the fuel.

Standing, he pressed his face against the inside wall, pushed his chest into the wood, stretched out his right leg . . .

When he touched stone, he shifted his weight.

His left leg buckled. He twisted, threw his weight forward, bounced out of the darkness and onto another landing where he collapsed breathing heavily.

The window on this landing faced back into the cliff.

He didn't look.

"Well, flame it, he actually learned from experience."

"That's unexpected."

"Don't get too excited until we find out what he learned."

Somehow, his brothers' commentary added weight to the silence.

After a drink of water, he layered new bandages over the bite. Approaching the creature in the lake smelling of fresh blood seemed like a stupid thing to do.

The Black Flame warned the enemies of Marsan an attack wouldn't be worth the risk. *Beware our strength. Remember what we did to Northport. We came down from the Mage Lands; do you know what we have hidden?*

Ryan suspected they were no stronger than any other city-state on the lake. Northport had been all Nonee and Nonee was no longer chained in the dark until she could be used again. The scholars were definitely hiding any number of things, but he doubted that they'd be of any use defending the city.

Perspective was everything.

The Black Flame had flickered.

The fuel for the flame was at the bottom of the stairs.

He was the Heir of Marsan as the Lord Protector had been before him.

"It's just stairs . . ."

GARRETT.THEN

Garrett had been in good shape when he left Marsanport and traveling had whittled away any remaining softness, but after so many burning stairs, stairs that mage-craft extended three or maybe four times the height of the cliff face, his legs ached and his knees felt as though sand had gotten into the joints, grinding off another layer of bone with every step.

And he still had the climb back to look forward to.

Ahead was the lake, lapping against the lowest landing. Fog obscured the far shore and the wind off the water jabbed cold, ethereal fingers through every gap in his clothing, chilling the layer of sweat between skin and cloth.

To his right, a closed door, the blue paint surprisingly unfaded.

He tossed an empty waterskin at it. It slapped against the wood and bounced back, landing at his feet.

No visible mage-crafted defenses.

Or more accurately, no recognizable mage-crafted defenses.

"Burn it." Sword in one hand, he closed the other around the handle, paused to wonder what he was supposed to do if the door was locked, and pushed it open.

The room beyond was a small rectangle. The wall ahead of him and the wall to his left, both looking out over the lake, were made of unbroken, multi-paned windows. To his right, the rock of the cliff face had been worked flat and smooth. Air that should have smelled stale after a hundred years smelled of nothing at all.

It had probably been a pleasant room once. A divan piled high with pillows took up much of the space. Next to it was a small bookcase, a table with a tea set, and a brazier tipped on its side with a clear-edged boot print in the spilled ashes. Captain Marsan's boot print? She'd brought the first piece of fuel out of the Broken Lands, so she'd been in this room. For a legendary leader, the captain had had surprisingly small feet.

He could see the desiccated body of a dead animal, cat-sized although not cat-shaped, but saw nothing resembling the fuel he'd come so far for. Were there secret chambers? If there were, why weren't they in the chronicle? Then he saw an embroidered silk throw covering a series of lumps on the floor behind the divan.

Captain Marsan could have covered the fuel for safekeeping.

One knee on the divan, he leaned over and lifted the throw, exposing the statue of a middle-aged woman with soft, plush curves.

The stone was . . . not stone. It was gray, yes, but slick looking. Slick feeling, and gave slightly under pressure.

Not a statue, then.

A body. Eyes and mouth both wide open. He could see a gap where a tooth was missing halfway back on the right side of the jaw. He could see the bumps on her tongue. He could see the rage in her eyes. Knew she'd burn the world given half a chance.

His throat clicked as he swallowed. This was the mage who'd built the tower.

The silk slid from suddenly nerveless fingers.

The Scholars of the Flame had said the fuel that kept the Black Flame burning had originally been the size of a small melon. Rounded, but not entirely round.

The size of a knee?

Her left knee was missing, the lower leg lying off to one side.

They were burning a piece of the mage as a symbol of Marsanport's might.

He felt laughter rising and swallowed it back. It wasn't funny.

"It's a little funny," he allowed, then wished he hadn't spoken as the silence absorbed his voice.

She'd been a mage, and the mages had destroyed each other and the land and driven the Five Thousand from their home. If she now fed the flame that protected the descendants of the Five Thousand, that was only fitting.

Besides, Captain Marsan had already dismembered the body. And Captain Marsan had known the mage in life. All he had to do was cut another piece off a stranger who'd been dead long enough now that she was an artifact, not a body. Cut off a bigger piece than his great-great-grandmother, so no one would have to do this again for years.

All he had to do.

Teeth clenched, he raised his sword. Neither the edge nor the point, when he jabbed it down to pry a piece free, left a mark on the silver-gray. Frustrated, he finally braced his sword hand against the divan, bent down, and grabbed the thigh above the missing knee. Silver gray *something* dimpled under his fingers. In the end, he needed to use both hands. When the piece of thigh broke free, he overbalanced and landed with his left forearm beside the head, their cheeks nearly touching in a parody of intimacy. This close, he could hear screaming, the sound distant as though the screamer raged from the bottom of a well.

Or had been turned to . . .

He leapt back, fell over the divan, and found himself sitting on the floor, holding what looked like a small silver-gray log. The ends were solid, no evidence of flesh or bone.

It was heavier than it looked.

He wanted to drop it, but doubted he'd be able pick it up again if he did, so he wrapped it quickly in the silk and shoved it into the leather sack that hung from his shoulder. The silk was the same color as the log. As the leg.

The exact same color.

What was it Arianna had said?

"That sounds like worship to me."

He'd scoffed at her then. Now, holding the log . . . the leg . . . the piece of leg . . . the fuel . . . he wasn't entirely certain she was wrong.

Gateway existed, although the Captain's Chronicle said it had been destroyed. The scholars said belief without substance was the first step on the return to mage-craft. But the scholars had given him the silk, and the sermon. He'd have to look into the scholars when . . .

The door blew open.

Water lapped against the threshold.

Garrett wrapped the fuel, shoved it into the sack, and scrambled to his feet.

The next wave rose higher.

The next higher still, and out of it, the tip curling and reaching . . .

RYAN.NOW

Ryan left the blue door open behind him. Sidling into the room, his back against the wall, he raised his sword diagonally across his body, and took a deep breath. *"Take a moment to assess the situation,"* said the captain's voice. He suspected *assess* in this instance did not mean his attention should jump from place to place like a bug on a griddle, and he forced himself to focus.

No one, not Captain Yansav or the guardians or Keetin or Nonee or, flame forbid, Lyelee could come to his aid, and if he failed, the Black Flame would go out and Marsanport would fall.

"Or Lyelee will follow you down the stairs."

"She's a lot smarter than you'll ever be, little brother."

"There's a lot in the Court who'd rather she was heir."

His brothers weren't wrong. Even he wasn't politically unschooled enough to miss that his Aunt Hamaline and her brother had convinced a number of the Court that Lyelee would be the better choice. Lyelee would, of course, refuse, Trina would inherit, and Aunt Hamaline would stand as Regent.

No one who wanted the job that badly should have it.

Ryan squared his shoulders. He'd neither expected nor wanted to be Heir of Marsan, but it had happened, and it was his responsibility as heir to return with the fuel for the Black Flame.

He just had to find it.

The sunlight streaming through the windows should have raised the temperature to greenhouse levels, but the air inside the room remained comfortably cool. It had probably been a pleasant room once, before the contents had been smashed. Smashed during the Mage War or when the Lord Protector retrieved the last piece of fuel? He couldn't know.

"And he'd really like to know," Ryan muttered, stepping cautiously forward. A piece of the scattered debris gave under his foot and he leapt back, staring down at an enormous dried sausage.

"Welcome to the Broken Lands," he muttered, chest heaving.

The sausage was about as long as his forearm, half as big around, and had collapsed in on itself. Three, no, four similar pieces lay scattered between the door and a destroyed divan. The middle of the divan had been crushed as though something heavy had fallen on it, the wooden frame a shattered vee. He couldn't see beyond it. As the broken shelves and the flattened brazier were clearly not the fuel he'd been sent for, he moved carefully across the room, sliding his feet against the floor, his body angled to keep the door in sight.

Behind the divan, a silver-gray statue of a woman sprawled on the floor. It had broken when it fell, and the left leg was missing. One arm crossed the chest and clutched at a brocade vest; the other was folded up, palm facing outward. Narrow lips were drawn back off creepily realistic teeth and the eyes were half closed. When he shifted, her attention followed him.

A portrait of Captain Marsan in his father's study had watched him disapprovingly no matter where he stood.

Except . . .

The captain's eyes had only seemed to move. The statue's eyes were immobile, but it knew he was there.

Not it. She.

She was the color of the fuel and part of her was missing.

Tanika Fleshrender. He knew it the way he knew he'd never be the Lord Protector his brother would have been.

Tanika Fleshrender.

That seemed like something the Heir's Chronicle should have mentioned.

Ryan shifted his sword to his left hand and wiped his right against his thigh, sweat leaving a damp smear against his trousers. His grip didn't seem any more secure when he shifted it back. If he died because he dropped his sword . . .

He could almost understand why the Lord Protector had broken a piece from the mage's transformed body. He, like Ryan, had been sent to replenish the fuel that fed the Black Flame and kept Marsanport safe. But what had possessed Captain Marsan to take a piece with her as she led the Five Thousand to the Great Lake, and then to set that piece on fire?

"She must have really hated you," he said, shoving at the ruins of the divan with the flat of his blade. Or really not hated her and wanted a remembrance of what they'd shared? Wanted Tanika Fleshrender watching over the survivors in their new home? There'd been a few details left out of the Captain's Chronicle as well.

But who'd left them out?

Ryan wet dry lips and stared down at the mage. Head tilted back, she scowled at nothing.. He shuffled a little further from her line of sight. All the hair on his body had lifted, new lines of sweat dribbled down his back and sides, and he felt like he imagined a mouse would feel in front of a snake.

"Is widdle Ryan scared?"

"Baby going to piss his pants?"

Donal had the last word. *"She's dead, you flaming dipshit."*

Waves slapped against the landing. Ryan spun around, suddenly aware he'd been standing with his back to the open door. Water dribbled over the threshold, but the landing was empty.

"Okay, I'm just going to . . ." Trying to keep both the door and the mage in sight, he moved around to the sta . . . to the mage's side, forced his left leg to bend, and sank to one knee. If he had to, he could push himself upright with his right.

Taking a deep breath, he placed his sword on the tiles.

If he touched her would he hear screaming?

How long had Harris screamed before his voice had failed him?

How much screaming had Nonee done inside the tank?

"Was eternal torment another experiment, then?"

No one answered. Ryan was actually pretty happy about that.

The Captain's Chronicle told how mage-craft had twisted the mages, that however wise they'd been in the beginning, they'd been worthy of nothing but hate and fear in the end. Some families, like Curtin's, kept the hate and fear alive.

At this moment, he wasn't entirely certain that Curtin's family was wrong. Curtin's death would keep the hate and fear alive a little longer.

Ryan stretched out his hand again.

Had Captain Marsan expected Tanika Fleshrender to wake? Had the captain taken a piece of her leg to hobble her? Could a mage grow a new leg? Was he supposed to take a piece of the other leg?

Was the flame a beacon so she could find them again?

He jerked back at the slap of flesh against wood, suddenly aware he'd leaned in so close he could see freckles scattered over both cheeks in a slightly darker gray.

Mages had freckles? Had her eyes mov . . .

Another slap.

He yanked his gaze off hers as a writhing mass of tentacles emerged from the lake.

Six . . . no seven . . . tentacles dove straight for him.

Ryan groped for his sword and slapped it sideways, shoving it out of reach under the broken divan. The tips of his fingers touched the hilt, but he'd have to take his eyes off the tentacles to reach it.

No time!

He shoved both hands under the mage's body. Lifted it. Threw it.

She was lighter than he'd expected. Or terror had lent him strength.

The silver-gray body slammed into the tentacles and hung suspended for an instant as time stopped. She'd landed facing him. Had her expression changed? Then fleshy, green-brown cables wrapped around her and snapped back out of the room. By the time Ryan got to his feet, only ripples lapped against the landing.

Then the ripples faded.

He retrieved his sword, and when he lifted it, the tip trembled. He stood motionless, breathing heavily, until it stilled.

Stood motionless a moment longer as he realized he'd thrown away the fuel he'd been sent for.

"Stupid."

"Useless."

"Typical."

Marsanport would fall.

"Because of you."

Marsanport would fall because of him. What would Donal do?

"Not screw up so flaming badly in the first place."

He kicked at a broken shelf. It caught on a piece of fabric and lifted it as it tumbled, exposing a silver-gray lower leg. Calf. Ankle. Foot.

It should have looked pitiful. It didn't.

Teeth clenched, he pulled the piece of silver-gray silk from the daypack and draped it over the . . . over the fuel. Bending, he put his foot on Tanika Fleshrender's ankle. It would've helped had he been able to think of her as *the mage*, but he couldn't. She had a name. He grabbed the upper edge of the calf through the silk and tried not to think of how his fingers sank into the transformed flesh. When it finally broke, he held what looked like a tapered log.

Halfway to the door, he looked back at the ankle and foot.

The embroidered blanket crumpled beside the divan made an awkward sling, but Ryan kicked the last piece of Tanika Fleshrender into the loop and whipped it out over the lake.

It tumbled. Ankle. Foot. Ankle. Foot. Ankle . . .

A single tentacle thrust out of the water and snatched it from the air.

His breathing loud enough to mask all other sounds, Ryan ran for the stairs, leaving the blue door open behind him.

Seventeen stairs up, he paused and looked out over the water.

Had that been an attack or a rescue?

LYELEE.NOW

Lyelee ignored the discussion around the door. Either Ryan would return or he wouldn't.

Voices began to rise. Destros ducked Keetin's waving arms.

Then she caught sight of Gearing. The sound of his movements covered by the argument, he was heading for the door to the right of the hearth. Stepping in front of her mentor, forcing him to stop or push her aside, she leaned in and murmured, "You had the words for all six of the weapons."

"What if I did?" His nostrils flared. "Scholars have access to information novitiates do not."

Novitiates didn't challenge Scholars, but the Broken Lands had changed the rules. "And if you'd been killed, leaving me with no way to control an approaching weapon?"

"I wasn't killed." His right arm pressed down on his satchel. "Making your argument irrelevant."

What else did he have in that satchel? Lyelee wondered. What else had been kept from her? "There were six weapons," she reminded him. "We've only accounted for two. And knowledge is always relevant. Isn't that what you taught me?"

"One doesn't teach a child to handle fire."

She was so astounded at being called a child, she let him brush by. Didn't stop him when he opened the door. She caught a brief glimpse of a set of stairs heading up as he pulled it closed behind him. He knew exactly where he was going. His satchel contained a floor plan of the tower.

Only Nonee was watching as Lyelee walked to the door that led to the workroom, and Nonee didn't try to stop her. The weapon was smarter than she looked.

Lyelee arrived in the long hall leading to the workroom with no difficulty, although twice she had to pause while halls rearranged themselves ahead of her into remembered configurations. She slowed at the point Ryan had begun to crawl and stopped two steps later when her perception of the available space remained the same. Had something as simple as a piece of

cork actually disabled the mage-craft on the lock or was this new, unob-
structed access part of an elaborate trap? Tanika Fleshrender liked elaborate
traps.

Had liked.

How similar were the likes and dislikes of the other mages?

How could they have allowed so much knowledge to be lost?

One of the wall carvings chittered, so close to the edge of hearing she
might have imagined it. If she had the time scholarship was entitled to,
she'd stop and make a detailed observation, but she had to be back in the
six-sided room when Ryan returned lest Captain Yansav convince him to
leave her behind. He might not be easily convinced, but he'd always
wanted the approval of those he saw as more powerful than himself. His
brothers had so exploited that weakness, she was a little surprised he'd
survived his childhood.

The door to the workroom was unlocked, the piece of cork still in
place.

"If such a simple solution can defeat your mage-craft," Lyelee muttered, pushing the door open, "perhaps you deserved to be defeated."

The room stank worse than it had. Logical, as the cover of the tank
had been buried with Harris. Although she was intrigued by the vat of
raw materials, the limited time available sent her straight to the books.
She tucked the book she'd left on the table into her satchel, and turned her
attention to the shelves.

The first four books were unreadable, the language unrecognizable.
Given time and access to the Scholars' Archives, she knew she'd be able to
work them out, but she had neither now.

Finger holding her place in the fifth book, she stopped to cough. Dust
may have refused to settle on the rest of the workroom, but not even
mage-craft could stop it from clinging to ancient books. Lyelee could appreciate the familiar, and a moderate amount of coughing at the disturbed
dust was definitely preferable to how Keetin still hacked up water. She
suspected one or more creatures similar to those Nonee had sucked from
Destros's leg now grew in Keetin's lungs. She looked forward to studying
it if it—or they—waited until after Nonee was safely back in Gateway
before bursting forth.

History come to life. As it were.

Fingertip trailing over leather spines while she decided what to try
next, she realized she'd dreamed of this. Among the fires and the shouting

and the cascades of images—it hadn't been a restful night—there'd been books. These books.

This book.

She recognized the tear on the top of the spine where the blue leather was worn thin. When she opened it, she knew the feel of the thick, yellowed paper.

This book was meant to be hers.

The words shifted on the page.

Lyelee froze, hand half-raised to rub at dry eyes.

When the words stopped moving, she could read most of the text.

Had the mages been here long enough, had their languages drifted enough they needed mage-craft to read their oldest books? Was that mage-craft now responding to a new reader, pulling a modern language from her mind, and shifting the contents of the book as close to that modern language as it could?

More questions with no answers. So much history stupidly lost.

Lyelee pulled out pencil and paper.

ARIANNA.THEN

Arianna had to assume Garrett had won the fight that had given him the split lip and black eye as he'd made it back up the stairs. "Hidden injuries?" she asked as both she and Malcolm moved to support him.

"Bruising," Garrett panted, resting most of his weight on Malcolm. "Left elbow's burned . . ."

Profanity, not a description, she concluded, sniffing the area.

". . . and my legs feel like cooked noodles. There's a large tentacled thing on guard down there . . ."

"Like a big squid?" Malcolm asked, eyes wide. "Like the boats bring from Southport?"

"No idea. Just saw the tentacles." He huffed out a tired laugh. "And when I say *saw*, I mean got tossed on my ass and hacked off a few."

"Did you kill it?"

"Doubt it." Sucking air through his teeth, he shifted his weight from leg to leg. "Also, I'm having every burning set of stairs removed from the Citadel when we get home."

"That's going to make getting to your chambers interesting." Norik released the draw as the door slammed shut—without assistance, Arianna noted—and lowered his bow. "Did you get the fuel?"

Garrett raised the arm on Arianna's shoulder and flashed flame at Norik. "No. I came back without it."

Norik snorted. "Let's see it, then."

"Let's get him off his feet first." Arianna maneuvered the three of them away from the door. Garrett's jacket hung open and she could feel heat and moisture rising off his body. If she squinted, she could almost see it. "Sit here by the window."

"No." Garrett pulled free and turned, slumping back until the wall supported his weight. "If I sit, I'm never going to get up again." His breathing beginning to even out, he yanked the hanging bag around to the front of his body and flipped back a fold of silk. The upper curve of the fuel looked like a silver-gray log made of shiny putty. Arianna could see the shallow imprint of fingers on both ends. It almost felt as though it needed healing. Almost . . .

"I thought it would be black," Malcolm muttered. "Like coal."

Uvili made a sound low in her throat. Garrett looked past Arianna's shoulder, met her eyes, and shook his head.

Another time, Arianna would have asked what he was denying. Another time, when Garrett's right eye wasn't swelling shut and the whole side of his face purpling. When she raised her hand, he jerked his head away like a child. If he thought she wasn't going to heal him, he could have another think about how useful a one-eyed swordsman would be getting them out of . . .

Something hissed high in the beams over the six-sided room. Something moved between the mage-lights and the ceiling.

She froze. "Did you hear that?"

The three men shook their heads. Norik raised his bow. Uvili glanced up, frowned, but shook her head as well.

The room had been empty all the time they'd been waiting. Uvili had been made so uncomfortable by Malcolm's questions about what Garrett might find at the bottom of the stairs that Arianna had suggested the younger man guard the door that led back to the kitchens. It got him out of the way, but he hadn't needed to be on guard. She'd felt safe. She didn't now.

She could feel something coming closer, drawn by Garrett's return. No. Her gaze returned to the bag he carried. Drawn by the fuel for the Black Flame.

A glance through the closest of the tall windows showed a path through an overgrown garden cloaked in shadow. The mage-lights had kept her from realizing that it was almost dark. "Uvili, can we get out that way?"

Uvili walked over to the big double doors between the two windows, pulled, and stumbled a step back when both doors swung open with little resistance. Weak sunlight and cold air spilled into the room. "Yes."

Arianna stuffed her kit into the top of her pack and swung it up off the floor. "We need to get out of here."

"Is it the dead? Are they coming?" Malcolm swung his sword, trying to cover all six corners of the room at once.

"No." Probably not, she amended silently. "The fuel's attracting attention."

"Attention?" Norik asked.

"Unwelcome attention?" Garrett added.

"Yes." Uvili scooped up her pack and Garrett's and stood in the doorway. She felt it too, Arianna realized.

"Any other kind in the Broken Lands?" Norik muttered. "Malcolm . . ."

"I'll get your pack!"

Garrett pushed himself off the wall. "Should've known it wasn't over. Let's go."

Malcolm looked around the room and sighed. "I liked sleeping inside. It's cold out there. Cold and damp and dark."

Hand in the middle of the younger man's pack, Garrett pushed him toward the door. "It's darker in here."

Arianna wondered what he'd brought up the stairs.

NONEE.NOW

Nonee kept her attention on the beams that crossed the six-sided room while waiting for Ryan Heir to return. The last time, she'd been overwhelmed by mage-craft and memories that had pressed on her from all sides, finding their way past the darkness and the chains. The last time, Arianna had given the warning. This time, Arianna was dead. She needed to be ready.

The captain opened the big double doors and sent Destros out for rocks to prop them open. If they had to leave quickly, they could. Nonee appreciated the captain's foresight. The doors seemed willing to open now, but might not when it became necessary. The others ate, kept trying the door to the stairs, and argued about going after the scholars.

"They're adults and knew the risk," Captain Yansav said at last to the two remaining guardians. "We can get Lord Marsan and the fuel home without them, and I'm not risking your lives on their foolishness."

"You can get Ryan home without me," Keetin Norwin-cee pointed out, arms crossed. "I could go after Lyelee, at least."

"If you want to go after the novitiate, Lord Norwin-cee, go."

He stayed.

Nonee liked the captain.

The heat of the afternoon pushed in over the threshold. Once, mage-craft would have stopped it at the door, keeping a constant temperature inside the building. That mage-craft had failed. Traps that ended in blood and terror had not. Nonee snorted. Typical.

Keetin Norwin-cee, who'd returned to yanking on the latch as though stubbornness could overcome mage-craft, fell on his ass when the door opened. He scrambled to his feet as Ryan Heir stumbled into the six-sided room.

Ryan Heir looked better than Garrett Heir had. Exhausted. Angry. Dripping with sweat. No visible injuries. Her nostrils flared. He stank.

He had the fuel.

"You look like shit."

The gaze Ryan Heir shot Keetin Norwin-cee was mostly relief, but the anger remained behind it. "Burn you." Wrapped in Keetin's arms, he shuffled forward, barely putting weight on his left leg.

"What happened?" Keetin demanded. "Are you hurt?"

"It's the bite. From the carving."

Nonee could smell the blood dribbling down his calf. She wanted Arianna. For Ryan Heir's sake as well.

Captain Yansav moved closer. "Do you have the fuel?"

Ryan Heir laughed. "Oh yes, Captain, I have the fuel." He jerked his gaze up to meet her eyes. "Did you know, Nonee? Did you know what the fuel is?"

"Yes." She'd known the moment Garrett Heir had brought it up the stairs.

"You didn't think that was worth mentioning?"

She frowned. "Garrett Heir knew. Why isn't it in his chronicle?"

Ryan Heir's lips drew up off his teeth. Once, a long time ago, she might have thought it was a smile. "That's a good question."

"Ryan!" Keetin shook him. "What is the fuel?"

"Tanika Fleshrender."

The door to the stairs slammed shut.

"May have just pissed myself a bit," Keetin Norwin-cee muttered after a moment. He twisted so he could look Ryan Heir in the face while still supporting his weight. "To be clear, you have a piece of a mage in your pack?"

"I do."

"The mage who created Nonee?"

"Yes."

"The mage who named herself Fleshrender?"

"Yes."

"That's . . ." Keetin Norwin-cee shook his head. ". . . disgusting. But not actually surprising, all things considered."

What had Keetin Norwin-cee been considering? Nonee wondered.

"So you defeated the tentacled creature." The captain sounded impressed.

"No." Ryan Heir shook his head.

"But if it was guarding the fuel . . ."

"It wasn't. Not exactly."

"Define *not exactly*," Keetin Norwin-cee managed before turning his face into his shoulder to cough. If she listened closely, Nonee could almost hear the water still in his lungs.

"It wanted the mage. When it . . ." Ryan Heir wet his lips. Nonee wondered what should have filled the pause. "When it dragged the rest of . . . of her into the water, I ran for the stairs."

Nonee frowned. "The rest of her?"

"All of her." Ryan Heir left no room for doubt.

Gone.

No chance of recovery. Of return. She breathed easier than she had since she'd realized what Captain Marsan had carried up the stairs so many years ago.

"Do you hate her?" Arianna had wondered.

"Made."

"That's not what I asked."

"Do you hate her?" Ryan Heir had asked.

Her feelings for her creator were complicated and always would be. Some of those feelings had no words to define them. Here and now, she felt relief. There'd been a chance that the mage-craft holding Tanika Flesh-render would change, could fade, or could be canceled by another bit of mage-craft turned loose in the war. If Tanika Fleshrender returned to herself, the loss of a leg would slow her only long enough for her to replace it. If the creature left her whole and she returned to herself at the bottom of the lake, she'd drown.

No one had ever asked, *"Do you fear her?"*

"Wait." Keetin Norwin-cee raised a hand, although there was no conversation to silence. "If the fuel's gone, what happens the next time the flame flickers?"

Ryan Heir's lip curled. "Maybe the scholars can work on that." He pulled away and glanced around the room. "Where are they?" He sounded more angry than concerned.

"The scholars?" Keetin Norwin-cee asked, gaze tracing the same path.

"No," Ryan Heir snapped. "The Citadel choir."

"Exploring," Nonee told him.

"The building?"

"Yes."

"You didn't stop them."

Captain Yansav stepped forward. "We didn't see them go, my lord. Scholars . . ."

". . . consider the pursuit of knowledge their only directive." Ryan Heir's lip curled. Nonee could see he no longer considered the word "scholar" enough of an explanation, and she wasn't the only one who noticed. Back behind the captain, Servan and Destros exchanged raised brows. "Nonee, can you go after them?"

"Yes." She could.

He waited. So did she. After a moment his mouth twisted into something close to a smile. "Will you go after them?"

She glanced up into the beams. The carvings were gone. "No. Removing the . . ."

The door that led to the workroom opened and Kalyealee who-could-be-heir stepped through. She met Ryan Heir's angry gaze, and said, "Do you have the fuel?"

"I do. Do you have what you went after?" He crossed the room, careful to move as though he were in no pain. Careful to show no weakness. Interesting. "What's in your satchel, Lyelee?"

It bulged. Corners protruded through the leather.

"Scholarship."

"Let's see it."

"No."

He made a face that reminded her of Arianna with an unwilling patient. Weary. Unsurprised. "Captain, have the scholar's satchel searched."

Kalyealee who-could-be-heir was surprised. "I forbid it!"

His lips twisted again. "I don't care."

"You can't . . ."

He cut her off. "I did some thinking while I climbed. The Lord Protector doesn't command scholarship; that's what it says in the Charter, but the scholars themselves aren't mentioned."

"It's understood."

"It's not mentioned."

"You're not the Lord Protector."

"I'm as close as it comes out here."

Nonee recognized the expression on the captain's face. Arianna had worn it every time Nonee had thrown off another chain. She watched Servan back Kalyealee who-could-be-heir against the wall by the hearth. Kalyealee who-could-be-heir protested loudly. Servan ignored her and held up a book when she stepped away.

"Is that the book you were looking at before?" Ryan Heir asked, as Kalyealee who-could-be-heir grabbed for it. Servan easily avoided her. She looked like a small child reaching for a denied treat, and from the way she suddenly stilled, she probably realized it herself. No. It was deliberate. She was trying to look like a small child reaching for a denied treat, her anger easy to disregard.

Suspicious.

Captain Yansav's narrowed eyes suggested she thought so too.

Ryan Heir needed to search the satchel, but his barely hidden relief said he could push no farther past his training. Not now. Not yet.

"I can translate it," Kalyealee who-could-be-heir declared.

"You want to take it to Marsanport."

It hadn't been a question, but Kalyealee who-could-be-heir answered it anyway. "Yes!" The silent *you idiot* filled the room.

"No. Mage-craft, in any form, will not be permitted within the bounds of Marsanport."

"This isn't mage-craft," she spat. "It's scholarship. And if you're going to quote the charter at me: Scholarship will examine the world as it is. The search for knowledge will have no parameters."

The final *ess* extended. Became a hiss.

Split into multiple parts.

Nonee looked up. "Get out! Now!"

Ryan Heir pointed to the door leading to the workroom. "Servan."

"Sir." Servan opened the door, tossed the book through, and closed the door.

"Packs on, people!" The captain's voice was a whip. "Let's go!"

"No!" Kalyealee who-could-be-heir pushed past Servan, but the door wouldn't open. "What have you done?"

"The tower won't let you escape that way." Nonee growled at the beams.

Kalyealee who-could-be-heir turned with the rest to stare at her.

"Servan, outside!" Propped against the wall, Captain Yansav had her sword in hand. "Make sure we're not walking into an attack."

"My bow . . ."

"Use a crossbow," the captain snapped. "You're still the best shot we've got. Destros, toss out any pack without a person attached. My lords . . ."

Keetin crammed an empty waterskin into his pack. "On it."

"Gearing," Ryan Heir began, when the door to the left of the hearth opened and Gearing fell through. From the blood on his knuckles, he'd been fighting to open it for a while. Tanika Fleshrender had always been amused by the independence of doors. She'd find the scattered pile of her books less amusing. Scholar Gearing bent to pick them up.

"Leave them," Ryan Heir commanded.

"I will not!"

Ryan Heir stepped forward and slammed the door. The books were on one side and both scholars were on the other.

"Scholarship cannot be silenced!" Scholar Gearing lurched toward the door . . .

"Destros."

. . . and found himself struggling in Destros's grip. He had, Nonee acknowledged, as little chance to free himself from Destros as he would have from her. "Scholarship is not to be impeded!" he shouted.

"Mage-craft is." Ryan Heir heaved his pack onto his shoulders.

"The Lord Protector will hear of this!"

"I'm counting on it."

The first snake dropped from the beams. It wore Tanika Fleshrender's face. Nonee caught it and crushed its head, dropping the inert carving to the ground as the second and third fell. They all wore the mage's face.

Fangs sank into her arm. She ignored the bite, grabbed a writhing length lunging for Ryan Heir, and slammed its head against the wall. They were all heading for Ryan Heir. No. Not Ryan Heir. The fuel.

More fell.

One crushed underfoot.

One ripped in half.

One thrown, and crushed as it returned.

"Nonee! All clear!"

As she crossed the threshold, she yanked the doors closed and felt the other door, the mage-crafted door, slam into place. Wondered if the surviving snakes would return to the beams.

The scholars continued to rage. No one paid them any attention. She thought they should.

"What the burning flame were those?" Keetin Norwin-cee demanded. He and Ryan Heir had moved the farthest from the tower. Still not far enough should the tower try something, but the gardens were usually safe.

"They were snakes." Nonee shrugged and ignored the vaguely egg-shaped rock tucked in behind a tangle of brambles, the face only barely visible. None of the others had seen it, and that was good.

"Carved snakes." Keetin Norwin-cee lowered Ryan Heir to a stone bench. "Carved snakes that came to life!"

"Yes."

"And attacked us!" He was clearly shaken, but Nonee knew some people just didn't like snakes.

"Yes."

Captain Yansav glared up at her. "They were trying to get to Lord Marsan."

Of course the captain had noticed. "No, to the fuel." She nodded toward the bulge in the waxed canvas bag. "To the remains of the mage."

Neither scholar looked surprised, although neither had been present when Ryan Heir identified the fuel. She was about to mention it, the words on her tongue, when Destros touched her arm. It was the first time he'd touched her.

"Are you going to deal with that?" he asked.

His hand was warm and a little damp, with familiar calluses. "That?"

"The snake."

Nonee glanced down, yanked the fangs free, destroyed the head, then crushed the body a handspan at a time until she could brush the last of the sawdust off her palms.

Even the scholars were silent when she finished.

Destros shook his head. "Are you okay?"

She flexed her arm, took the piece of cloth he handed her, and wiped the wound clean. "Yes."

"You're still bleeding. Here . . ." He pulled out another piece of cloth and waved it at her arm. "Let me?"

It wasn't necessary, but she let him bind it and saved the memory of his fingers against her skin. Arianna would have told her there was a chance. She knew better.

"If we move now, and the traps haven't been reset . . ."

"No one to reset them," Nonee told her.

"Then we can make it to our last campsite before dark." The captain's voice was matter-of-fact, as though large, carved snakes came to life around her every day. The others visibly calmed. "Lord Marsan, do you need your pack lightened?"

"No, thank you, Captain. I'll . . ." Ryan Heir stood, shifted the weight on his shoulders, and his leg buckled. "Maybe a little," he amended as Keetin caught him.

"Destros?"

"On it."

Nonee watched Destros for a moment, then turned to see Captain Yansav scowling at the path, at the grass, at Harris's grave, at the distant edge of the disturbed soil. Finally, the captain turned to scowl at her. "Are you sure it's safe?" she asked.

Nonee shrugged. "These are the Broken Lands."

"So, that's a no."

"Yes."

RYAN.NOW

Ryan stretched out his left leg and rotated his foot to ease the muscle around the bite. It didn't do anything for the way his ass protested its sudden impact with the ground, but it eased the painful cramping. A little. Captain Yansav had moved them quickly down the hill, quickly enough he'd had to ignore the flashes of pain that shot up into his hip or be left behind.

"You're bleeding again." Keetin dropped to one knee, lifted Ryan's left foot onto his thigh, and tugged off his boot. "It should have scabbed over by now."

"There's a piece missing." At least the blood was running into his boot, not leaving a trail for . . . for things to follow. Fresh lines of moisture softened the stiffened fabric of his trousers, painting a darker pattern within the multiple shades of reddish-brown. The lopsided circle of swollen flesh surrounding the wound was hot to the touch, but he didn't think it was infected.

"Drink some water." Keetin scrubbed at the lines of old blood with the stained bandage as new blood oozed up. "You need to replace the fluids you're losing."

Ryan obediently uncorked a waterskin. The clear, cool water had warmed and tasted of leather. It was still the water Nonee had mage-crafted, but the familiarity was comforting.

"Aw. Does the baby boy need comforting?"

"Is he going to cry?"

"Should we toss his blankie in with him?"

"Did I hurt you?" Keetin's hands were warm around his ankle.

"No." Had he flinched?

It had been cold and wet at the bottom of the old well and he'd been down there, clutching the woolen blanket off his bed, until the stable master had found him and gone for a ladder. His father had wanted to know why he hadn't climbed out on his own. *They're just trying to toughen you up.* He'd been six. His mother had been dead for two years.

Keetin looked ready to argue, but tucked his head into his elbow and coughed for a few minutes instead.

"Use this."

Ryan jerked, nearly kicking Keetin in the crotch; the coughing had covered Nonee's approach. He frowned at the familiar crushed leaves and flowers piled on her extended palm. "Yarrow?"

"Yes."

"Is it safe to pick it here? Are we far enough from . . ." He nodded toward the mage-tower on the top of the hill.

"No. The yarrow picked here will turn your leg to wood."

He sighed. "Wood doesn't bleed."

"Or feel." She glanced at the nearest trees and added, "Usually."

Keetin wiped his mouth on his sleeve and glared up at Nonee. "We've been collecting wood. Burning it."

"Yes." She nodded at the herb. "This is from Arianna's stores. Pack it in and around the wound."

"I know." Keetin held out his hand and Nonee dropped the yarrow into it.

Ryan frowned. In spite of the bandages, he thought he could feel blood dribbling down his leg. "What if this doesn't stop the bleeding?"

She shrugged. "You'll live."

"That's not very comforting," Keetin muttered, exposing the hole again.

"It is to me," Ryan told him, then sucked air through his teeth as Keetin pressed the mashed plant into the wound. "What about your arm?" he asked, nodding toward the mangled skin of Nonee's forearm, ridges black against the gray where the fangs had sunk in.

"It'll heal. Two, three days at the most."

"Nonee!" Servan jogged over, holding a loaded crossbow like it was a dead fish. "That patch of fog you told us to keep an eye on is gone."

Nonee frowned out over the lake. "Probably good."

"And so are the birds that were circling the other tower."

"Not good."

"You don't think," Ryan began.

Servan cut him off. "Down!"

The next few moments were a mix of swearing and crows screaming defiance.

Then a hunter hit the ground, sky-colored feathers red around the quarrel protruding from its breast.

"You could see it?" Ryan asked the archer, yanking his sword free as he stood.

"I could see there was something blocking my view of the crows." Lip curled, Servan kicked her toe into the stirrup and reloaded. "I hate these flaming things. If I had my bow, I'd have fired half a . . ." She shot again. ". . . dozen times by now. Burn it!" A feather nearly as long as Ryan's arm drifted down to brush past Nonee's shoulders as another hunter pinwheeled out of the sky. "Can't see them well enough to hit the flaming things!"

"Sev!" Destros traded his loaded bow for hers. And again. And again.

Three crows dove for Ryan's head. Before he could swing at them, Keetin yanked him back to the ground.

Where he came face to face with a crow perched on the fuel. It . . . no, not an it . . . they had golden eyes. Crows didn't have golden eyes.

He knelt, shifting his grip on his sword . . .

Felt pain draw a line across his cheek.

Saw Nonee's hand dart out, heard bones crack, saw her slam down a third hunter with enough force that feathers fountained up from the broken body. The bird was large enough, heavy enough, that Ryan felt the impact shudder through the ground.

The crows stopped circling and landed.

"No!" Nonee closed her hand around Servan's crossbow, holding the quarrel in place.

Ten . . . thirteen . . . fourteen . . . The fifteenth hopped off the fuel and joined the flock.

They were large for crows, but they were definitely crows, not ravens. They had the fan-shaped tail, the blunter wingtip and the narrower chest. They grumbled to themselves—Ryan could almost hear words in the rattles and clicks—heads constantly in motion as they turned one eye and then the other on the people surrounding them. "What are they waiting for?" he whispered.

"Food." Nonee swept the crushed hunter toward the flock with the side of her foot. "Destros."

He tossed the second.

Servan and Captain Yansav grabbed the third, carefully gripping where the wing met the body to avoid the sharpened feathers, and heaved it closer.

The contrast put the hunter's size into perspective, their bodies as large as a five-year-old child's, their wingspan easily as wide as Nonee was tall.

"We need measurements," Gearing began. "Samples and . . ." He fell silent when all fifteen crows turned toward him.

They arranged themselves five to a body. Ryan expected squabbling, but the birds were quiet and efficient.

Captain Yansav shook her head. "We should . . ."

"No." Nonee cut her off. "Be still."

In what seemed like an impossibly short time, nothing of the hunters remained but white shards of bone, barely visible amid the drifts of feathers.

"What if they're still hungry?" Destros asked quietly.

"Boe Mah Sing made them carrion eaters, exclusively." Nonee shrugged. "Don't die."

"I kind of love it when she pops out a burning big word," Servan muttered.

All fifteen crows turned toward Ryan. He wanted to step back, but he couldn't move his feet. Then he remembered that Nonee had said be still; it seemed his feet were smarter than his head. They stared at him for a long moment, then in unison dropped their collective gaze to the bag that held the fuel. Held a piece of the mage. "No. You can't have it."

The crow that had been on the bag—hard to miss the golden eyes—spread their wings and hopped over to stand looking up at Servan.

"Be still," Nonee repeated quietly.

Head cocked toward Servan, the crow made a distinctly questioning noise.

Servan nodded at Ryan. "Nothing to do with me," she said. "He's in charge."

They turned and swept a glittering gaze from person to person, ending with their head tilted back so far their beak pointed straight up as they locked eyes with Nonee. The not-quite-a-crow and the weapon stared at each other for a moment.

The double clack of beak sounded like bones slamming together. Then, screaming "Jah!" the crow leapt into the air, wingtips nearly brushing Nonee's face.

The flock followed.

"Will they be back with more hunters?" Ryan asked when the sound of wings and complaints faded enough he thought he might be heard.

Nonee shrugged. "They want what you carry."

"They're crows!" Lyelee snapped, reaching for a white feather. "They're intelligent birds, but they're still birds. They can't know Ryan's carrying something if they can't see it."

"They're mage-crafted crows," Ryan reminded her, trying to make it look as though he'd decided to sit rather than been unable to stay standing.

"They sure as shit don't eat like regular crows," Destros muttered, firing the last loaded crossbow into the dirt.

"Aloga ants." Captain Yansav looked a bit wild-eyed. "Aloga ants can strip a corpse to the bone in minutes."

"And there goes any urge I ever had to visit Shurlia," Keetin muttered, sitting beside him. Ryan leaned closer. The two of them on the ground made it look more like a choice.

"Mage-crafted crows can see through canvas? Because that's a ridic . . . Ow!" Lyelee stared at the blood beading up on the end of her finger.

She looked so annoyed, Ryan stifled a giggle. The Heir of Marsan didn't giggle. He clearly needed sleep. Food first, then sleep.

"The hunters are weapons," Nonee told her.

"Well, you'd know."

"Lyelee . . ."

"Am I wrong?" she asked, and stuck her bloody finger in her mouth.

Keetin began to answer—a scholar's question was *always* answered— but Ryan gripped his wrist and cut him off. "I take it that when the Lord Protector came this way, he was not attacked by hunters or swarmed by crows."

"Fifteen is not a swarm," Gearing grumbled. He and the captain were sitting as well. "And you've read the Heir's Chronicle, did you read about an attack?"

Ryan smiled at him. "No, I didn't."

Grip on his satchel tightening until the leather buckled, Gearing opened his mouth, shook his head, and closed his mouth without speaking. Whether he was reacting to the smile or the tone, Ryan neither knew nor cared.

"Tough guy."

"Sure he is, when facing a decrepit old man."

"A new low, little brother."

Lyelee jabbed her wet finger toward him. "It was the Frost Moon and there was a storm. Or did you skip that part?"

The storm had definitely been mentioned.

Ryan glanced over at the spray of feathers and bone. "We could use a storm."

"No," Nonee growled.

"You really do excel at saying the wrong thing."

Josan snickered. *"Open mouth, insert other foot."*

"How does he have room for all those feet?"

Ryan flushed. "Sorry. Nonee, is there somewhere safer in case the crows return? Somewhere we could get to before full dark?"

"No."

"Crows don't fly after dark," Gearing grumbled, staring at the ground.

"Mage-crafted crows, Scholar." Keetin stretched out his legs and crossed them at the ankle. "For all we know, they might turn into canna dancers after dark and return to seduce us."

Gearing raised his head, some of his old certainty resettling on his face. "Don't be ridiculous."

"Canna dancers," Keetin repeated. "Oil and flowers and not much else." He winked, Gearing snorted, and Ryan gave thanks that Keetin had agreed to take the Mage Road. It would have been so much harder without him.

If they couldn't get somewhere safer, they might as well stay here. Harris would've had the fire going by now . . . He swallowed, hard enough to hurt, and glanced over at Captain Yansav. He had no idea what she saw on his face, but she nodded and stood, her right foot barely touching the ground. "Destros. Make camp."

"Aye, Captain."

"Nonee, will that talented stone of yours work again?"

"Twice more, Captain."

"Good. Lord Norwin-cee, fill Harris's kettle and pot with the remaining water, all empty skins to Nonee. Servan, you're on watch. Shoot anything approaching from the air."

"With this?" Servan glared at the unloaded crossbow dangling loosely from her right hand and reluctantly raised it. "All things considered," she sighed, with exaggerated disdain, "like giant, fast-moving, highly maneuverable murder birds, it's got a dangerously short range and it's stupidly slow to reload."

"You have another longbow under your tunic, Servan?"

"Or are you just happy to see me," muttered Keetin over the sound of pouring water.

Servan snorted out a laugh. "I do not, Cap."

"Then make the best of it. Lord Marsan, if you could shift over behind Servan so she doesn't shoot you by accident, I'll have a look at your leg."

His calf was swollen around the edges of the wrapping and hot to the touch, so Ryan swallowed his objection and carefully moved where indicated. "And your leg?"

"When you've been seen to, you can return the favor." She shifted more of her weight to her good leg. "Scholars . . ."

Lyelee dropped a feather and piece of bone into her satchel. "I'm going with Nonee."

"You're gathering wood." She nodded at Gearing, who'd been able to pick up a beak without rising and was holding it up to the fading light. "Both of you. Since you both have two good legs."

"You, Captain, don't . . ."

"If you can carry books, you can carry wood," Ryan snapped before Lyelee could say what the captain wasn't. "And remember the fire will be protecting you along with the rest of us." He breathed a sigh of relief as she spun on one heel and stomped toward the tree line. Gearing followed, moving considerably slower. "Stay in sight," he called.

She flicked fire over her shoulder.

"Captain Yansav." Nonee tossed the captain a corked glass vial. "Oregano oil. It'll help if the bite's infected."

"And if it's infected with mage-craft?" Keetin asked, handing her the empty waterskins.

Nonee nodded toward Destros. "Those axes will cut through bone."

Ryan clenched his teeth to keep from throwing up.

❧

They'd had to leave the books, but what else had the Scholars hidden in their satchels? Leg throbbing, Ryan stared up at the stars. If he asked, they'd say it was none of his business. If he ordered the contents exposed, they wouldn't cooperate. If he forced a search, how would the others react? Was he alone in his suspicions? He couldn't be the only one who feared the scholars were teaching what they wanted known. Was he overreacting?

"It wouldn't be the first time."

"Donal's mean to me!"

"Josan took my clothes!"

"Corryn locked me in the root cellar!"

"It's too high. It's too hard. It's too cold. It's too hot. The scholars are lying to us."

But they were lying. They were hiding parts of the chronicles. Adding their own words. And if the Scholars were lying, maybe it had been too high, too hard, too cold, and too hot . . .

"You keep telling yourself that, slug."

"Maybe I will," he muttered, grunted as Keetin poked him, and finally closed his eyes.

He dreamed of the Heir's Chronicle, words sliding off the pages as he turned them. He dreamed the fuel turned to flesh and blood in his hands. Then the blood wrote words on his hands, but although he knew it was a warning, he couldn't read what it said. Then the blood turned to crows, rusty black feathers tinted red. He could hear water lapping against the stairs as their beaks drove into his flesh again and again and again . . .

He sat up. Beside him, Keetin's body shook as he coughed, not asleep but not awake. He could hear Gearing breathing heavily, each exhale almost a growl. Destros whimpered, Servan swore, and Captain Yansav whispered words he didn't understand. Only Lyelee slept quietly. Leaning closer, he saw her mouth curve into a satisfied smile.

Curtin wasn't fidgeting with his vest. Harris wasn't snoring.

He'd failed them both.

Kicking free of his bedroll, he got to his feet and sucked air through his teeth at the sudden stabbing pain. He limped past legs and packs and weapons to where Nonee stood, silhouetted against the sky, eyes turned toward the distant headland. Sweat plastered his tunic to his back and it took a conscious effort to unclench his teeth.

"You should be sleeping," she said quietly.

"True, but I should be at home sleeping under a fan and my mother should be the Heir of Marsan," he muttered. "Life burns us all."

"Coward."

"You'd send your mother to the Broken Lands in your place?" Nonee sounded curious, not accusing. Not like his brothers.

Ryan snorted. "My mother would finish breaking the Broken Lands. She was . . ." Fading. Most of his memories of her were stories he'd been told. He nodded toward the bag between Nonee's feet. "If we left that here, would it be easier to get out?"

"Yes."

He knew that. "This is the last piece of fuel. The Black Flame will go out. It might as well go out now as later, right?"

Nonee shrugged.

"But then Curtin and Harris would have died for nothing."

She shrugged again. If he could see her expression, would it agree that they'd died for nothing? The Black Flame was the symbol of Marsanport's strength, but in and of itself it was . . .

Nothing.

No easy way out. He'd bring the fuel home. Become the Lord Protector. Ease his people into believing they didn't need the flame before it burned out one last time. But how?

"Your leg keeping you awake?"

"More my head."

Her noncommittal hum was vaguely comforting. "This would be the time to live in the moment."

"This moment, also not so great." Actually, he amended silently, this moment was kind of nice. A light breeze blew in off the lake, the sky was clear, and nothing was trying to kill them. "Should we have kept moving through the night?"

Nonee stood silent and motionless for a long moment. "No," she said at last.

But she'd considered it. Ryan sighed and adjusted his stance until only his left toe was on the ground, the new angle changing the pain. "There must be good things in the Broken Lands. Things that weren't destroyed or polluted by mage-craft."

She cocked her head. "Why?"

He sighed. "I don't know. Wishful thinking? Nonee, why did the tower let the scholars wander around?"

"Let?"

"Allow. You know what I mean. There were traps and impossible halls when we were trying to save Harris, but the scholars danced in and out again unopposed."

"You think you know why."

"No, I . . ." When she turned to look at him, he fell silent and shook his head. Picked out the archer in the pattern of stars. And the lion. And the olive tree. And the pomegranate. He'd only ever been able to see a formless mass of stars where the pomegranate was supposed to be, but considering pomegranates, maybe that was the point. "The chronicle," he began. And had to begin again. "The chronicle says the Lord Protector left you behind because you could better protect Marsanport in Gateway. Maybe it wasn't just physical abominations he wanted you to keep penned, but mage-craft itself. Maybe . . ." He turned the thought over. "Maybe the mage-craft wants out." He waited for her to tell him he was wrong. Nonee's leather creaked as she shifted. It was quiet enough beyond the camp; Ryan heard the soft splash of something breaking the surface of the lake. He bit back a hysterical giggle and said, "Nonee?"

"No." To his surprise, she kept talking. "And yes. The mages were powerful. People want power."

"And some will see mage-craft as a way to get it. I know. That's why Marsanport keeps people away from the Mage Road."

She snorted. "Try to sleep, Ryan Heir. If the nights are short, the days are long."

LYELEE.NOW

Lyelee dreamed of books piled on a table in the Scholar's Hall. Familiar books.

"I have reclaimed our history," she told the faceless scholars surrounding her. "I have applied scholarship where others hid in fear and superstition."

The books disappeared, leaving behind a single sheet of thick paper.

The surrounding Scholars began to fade.

"No!" Lyelee slapped her palm on the table. "This is enough! With this I prove there is nothing inherently evil in mage-craft. With this I put together an expedition of scholars, only scholars, who will study the Broken Lands, not merely walk in and walk out again. Scholars who will study and learn and in time *control* the Broken Lands. The history of the Broken Lands is our history, and we will not be denied."

"The Lord Protector," whispered someone in the crowd.

"The Lord Protector does not control scholarship! Scholars remain separate, untainted by politics, unrestrained by fear. We are governed by knowledge alone and our very charter states we cannot be prevented from seeking it out. This . . ." She held up the paper. ". . . is the key that will unlock our past!"

And the faceless scholars were in a wagon moving up the Mage Road pulled by the shadows of creatures that were not quite horses. And the wagon took them past Gateway, past those who benefited from their heritage even as they denied it, and into the Broken Lands. And those trapped in wood and stone were set free and in their gratitude threw open unseen doors.

And she had the time to find the information she needed.

And Nonee became again the weapon she was meant to be, commanded by scholarship, given purpose, guarding scholars from the fearful . . .

Lyelee's eyes snapped open as the Nonee in her dream grew to even greater size and smashed through the wall around Gateway, the roar of falling stone becoming Gearing's snores. She blinked, shifted so a broken piece of the Broken Lands no longer dug into her hip, and focused on the dark stain of Nonee's silhouette against the night sky.

Would they allow such a weapon to roam free in Gateway if they had no way of controlling her?

She, personally, had no emotional attachment to children, but scholarship supported the belief that no one would allow their children around such a weapon unless they could control it.

When the scholars return, she decided, closing her eyes, *they'll begin by claiming Gateway's archive.*

And then claiming the weapon.

They'd be a force against ignorance.

RYAN.NOW

Ryan's leg felt better in the morning.

"Better being a relative term," he admitted as Keetin checked the bandage.

"Can you walk on it?"

"Going to have to, I'm not staying here."

Keetin turned his head to cough, then looked up and grinned. "Atta boy."

Nothing attacked before breakfast, or after breakfast, or while they made their slow way back down to the broken bridge. Nonee remained outwardly placid. The guardians jumped at shadows, Keetin coughed, and Gearing kept his eyes on the ground as though his feet needed the incentive of sight to keep moving. Lyelee looked determined.

Ryan didn't trust that look. At ten, a determined Lyelee had pushed him off the end of the pier to see if his brothers' taunts about his inability to swim were true. Had one of the women who fished his father's quota not pulled him out, he'd have definitively proven it.

"Why are you scowling at your cousin?" Keetin asked.

"I'm not. I'm scowling at a scholar."

"Is that even allowed?"

It was. But the scholars discouraged it. Discouraged criticism. Discouraged what they deemed to be unnecessary questions from the moment children sat down in their classrooms. Was that what Captain Marsan had intended?

"Ryan?"

Ryan shook his head.

They rested at the bridge. Ryan eased himself down onto a chunk of dressed stone he didn't remember from their trip *to* Tanika Fleshrender's tower. Hopefully it wouldn't shift into a mage-crafted rock monster and eat his ass. He wanted to close his eyes and let the sun bake some of the pain away, but knew relaxing would be a mistake. He needed to be ready for . . . whatever. Propping his left foot on his right ankle to change the pressure against the bite, he looked at Captain Yansav's knee, flesh swelling around the edges of the wrap that kept her from bending the injured joint, and wondered if either of them would be able to manage the hop, skip, and jump it would take to get across the break.

About to suggest she sit as well, he closed his mouth as she snapped, "Servan, what the flaming hell are you doing?"

"Feeding oatcake crumbs to a bird, Cap."

"Birds attacked us, Servan."

"Not this bird, Cap." She flinched back from the captain's expression, bent her head to the small speckled bird on her palm, and murmured just loud enough for Ryan to hear, "Off you go, little one. We're tired and hurting and not too happy because of it."

Ryan watched the bird fly away over the swamp, half waiting for a tentacle to rise out of the water and grab it—although it would be less than a snack for the creature. Actually, they'd only seen tentacles; they'd assumed the tentacles were attached to something. He tried to bite back the snicker, but it slipped past his teeth.

"Ry?"

"Free-ranging tentacles." He pushed Keetin's hand away from his forehead, no longer amused. "I'm not feve . . ."

"Nonee." Servan pointed out into the swamp. "Fog."

Ryan couldn't see fog, but if Servan could, it was definitely there.

Nonee held out a hand. "Give me your pack, Ryan Heir." The other hand reached toward the captain. "And yours."

The captain bristled. "I don't . . ."

"Give her your pack, Captain." Ryan shrugged out of his straps. "You and I, we're working on a leg and a half each and Nonee can't fight fog." He frowned as the captain waved Destros to the other side of the bridge, glanced into the swamp, then up at Nonee. "Can you?"

"No."

He patted the bulge in the daypack. "Is it drawn to . . ."

"Yes."

"However mage-crafted it may be," Gearing grumbled as Servan helped him to his feet, "fog has no agency."

"Mage-craft does," Nonee told him, taking his pack as well. She snorted when Lyelee offered hers. "You're young enough to carry it."

Unless you've other things weighing you down, Ryan thought, using Keetin's arm to rise.

"And now you're talking to yourself," Donal mocked.

First Destros. Then Nonee with the packs. Then the scholars—Gearing reluctantly releasing one hand from its death grip on his satchel in order to keep his balance.

When Nonee wrapped an arm around his waist and scooped him up against her side, Ryan gritted his teeth and kept silent. The captain, on Nonee's other side, did not.

"You ask first!" she snarled as Nonee set them down.

"No time."

He could see the fog now, skimming the top of the murky water connecting the swamp to the lake. Keetin had nearly cleared the break, Servan right behind him.

Ryan felt Nonee's hand on his back, pushing him gently toward his pack. "Keep moving up the road."

The fog was noticeably closer. Ryan had seen a lot of fog in his life; it could come in off the Great Lake surprisingly fast. But not that fast. "The chronicle said it can only move over water."

Her nostrils flared. "Go!"

"Sir." Destros lifted his pack and Ryan shoved his arms under the straps, his eyes on Keetin.

Neither scholar had paused after crossing the bridge, although they hadn't gotten very far either. Gearing, still without his pack, held Lyelee's arm, and Ryan would have been reassured to see she hadn't shaken the older scholar off if he hadn't been concerned about her interest in the fog.

As he and Captain Yansav limped away, Destros behind and between them, Nonee moved back toward the bridge. He heard Keetin shout, tried to pivot, and would have fallen had the big axeman not grabbed his pack and kept him on his feet.

"She's just speeding things up a little, sir. They're fine."

"Picked them up?"

"Scruffed them like kittens. It's adorable."

"I am not adorable!" Servan shouted.

Keetin called something Ryan couldn't make out, but Destros laughed, so he assumed Keetin had protested that he, at least, was adorable.

They stopped again by the old pier, gathered on the far side of the road, as far from the water as possible. Ryan thought of how the cold water would feel against the bite on his leg and took a step toward it that he turned into an awkward pivot back the way they'd come.

The fog had engulfed the bridge, a roiling tail trailing back into the swamp.

"How does fog look menacing?" he wondered.

"Like that," Keetin muttered. "Just like that."

"Nonee, there's another patch of fog moving in across the lake. You sure it'll stay over the . . ." Servan stuffed her toe in the stirrup of her crossbow, yanked back the string, loaded, snapped it up, and fired, muttering, "Too flaming slow and the range is flaming shit."

The hunter hit the water not far from shore and floated, wings spread. Ryan heard crows cry out, but the flock stayed high.

"It hasn't taken it because it's trying to lure them closer. It's what I would do," Lyelee added when Ryan turned to look.

"If you were a mage-crafted tentacle creature?"

"Obviously."

"Keep moving," Nonee said.

❧

Ryan stumbled into the old campsite, let his pack slide off his shoulders, sat on one of the rocks Nonee had placed when they were there . . . two nights ago. Two nights. He didn't quite believe it.

". . . and eventually, we'll set up a research facility in the tower." Gearing's voice drifted over to him. "The Scholarship of the Broken Lands will gain novitiates when we return."

Nonee grunted and Ryan glanced up at her face. "Research facility not happening?"

"They can try."

"Without your help."

She didn't respond, but he supposed that was so obvious a statement she didn't need to.

Something with too many teeth charged out from under a bush and a crossbow bolt pinned it to the ground. It had fur, the body looked vaguely like a rabbit, the head was enormous. Nonee pulled the arrow free and stomped the writhing body flat.

"Good shot," she called to Servan.

"Thanks, I hate this bow. Can we expect more?"

"No. Solitary hunter."

"Was it after the . . ." He cupped his hand over the bulge in the daypack and had a sudden memory of the woman at the well—the *talented* woman—cupping the bag she carried in much the same way. "Never mind. Of course it was. Are the shattered drawn to Gateway because of the people with talents?"

"Yes." Nonee kept her eyes on the road, both the road they'd traveled and the road they were going to travel.

"Maybe you should . . ."

"No."

Fair enough. They'd survived this long without the benefit of his opinion. "What are you watching for?"

"The road hasn't changed."

"Isn't that a good thing?"

"Maybe."

ARIANNA.THEN

Arianna shuffled her feet to keep her toes from freezing, and wrapped her arms around her chest. Since leaving the mage-tower, the weather had gotten progressively worse.

"We should've gone back the way we came," Norik said, securing his pack. "At least we'd know what to expect."

"The way we came killed Petre," Malcolm growled around a mouthful of dried meat. The two older men exchanged a look that Arianna interpreted as:

"Do we let this go?"

"He's still grieving."

"Court . . ."

"This isn't Court."

"You'll have twenty-eight days on the road to repair the hierarchy," Arianna said quietly. "Let him be angry if he needs to." When they exchanged another look, she sighed. "You have very expressive silences. Now, can we get moving? I don't like the look of that sky." When Uvili grunted, she frowned. "What is it?"

Uvili pointed toward the roiling mass of black and gray clouds out over the lake.

"Yes, that's the sky I don't like the look of."

The big woman huffed out a breath and said, "Mage-craft."

"That's a mage-crafted sky?" Garrett asked, coming to stand next to Arianna. "Then I don't much like the look of it either."

"D'lan Gee," Arianna said thoughtfully. When Garrett opened his mouth, she raised a hand to silence him, working through the faded memories of childhood lessons. "They worked with weather. Is that a piece of their mage-craft out there, Uvili?"

"Yes."

Garrett shook his head. "They've been dead for a century."

"So were those skeletons." Norik joined them. "And that didn't slow them down. That storm looks like it's heading right for us."

"Yes." Uvili pointed toward the daypack slung across the front of Garrett's body. "That."

"That?" Garrett frowned down at the pack. "The fuel? It's drawn to the fuel? How do you know?"

Uvili had some pretty expressive silences herself. Arianna giggled again and stuffed her mitten in her mouth to muffle it. She was so very tired.

Norik turned to stare down the road they'd been cautiously following. It was a mage road, the same as the road to Marsanport, and Arianna both did and didn't trust it for that reason. Uvili seemed to trust it, although her still limited vocabulary prevented her from telling them where it led. "It looks like there's some kind of shelter on the other side of that bridge," the archer said. "We put the effort in and we should be able to get there before the storm reaches us."

Garrett shook his head. "We're not taking shelter, we keep moving. We have to get the fuel home."

"Or Petre will have died for nothing," Malcolm muttered behind them.

Before either of the two men could respond, Arianna stepped back and pushed up against Malcolm's side. The packs made hugging difficult, but he needed the comfort of touch.

Norik glanced at them and nodded, then turned his attention back to Garrett. "We can't get it home if we freeze to death."

"No one ever," Garrett began, then stopped. Although she could only see his profile, she could tell he'd just realized they were a lot farther north than he was used to.

"Good. Let's get moving, then." She could just make out the corner of a building through bare trees. Tucked between the road and the lake where the road dipped down into a valley between the two headlands, pilings jutting out of the water like wooden ribs suggested it was a boat house or a warehouse. Either way, she had a destination, and she nudged Malcolm until he fell in beside her.

They'd barely gone a dozen steps when Garrett caught up. "Keep an eye on her," he snapped at Malcolm as he passed. She hid a smile. He hated her being out front. She continued to give him the benefit of the doubt and assume it was for the very sensible reason that she was a healer. "Shouldn't you and the fuel be in the middle where you can be protected?" she asked the back of his head.

"I don't need protecting. You do. If the dead guard the way to this as well . . ."

"My staff will be as much use as your sword in that case."

"And more use than arrows," Norik called cheerfully from the rear.

"You're not helping," Garrett yelled back without turning.

"I'm nothing but helpful."

"Like tits on a bull."

This time she didn't hide her smile, and beside her Malcolm huffed out a tiny, broken laugh. As the banter stopped, she assumed that laugh had been the goal and felt a sudden surge of fondness for the two men and the not-quite-a-boy beside her.

And was mortified by the tiny, horrid part of her mind that said if Garrett, Heir of Marsan, and the fuel for the Black Flame, was out in front, then the lingering mage-craft he—and it—attracted wouldn't have to go through the rest of them first.

Uvili moved up and down the line. Up on their left, down on their right. No one asked what she guarded them against. Arianna suspected Uvili herself didn't know.

By the time they crossed the bridge, Arianna had to lean into the wind, snow stinging her face.

By the time they reached the overgrown lane leading to the building, she realized: "The snow is getting colder! It's stopped melting when it touches bare skin."

Garrett looked past her to Malcolm, to Norik, then at Uvili, who was suddenly by his side. She nodded at his silent command and pounded up the lane.

"Huddle close." Arianna reached out and pulled the fold of Garrett's hat down over his ears.

"I don't like . . ."

"You'll like not having ears less."

Norik backed in to the huddle, facing the storm.

Arianna wondered what he thought he was going to shoot. At least his beard was thick enough and grew high enough to protect most of his face. And he knew how to wear a hat.

"Safe."

She stifled a shriek as Uvili appeared, a gray bulk in the white, the storm beating against her and having as little visible effect as it would have had against an outcrop of rock.

The building's outside wall, the wall nearest the lake, had boards missing, and the storm followed them inside. Uvili led the way to an inside wall, opened a door, and slammed it closed once they were all through. The storm hissed against the barrier. *Hissed angrily,* Arianna thought. She'd heard angry hissing before—her mother kept geese—but never from a storm. The other outer wall on the far side of the room was solid, even the glass in the window miraculously whole. Not that she could see much through the . . .

She leapt back as the storm hit, and bounced off Garrett, who steadied her. Together they watched wave after wave of white slam against the window.

"Will it hold?" Malcolm asked almost plaintively.

"Yes," Uvili said.

"How do you . . ." Garrett shook his head. "It's mage-crafted."

"Yes."

"And not by the mage of storms." He released her—Arianna hadn't realized he'd still been holding on. "Do you have a name for the mage of shelters?"

"I'm a healer, not an archivist."

"Fair enough." He kicked at the floor, slivers of wood scuffing off the surface. "We can't light a fire. This whole place will go up."

"I'd almost welcome that." Norik slid out of his pack and helped Malcolm out of his.

All three had gray patches on their cheeks where the snow had lingered a moment too long. She dropped her pack to the floor and knelt beside it, rummaging until she found the jar she wanted. "Rub it into any exposed skin." She tossed the jar to Norik. He had the least skin exposed; he'd be done fastest. "Rub into the edges of your beard where the growth is thinner." Into most of Malcolm's beard, but she didn't say that. One of the men would see to it. "And check the back of each other's neck in case the snow found a way in."

"And you?"

She ignored the bright points of pain on her face. "I'll heal from the inside."

Garrett grunted and caught the jar. "You were ready for this."

"I was ready for freezing nights. Not for this."

Malcolm complained under his breath as Garrett all but oiled his beard with the cream. Arianna suspected the complaints were as much to keep his lord from noticing how his teeth were chattering. The older men had more weight to act as insulation, but Malcolm was lean and wiry and not entirely grown. She drew a blue glass flask from her pack, and broke the seal around the cork with her thumbnail. "Drink this," she said as she passed it to him. "One swallow."

He dutifully drank. "Tastes like . . . grass. What is it?"

"You should ask before you drink," Norik teased.

"It's tonic." She took the flask back and passed it to the archer, knowing Garrett wouldn't drink until after his people did. "It'll warm you from the inside. One swallow," she cautioned again. "It's strong."

"What's in it?" Garrett asked, as he received the flask in turn.

"Heat."

He stared at her for a long moment, then tipped the flask to his mouth and swallowed.

"Uvili?"

"No."

"And you?" Garrett demanded as she tucked the flask back in its nest of lamb's wool.

"I'm not a frail southerner. I've lived in the shadow of these mountains all my life."

"And you're a healer." He sounded more questioning than accusing. That was good. It didn't matter, but it was good.

"And I'm a healer."

Malcolm's pupils had dilated and his shoulders had come down as muscles unlocked. He sagged against his pack and tugged at a loose thread on his jacket.

"We should sleep while we can," she advised.

The whole building shook as the storm fought to find a way in.

Garrett snorted. "We should stay awake in case the roof comes down."

Arianna couldn't argue with that.

⚒

"We need water."

They had less than half a skin remaining, although they'd filled them in the tower's kitchen. Arianna had kept them drinking, making sure they weren't adding dehydration to exhaustion. They'd intended to fill their skins when they reached the lake, and she should have known what happened to intentions in the Broken Lands.

"We'll melt snow." Garrett's tone was almost soothing and she wondered if she'd allowed her self-condemnation to show on her face.

From where she sat in front of their huddle, acting as both guard and barrier against the storm, Uvili grunted, "No."

"No, we couldn't melt it or no, we shouldn't drink it?"

Uvili turned and shot Garrett a look that so matched her nana's *What did I just say?* Arianna couldn't stop a snicker.

He raised his hands in surrender. "Okay. No."

"Do you hear that?"

"I don't hear anything."

"Exactly." Norik leapt to his feet, tumbling a dozing Malcolm almost onto Arianna's lap. "The storm's stopped." He crossed to the window, leaned in until his forehead nearly touched the glass, and swore. "The outside's frosted. I can't see a flaming thing."

The outside was frosted? That wasn't how frost worked. And the silence had a weight Arianna didn't like. "Uvili?"

Uvili rose slowly, then stood head cocked. After a moment, she shook her head. "Stopped. Now."

"Now is all that matters," Norik told her, heading for the door.

"Wait!" Malcolm had surged to his feet, hands clenched into fists by his sides. "What if it's trying to lure us out?"

"It's weather," Norik protested.

"It's mage-crafted weather," Arianna reminded him.

"And yet, we still need water and I need to see the sky. Would it hurt to look?"

Uvili shrugged.

"Good enough for me. Garrett?"

Garrett rose slowly, using the wall to help him stand. Arianna could see that the stairs had left him needing heated oil rubbed into his legs and back, but the Broken Lands weren't likely to allow that level of vulnerability, not now they had the fuel. He glanced around the room, gaze skipping past the far corner they'd designated the emergency privy. It wasn't a small room, but Arianna had begun to feel the walls move in and could see the three men felt the same. "We can look," he said at last.

It needed Uvili's strength to open the door against the drifted snow, but the rest of the outer room was clear and it wasn't snowing beyond the broken wall. Arianna took a deep breath of fresh air and forced herself to walk carefully across the buckled floor.

They stood in a syrupy calm within a circle of roiling cloud, white and heavy with snow where it touched the water's surface and growing progressively darker the higher Arianna looked. "This isn't natural."

"No burning shit," Malcolm muttered.

"We've seen storms do this," Norik insisted, hat off, fingertips scratching through matted curls.

"This?" she demanded.

"Not exactly this," Norik admitted. "But it doesn't much matter. We need water."

Garrett's hand dropped to the daypack. "We don't have time to be trapped here. We need to break free."

"We need to let the storm play out," Arianna told him. The snow-burned skin had faded back to brown, but the marks remained visible. "We won't survive out in it." Uvili would. She might. They wouldn't.

"Breaking free, hunkering down . . ." Norik spread his hands. "We'll need water while we're doing it."

"There's tentacles in that water," Garrett reminded him. "It's the same lake here as at the tower."

"And if those tentacles are small enough to get into a waterskin, we need to revisit the daring tale of your fight."

After a moment, Garrett nodded. "Malcolm, get the empty skins. Uvili will . . ."

"Uvili will." Norik folded his arms. "And I'm going with her."

Garrett huffed out an impatient breath. "Fine."

"Sir?" Malcolm clutched at Garrett's sleeve. "If we all go, we'll fill the skins faster."

"Risking this idiot's enough. He's never done well when he thinks he's trapped. You should see him at formal dinners. He's faked choking so he could leave the room. Another time, Miria Halin-cer backed him into a corner at a party—tiny woman, half his size—and he nearly climbed a tapestry to get away."

Arianna grinned. "So you'd say he's handling this fairly well?"

"I would."

"If the storm breaks . . ."

"He's quick on his feet."

The calm was still holding when Norik and Uvili reached the pebble beach. Norik dropped to a knee, stretched out a long arm, submerged the first skin. Pulled it out. Submerged the second. The third.

A creature made of storm charged down from the road. Then a second. And a third.

Uvili's fist slammed into the first chest and it shattered. She threw the second creature to the ground and stomped it into an icy smear.

"She's got this," Garrett said quietly, and Arianna knew he was reassuring himself as much as Malcolm and her.

As Norik reached for the last skin, a billow of white fog surged out of the storm and engulfed him. He fell forward, toward the water. There was no splash.

He screamed.

Uvili shattered the last creature and reached into the fog, and yanked Norik out by one foot.

Garrett started forward, but Uvili was already more than halfway back, a screaming Norik in her arms.

The storm crashed in around them.

⚜

"It's like an acid," Arianna ground out through clenched teeth. Her hand on Norik's wrist lowered the pain enough he'd stopped screaming, but he still whimpered and she didn't know how long she could maintain the contact. She'd never dealt with this level of agony. He should have been unconscious, or dead already, but he wasn't. He stared up at her with milky eyes under the stubs of lids.

His nose was gone. His ears. Lips. The skin of his hands. Exposed flesh seeped blood. Kneeling across from her, Garrett slid his knife under Norik's clothing. Cut fabric fell away, and the edges of Norik's skin turned gray, then white, then crumbled to powder as the effect of the fog spread like the edge of a slow fire.

Garrett's lip bled where he'd driven his teeth into it. "Heal him!"

"I can't!"

"Then what good is this talent of yours!"

She fought to calm her breathing before his words filled her head and kept her from providing what little help she could. "It'll keep eating him alive until he isn't alive and then it will dissolve what's left. It won't stop," she panted. "I can't stop it."

Blood gurgled within the ruined throat. Oozed out between loosened teeth.

Garrett stared for a long moment into Norik's eyes, then leaned in and kissed him gently on what remained of his forehead. "Uvili."

She was kneeling at Norik's head before Arianna realized what was about to happen. The crack of breaking bone sounded over the howl of the storm and Arianna sagged with the sudden release from the pain, swallowing bile.

"How do we bury him?" Malcolm whimpered through his tears.

"We don't, he'd hate it." Garrett rolled back onto his feet and stood. Tears ran down his face as well, but Arianna could see that he'd locked away the grieving he needed to do—the howling at fate, the cursing at the gods. He'd do what he had to for as long as he had to. The breath he drew in was shaky. The breath he blew out was not. "Take the body outside," he told Uvili. "Let the storm have it. Let the scavengers eat it. Let it be spread so far that Norik's spirit will know he can never be trapped again."

~~✦~~

Arianna had needed Garrett's help to rise, and if he tugged her into his arms and held on too tightly for a moment, she needed the comfort as well. He moved to Malcolm when he released her and pulled the younger man close, lips moving against Malcolm's hair.

They didn't have gods in Marsanport. She wondered who he prayed to.

Leaning on her staff, she gave them what privacy she could and watched the door for Uvili's return. Sweat-damp undergarments clung to her body, and she clutched the polished wood to keep from clawing at the memory of pain on her skin.

Wood cracked.

The floor in the privy corner exploded outward and an insect . . . a mole . . . an impossible combination of the two emerged. As long as Uvili was tall, what served it for shoulders rose as high as Garrett's waist. Enormous claws clattered, multiple tiny eyes glittered.

Arianna slammed its head with her staff. Danced back. Again. Again. Claws caught at her skirts. She tore free. And hit it. And hit it. And hit it.

She couldn't save Norik.

She couldn't save Petre.

And hit it. And hit it.

AND HIT IT!

Then large arms wrapped around her and pulled her back against a solid chest as Garrett and Malcolm rushed forward, swords drawn. Arianna stopped struggling and sagged in Uvili's grip. They needed something to defeat as much as she did.

The insect-mole bled black. Like Uvili.

"What is it?"

Uvili shrugged. "Dead."

Malcolm laughed, edging on hysteria. Garrett wrapped an arm around his shoulder and drew him up against his side, angled so that both of their sword arms were free. Arianna pulled a packet of oatcakes from her pack, and offered one to each of them.

"I can't." Malcolm shook his head.

"It'll help."

He looked to Garrett, who glared at her, then took a cake and bit into it. Malcolm sighed and held out his hand.

She couldn't taste the oats, or the honey, or the dried currants. But it *would* help.

"Out?" Uvili asked, standing over the misshapen body.

"Out," Garrett agreed. "But not gently."

Uvili was still chewing when she returned, and it took Arianna a moment to realize why. She tried to feel pleased Uvili had eaten and didn't quite manage it.

"The hole leads to a big tunnel." Garrett stepped carefully back from the shattered edge. "Impressively big. Big enough Uvili could crawl through it."

"You're not suggesting," Arianna began.

Garrett ignored her, beckoning Uvili closer. "Is it empty?"

She broke the edges of the floor back until she reached solid wood, then leaned over the hole. Her nostrils flared. "Yes." But it sounded more like *now* to Arianna. It was empty now.

"Will it take us past the storm?"

She cocked her head, then leapt in and disappeared. Arianna held her breath until she emerged, the leather over her shoulders dusted with earth.

"Yes."

"You weren't gone long enough to reach the other end."

"Air."

"You could tell from the airflow?"

Her forehead creased. "Yes."

"We don't have torches." Malcolm squared his shoulders. He wasn't afraid. He was just pointing it out. "It'll be dark."

Uvili reached out of the hole and gently touched his foot. When she had his attention, she tapped her chest.

"She sees in the dark," Garrett said quietly, his tone not quite matter-of-fact. Faced with following Uvili through a dark tunnel dug by an insect-mole she'd tried to beat to death, Arianna appreciated his attempt.

RYAN.NOW

Ryan woke to the sound of distant screaming.

Harris.

No. Harris was beyond screaming. The fog had taken Lord Norik Yeesan-cer not far from here, and the last time Ryan looked back before they lost the light, the fog still engulfed the bridge.

Was Lord Yeesan-cer still screaming in the fog?

He moved closer to Keetin, seeking warmth in spite of the heat, breathing as Keetin breathed, trying not to hear anything but the damp in and out of air.

LYELEE.NOW

Lyelee had never liked teaching, it took time away from her own search for knowledge, but she did like the way the first-year novitiate scholars watched her as though they knew she'd be able to cut through the fog of their childhoods and lead them to scholarship.

She turned and pointed to Harris, hanging bleeding at the front of the classroom. "The question is always, what can we learn from this?"

When the novitiates continued to stare silently, she smiled.

"Mage-craft kept this man alive long after he should have died. How? This is knowledge worth acquiring."

"So we can keep people alive?" The novitiate had a gray cast to her skin and her lips had begun to pull back off her teeth.

Lyelee frowned. "Application is irrelevant. We acquire knowledge for the sake of knowledge."

Harris screamed.

NONEE.NOW

Nonee watched Destros splint Captain Yansav's knee to keep her from bending it. It wouldn't heal until she could stay off it. She couldn't stay off it until they were out of the Broken Lands. The captain understood.

"How do we get back to the tower?" Ryan Heir asked, staring up the road to the headland. "Can we go back through the fungus people?"

"No."

"Because we broke them?" Servan asked.

They were staying close, no more than an arm's reach from each other. Only Kalyealee who-could-be-heir stood a little apart. "Yes."

"Could we follow Captain Marsan's path?" Gearing's eyes were deeply shadowed. She wondered what he'd dreamed of. "You know the way."

She thought of the path they'd followed, a path created by mage-craft no longer in the control of the crafters. "No."

"But . . ."

Leather creaked as she pulled aside the shoulder of her tunic to expose the puckered scar. It was the only scar she had. "No."

"But . . ."

"She said no." Ryan Heir met the scholar's gaze and the scholar looked away. Then he returned his attention to the road. "How, then?"

❧

"And my mother tried to keep me from the ball field. Little did she know a misspent youth would result in the skills needed to smash a mage's window." Keetin Norwin-cee bounced the rock on his palm, then threw, shattering another sharp triangle of glass.

Nonee pointed past the trees at the distant line of dark towers. "The mage lived there." She frowned at a smear of guts on her hand and wiped it off on the grass.

"Smash a window in the mage's auxiliary building that he never lived in, then." His next rock took out the point jutting up from the bottom of the casement. Although the window was almost three times his height from the ground, he was fast and accurate.

"I know you said it's the murder birds that are the threat . . ." Destros pointed a bloody axe toward the edge of the garden, where more crows had just landed to join the flock already watching. ". . . but that lot's starting to bother me. Why aren't they eating the rats?"

"Maybe they don't like the taste of rat." Crossbow in hand, Servan searched the sky. "Maybe they don't want to ruin their appetites for the main course."

"We're running out of time," Captain Yansav said quietly. Looked up and met Nonee's gaze.

Nonee nodded. "Yes." She lifted her pack and threw it through the window, taking the rest of the glass with it. Ryan Heir handed her his. Wheezing as he breathed, Keetin shoved him down onto the end of a shattered bench, snarled, "Stay off your leg!" and gathered the rest.

"Nonee!"

She ignored the sound of wings and the sound of crossbows, and propped the tree she'd carried from the far side of the garden up against the window sill. She'd ripped it free of the earth just before the rats attacked. Had snapped off the crown and the roots. Too many branches remained, but it would serve. "Climb!"

Then the sound of wings became too much to ignore. She leapt and pulled a hunter from the sky.

Kalyealee who-could-be-heir was first into the building, scrambling up the tree at an impressive speed.

"They're dodging the quarrels!" Servan shouted.

Keetin Norwin-cee had perched halfway up, thigh braced against a branch. He steadied Gearing . . .

"If they're dodging, they're not attacking!" Destros shouted back.

. . . hauled a protesting Ryan Heir past him and over the sill . . .

"Burning shit!"

"Servan!"

"Knocked my helm off. I'm okay."

"You hate your helm."

"Didn't say it was a bad thing."

"Nonee!"

Ryan Heir stood in the window. She could hear Keetin Norwin-cee coughing behind him and the sound of broken glass being swept aside.

She grabbed a beak just before it touched her throat, ignored the lines the edges opened in her palm, and slammed the hunter into the wall. "Get clear of the window!"

Then she kicked the tree away, grabbed Captain Yansav, and threw her, the arc low enough she barely cleared the sill and would hopefully slide across the ballroom floor rather than crash into it. The captain's response got lost behind the scream of a hunter as Nonee ripped a wing off and stomped it flat when it hit the ground.

She grabbed Servan.

Threw the dropped crossbow into the building after her.

She didn't want to throw Destros.

Didn't want to remind him what she could do. What he couldn't do.

Didn't want him to die. She ducked under an axe swing and smelled blood.

Not hers.

His.

"You're hit!"

"Beak," he grunted as half a hunter hit the ground. "In under the edge of my vest."

How could feathers make so much sound against the air?

How many feathers were needed to make that much sound against the air?

She clamped his arm against his side to slow the bleeding and found he was large enough her arm didn't go completely around him. He wrapped both of his arms around her waist. It was almost an embrace. If not for the bloody axe tucked where it would do the least amount of damage. She leapt. Her free hand caught the lower sill. She kicked out, clipped a hunter with her heel, and heaved herself up and in . . . landing on Destros. She rolled them, putting her back to the floor, braced a foot against the sill, and shoved them away from the window. Keetin Norwin-cee swung his sword; a hunter's head bounced across the floor. Ryan Heir jammed a screen into the opening, the protruding bits of broken lattice securing it on either side.

From the sound of the swearing, Servan and the captain were alive.

"Nonee."

Destros had a feather in his beard and his helm had dipped down until the front edge rested against the bridge of his nose, his eyes barely visible.

She let him go.

Outside, the crows began to feed.

RYAN.NOW

Ryan had bit back a scream when Captain Yansav and then Servan had come flying through the window. Just barely clearing the lower edge, they'd skidded more than crashed when they landed and had looked, for a moment, like bodies. Like two more he'd lost.

Servan's nose still dripped blood and Captain Yansav was spreading one of Arianna's creams on her elbow—not the elbow of her sword arm, Ryan noted thankfully.

"How did you know that wouldn't kill them?" he demanded, standing close enough to Nonee's shoulder that the others shouldn't be able to overhear him asking about their possible deaths.

Nonee shrugged. "There was a chance. The hunters were a certainty."

Fortunately, the hunters seemed to follow an *out of sight, out of mind* doctrine, as the screen he'd dragged from the other side of the ballroom wouldn't hold against a determined attack by a flock of non-mage-crafted sparrows.

"Because you're useless and you grabbed a useless barricade."

They'd been nine when they left Gateway; now they were seven. Could Donal have kept Curtin and Harris alive?

"Yes."

No, he didn't think so.

"You don't think. You never have."

Right now, at this moment, the seven of them were safe. Weapons had been cleaned, water drunk, and everyone's breathing, even Keetin's, had returned to normal. Destros's scale vest hung from one shoulder as Captain Yansav packed his wound. The hunter's beak had lifted flesh off of the bone, but the guardian had pressed it down himself and insisted it was nothing. Servan stood guard by the window. Gearing lay on the floor, clutching his satchel. Ryan opened his mouth to order the satchel searched, and closed it again. Scholars. He couldn't. Lyelee paced the perimeter. Ryan assumed she *searched for knowledge*, but he didn't much care about what she could find in faded paint and crumbling plaster.

"How fast does fungus spread?" Keetin called from the ballroom door. "This wood's getting damper and I think we're about to be overrun."

"I think we can out-pace fungus," Gearing told him, struggling to sit.

"I think we should leave. Now." Ryan turned toward the far end of the room and remembered. "There's no door."

"There's a door," Nonee told him.

She'd looked almost embarrassed as Destros rolled off her. Embarrassed because she hadn't asked before throwing the guardians through a second-floor window? They weren't happy, but they understood. He almost wished she'd thrown the scholars. Their argument about angles and vectors and why she shouldn't have done it would have been a welcome diversion.

Nonee didn't stop at the place the door should have been, but slammed into the wall with enough force another of the windows cracked. That drew everyone's attention. She stepped back, and slammed her fists down again and again until the wall crumbled into a pile at her feet. There was still no door, only a hole and a shimmer like oil on water.

"And they say mage-craft is destructive," Lyelee scoffed.

"Nonee is mage-crafted," Gearing reminded her.

Ryan turned to speak to Keetin in time to see the ballroom door bulge and a piece of ornate molding fall to the floor.

"Wood should not go splat." Keetin backed away.

"It shouldn't," Ryan agreed. "Packs on, let's go. The . . ." He waved at the hole, at the oil shimmer. ". . . door is open."

"We have no idea where that goes," Gearing grumbled.

"Fungus is always an option," Keetin said cheerfully, hauling him to his feet.

"Fungus is not an option."

"Then get your wrinkled old ass in gear."

Ryan let Gearing's diatribe on the respect due scholars drive the prospect of being engulfed by fungus, of becoming like the bodies in the glass house, from his mind. The need to trust centuries-old mage-craft was all he could handle at the moment.

Captain Yansav buckled Destros's vest and levered herself to her feet using his shoulder. "He's fine," she said in response to the silent question. "As we have no idea what we'll meet, Nonee, first through. Destros, point. Servan, rear. Scholars, then Lord Keetin and myself. Lord Marsan . . ."

Ryan waved a hand at the daypack. He had to carry it; he wasn't going to touch it again if he didn't have to. "I'll keep the thing that attracts attack on this side of the door as long as possible."

Servan raised her crossbow. "Request permission to take point, Cap."

"Permission denied." She swept her gaze from face to face. "Count of three before you follow."

"And can Nonee destroy whatever horror is facing us on the other side in a three-count?" Gearing asked sarcastically.

"She'll have a six-count," the captain told him flatly, "after Destros joins her."

Servan snickered.

"Are you all right?" Ryan asked as he waited by Nonee for Destros to reach them. She held up her hands. The knuckles were unmarked. "That's not what I meant."

She closed her eyes for a moment, and said, "Yes."

※

They stood in a room barely large enough for people and packs and the last piece of Tanika Fleshrender. The walls, floor, and conical ceiling were wood, the boards warped and curling, and in some places, missing entirely. A narrow window ran across the top of each wall, including the one they'd just come through. This impossibility, more than the attacks, gave Ryan a personal understanding of why Captain Marsan had hated mage-craft. Mage-craft made reality malleable. "This isn't the tower."

Nonee sighed, one hand against a wall that looked as though she could push it over. "It is."

"It doesn't look like the tower," Lyelee pointed out. "The tower was stone."

"Was stone." Nonee shrugged. "Don't judge on appearance."

Lyelee's lip curled. "Ancient mage-crafted wisdom?"

"Common sense."

"And does common sense have a way to deal with yet another missing door?"

Keetin threw up his hands, miraculously not smacking anyone. "We don't need Nonee for that. I could cough at one of these walls and take it down."

"Leave that as a last resort," Nonee told him.

"I'm onto you." He tapped his knuckles against her arm. "You want to keep all the glory."

He was trying too hard to lighten the mood, but Ryan appreciated the attempt.

"It's the tower," Servan called. Fingers clutching the sill, she'd used a buckled board to boost herself up until she could see through the small, misshapen window. "I can see the clearing and the path that goes down the hill to Curtin's grave. We go back through the cave and we're almost out."

"Is there another way?" Ryan didn't want to go back through the cave.

The room swayed. A nail popped from a bulging board and clattered against the captain's scale.

Keetin wrapped his arm around Ryan's chest and kept him on his feet. "You had to ask."

The floor tilted and they staggered toward Servan.

"Does this mean the tower wants the fuel?" Ryan shouted above the sound of splintering wood.

Nonee handed the captain off to Destros. "Yes."

"Buildings don't have agency!" Gearing grabbed for Lyelee. Lyelee moved out of his reach.

Nonee threw herself at the wall.

The wall absorbed the impact.

Ryan clutched at Keetin's arm. "Destros!"

"It's a battle axe," he grumbled, passing Captain Yansav back to Nonee as they gave him what room they could. "It's not . . ."

The floor dropped. Gearing collapsed. Ryan clenched his teeth against the pain shooting up his leg.

The room tilted.

Ryan felt Nonee gather him in against her. He grabbed Keetin's sleeve and pulled him close.

Wood shattered. Metal screamed. The room lurched and dropped. Nonee twisted while they were in the air, and when they landed, she was facing the rising angle, Captain Yansav under one arm, Ryan, holding Keetin, under the other.

Destros grunted. Servan swore. And the room began to move. Slowly at first, then it began to pick up speed. A board popped off the side wall, and Ryan saw a tree fly by. The side of his face mashed into Nonee's un-yielding chest, he realized she'd done what she could to ensure that what-ever they hit, it would hit her first.

"We're sliding down the hill!"

"On what?"

"The mossy path!"

"The mossy path is too narrow to hold us!"

"No flaming shit!"

The guardians were barely audible over the splintering, shattering, and smashing. Ryan understood the urge to shout into the wind, but he had nothing, however banal, to say.

"Going to cry instead?"

Get burnt, Donal.

Then the room tilted again and they were careening . . . up?

Still moving, but slowing.

Was it almost over? This time, he clenched his teeth on a laugh. Was the tower about to drop them over Gateway's wall? If not, it wasn't over.

Slowing.

Slowing.

Stopped.

Another lost nail clattered across the floor.

Ryan took a deep breath. "All right," he said, "that wasn't . . ."

And they dropped, straight down.

The floor shattered with the impact, the walls exploded outward, and the conical roof continued the original motion.

It was dark, and dusty. Ryan licked dry lips, his pulse pounding in his ears.

Nonee carefully released them, stood, and threw the roof aside.

Thew it far enough aside, the sound of it landing was no more than a distant crash. Ryan lifted his head and looked around.

They were in the red dirt circle where the pond of the chronicle had been, sprawled in a pile of broken wood to the left of the cave entrance. Crushed vegetation and gouged earth showed where they'd gone over the edge of the cliff.

"Mage-craft saved us." Gearing's voice combined disbelief and awe.

Something had. It might as well have been mage-craft because no-where actual rules applied would they have survived that.

"Is anyone hurt?"

His leg, the captain's knee, Keetin's lungs, Lyelee's fingers, Destros's healing puncture: no more than they'd had before they'd started.

"Nonee?"

She hadn't moved since she'd thrown the roof. She stood with her chin up, her nostrils flaring . . .

And a dragon surged out of the cave.

GARRETT.THEN

Garrett swore as his knee came down on a stone. Not his first bruise nor likely his last; more and more stone had begun appearing in the packed dirt of the tunnel floor. Then his hand touched what was clearly a shaped block and he opened his eyes.

Still pitch black. They weren't out . . .

No.

He could see gray in the small spaces Uvili left around her.

Below his hands and knees, masonry. A ruin?

The angle of Uvili's silhouette changed. She stood and disappeared into shadow.

Garrett followed. He'd wanted to bring up the rear. Next to the weapon, he was the best fighter they had remaining.

"They're after what you're carrying," Arianna had reminded him. "If you're at the end, they'll pick you off."

"What will?"

"Does it matter?"

He could have had Arianna or Malcolm carry the fuel, put them in the safer position, and freed his sword, but even as his hands had gone to the strap, he was unable to follow through. So he crawled after Uvili, Arianna crawled after him, and Malcolm, who wasn't yet twenty, who'd lost a friend and a mentor, brought up the rear.

As he stood, he dragged down the strip of cloth that had covered his mouth and nose, keeping out the dirt. He knew there were tear streaks through the dirt on his face. He'd mourned Norik as he crawled—not as much as he wanted to, but as much as he dared.

He stood in a stone room, the blocks tumbled in one corner where the tunnel emerged, and in the opposite wall a narrow, arched door. Narrow enough, Uvili would have to remove her pack and slip sideways through it. He had no idea where the light was coming from, was only thankful it was dim enough that—after what seemed like days in the darkness—he could see.

Arianna brushed up against him as she emerged, and as much as he wanted to step closer, he stepped aside to give her and Malcolm space.

"Glad to be out of there," she sighed, shaking dirt from her hair. "It smelled of the grave."

"Where are we?" Malcolm asked. His cheeks were tear-streaked as well.

Uvili touched the wall beside the arch, head cocked. "Tower," she said after a moment.

"The mage-tower?" Garrett fought to catch his breath. Fought to find enough breath to speak. "We're back at . . ."

"No." She frowned. "Tower." Held out her hand and turned it over. "Swamp."

"This is the tower that sent us to the swamp?"

"Yes."

They'd traveled for two, almost three days in the swamp, so . . . "We were underground for days?" Without eating, or sleeping, or pissing?

"No." Uvili shrugged, dirt falling from her shoulders. "Mage-craft."

The tower. The hill. The cave. A day to the Broken Line. They might survive this . . .

Those who remained might survive this.

⚮

Garrett watched Uvili's shoulders brush the walls as she led the way up the spiral stairs. The stone dipped slightly in the center of each step, worn by those who'd climbed the stairs before. These weren't the stairs they'd climbed before, but he'd begun to realize "before" had little relevance in the Broken Lands.

Behind him, Arianna's staff came down on each step, like the length of wood was the only thing keeping her on her feet, and behind her, Malcolm's heavy breathing had the wet sound of grieving in each exhale. They were exhausted, they were all exhausted—all but Uvili, who continued to climb as though she'd just left Marsanport. What would it be like to be her? he wondered. Strength and endurance, invulnerability and, as she didn't age, immortality. Of course, she might have aged in ways no one could see. Already gray and hairless, those markers were denied her, and her face held too few expressions to line her skin—if her skin could be lined.

According to Captain Marsan, the other five weapons had been destroyed. Uvili was the last of her kind.

A weapon with a name.

She hadn't had a name before.

She'd been gentle when she'd given Norik peace.

What would it be like to live forever as the Lord Protector's weapon?

Lonely. Garrett was too tired for anything but the truth.

She'd been alone for years when he found her, a useful tool tossed aside to rust, all but forgotten.

She'd been a weapon he'd looked forward to wielding while they'd traveled on the Mage Road, even if he could only aim her at large game, and once a large mountain cat. She'd chased it off and hadn't been able to catch it, but now he wondered if she hadn't wanted to catch it, if without a direct order to kill, she'd decided on mercy.

He hadn't seen her as a person until Arianna had refused to see her as anything else.

Arianna.

She practiced something very like mage-craft and that terrified him. If she practiced such arts in Marsanport, the Scholars would discover her, accuse her, and send her for judgment. To the Lord Protector. In time, to him.

But still, he wanted to show her Marsanport, to prove to her that something good had been built from the ruins of Northport. He wanted her to look at him like she did at Uvili. As though he had the infinite potential to be something great.

He'd never felt like that before.

There was that word again.

Before.

Norik would laugh his ass off.

Garrett brushed the back of his hand over his cheek as he realized that Norik *had* been laughing his ass off at him, the flaming little shit. Norik had seen what he'd only just discovered.

Then the stairs ended and they gathered in a long, arched corridor, the ceiling higher than Uvili could reach. One end disappeared into a darkness that made his skin crawl, the other curved around a corner, diffuse light seeming to come from the warm, yellow stone.

Uvili turned toward the corner, and while Garrett hadn't wanted to go into that darkness, it wasn't much of a relief to have it at their backs.

The corner led to more hall.

But they'd left the darkness behind.

"We need to rest."

Uvili lifted her head, her nostrils flared, and, reluctantly, she nodded.

He was about to ask if they were in danger when he realized that was a stupid question. Of course they were in danger.

They drank sparingly, chewed on dried meat, and Malcolm poked at a pile of what looked like turtle shells, ripped from the turtle and shattered.

"It's the outer carapace of the creature that dug the tunnels," Arianna said, carefully examining a large piece. "The meat's been clawed off it." She turned it so they could see the marks.

There were claw marks high on the wall as well, at about the level of Uvili's head.

Too soon, they hauled themselves back onto their feet and kept moving.

The hall kept curving to the right.

"This would never fit inside the tower," Malcolm protested. "Not the one from before."

Before seemed to be haunting them.

When Uvili stopped again, chin up, nose in the air, they drew in a deep breath in unison.

Arianna caught his eye and half smiled at the absurdity.

He half smiled back.

The smell that had stopped Uvili had a pungent familiarity. "Cattle. And the barracks."

Arianna frowned. "We cleared a nest of shattered out of the ruins a couple of years ago. It smelled sort of like this. Like the den of something not quite right."

Cattle in the barracks.

Garrett shifted his grip on his sword. "Is there a way around it?"

"The only other way is through that darkness," Arianna reminded him. "And I don't think . . ." She shook her head. "I don't that's something Uvili can fight."

"Let's keep moving, then. If the good people of Gateway can take out a nest, I'm sure Uvili will have no problem."

Uvili shot him a look that would have come with raised brows, had she any. She'd probably learned it from Norik.

"At least they're stinky enough to give warning," Malcolm muttered. The boy's voice was thin, he was nearing the end of his rope, but he was trying. All any of them could do.

More shell. A pile of bones, most of them cracked for the marrow. More scoring high on the walls. It was growing warmer. Under layers of wool, sweat ran down Garrett's sides.

They turned another corner and the hall ended in an arched doorway leading into an enormous room. A pair of deep gouges, an arm's length apart, marked the top of the arch. Beyond it, straw and cloth and bone and items Garrett couldn't identify had been piled against the walls of the room.

Uvili held up her hand, and they froze.

"Snoring," Malcolm breathed before Garrett could identify the sound.

"If they're nocturnal," Arianna said softly, her breath warm against his jaw, "they may sleep while the light's on."

"Who turns it off?"

"Let's not borrow trouble."

"Sir." Malcolm pointed past him. On the far side of the room was a door. A normal wooden door with a flat top, not a flaming arch.

When Uvili moved forward, they all moved with her.

Silently. Toward the door.

The snoring came from the largest pile of straw.

As they neared it, Garrett thought he saw the top of a discarded bull's skull, the great branching horns discolored by age. No, not a skull, he realized as they came closer, a bull's head. The largest he'd ever seen. And by the head, an arm, as large as Uvili's but a darker yellow-brown than the straw. Who, or what, had the head and arm been torn from?

Then he saw the nostrils flare.

A man sprawled naked on the straw, huge chest rising and falling under the ropey scars that attached the bull's head to his torso. His legs ended in bull's hooves, the scarring above them rising to his knees. Claws emerged from gnarled flesh at the end of his fingers.

They were halfway to the door.

The nostrils flared again.

And the eyes opened, red-rimmed and insane.

Garrett froze—at the anger, at the pain, at the knowledge that someone had done this. Then the creature snorted and scrambled to its feet.

His feet.

If Uvili was a person, this too was or had been a person.

As if called by his thought, Uvili grunted and moved until they were hidden behind her bulk from the man-bull's sight.

"We need to run." Arianna's voice in his ear.

"When battle's joined," he breathed. "Not before. We don't know if he'll give chase."

Uvili seemed willing to wait until the man-bull found his balance. Hooves weren't intended for standing erect. Perhaps she thought it would be all posturing until he was provoked. Perhaps she felt the same horrified sympathy Garrett felt.

And then the man-bull charged. Uvili twisted to avoid the horns, got her arms under his, and the two of them crashed across the room, slamming into the opposite wall.

"Run!"

The man-bull roared. Uvili roared back.

The door was locked. Five thick rings of iron curved into the wood and back out again. The rings turned when he grabbed them, and under the encrusted dirt, he could see simple runes pressed into the metal.

"It's a puzzle!" Malcolm shouldered him aside and bent over the rings. "My little sister . . ."

Another roar drowned him out and Garrett turned to see Uvili held one of the man-bull's wrists in each hand, his arms pulled wide, her head tucked in against his chest to avoid the horns. His hooves found little purchase on the stone floor as she pushed him back.

Thick, yellowed claws flexed above her grip. He could hurt her, Garrett realized. Like the dead who'd guarded the way to the tower, he could tear through mage-crafted skin. Unlike the dead, who fought without desire, Garrett could see the man-bull wanted to rend and tear and destroy.

"I'm through!"

"Garrett!" He started when Arianna touched his arm and reluctantly pulled his attention away from the battle. Malcolm had already gone through the open door and stood in a familiar stairwell.

"There's no rings on this side," he cried when they joined him. "How do we lock it?"

"We assume it locks from the other side," Garrett told him.

Arianna grabbed his arm. "Do you want to risk that?"

"Do we have a choice?"

They didn't.

She nodded, put thumb and forefinger in her mouth, and whistled.

Uvili ducked lower, rammed her shoulder into the man-bull's stomach, bent her knees and heaved, releasing her grip on his wrists at the last possible second. The man-bull tumbled as he hit the floor, and Uvili ran.

He dug his claws into the stone to stop himself. Got his feet under him again. Ran for the door with his knuckles against the floor for balance, blowing foam from red-rimmed nostrils.

"Get it closed!" Garrett roared, as Uvili slammed into the opposite wall, unable to stop in time.

Malcolm grabbed the door beside him and they heaved. Hinges screamed. Arianna joined them. It moved another handspan.

Then Uvili's hands hit the wood above their heads and they stumbled together as it swung . . .

. . . shuddered from an impact, and stopped. An arm thrust though the gap, claws dragging deep gouges into the stones of the wall.

Uvili grunted.

"Move away," Garrett commanded. "Give her room."

With the door cleared, she threw her full weight against the wood. The gap narrowed.

The man-bull bellowed. Garrett's ears rang and the stone by his shoulder vibrated.

The gap narrowed a fraction more.

He'd have to withdraw his arm or lose it.

The noise as the door slammed closed sounded like a portcullis dropping—metal against stone.

"Locked," Arianna panted. Her eyes widened. "You're hurt." Black blood stained the leather around a gash in Uvili's side. "I need to pack that!"

"No." She pointed down the stairs. "Go."

"She's right," Garrett said before Arianna could protest. "This whole tower is mage-crafted. We need to get out. Now. Uvili, point." If she collapsed, he didn't want her behind them.

She glanced over at the door, at the claw marks, paler gouges in the gray, and nodded.

❧

While Malcom dozed in a patch of sun, Garrett watched the clearing, the woods, the tower, and the path down the hill. The best he could say of their position was that nothing could sneak up on them. They were resting on a rocky outcrop at the top of the path, Uvili crouched just off it on frost-killed bracken while Arianna patched her wound, stubbornly racing against Uvili's ability to heal.

The tower looked like it had before, with no sign of the creature's lair or the halls leading to it. Garrett understood Captain Marsan's hatred of mage-craft. People needed reality to remain constant.

"I don't understand how we got here," he muttered.

Arianna spat out a chewed mouthful of leaves, pressed them into Uvili's side, and said, "I think that when we escaped the storm, it sent us to the nearest, greatest threat."

"It?"

"The Broken Lands."

"I'd rather not believe the Broken Lands has a personal perspective on what we do."

"So would I. However."

"However," he repeated.

She wrapped a strip of cloth around Uvili's middle, having cut away the leather while still leaving her clothed. Uvili had been naked when Garrett found her, naked until he commissioned her clothing, although he hadn't thought of her as naked, more like an axe without a handle.

Uvili protested as Arianna tied the cloth off.

Arianna shook her head. "I know, but his claws were filthy, and if they can wound, they can infect." She sat back on her heels and glanced over at the tower. "Who would do something so horrible?"

"Captain Marsan believed mage-craft corrupts everyone who practices it."

"And what do you believe?"

He thought of the man-bull struggling to stand. "That she was right."

"To create such a . . ." Her eyes widened. She scrambled aside and vomited. Garrett moved to her side and held her hair as she emptied her stomach, then handed her a waterskin as she straightened.

"The mage who did this . . ." She paused, took another mouthful and spat. ". . . had to have been a healer. I mean, not just a healer, but healing was the strongest among the talents they had. To force flesh to join, to force a living being to exist in such agony for so long . . ." Her voice trailed off and she turned to stare past him at Uvili, dark shadows under her eyes. "I almost wish you'd killed him."

Uvili sighed. "Yes."

"Could you have killed him?"

She frowned and stared back at the tower. "Yes."

"Could you have survived killing him?" Garrett asked. When her frown deepened, he nodded toward the wound.

After a long moment, she shook her head.

"The lock is on the inside," Arianna said softly. "All he needs to do to be free is figure it out. I almost hope he does."

"Yes."

Enough daylight remained to reach the bottom of the hill. Day or night, the passage back through the cave would be in darkness. He stood, offered a hand to Arianna, and nudged Malcolm's leg. "Let's go."

Uvili grunted as she stood. Without thinking, Garrett clasped her elbow to steady her. "Does it hurt?"

She snorted, an almost delicate sound from someone her size, and looked at him like he was an idiot.

He felt like one.

"Weren't there stairs before?" Malcolm asked, one foot on the path worn into the side of the hill.

"Yes. Stay close." He couldn't lose anyone else.

❧

Norik, or what remained of him, screamed. Bones wearing Petre's face demanded to know why his lord hadn't saved him. He saw Norik's blackened heart beating in his chest. Petre's eyes dissolving, running down his cheeks. Why had they died? they demanded silently. Why was a symbol worth more than their lives?

He was the Heir of Marsan. Why hadn't he saved them?

He fell to his knees, taken down by the weight of their anger. He struggled and fought and felt their blood on his hands and face.

Uvili held him against her chest as they emerged from the passage into the cave under the waterfall. Her back against the wall, she slid to the floor, and cradled him as he sobbed.

Even through his grief, he knew she'd saved him. He'd still be in the passage, held by guilt, had she not carried him free.

She saved him. She fought for him. Actions she'd been designed to perform.

Where had she learned to give comfort?

LYELEE.NOW

Lyelee knew she should have been cataloging—noting the dragon's size, shape, and color—but she wasted a moment appreciating the dragon's beauty. Its body was longer than two horses although not much wider. It had four legs, the rear pair heavier and more muscular than the front. All four feet had long, articulated toes ending in slender claws. One of the front toes looked like it could act as a thumb, but she couldn't be certain until she saw its grip. Its scales were red shading to gold on the extremities and Lyelee wondered if the red had been drawn from the soil—the soil that had been red was now pinkish gray. It had two large golden eyes, two flared nostrils, and a wide, fanged mouth. The tongue was long, like a snake's rather than a lizard's. Huge red membranous wings half unfurled as it flung itself from the cave.

The ground trembled when it landed, although it should have been bird-light in order to fly.

Her pack already discarded, Nonee charged forward. The dragon twisted to the right. When Nonee followed, its tail whipped around and slapped her nearly to the tree line.

The dragon roared and Lyelee laughed. Scholars took pride in discovering new knowledge, but she'd discovered old knowledge, and made it new again by applying it. Infinite possibilities were within her grasp. Things that had always seemed annoyingly just out of reach came into focus.

"Novitiate!" Gearing clutched at her arm and pulled, but she was securely rooted in place. "Novitiate! Move!"

She frowned as a crossbow quarrel bounced off the scales on the dragon's chest. Servan's aim was true, but her weapon useless.

"Kalyealee Marsan-cee!"

In seven years, had Gearing ever called her by her name, without *novitiate* tacked on before it? Reluctantly, she tore her gaze from the dragon and turned toward him. His eyes were wide in panic, his face damp with sweat. There was blood in his beard from a split lip and he shook hard enough she could actually see the movement.

"We have to get to safety!"

When he swayed, still clutching her arm, she understood. Battered and bruised from the fall, he couldn't get to safety without help. He'd thought of her safety only as it applied to his. She considered pulling free of his grip and leaving him to stagger to a prudent distance on his own, but he held on with both hands and she'd always found it difficult to free herself from his . . . oversight. Wind whistled past her ear. She swayed in the backwash from a wing strike at Keetin. Keetin threw himself flat. He was more intelligent than he looked. With the greater part of her attention still on her dragon, she dragged Gearing past the wreckage of the tower room. It appeared to be nothing more than the shattered wood of walls and floor, but that was clearly camouflage, hiding the mage-craft that had created and then destroyed it. She'd examine it more closely later. When they reached the perimeter of the absent pond, Gearing sank to the ground, panting.

Nonee had returned to the fight. She was fast. The dragon was faster.

Ryan had his sword out. What did he think he could do? The narrow swords he and Captain Yansav preferred required precision and Ryan had never been precise.

Nonee slammed the dragon's head aside and was slapped again, the dragon's tail whipping under her futile attempt to grab it.

It lunged at Ryan.

As Destros swung an axe toward the prominent joint in the front leg, Captain Yansav slipped in under the dragon's lunge. Lyelee assumed she was aiming for the throat, where logic dictated the scales would be thinner. Lyelee wondered if logic could be applied to a dragon, then reminded herself that logic could be applied to everything. Even dragons..

The dragon roared. Destros hadn't made contact, so the captain must have done some damage.

The captain flew back, trailing blood, her left leg gone below the knee. Ryan reached her side, fumbling under his vest for his belt, almost before she hit the ground. She still held her weapons—sword in one hand, long dagger in the other—although what she thought she could do with them in her condition, Lyelee had no idea.

Servan pushed between Destros and Keetin and headed straight for the dragon.

When Destros charged after her, Nonee stopped him.

Interesting.

Arms out, hands empty, Servan moved closer.

The dragon seemed confused.

Which proved its intelligence, as far as Lyelee was concerned.

"Hey there, beautiful." Servan's voice slipped between the sounds of wings and cursing and Gearing's heavy breathing. "Calm down now, sweetheart. We don't want to fight you. Mostly because we'll lose and you'll eat us, but the point stands. Calm. Calm. No more fighting now . . ."

The dragon's mouth looked large enough to close around the approaching guardian from head to hips. To Lyelee's surprise, it settled down onto its forelegs, wings mantled, and cocked its head. Even its tail stilled—all but the tip, which continued to trace figure eights in the air.

Servan stopped two or three body-lengths away. Her body-lengths, not the dragon's. "Maybe you should find a safer place to be, huh? A better place for dragons. No swords, no axes, no arrows, just open skies and comfy caves and plenty to eat. Does that sound good, sweetheart?" She waved one of her extended hands.

"Shoo?" Keetin muttered.

The dragon stared at Servan for a moment longer, blinked gold eyes, then reared up . . .

Destros shifted his grip on his axes.

. . . and leapt into the air. At the height of its leap, it unfurled its wings and brought them down, tips nearly touching the earth.

Lyelee squinted into the clouds of dirt.

It rose higher and higher. When it finally leveled out, it was an arrow-shaped shadow against the sky, aimed toward the mountains.

As the dirt settled, she saw Ryan had thrown himself over the captain. Nonee dropped down beside them, pack in hand, and everyone else—herself and Gearing included—stared at Servan.

Slate, no matter his mood, had never attacked her.

"What?" Servan demanded. "She's a baby, and she was frightened."

"How could you tell?" Destros's voice wasn't entirely steady.

"How could you not?"

Servan was right, Lyelee acknowledged. It was a baby and she'd created it and now it was gone before she could study it. Servan would face consequences for that. Cause and effect.

"A baby." Destros shook his head, the axe he still gripped sagging until the blade touched the ground. "It's a dragon."

"It didn't breathe fire," Keetin pointed out, swaying where he stood.

"Living tissue can't contain fire," Lyelee called. That seemed safe to conclude even without experimentation. "It's impossible."

"So's a dragon," he responded, half turning toward her.

"Obviously not." Living tissue could contain gases, though, and if the teeth were flint and steel . . . No. The inside of the mouth would cook. On the other hand, mage-craft . . .

"Nonee." Destros visibly pulled himself together. "Will it be back?"

"No." Nonee rummaged in her pack with one hand, the other clamped down on the captain's leg.

Lyelee moved closer until she could see the blood oozing out, in spite of Ryan's belt and Nonee's grip, and noted that the bone had been cleanly cut with no shattered edges. The dragon's teeth had been very sharp.

"She's heading for Dybrin Amsputov's tower in the mountains," Nonee continued, and Lyelee glanced toward the distant peaks. "He made dragons."

"You might have mentioned that," Keetin said, a waterskin halfway to his mouth.

"You had no reason to go to the mountains."

He sighed and surrendered. "So why were there no dragons in the Captain's Chronicle?"

"Captain Marsan never met a dragon."

Met? The others might not have understood how the weapon used the word, but Lyelee did. "How intelligent are they?"

"More than a cat."

"That's a very open variable."

Nonee shrugged, gently pushed Ryan away, and cupped a hand over the captain's stump.

Ryan sat back on his heels, obviously ready to help. Lyelee wondered what he thought he could do. "Something Arianna prepared for this trip?" he asked quietly, as Nonee covered the stump in what looked like a clay slurry speckled with plant matter.

"Yes."

"Destros . . ." The dark, rich tones of the captain's skin had dulled and taken on a grayish cast. Her voice caught in the back of her throat. "Make camp. Servan, on watch."

"Aye, Cap. But . . . here?"

"Safest place in the Broken Lands," Nonee said. "The dragon ate everything that might attack and chased away everything she didn't eat."

Lyelee hadn't been able to check the hole where she'd buried the dragon's tooth without causing questions she couldn't be bothered to answer. The dragon itself would have to stand as evidence the tooth was gone. She poked another stick into the fire and glanced across it at Captain Yansav. "Fortunately, you lost the leg you'd already injured."

"Harsh," Servan muttered.

Captain Yansav glared up at her and Lyelee rolled her eyes. "Now you don't have to be concerned about your bad knee giving out."

The captain shifted the glare down to where her bad knee had been, as though simple fact annoyed her.

"Sleep." Nonee stepped between them and held out a cup to the captain.

"If I'm drugged," the captain began.

Nonee cut her off. "You'll sleep."

"And if we're attacked? If something new comes for the fuel?"

"Don't worry, Cap," Servan called. "I'll shoot it in the eye."

"Or give it a biscuit." Keetin dropped another load of dead wood by the fire.

Servan laughed. "Not likely. There's burning-all biscuits left."

They were all ignoring the obvious, refusing to ask the questions. She'd tried but Ryan had stopped her, threatening her with a gag when she'd reminded him he had no authority over scholarship. The set of his jaw beneath his scruffy beard had convinced her he was serious. The Scholar's Hall would deal with him when they returned to Marsanport. Him and Servan both.

"Where are you going?"

Lyelee rolled her eyes and turned toward Nonee, refusing to startle when she realized how close the weapon had come. When she'd slipped out of her bedroll, Nonee had been a shadow on the far side of the camp. "I'm going to the latrine. Would you like to hold my hand? I'm going to be a while."

"More fiber," Gearing muttered.

They turned together to stare, but when a wheezing breath became a snore, returned their attention to each other.

"The satchel?" Nonee nodded toward it.

Lyelee patted the worn leather. "Woman supplies." She bared her teeth in a false smile. "You wouldn't understand."

Nonee stepped back and bared her teeth as well.

As Lyelee walked into the darkness, following the shadow the firelight threw in front of her, she had the strangest thought that she could feel Curtin watching suspiciously.

Safely behind the bush that kept the privy private, she moved away from the smell of excrement, pulled out her candle and tinder box and set them on a flat stone. She had to place her open notebook dangerously close, but after a moment that wouldn't matter.

Scholar's shorthand had allowed her to fill her notebook with mage-craft, knowing full well Ryan would deny her right to the actual book.

If she could create a dragon, what else could she do?

Anything else.

She should wait until she had more than a social contract of privacy. Wait until they returned to Marsanport, until she'd secured herself inside one of the experimental spaces in the Scholar's Hall. As a Scholar of History, of the Broken Lands, she'd never used one. That would change.

She *should* wait.

But she wasn't going to.

Not after seeing the dragon.

On her knees, she read the relevant notes again, then spat into her right hand and rubbed her palms briskly together twenty-one times, holding the intended result in her mind. Her skin warm, she reached out and lifted the flame from the candle.

History taught that mage-craft was difficult, that it required complex preparation and a surrender of a part of the mage to eldritch forces.

It wasn't. It didn't. But then, she was a scholar, not a mage.

She poured the flame into her other hand. And back.

It was beautiful.

"Novitiate!" Eyes wide, clutching his satchel against his stomach with both arms, Gearing stared at the fire burning in the center of her palm.

She couldn't be discovered now, not here, not with these people, not before she presented her regained knowledge to the Hall.

Her small flame became a pillar of fire with Gearing at its heart. He screamed as he burned. The heat from such a blaze should have crisped the leaves on the surrounding bushes, should have crisped her, but it was only a pleasant warmth. Barely warmer than the night around her.

Nonee arrived first and held Destros and Servan back when they followed. "Don't touch it! You'll become part of it!"

"What do we do?" Ryan demanded, arriving late. Limping. Damaged.

"Let it burn," Nonee told him.

"But . . ."

"It won't take long."

Gearing had stopped screaming, his image gray and featureless within the flame.

Lyelee pressed her fingers to her throat and counted. At thirty-one, the center of the flame turned from white to yellow. At thirty-six, to orange. At forty-three, it went out.

She blinked away afterimages in the sudden darkness.

The smell of cooked pork hid the smell of the latrine.

Servan vomited and Lyelee used the distraction to slip her notebook away.

❧

"Yes, I had a candle lit. You try dealing with bloody rags in the dark."

"She's not wrong," Servan muttered.

They were gathered around Captain Yansav, who'd been left behind during the rush toward the pillar of flame.

"I saw Scholar Gearing come around the bush," Lyelee continued. "He pulled a piece of paper from his satchel. I saw his lips move, then he spat in one hand, rubbed his hands together . . ."

"What did he do with the paper he was holding?" the captain asked.

"He tucked it into his armpit. I assume it's still there."

"He rubbed his hands together . . ." Ryan prodded. "And after?"

"He held a hand out and my candle flame leapt into it. Before I was finished with it, I might add. He seemed surprised, as though he hadn't expected it to work, called out *novitiate*, then the flame engulfed him. He must have taken notes while he was in the library, but his satchel's ash so I can't check."

"Did you take notes in the workroom?" the weapon asked.

"Of course I did." She pulled out her notebook, and opened it. Holding it so everyone could see the page. "Here, I identified the contents in the glass jars. They were remarkably well preserved given how long they'd been in there. Here, I made calculations to determine the rate of Harris's blood loss during the time he hung on the spikes given that when we arrived he still had enough blood remaining to allow his heart to beat. Of course I had to approximate the diameter of pipe between the drain and the tank and . . ."

"Enough." Ryan raised a hand, shaking his head as though denying the manner of Harris's death. Lyelee had come to realize that widespread denial was endemic in Marsanport. That would have to change.

The weapon's nostrils flared, but she let Ryan's order stand.

"Your notes are in condensed script." Captain Yansav looked as though she were about to reach for the book, but changed her mind at the last minute. "We have only your word that's what they say."

"Are you accusing a scholar of lying, Captain?"

"No," she said after a long moment. "I'm not."

Lyelee smiled. "Good."

"You don't seem overly upset by Scholar Gearing's death," Keetin said quietly, and coughed into his sleeve.

"Because you know what I'm feeling, is that it?"

"No, but . . ."

"Scholar Gearing killed himself by investigating a historical resource in an uncontrolled environment. I have little sympathy, given the way he was always after me to follow procedure!" She turned away from the fire, hand out to stop anyone from coming closer. Of course she was upset. In all the excitement, it had slipped her mind that in the eyes of the Scholar's Hall, Scholar Gearing held the only Scholarship of the Broken Lands. Who was going to approve her thesis now?

RYAN.NOW

Ryan rolled up onto his feet and squinted at the horizon. He wasn't positive he'd slept after Scholar Gearing's death. Exhaustion pulled at him, the bite on his calf throbbed in time to his heartbeat, and it felt as though he'd had a steel spike slammed into his head. He knew he should try to sleep; they had a long day ahead. He also knew sleep wasn't going to happen.

None of them had thought to dig another latrine pit. He should have thought of it. Donal would have thought of it.

"You were too busy whimpering like a baby."

"You watch a man immolated by mage-crafted fire," he muttered under his breath, before the twins could chime in, "and you'd whimper too."

A blackened circle of grass marked the spot Gearing had died. A perfect, unnatural circle.

Unnatural seemed fitting.

Lyelee had gathered what little ash there'd been, using a piece of paper to scoop it into a waxed container, working by the light of Keetin's torch. *"I'll take this back to the Scholar's Hall,"* she'd said. *"There'll be tests to do."*

Sentiment was not something Lyelee indulged in.

Leaves rustled, a bird called in the distance, and the hair rose on the back of Ryan's neck. He had to breathe deeply for a few moments before he could empty his bladder.

Limping back to the camp, he realized it had been surrounded by a shallow trench. Squatting, sucking air through his teeth at the pain, he leaned in as close as he could, and in the dawning light saw footprints. Nonee's footprints. She must have spent the night circling the camp, laying out a warning.

Cross this and you face the last of the great mage-crafted weapons.

He hadn't seen her or heard her, so he must have slept. Nice to have the confirmation, but it did nothing to ease his exhaustion.

Nonee stood by the edge of the vanished pond.

Ryan straightened slowly, teeth clenched against the stab of pain, and picked his way across the camp.

It wasn't too quiet—muttering and thrashing defined sleep in the Broken Lands—but something was wrong. The sounds didn't . . .

Didn't include Scholar Gearing's breathy snore.

Or Harris rising early to build up the fire.

Or Curtin scowling at Nonee's back.

Or Captain Yansav's leg, for that matter. Not that he'd ever been aware of her leg independent of the captain.

He'd lost three lives. And a leg.

He really needed more sleep.

When he reached Nonee's side, he turned to face the camp so they'd have eyes in two directions.

"Maybe you should fight with your eyes instead of your sword."

"Maybe he should hide instead of fight."

"Makes sense, he should stick with what he's good at."

"Are you all right?" he asked. They stood close enough, he felt her turn toward him. "You have history with the horrors of mage-craft."

"Kalyealee who-could-be-heir is a scholar of history."

Ryan couldn't get that to make sense so he grasped what he could. "Why do you call her Kalyealee who-could-be-heir?"

She shrugged. "It's important to remember."

"To remember who's in charge in case I die?"

"To remember why you need to be kept alive."

"She's not so bad."

"She shouldn't be the Lord Protector."

"She'd be bad at it," Ryan admitted. The Lord Protector cared for their people, the intent was right there in the title. Scholars cared only for knowledge. "She doesn't want the job. If she did, I'd be dead by now."

"Yes."

He frowned. There was a truth in both his joking comment and in Nonee's response he couldn't quite reach.

❧

Captain Yansav leaned away from Nonee's reaching hands. "You will not carry me."

Nonee shrugged. "You can't walk."

"And if you need to fight?"

"You can be dropped."

The captain barked out a startled laugh. "Do I have your word?"

"You do." Hand over her heart, Nonee gave a shallow bow.

"I'd almost like to see that." Keetin swallowed a mouthful of tincture, made a familiar face at the taste, and added, "Almost." He had deep, purple shadows under his eyes, more obvious than the shadows the rest of them carried because of his paler skin.

His cheek above the upper edge of his beard was warm and clammy under the back of Ryan's hand. The warmth might have been the heat of the new day, but Ryan knew it wasn't. "How do you feel?"

"Same old, same old. Like I have a brick in my lungs."

"If you need to rest . . ."

"How's your leg? Painful? If you need to sit . . ."

Ryan smiled. "Point taken. Just . . ." He sighed and rested his head on Keetin's shoulder, unable to deny himself a moment's comfort. "Don't die."

"I don't plan on it."

A buckle dug into his forehead. "Neither did Gearing."

"Spontaneous mage-craft."

"Is that what we're calling it?"

"It's a kinder way to define it in the chronicle. His family wouldn't want to know he actually attempted mage-craft."

"Did he?" Ryan had his doubts. Doubts too unformed to be spoken.

"I guess we'll never know. Unless Lyelee can get his ashes to talk."

"Is that possible?"

"How would I know?" Keetin leaned back and grinned at him. "Don't suggest it to her."

And there was that touch of truth again.

"Can you get through?" Ryan asked as Nonee ripped a questing root from the ground. The willows had become an impenetrable barrier along the missing river.

Nonee scowled. "Light a fire," she said. "Wood burns."

People burned. If the fire was hot enough.

"What is it?" he asked Lyelee as he tore strips off his shirt to make torches.

"If we had the flame Gearing used . . ."

"No."

"Mage-craft is not . . ."

"I think last night proved it is."

"You *think*." She shook her head. "You don't think. You don't reason. What kind of Lord Protector keeps his people from using tools out of fear?"

"One who learns from history."

Her eyes narrowed and she stomped away.

"Good one," Keetin murmured.

When they finally reached the cliff—smelling of smoke, with minor burns and lash marks from roots that died trying to reach the fuel—the gully they'd climbed down had disappeared.

"We can't get up that." Ryan squinted first up at the rock face and then along it. It wasn't just that the rare cracks in the rock ran vertically, offering no handholds, but that the top of the cliff leaned out toward them. It was higher, too. He was certain of it. "We'll have to keep following it and hope . . ."

"No."

"No hope?" he sighed, shifting his weight off his bad leg. It wasn't hard to believe the Broken Lands had raised a barrier to keep them penned until something better able to take the fuel arrived. There'd be a last stand with their backs pressed against the rock, their bones joining the shattered bones and teeth at the base of the cliff.

"No point in going on," Nonee told him. "The tree is a fixed point, we have to reach it."

Ryan wanted a long hot bath, clean clothes, and a meal not cooked over an open fire. He wanted Curtin, Harris, and Gearing back. Most of all, right now, he wanted to sit down, but he couldn't because that would put the fuel, and his ass, closer to any questing roots. He looked up. Heard the twang of a crossbow and heard Servan call, "Six quarrels left," as one of the impossibly toothy doves that had been attacking all morning plummeted toward the ground. "Can you get us up there?" he asked wearily.

"Yes."

"Do it."

Nonee set Captain Yansav down on a large slab of flat rock, tucked her pack behind the captain's back, and ignored her snarled, "I can sit on my own." The captain's long dagger had blood caked against the pommel. The doves had been . . .

He didn't want to think about the doves. He was having the dovecote in the Citadel torn down.

"Stand by Captain Yansav," Ryan ordered the others as Nonee approached the cliff. "The roots can't get you through the rock."

Keetin squatted to rap his knuckles against it. "You sure about that?"

"Nonee is."

He'd expected her to punch a staircase into the rock, but it looked more like a fight, forcing the cliff to give her access. Rock fell in large pieces that hit the ground and shattered and flew from the cliff face in shards that had them build a hasty barricade of the packs.

"Lyelee! Get behind the barricade!"

She stood, arms folded, watching Nonee, and shot him an impatient dismissal when he said it again. He wanted to think she was so wrapped in the shock of Gearing's horrifying death that she'd forgotten self-preservation. He didn't think it, but he wished he could. He could deal with shock.

When she finally joined them, she carried a rock the size of her head. Before he could ask why, she dropped it. It split into two equal pieces.

"Rock doesn't break that way in nature," she said, prodding the pieces with her boot.

"You're a Scholar of History."

She curled a lip. "Historically, rock doesn't break that way."

"It's mage-crafted rock," Keetin reminded her, opened his mouth to continue, and began to cough, his whole body shaking.

"And if mage-crafted rock were to be quarried along its fault lines, it would produce building materials in half, no, a quarter of the time."

"And then split when you least expected it." Ryan moved closer to support Keetin as he doubled over. "And no one would put a quarry in the Broken Lands."

"Because no one has enough foresight to overcome irrational fear."

Destros cleared his throat, and when Lyelee turned toward him, asked, "Irrational?"

"It means . . ."

"I know what it means, Scholar." He stomped on the tip of a questing root, his weight almost holding it in place, then used his axe to sever it back as far as he could reach. "Don't agree with the way you're using it."

"And I don't care if you agree or not."

He smiled at her, showing more teeth than usual. "Figured that already, Scholar."

Not only rock fell. Ryan saw flashes of ivory and once a long, pale bone that tumbled and shattered when it landed.

Nonee reached the top of the cliff, paused, gathered herself to leap down, and . . .

"Wait!" Ryan pointed. "It that what I think it is?" The angle of the cliff meant he could only see the top of the egg-shaped rock. And the face.

The captain's string of Shurlian profanity was weary but emphatic.

"This time," Lyelee announced, "I will examine it."

It had said *Free me.* Had it begged or commanded?

Tanika Fleshrender had been screaming in rage.

"Nonee! Throw it off the cliff!"

Nonee stared down at him for a moment, then she nodded.

She couldn't lift it. Ryan could see her straining. Hear her grunting.

She couldn't lift it, but she could move it. More of it came into view as it slid closer to the edge of the cliff.

"Don't you dare!" Lyelee shrieked, darting forward. "Nonee! I'm warning you!"

Ryan folded his hands into fists. "Destros."

Lyelee shrieked as Destros carried her back beside the captain. Shrieked as the rock began to tumble. As it fell. As it hit the ground and crumbled in place.

Stopped when a hundred or more writhing roots dragged the pieces away.

"Didn't see that coming," Servan said quietly.

Ryan almost had.

Nails digging into Ryan's arm, Lyelee leaned close and snarled, "I will tell the Scholar's Hall what you've done, and you will pay for destroying a unique artifact. You will pay."

"Ryan's going to get it," Josan sing-songed.

"Get burnt." He yanked his arm free and met Nonee where she'd landed, halfway between the cliff and the captain, the impact making the area temporarily safe from the roots. Her chest visibly rose and fell.

"Keep Kalyealee who-could-be-heir away from the bones," she said before he could ask if she needed to rest. "Don't listen to what they say."

"To what the bones say?"

Instead of answering, she raised her head. "Servan! Wear your pack. Not enough in it to matter."

"Why do *I* have to go first?" Servan asked, sighing.

"Best to put the archer on the high ground."

Servan swore once during the ascent—Ryan admired her restraint. Nonee disappeared when they reached the top, and a moment later, something with three legs and a long whip-like tail arced through the air and into the nearest clump of willows. Branches bent to meet it.

"Those willows moving closer?" Destros wondered.

Keetin sucked in a watery breath. "They're trees."

"And?"

"We're clear!" Servan called.

"Stay away from the cliff." Ryan moved back to Captain Yansav as he spoke. "We don't know what's coming over next."

"Yeah, we do," Keetin said as Nonee landed.

From the way the captain went limp about halfway into Nonee's return journey, Ryan suspected she'd passed out.

He hadn't realized he'd stepped back off the slab until a root wrapped around his ankle and dragged him toward the trees. Destros grabbed him under the arms—he bit back a scream, caught between the root and the guardian's hold. Keetin flung himself to his knees, hacking at the root with a knife. Other roots began to climb his body, using him to get to Ryan.

A flaming quarrel hit the nearest tree.

The roots whipped back.

Only Destros's strength kept Ryan standing when they reached the slab, although part of that could have been Keetin hanging off his arm, trying to breathe.

"I could . . . carry the fuel. Allow . . . you to recover from the . . . constant attacks."

The fuel was his burden. He hadn't questioned that. No one had questioned that. No one even acknowledged it if they could help it.

"Ryan?"

"No."

The ground trembled as Nonee landed for the third time. She pointed at Lyelee. "You next."

Servan could protect the captain if it came to it.

Ryan frowned. Where had that thought come from?

"Could be worse," Keetin wheezed. "Could be sky-darkening clouds of flesh-eating insects. Nonee!" He raised his voice. "Why didn't the mages create swarms of flesh-eating insects?"

"Too hard to control."

"This is controlled?" he asked as Nonee started to climb.

"It was."

LYELEE.NOW

Lyelee appreciated control. If the mages hadn't lost control, Captain Marsan would have continued to lead Tanika Fleshrender's personal guard and Lyelee would have been born in the Mage Lands, where fear had never forbidden knowledge. Captain Marsan's fear had driven her all the way to the Great Lake. Her fear had destroyed Northport and forced the people she supposedly protected to turn their backs on their history. *Magecraft destroys*, she'd said. When the truth had actually been that six specific mages had lost control. As though there'd only ever been six mages.

Lyelee understood control.

The weapon released her at the top of the cliff. Lyelee peeled herself off the leather—the weapon might not sweat, but she did—twitched her vest back into place, and walked in from the edge, satchel tucked under her right arm. She'd concealed the bone—a full finger section joint to joint, retrieved while Destros and Keetin freed Ryan from the roots—under the bandage around her broken fingers.

"Power," said the bone. *"You could reclaim history if you only had enough power."*

"Don't wander off, Scholar. We have no idea what other changes the land has made." Captain Yansav sat propped against a stump, armed and armored, maintaining the illusion of an effective guardian. She even wore her helm, although she could barely hold up her head.

Lyelee had no patience with those who refused to acknowledge a changing reality. "This would be the best time to discover those changes, before the fuel begins to draw unwelcome attention."

"Not on your own."

"I'm not under your command, Captain."

"You're under my protection, Scholar, and I can't protect you if you wander off."

She thought of Gearing bursting into flames and smiled. "I can protect myself."

"Don't wander off, Scholar."

"How do you plan to stop me?" Lyelee asked, curious. Servan stood at the edge of the cliff, a small fire burning at her feet, crossbow cocked, a rag-tipped quarrel in her other hand, doing what she could to protect the Heir of Marsan. Captain Yansav had lost a leg to a dragon—her dragon—

and was unable to stand on her own. Then Lyelee realized what she should have asked. "What are you afraid of?"

"Knowledge," said the bone. *"Knowledge she doesn't control."*

The captain's eyes narrowed. "Wander off and you could die."

No, she didn't think so. The Mage Lands had welcomed her—she had only a minor injury, she'd faced no terrors. The Mage Lands knew she could return them to what they'd been, a place where knowledge had no foolish constraints. "Tanika Fleshrender could have regrown your leg."

"Might be a goat leg, though," the weapon grunted as she reached the top of the cliff for the fifth time.

"She could do that?"

"Not successfully. Kept trying.. Arianna said it was easier to make adaptations than changes." She set Keetin on his feet. He waved off her help as he bent over coughing.

"She could clear his lungs," Lyelee said thoughtfully. Had the mage been a healer, searching for new ways to make flesh obey?

The weapon snorted. "She'd remove his lungs."

Lyelee folded her arms. "To study the problem."

The weapon stared at her for a long moment, then dropped back off the edge of the cliff.

"Pass," Keetin panted. Straightened. "I like my lungs where they are. How is it up here?"

"Quiet, Lord Norwin-cee."

He nodded at the captain. "Glad to hear it." He wiped a bit of blood off his cheek—whether he'd been cut by the roots below or during the weapon's carelessness hauling him up the cliff, Lyelee couldn't tell. "Nice shot," he said as Servan dipped the rags into the fire, leaned out, and pulled the trigger.

"Four bolts left."

"Can you make more?"

"If I get the time."

"Then when we make camp . . ."

"And wood that isn't trying to kill me."

"Oh, sure, ask for the impossible."

"Impossible," said the bone, *"is a word used by those who refuse to admit knowledge is infinite."*

"Lyelee?"

She shook herself free of infinite possibilities. "What?"

Keetin's brows had drawn in far enough to crack surface layers of the sunburned skin on his forehead. "You had a funny look on your face."

"Your face is a funny look." She pivoted on one heel and headed for a potentially mage-crafted rock formation in the near distance.

"Lyelee." And now Ryan was at the top of the cliff. Lovely. "If you think you're heading off to *search for knowledge*, think again."

She curled her lip at the emphasis. He wouldn't recognize actual knowledge if a scholar presented it to him in a lecture hall with visual aids.

"We're staying together," he added.

She pivoted again, and glared. "I'm a Scholar of the Broken Lands. I am the only Scholar of the Broken Lands remaining."

"Because Gearing is dead."

"Obviously." What a stupid statement. Gearing had been reduced to ash.

"Time," said the bone. *"Time never has to run out."*

All her life, Lyelee had felt she didn't have enough time. "If you stop me from studying the Broken Lands, the very thing I was sent here to do, I will speak to both the Scholar's Hall *and* the Court about your obstruction."

"You do that." Then, turning away from her, he said, "We'll try to make it to the fixed point of the tree before dark." Ryan took a swallow from a waterskin and passed it to Keetin. "We'll keep to the fastest pace we can manage."

"And learn nothing on the way," Lyelee muttered, retrieving her pack.

The weapon folded its arms. "Throw the piece of root trying to climb from your satchel off the cliff, Scholar."

She looked down. The root was *not* climbing from her satchel. When she looked up, they were all watching her.

"Lyelee," Ryan sighed. "Throw it off the cliff."

"It's dead."

"Dormant," said the weapon.

"Lyelee."

If she said no, what would they do? She didn't like the look on Ryan's face. "Knowledge is not to be feared," she said, pulling the length of root from her satchel. "But you let fear rule your lives."

When it hit the ground, other roots rose up to drag it into the dirt.

"Knowledge," said the bone, *"should be kept from those too ignorant to understand."*

Fortunately, she'd slipped another piece of root through a tear and into the hem of her shirt.

The cliff rumbled as she stepped away. And again as she put distance between her feet and the edge. It bucked and groaned and dropped her onto her ass.

Destros scooped up the captain. The weapon supported Ryan and Keetin.

She should have been the first escorted to safety. When she returned to Marsanport, changes would be made, expectations adjusted, and the respect due to scholarship strengthened. They would teach the children properly.

"Knowledge," said the bone, *"should be shared with caution."*

"Scholar!" Servan grabbed her arm. "Come on."

Lyelee yanked free. "I don't need your help, Guardian."

"Knowledge," said the bone, *"fulfills all needs."*

"Suit yourself, Scholar. Easier to guard the rear with both hands free."

When they reached solid ground, Keetin shoved Ryan down on a stump and dropped to a knee at his feet. "We should check your ankle before we go on. That root had quite the grip."

Ryan laughed, almost convincingly. "If I take my boot off, I'll never get it back on again."

Keetin grinned up at him, one hand raised to shade his eyes from the sun. "A mage-bite on one leg and a root-strangled ankle on the other; you need a third leg."

He winked. "Got one."

"Me too," muttered the captain. "One left, anyway."

Servan barked out a laugh.

They were attempting to reassure themselves with absurdity.

"Knowledge," said the bone, *"understands strength."*

"Nonee can't carry both of you." Keetin helped Ryan stand. "Can you keep going?"

"I can do what I have to."

"My hero."

"Bite me."

No one had flicked flame since Gearing's death. As though it would matter.

The weapon settled Captain Yansav against her torso in what looked like moderate comfort. Except weapons, Lyelee noted, didn't offer comfort.

"Call out if you have to stop," it said, as Destros handed the captain her long dagger. "No one gets left behind."

Lyelee stroked the bandage with her thumb, rubbing it along the ridge of bone.

"We died so you could find us," said the bone.

"What would happen," she asked, "if you picked Ryan up and ran for the Broken Line? Would we be able to follow without being attacked?"

"Actually, that's a good question," she heard the captain mutter.

"It is," the weapon agreed, as though its opinion mattered. Lyelee wanted access to the information it carried, she had no interest in what served it as thought. "Unfortunately, you'd still be attacked."

"That figures," Keetin sighed.

"But they'd be the type of attacks we faced on the way in," Lyelee pointed out, unsurprised she had to. "Undirected environmental attacks. Merely the Broken Lands flexing old mage-craft."

"Merely?" she heard Destros ask. As he'd never take that tone with a scholar, the question clearly hadn't been directed at her, and she ignored it.

"Curtin and Harris both died before I had the fuel." Ryan's expression was equal parts anger and . . . Concern? Speculation? No. Suspicion. What, Lyelee wondered, did he have to be suspicious about? The weapon was more prone to taking initiative than she was comfortable with, granted, but it had acknowledged the Last Command, and given how long it had been without direction, that was as much as they could hope for.

"Don't forget we were attacked before we crossed the line." Keetin tapped his chest, coughed, and said, "I'm holding that memory close to my heart."

"Humor," said the bone, *"is the shield of incompetence."*

They didn't reach the tree until dark the next day and only then because the days stretched so long. They'd stopped, drunk, chewed some of the disgusting food remaining, and then did the same thing again. And again. The attack by shuffling clods of dirt had been more farcical than dangerous. The weak force that held them together was easily disrupted by a blow—Destros had taken one down with his fist—and once scattered, they couldn't pull themselves back together.

"I don't like leaving that behind us," the captain said, glaring down at the seven twitching patches of ground from her perch in the weapon's hold. "Will they reform?"

The weapon shrugged.

Destros flicked away a bit of dirt he'd scraped out from under his fingernails. "If they reform, I'll knock them down again. And again, until they stay down."

"So we wait around watching dirt?" Servan sighed. "Eventually, something actually dangerous will show up."

Lyelee rolled her eyes. "I'm going behind that bush to pee while you argue. Don't leave without me."

There was no twitching dirt behind the bush. It didn't matter. She'd kicked out at one of the creatures and still had a bit of it struggling in the fold of her boot.

They didn't so much make camp at the tree as collapse where they stood, leaving the weapon on guard. Semi-conscious, Captain Yansav kept turning her face from the water Servan offered. Ryan panted, clearly in pain in spite of the healer's tinctures forced on him by the weapon. Keetin coughed, but that had become background at this point. Like Destros's snoring.

Lyelee stared up through the branches. The tree was a fixed point. It had power enough to defy the changes of the Broken Lands. How? More importantly, how could she free it?

The Broken Lands had so many secrets she wanted to uncover.

She wanted to read every book in Tanika Fleshrender's workshop. She wanted to find Boe Mah Sing's mews and discover how he controlled the crows. She wanted to follow her dragon to the mountains.

She wanted a lot of things.

"Knowledge," said the bone, "needs to be free."

She turned her head just enough to see the bag hanging from Ryan's shoulder, the contents lying as far from his body as the strap allowed.

GARRETT.THEN

Garrett looked out over the meadow and shook his head. "That's a lot of open ground to cross." He had blisters on his right hand from a pale gray branch he'd picked up to throw on the fire. He gripped his sword hilt harder, pressing the blisters against the wrapped leather, the pain forcing awareness through the exhaustion.

"It is," Arianna agreed, a line of warmth against his side.

"At least we'll see them coming," Malcolm pointed out, mirroring Arianna's position.

It would have been smarter to stand far enough apart to be able to swing swords and staff, but they'd all dreamed of freezing, of skin and bones cracking in the cold until the snow cover grew deep enough to offer the illusion of warmth. None of them would have woken had the lizard-dogs not howled as they attacked. Even then, Garrett hadn't been able to throw off the dream before Uvili had sent the surviving members of the pack into retreat.

Another tear in Arianna's skirt, where the thick wool had kept teeth away from her flesh, showed how close they'd come.

Malcolm had been the hardest to wake, his teeth chattering until dawn.

Garrett wasn't sure if they stood close now for warmth or comfort. Nor did he suppose it mattered.

"Across the meadow, a half a day's walk, and we're over the line."

"One continuous battle, then, as the Broken Lands throws everything it has at us." He grinned as the other two twisted to glare at him. "If you think I'm going to provoke things by suggesting it'll be easy, think again."

"You're trying to lull the Broken Lands into a false sense of security?"

"Worth a shot."

After a moment, Arianna nodded. "Truth."

"We know the lizard-dogs are out there," Malcolm murmured. "Why aren't they making noise? It's too quiet."

"Yes," Uvili rumbled behind them.

So much for an attempt to raise spirits. "They're nocturnal."

"Does that matter? If they want to take the fuel, they're almost out of time."

"So we'll be more careful." Garrett glanced up. The sky over the meadow was gray and the clouds looked low enough to touch. "At least it's not . . ."

Arianna clapped a mitten-covered hand over his mouth. "Don't say it."

He wanted to pull her closer still, brush her hat aside, bury his face in her hair. He wanted to take the time to mourn for Norik, who'd been the brother of his heart, and for Petre, the youngest of seven, who'd had his whole life ahead of him. He wanted to walk into the Citadel, Malcolm and Arianna by his side, and throw the fuel at his father's feet and dare him to continue favoring his sister as Lord Protector. He wanted to make changes, although he wasn't yet sure what those changes would be.

He wanted a lot of things.

The meadow had been frost-touched. What had been lush green was now brown and scraggy, offering little cover. At this point, he wouldn't be surprised if the ground itself attacked.

He said, "Uvili. Let's see what you can scare up. You two, arm's length apart in case whatever it is isn't scared enough."

Uvili could make the ground tremble, but she could walk quietly when she wanted. The only sound as she moved out into the meadow was the snap and crackle as she crushed dead weeds and grasses into a broad path. Malcolm was right, Garrett acknowledged. It was too quiet. She paused about a third of the way across, turned slowly and sniffed the air. He couldn't make out her expression, but he'd bet she was frowning. Then she squatted and, head cocked, peered through the dead grasses. Stalks swayed, seed heads tossed in the cold wind that whipped across the open ground.

"She's unhappy about something," Arianna murmured.

Garrett snorted. "When isn't she?"

"Oh, I don't know . . ."

He could hear Arianna's eyes rolling.

". . . maybe when she isn't trying to save the life of the son of the man who kept her in chains while he carries a piece of the mage who tried to twist her into a thing with blood and pain."

"Tried," Malcolm said softly.

"Tried," Arianna repeated.

"She's still a weapon," Garrett cautioned them.

"Only if that's how she's used."

"That wasn't a judgment. She's a weapon as you're a healer. If you build a wall, or plant a garden, or weave a blanket, you're still a healer. You can use a sword to cut fruit, but it's still a sword." When Uvili straightened, he realized he'd stood motionless for as long as he could. He had to keep moving. He had to get out. He had to get the fuel out. "Let's go."

She didn't look any happier when they joined her.

"What is it?"

She shook her head.

Had the sun been out, they'd have seen them sooner, but with only the dull gray of the clouds to reflect and with movement hidden in the wind-tossed grasses, they got close.

Halfway across the meadow, Uvili froze.

Arianna clutched his arm. "Garrett."

"I see them."

Snakes. A dozen, maybe more, as big around as his thigh, coming at them from the north.

"It's too cold for snakes to be out." She released him, although he could still feel the warmth of her touch, and brought her staff around to grip two-handed.

"They look like they're made of glass."

Malcolm giggled, high-pitched and nervous. "It's too cold for glass snakes to be out."

And Uvili said, "Run."

Arianna was fast, even with the heavy skirt swirling around her legs. Garrett wanted to see her run in the summer, long legs flashing, skin glistening, tumbled mass of curls flying behind her. He wanted to see her in the Citadel, dressed in silks from Nerathee, cutting a swath through the posers and sycophants of the Court. He wanted . . .

Uvili roared and stomped.

The ground quivered.

He half-turned in time to see her grasp two of the snakes under their heads, and as their bodies wrapped around her, she slammed their heads together.

He got a hand on Malcolm's pack and shoved him hard. "Get down!"

Crushed grass caught in his throat as he hit the ground, but he'd worry about that later. Shards of glass flew over his head.

His pack now empty enough to allow it, he rolled onto his back and saw Uvili throw the next snake. He didn't hear it break.

He was on his knees when a snake rose up where his feet had been moments before.

This close he could see a faint pattern of scales, as though the glass had been pushed into an etched mold. Its head was the size of his torso, and its eyes were black. Completely unrelieved black, dark and rich and warm and he couldn't look away. They offered rest. Peace.

It couldn't blink. He didn't blink.

It opened its mouth.

What did glass snakes eat?

Screaming, Malcolm slammed the snake in the side of the head with the flat of his sword. The steel rang and the snake's head whipped around, undamaged. Garrett realized the boy had swung too wide and couldn't get his sword around to defend himself. He struggled to stand.

Arianna took Malcolm to the ground, under the strike.

The snake ignored them as they rolled clear, head turning back to him with impossible speed. No longer playing, it dove forward. Living glass touched his chest and was snatched away to be spun around Uvili's head by the tail.

It landed too far away for the shards to reach them.

Glass amplified the sound from the surviving snakes until it filled the meadow and Garrett couldn't tell where it actually came from.

Uvili scooped Malcolm up under her arm and said, "Run."

"Arianna!"

"Right beside you!"

And they ran, glass shards driven into the ground under their boots. When they reached the other side of the meadow, miraculously whole, he turned to see four glass heads rise above the grass.

With Malcolm still under her arm, ignoring the way he struggled in her hold, Uvili turned as well and stomped. One. Two. The ground boomed under her feet.

The snakes rose up, as high or higher than his head. They were beautiful, Garrett realized, although that made them no less horrifying.

Uvili stomped again. A warning. A threat. *You break.*

And the snakes sank out of sight.

She held Malcolm close as he screamed and shouted and fought to get back into the meadow.

Finally, he sagged and sobbed.

Uvili shot Garrett a look that, for an instant, reminded him of his mother telling him not to be an idiot. Taken aback, it took him a moment to understand what he needed to do. Then he moved closer and called, "Malcolm."

He flung himself out of Uvili's arms and into Garrett's. "It could have killed you!"

"It didn't. You saved me."

"I can't lose . . ."

"I know. Shush. I know." They needed to keep moving, but he could no more lose Malcolm than Malcolm could lose him, so they stayed within the dubious shelter of slender trees. He heard Uvili stomp—one, two, a third time—and might have heard breaking glass, but he didn't look up. When Malcolm's sobs died, Garrett held him out at arm's length, and traced a cut across one cheekbone with his thumb, the dampness below it a mix of blood and tears. At some point, he'd been caught by a piece of flying glass. "Arianna needs to have a look at this."

"Will it scar?"

"Yes. But it'll be the kind of scar you can tell stories about."

Malcolm shook his head, sucking air through his teeth as the movement pulled at the edges and a line of blood drew a darker line across his skin. "I'm never going to talk about this."

"And it's not going to scar," Arianna snapped, taking Garrett by the wrist with one hand and slapping a clay pot into his palm with the other. "Hold this."

They were so close to the line. They needed to keep moving.

They needed to slap a temporary dressing over emotional wounds before they could go on.

RYAN.NOW

Ryan stared out over the meadow in disbelief. The lush grasses drooped, flower petals were limp and brown. The butterflies were gone and the buzz of other insects had been silenced.

"It's been hot and dry," Keetin said beside him.

"It's only been . . ." He frowned. Tried to count how many times they'd slept, but the number kept dancing just out of reach. "Are we sure it's the same meadow?"

He hadn't been entirely serious, but Nonee stepped out of the trees and drew in a deep breath, nostrils flared. "Probably."

"Not really helpful," Keetin pointed out.

"The tree is a fixed point, the line is a fixed point. The rest is . . ." She paused. Frowned. ". . . unsettled."

"Well, that dragon was certainly unsettling."

"Yes."

Even Nonee looked unsettled. That was . . . unsettling.

"That's a lot of open ground." Servan tipped her head and squinted up into a cloudless sky. "What about the hunter birds?"

"They're on the other side of the tower," Destros protested.

"The tower that was stone when we went, wood when we returned, and dumped us at the feet of said dragon?" Keetin asked.

Ryan hated that he had a point. "Nonee?"

"Destros is right. The birds are too far away."

"What about the bird you killed in Gateway?"

"They only hunt at night."

He didn't quite touch the bulge of the fuel where the daypack rested against his hip. "Even now?"

"Probably."

"Again, that's not . . ." Keetin began, then lost the rest to coughing. Ryan tried not to see the blood on the back of his hand when he stopped.

Destros reached for the captain. "If you need to be on guard, I can carry . . ."

"You can." The captain cut him off. "You could carry me across the meadow at a run if you had to, but you'd be shit in a fight afterward. What's more, I trust Nonee to drop me if she needs to. You'd set me down carefully and die in the process."

"That's not," he began, then shook his head. "Yeah, that's fair."

"Let's get moving, then." Ryan shifted his pack, much lighter now, thank the flame—he couldn't carry a full pack plus the weight of the fuel. Although the fuel had seemed lighter this morning. He hoped he wasn't growing used to it. Was that what it meant to be Lord Protector? Growing used to the weight of things beyond your control? "Once we're across the meadow, we're almost out."

"Distance is relative in the Broken Lands," Lyelee stated in the scholar's voice that refused argument.

Ryan shivered, glad that Keetin would walk between them. The Broken Lands seemed to emphasize all the parts of his cousin that had terrified him as a child.

LYELEE.NOW

"*Power*," said the bone, "*must be fueled.*"

Something had already drawn power from the meadow.

Lyelee's eyes narrowed, her attention not on Keetin's back, or his pack, or his admittedly fine ass, but on possibilities.

"*Release the fuel*," said the bone, "*while the land can still help!*"

"Don't tell me what to do."

"Scholar?"

"I wasn't talking to you."

Servan muttered something. Lyelee ignored her and stepped out of line. "Scholar!"

"Samples!" she snapped, bent to pluck a seed head, and froze. The air was still, completely still, but the grasses swayed and twisted, the motion growing more violent as it moved away from her to join a writhing patch of meadow. She'd like to see the crystal snake again—she'd had no time to study it—but it wasn't the snake that rose. It was a human-shaped form, at least as human-shaped as the weapon was, made of plants, and it left a patch of bare ground behind as it stood.

"Incoming!" Servan yelled.

It roared, the sound like a storm bending the tops of trees.

The crossbow quarrel went through it, the tangle of green and brown that made up its body shifting to open a passage. Unless Servan managed to light one of her final three quarrels on fire, she'd do no damage.

Servan had no time to light a fire.

She didn't need Servan. Or time.

She spat and rubbed her hands together, the fire she created white hot at the core. She threw it as the creature charged forward, and if some of its plants were too green to burn in a normal fire, this wasn't a normal fire. She half saw the weapon leap back as the creature burst into flame.

The fire burned hot and fast. When it burned down to a dusting of white ash—it had been consumed much faster than Gearing, but given their respective compositions that made sense—she felt the weight of attention on her back. Scholars were used to attention. She turned.

Eyes were wide. Mouths were open. Sword points and Destros's axe blade touched dirt. Only Captain Yansav, on the ground, missing half a leg, held her weapons at anything approaching ready. The captain had never learned the respect for scholars drilled into the children of Marsanport from birth.

Lyelee made a mental note to have incomers properly instructed by the Scholar's Hall.

The weapon's eyes had narrowed.

Ryan took a single step toward her. "Lyelee?"

"*Release the fuel,*" said the bone again, "*while the land can still help!*"

She flicked her satchel open. She'd pulled the fuel from Ryan's daypack during the night while the lizard-dogs howled in the distance and the weapon paced a circle around the camp and the tree. The fuel had fit perfectly in her satchel, although it shouldn't have. Clearly, she was meant to have it. Lying on her side, faking sleep, her body hiding her actions, she'd scooped up dirt, packed it tight, wrapped it in the silk, and slid the substitute back into the pack. Ryan would never notice. Ryan paid no notice to what he carried. Ryan was a fool.

The fuel had warmed over the morning to almost body temperature. She drove her fingers into the greasy, yielding mass.

"Feel it," said the bone. *"Open yourself to it."*

"Imprecise," Lyelee muttered. But she *could* feel it, rising up her arm. *Open to it* made sudden sense in light of this new information. It rose to her shoulder. She could more than discover the history of their people, she could recreate it. She could . . .

NONEE.NOW

Nonee lowered Kalyealee who-could-be-heir to the ground.

"Is she dead?" Ryan Heir asked quietly.

Not *did you kill her.* Nonee appreciated the difference. "No."

"Choked her out," said Servan, nodding too fast, her voice too high.

Ryan Heir took another step closer. "That was mage-craft."

"Yes."

Then slowly, testing each word. "She killed Gearing."

"Yes."

"On purpose?"

Nonee glanced over at the ash. Did it matter? "She didn't care that she'd killed him."

That mattered.

RYAN.NOW

Ryan assumed Keetin was too exhausted to pace, that twitching was as much as he could handle.

"We need to leave." Keetin's face darkened and he forced the next sentence out before he began to cough. "We need to get across the Broken Line and into a place where shit like that does not happen."

"It's not the place," Nonee said. And then, "Not anymore."

Ryan nodded. "We need to know what we're taking across the Broken Line. What we might be turning loose on the world." He'd shaken the packed clump of dirt out of the silk, and used a fold to move the fuel back to the daypack, the weight settling on his shoulders again. He couldn't believe Lyelee had been able to take it without him knowing. Not through use of mage-craft, but through his own inability to keep it safe.

"You mean through your incompetence."

"And you're supposed to keep Marsanport safe?"

"Yeah, like anyone believed he could."

Keeping Marsanport safe was for after he returned. Now, he had to keep these specific people safe. "We need to get out of the meadow. We're too exposed and . . ." He couldn't say her name. "And *this* proved there's mage-craft here. Let's get in under the trees."

Feet braced, crossbow ready, Servan swept her gaze around the meadow. "Will it be safer under the trees?" she asked.

"No."

Her gaze swept over to Nonee. "And yet I'd feel safer under a little cover."

Did it matter? Ryan wondered, looking down at his cousin. They were taking the danger with them. "Divide what's in her pack." Lyelee was taller than the captain, but less heavily muscled and wearing linen and leather, not armor. "Destros, can you carry her?"

"Yes, sir."

"She won't stay out for long," Nonee cautioned.

"Get in under the trees," Ryan repeated, trying not to read attack into every rustle of grass. "We'll deal with it then."

❧

"She'd be more comfortable with her hands tied in front of her." Still breathing heavily from his last coughing fit, Keetin leaned back against a tree and waved a hand toward Destros wrapping another loop of rope around Lyelee's body while Nonee held her off the ground. "Look, I know we have to take precautions, but she's a scholar and a Marsan and entitled to at least a little consideration."

"She has to see her hand to make the fire. There are rules." Nonee set her down and tugged the rope tight. "She made the rule, she has to keep it."

Standing by the captain, concerned about the lines of pain around her mouth and eyes, Ryan frowned. "Lyelee made the rule?"

"Kalyealee who-could-be-heir stared at her hand before the fire appeared. If this was only the second time, she'd have repeated what she did to make it work the first time."

"If?"

"No way to know for sure."

"I think we'd have noticed another pillar of fire!"

Nonee shrugged.

"Doing something twice makes it a rule?" Keetin asked sarcastically.

"Yes."

"And mages make their own rules?"

"Yes."

"Can't see that ending well," Destros said, rising to his feet.

Nonee snorted. "It didn't."

They had no fabric clean enough to use as a gag. *She killed Gearing,* Ryan reminded himself. *On purpose? Did it matter?* He suspected it shouldn't, but it did. Lyelee was still his cousin. And she was still a scholar.

Finally, Nonee used the last of the bandages. "No more bleeding," she ordered.

"I'm good with that," Servan called from the edge of the trees.

Before he could think too hard about what he was doing, Ryan dumped Lyelee's satchel.

The splinter of wood had come from the shattered tower room. The piece of glass, from the ballroom. A feather. A rat tail. There was a tooth from the skull that had been thrown onto the road by the other weapon. A stone, one edge freshly broken.

"From the landslide when the trap took Harris," Nonee said.

No one asked how she knew.

A small piece of fungus wrapped in waxed cloth and sealed into a box.

"At least she was being careful," Keetin said.

In a sample bag, blood-soaked cloth.

In still another, other things soaked into cloth.

Whose blood? Ryan wondered. *What other things?* He couldn't read her notes, but the child's writing in the ancient notebook was decipherable.

"She made the dragon."

"No." Keetin shook his head. "Fire, sure. Give me flint and steel and I can make fire. But there's no possible way she made that dragon."

"There's instructions. She made the dragon by burying a dragon's tooth." He looked up, crumpling the page. "Nonee?"

"There's two ways dragons grow."

Keetin rolled his eyes. "When a mommy and a daddy dragon love each other very much . . ."

Nonee cut him off. "And when a mage plants a dragon's tooth."

Ryan's throat clicked when he swallowed. "Lyelee's a mage."

"She's a scholar," Keetin protested.

"Yes." Nonee picked up the piece of stone and crushed it. "No person is ever one thing only."

"You're saying she's a scholar *and* a mage." It didn't seem possible. Scholars taught that mage-craft was an abomination of the natural order. But neither did it seem as impossible as it should, Ryan acknowledged. Not given the fire. And the dragon.

"What did this to her?" Keetin demanded. When Ryan put a hand on his shoulder, he shook him off. "She was fine when we left home! She was fine in Gateway! What in the Broken Lands made her this way?"

"Nothing. She was always and always would be a mage."

"No!" Keetin shouted his denial. "No one practices mage-craft in Marsanport."

"Maybe that's why she wasn't very good at it," Destros offered. "Not enough practice."

"Not what I meant, Guardian! And you know it."

Destros sighed and folded his arms. "When you learn a new skill, if you have any ability at all, you're hopeless until the moment you suddenly get it. The Broken Lands allowed her to *be* a mage."

Nonee ducked her head. "Yes."

"The mages are dead! They're . . ." Keetin folded forward, coughing so violently, he had to drop to his knees. Because he could do nothing about it, Ryan continued to ignore the blood.

Nonee waited until he stopped coughing. Until he could breathe again. Until he sat back on his heels, eyes watering. "The mages who built the road," she said, "and who allowed Gateway to flourish, and who built sanctuaries in what became the Broken Lands, they were never the only six."

"They were only the six who came here and consolidated their power," the captain said quietly, rubbing her thigh above the clay.

"Then there are other mages in the world." Ryan turned the thought over and didn't much like it. He remembered Harris hanging, still alive, on spikes that should have killed him.

"Arianna said mages were rare. Minds break trying to alter reality." Nonee spread her hands. "Rare is more than none."

She'd never been out in the world, Ryan realized. None of them had. Except for Captain Yansav. "Are there mages in Shurlia?"

For a moment, he thought the captain wasn't going to answer. She never spoke of Shurlia. He didn't blame her; her family had been slaughtered, the queen she'd served killed and a new queen put in her place. Finally, she sighed and said, "There are *apaya*. Seers. Advisors. Not the same thing."

How different? he wondered. And would his great-uncle live long enough for him to find out? He knew a little of Gateway and less of the Broken Lands and nothing of the world outside Marsanport. "Now what?" he asked, thinking Lyelee secured looked more like herself than she had over the last few days. "Can the healers in Gateway . . . heal her?"

Squatting at Lyelee's side, Nonee shook her head. "Mage-craft can't be healed. It is."

Could anything be completely evil? Leading five thousand broken people away from Gateway had to have influenced Captain Marsan's beliefs. "Your people have *apaya*, Captain. And Lyelee saved us from the grass creature with mage-craft."

"She killed Gearing with mage-craft," the captain said softly.

And hadn't cared. That was the sticking point. Mage-craft wasn't a skill, or only a skill, it was a way of thinking of the world and the other people in it. It wasn't only about what Lyelee had done, but how she'd reacted to the doing of it.

He wondered what had been in Gearing's satchel.

≈≫

It was almost dark when they crossed the line.

"Make camp," Ryan said, staggering past the boulder. Sweating heavily, unable to put weight on his left leg without pain shooting up into his hip, his stomach protesting the dried fish he'd eaten while they walked, he couldn't take another step.

Keetin dropped to his knees, fighting to breathe, air whistling wetly in and out of his lungs.

Servan helped Destros lay Lyelee on the ground. Her eyes were closed but Ryan suspected she was awake.

Captain Yansav was asleep—because he preferred that to her being unconscious.

Only Nonee looked unaffected by the day.

They weren't necessarily safer on this side of the line than they would be on the other. They'd been attacked here, in this very spot, on the way in. But the lizard-dogs, for all they lived on both sides of the line, were animals. Made by mage-craft, deliberately or accidentally, during the wild years after the war, yes, but they killed with tooth and claw and ran when they recognized a more dangerous predator. They were vicious, but they were a threat Ryan could understand.

The marks of Lyelee's fingers were still in the fuel.

LYELEE.NOW

Lyelee regained consciousness slowly, light and dark flickering over her lids. Sunlight through leaves, she realized. She was no longer in the meadow. The fire rose in her mind and she watched it for a while. Knowledge reclaimed, it was beautiful. What were its limits? The grass creature had been consumed in a heartbeat. A body was primarily water and yet Gearing had been reduced to ash as though he'd been made of kindling.

Did it burn through every fuel at the same rate?

Scholar Mirriben, a Scholar of Language, was so large he had to have furniture specially constructed.

Would he burn at the same rate as the grass creature? As Gearing?

She had a lifetime of research ahead of her.

Slowly, she became aware of uneven movement, of arms around her, of scale against her cheek, of the smell of sweat, and the faint, lingering scent of beard oil.

Destros.

Why was he carrying her?

It hurt when she swallowed. There was fabric in her mouth that tasted faintly of honey.

Had she been injured?

No. The weapon. It had attacked her from behind.

She'd been looking at Ryan when the pressure around her throat had brought darkness. He'd looked . . . relieved.

"Ignorance," said the bone, *"leads to fear."*

She'd like to say she was surprised by his reaction, but she wasn't. He'd always walked the safe paths, afraid of confrontation: hiding from his brothers, trying to appease the Court when they let him know he wasn't the Heir they expected, never looking beyond the narrow parameters that defined comfort.

"Fear," said the bone, *"leads to violence."*

He'd been afraid of what she'd learned, of the history denied that she'd reclaimed. He'd ignored the way she'd used that knowledge to save them and ordered the weapon to attack. Ordered the weapon to lay hands on a scholar. Then he'd had her tied and gagged to keep her from challenging his fear. What would his desperate clutching at ignorance do to the people of Marsanport? Her mother was right. He couldn't become Lord Protector.

Her eyes were too heavy to open, so she watched the fire burn.

She'd been drowsing when Destros and another pair of hands set her on the ground. Drowsed a little longer until she felt hands removing the gag. She coughed, licked her lips, and glared at Ryan as he lifted her shoulders off the ground.

A demand that he release her became an unintelligible rasp.

"Drink first," he said, holding a waterskin up to her mouth.

The water was no longer cold and fresh. Apparently even the mage-crafting couldn't stand against time. The people of Gateway might call them talents, but she knew what they were and how they could be used.

"Hypocrisy," said the bone, *"is the refuge of the morally bankrupt."*

Her throat ached when she swallowed.

"Release me," she demanded when she had her voice again. "You don't disrespect a scholar this way."

"Scholars don't set fire to their mentors."

She thought about maintaining the illusion that Gearing had set the fire. There was no point. They'd seen her in the meadow.

"I saved you."

"Possibly." He sighed and continued before she could suggest he had no idea of what the word meant. "If we untie you, will you swear you'll do no more mage-craft?"

They were all watching. Even Captain Yansav, who'd fed her dragon. She rolled her eyes. "Don't be more of a fool than usual, Ryan."

"So you won't swear?"

"Not to you. The Heir of Marsan has no control over scholarship."

He sighed. Offered her the waterskin again, then sat back on his heels. "She stays tied."

"Because you're too weak to face your ignorance."

"And gagged."

"Because you've always taken the easy way."

He shook his head and stood, closed off to knowledge. Even self-knowledge. Not a surprise.

She shifted, cataloging her aches and pains. "I have to use the latrine." Bodily function was not something he could argue with, and he was too soft to deny her relief, in spite of his misgivings. Marsanport would be overrun by enemies within a year of his becoming Lord Protector.

"Then Nonee goes with you."

"No. Servan." She narrowed her eyes and dared him to argue that.

He didn't. "Fine. Servan, untie only her legs until she's at the latrine pit, then her arms."

"Sir?" Servan stepped closer.

He squatted beside her again, in the position the weapon favored. Had it corrupted him somehow? Another reason he should never be Lord Protector. "Your word as scholar that you won't bring the fire. Or I'll blindfold you."

"Uh, my lord . . ."

"In the time it takes her to remove the blindfold, Servan, you should be able to take her down."

"Yes, sir."

"You're taking this too far," she heard Keetin mutter as Servan led her away.

At the latrine, she flexed her shoulders, met Servan's eyes as she dropped her freed hands to her trousers, and jerked her head. "If you don't mind."

Servan didn't budge. "Nothing I haven't seen before, Scholar. Bugger-all privacy in the barracks."

Fine. With an audience then. At least it was an audience who under-stood what she observed. Not to say the weapon wasn't an amazing con-struction and she looked forward to learning just how that construction had been achieved, but the presence of another woman . . . She frowned as the thought trailed off, uncertain of where it had been going.

Returning to camp, her arms tied again, they passed the place where she'd dissected the lizard-dog, soil marked where the blood and other fluids had soaked into the ground. She stumbled, dragged the toe of her boot through it, and allowed Servan to tug her back to the path.

"The line," said the bone, still tucked in against her fingers, *"is arbi-trary."*

As she was bound, she jiggled her foot until a little bit of stained dirt fell from her boot.

"Innovation," said the bone, *"is the child of knowledge."*

RYAN.NOW

Wrapped in blankets, Ryan snuggled deep into his childhood bed, trying to find a comfortable spot among the toys and books and severed legs he'd gathered around him. Hiding things he cared about had become second nature. If he didn't, the moment his brothers realized something was im-portant to him, they destroyed it. He just couldn't get . . .

"Comfortable?" Donal grinned down at him. "Of course you are, you're always *comfortable.* Flame forbid you should ever take a risk. Come sailing with us."

Donal's face began to bloat. Ryan clutched at the blankets. "No."

"No?" Donal laughed. "You don't get to say no, slug." He pulled the seal of the Lord Protector out from among the pearls woven into his beard. "I wasn't asking, so let's try this again. Come sailing with us."

Unable to open his mouth, Ryan shook his head.

"You had your chance." The three long locs Donal kept high on the right side of his shaved head swung forward as he bent to set the seal on Ryan's chest.

It was heavy, so heavy. Ryan felt himself sinking, but his arms and legs refused to move.

"You're lying on dragon's teeth," Lyelee told him, rolling her eyes. "Use one. Use all of them. For once in your life, take control."

The teeth dug into his back.

"You're afraid," she scoffed. "Knowledge is meant to be used. Taken apart. Examined." She held the elderly cat she'd dissected at ten, its organs spread out in her arms. The cat silently begged Ryan to end its pain. "Last chance," she said, hands on either side of the seal.

Ryan overcame his terror enough to shake his head again.

Lyelee smiled as she began to push, and he sank under the surface of the Great Lake. The pressure of the water held his mouth closed and plugged his nose. He couldn't breathe.

Couldn't breathe!

Couldn't . . .

He spat out dirt and gasped and spat again. Dirt fell all around him and the pain from the bite in his leg made it hard to find thought among the shards of red. Slowly, still spitting, still gasping, he realized he hung upside down, Nonee holding him by the ankles.

He could hear shouting, and Keetin wheezing. Ignoring bright lines of pain, he squeezed the grit from his eyes in time to see Destros kneel by his head. The guardian's hands shook as he lifted them and wrapped them around Ryan's face.

"That's it," he said. "You're okay." Then he sat back on his heels. "Let him down, Nonee. I've got him."

Nonee lowered him into Destros's arms, where he spat and gasped again, blew plugs from his nose, then began to cough.

"Get it out," Destros murmured, rubbing his back.

When he finally forced himself to stop and settled lightheaded back into the guardian's hold, he blinked away tears to see Keetin kneeling in front of him, holding out a waterskin.

"Rinse and spit."

That brought on more coughing.

Keetin attempted and didn't quite achieve a grin. "Sucks, doesn't it?"

It did. "Tastes like dirt."

"Well, yeah." He held open his arms.

Ryan fell from Destros's hold to Keetin's embrace and, as arms wrapped around him, remembered the struggle for comfort in his dream. *This*

hand he had on the ground to brace himself. When he wiped the sweat from his forehead, there were streaks of mud on his fingers.

Lyelee snickered behind her gag.

※

Dawn meant they could put it off no longer.

Nonee threw the last of the shredded bark into the pot and split it between him and the captain. When Ryan tried to protest, she raised a silencing finger. "You need to be clearheaded for this."

"It's not so bad."

She cocked her head and he surrendered. He couldn't actually tell where the pain that throbbed through his body originated. He knew, but he couldn't *tell*. With a stomach full of warm liquid, it began to retract to a bright, burning point surrounded by a dull throbbing ache he could think through. He stared into the dented mug, sighed, and swept his gaze around the fire. "We all know what she's becoming."

"Is," Nonee said.

"What she is," he amended.

Keetin was going to protest, Ryan could feel it rising, but instead he shook his head, reached out, and brushed a bit of dirt from Ryan's hair.

Nonee's gaze locked onto Lyelee, tied and apparently sleeping just outside the circle. Ryan doubted any of them believed she was *actually* sleeping. "She'll get stronger as she becomes more aware of what she can do."

"Which is?" Captain Yansav demanded.

"Anything she wants."

"What happened to those other mages? The ones who weren't the six, but who weren't driven mad?" Ryan glanced at Lyelee and added, "Not completely mad."

"Arianna said that with luck, they were stopped early enough to limit the damage."

"Without luck?" Servan asked.

"The archives hold the story of a city that sank into the sea. Thousands dead." Nonee paused. They waited. "The archives say the six studied the city to discover how it was done."

Keetin looked over at Lyelee. "To stop it happening again."

"No."

No, Ryan repeated silently. *The mages intended to use the knowledge they found.* The inventor of the crossbow might have been appalled at how it killed so easily even in the hands of the unskilled. They'd carried four of them into the Broken Lands. "How do we stop her?"

Nonee said nothing.

He could hear birds singing, greeting the morning. Or planning world domination. They could be singing on either side of the Broken Line. Or both sides. Everyone around the fire knew what Nonee's silence meant. He could read the understanding on their faces. He shook his head. "That can't be the only way."

"Confine her in chains and, eventually, she'll bend the iron to her will. Confine her in stone and she'll work it to dust." Nonee flattened a small bulge of rising dirt, leaving an imprint of her fist in the ground.

"Can we convince her . . ." Destros paused, frowned, and finally finished, ". . . to not be what she is?"

"No."

"Can the other scholars convince her?" he asked.

"We won't survive to get her to the Scholar's Hall," Ryan told him, keeping his voice even with an effort. "She'll ride alone into Marsanport, holding the fuel."

Keetin's hand closed around his arm. "You can't know that."

"Look at her."

Lyelee's smile had edges. Her eyes were open. He'd seen madness before when it was a sickness of the mind that could be eased if not healed. This wasn't that kind of madness, and Ryan was afraid that if he looked into her eyes too deeply, he'd see the infinity she found and be lost to it as well. There had to have been a reason so many people had followed the six.

"Yes."

He turned to look at Nonee. "I said that aloud?"

"Yes."

"We only have your word for this," Keetin growled at her. "For any of this."

It was Ryan's turn to grip his arm. "Do we?" he asked gently. "Look at her. Remember the dirt, and the fire, and the dragon, and Scholar Gearing."

"An accident."

"Possibly, but she didn't *care.*"

Keetin closed his eyes, shook his head—Ryan knew it wasn't the facts he denied—and gave himself over to coughing.

"She can hear us," Servan said quietly. "But she just keeps smiling. Why isn't she worried?"

"She knows me," Ryan told her, stood, turned his back to the fire, and watched the sun clear the horizon. The birds had stopped singing. A trio of dragonflies flew into the clearing, translucent wings glimmering. He could smell green growing things, smoke, and fresh-turned dirt. He'd stopped smelling himself some days ago, so there was that to be thankful for. The sharp pain in his leg had begun to spread again, although the bitter taste of the willow bark remained on his tongue.

"We know what we have to do," Captain Yansav said heavily.

Ryan didn't give a burning shit what Donal would do. Donal wasn't here. He was. And Lyelee was.

"Arianna said that with luck, they were stopped early enough to limit the damage."

They'd have to make their own luck.

Turning to face the others, Ryan felt that he should be wearing the tabard that declared him Heir of Marsan—had it not been left in Gateway with the wagon and the horses. Except the tabard didn't make him the heir. He *was* the heir, like it or not, and he suddenly understood Nonee's assertion that *it's what she is* like he hadn't before. "We don't take a vote. We don't all have to agree. It's my decision." Like Harris had been his decision. "I need your understanding, not your approval."

Captain Yansav stared at him for a long moment, then said only, "Lord Marsan."

The two guardians stood and touched fist to chest.

Finally, tears streaming down his face, Keetin nodded.

"You have a weapon." Nonee straightened out of her squat, her size a comfort. "Use it."

"You're not an it," Ryan told her.

"I could use my axe to . . ."

"No." Cutting Destros off, Nonee held out her hands. "So many dead here already. One more . . ."

Ryan pushed her hands down—because she allowed it.

She cocked her head and stared at him. Neither of them spoke. They both knew what was about to happen.

"You can refuse," he said at last.

"Yes."

Her choice. If he took that from her, how much better was he than his ancestors who'd kept her chained? At least she wouldn't bear this death alone, he'd hold it with her. Like he'd hold Harris. "Thank you."

She nodded.

"Destros, help me stand." Captain Yansav settled her helm and held out a hand. "I'll witness."

"We'll all witness." More than the water rotting his lungs roughened Keetin's words.

"Yes," Servan said. A dragonfly had landed on her helm. It took off in a whirl of wings as she stepped forward.

"Remove her head," Ryan said, not recognizing his voice. "Bury it separate from her body. Tanika Fleshrender," he added before anyone could find words to protest, "was still alive." He touched the bulge in the day bag. "She was this, and she was still alive."

Lyelee kept smiling.

"What will the chronicle say?" Keetin asked as they watched Destros and Servan finish digging the grave as far from the stain the lizard-dog had left as they could and still be in the clearing.

Ryan swallowed. He had to keep swallowing so as not to throw up. "The chronicle will say that the mage-craft she faced in the Broken Lands killed her. Like it killed Curtin and Harris."

By the time Lyelee had been settled in the grave, Nonee had returned with her pack full of fresh purkin flowers. She covered both the body and the head and then poured in the last of the distilled oil.

"She taught me how to play mancala." Ryan dropped in the first handful of dirt. They'd been seven or eight and they'd sat under the big table in the library and played for hours. She'd won every game.

Balanced on her remaining foot, tucked up against Destros's side, her eyes tight with pain, Captain Yansav threw in the second. "She had a way of reading the chronicles that made me feel as if I were there."

"She showed me how to tie Bondtian tassels." Servan plucked a tassel from her belt and threw it in with the dirt. "She'd never done it before, but I only had to tell her what I thought I was supposed to do once and she got it . . ." The guardian snapped her fingers. ". . . like that."

"She did a beautiful harmony on *The Golden Tower.*" Destros almost smiled. "For all she argued how the song got the history wrong."

"She was right, though." Keetin paused to cough. "Like she was right about roasting the cattail roots." His voice rose in a fair imitation. "Of course I researched wilding foods before we left, didn't you?" He managed a wobbly laugh without sending himself back into a cascade of coughing. "She made meals on the road a lot more interesting than they would have been and she was right about a lot of things."

"She was," Nonee acknowledged, to Ryan's surprise. But that was all she said.

Not one of them, Ryan realized, as they filled in the grave, had said her name.

"*Mage-craft,*" said the bone, "*lingers..*"

Ryan stumbled over nothing, sucked air through his teeth at the flash of pain, and said, "Is it the lizard-dogs again?"

Something was stalking them—behind, beside, before, a rustle in the underbrush and the occasional low-pitched grumble. They weren't trying to hide their presence.

"Yes."

"I thought they hunted at dawn and dusk."

"They're aware of the fuel." Nonee waited until Destros had finished cursing. "But they don't want it back."

"So you're saying . . ." Keetin paused to draw in another shallow breath. ". . . don't worry about the lizard-dogs, they'll . . . only try to kill us?"

"Yes."

When they reached the grove Nonee had created for Arianna, they stopped for the day. No one suggested using the hours of remaining light to cover the final distance. Captain Yansav moaned when Nonee set her down. Keetin's skin was clammy and his grasp on Ryan's arm had been all that had kept him on his feet.

At dawn, when Destros and Servan were awake and armed—and Keetin wheezed, and the captain's nostrils flared, and Ryan felt as though feeding his leg to a dragon was an excellent idea—Nonee said, "Stay here."

"Anyone else feel the earth move?" Keetin laughed, then collapsed, coughing, as Nonee disappeared into the distance, feet pounding against the dirt.

They stayed.

Servan fed a ground squirrel a piece of broken biscuit.

"If it eats your hand," Destros grunted, "it'll be no more than you deserve."

Lyelee would have filled the silence, either asking for information or telling them what she knew. As Lyelee was . . . wasn't . . . the silence settled.

Ryan dozed with his eyes open. When he closed them, he saw Lyelee's head at the bottom of a hole, eyes open, her expression annoyed. Nonee had wrapped both head and body before she'd allowed any of them close, and he appreciated the thought, but it hadn't really helped. He'd ordered her killed and she'd haunt him for it. As she should. If executions came without consequence, there'd be too many of them. Which was a fine thought, he acknowledged, the sort of thought a Lord Protector should have, but he wondered if he'd ever be able to sleep peacefully again.

Tears kept running down under his collar, although he couldn't remember crying.

She'd been his cousin.

The sun was high when Nonee returned draped in waterskins, followed by six people carrying three stretchers, and a stern-looking, middle-aged man who announced he was a healer and they could all just stay right where they were until he looked them over. He tapped approvingly on the clay covering the captain's stump, muttered to himself at the sound of Keetin's chest, and scowled at the hole in Ryan's leg still weeping blood.

"What bit you, boy?"

"A building."

"Of course it did." He nodded at the daypack. "Nonee says that stays with you. She right?"

"Yes."

"Fine. Make my life difficult." He gestured at the guardians. "You two, empty what can't be left behind into Nonee's pack."

Servan stared at him for a long moment, then said, "No. We can carry our share. She isn't a pack horse."

"Did I say she was?" He shook his head. "Suit yourself. Nonee! You willing to pick these two idiots up if they fall over?"

"Yes."

"Not my problem, then." He pulled three corked, green-glass bottles out of his daypack, unsealed them with a thumbnail, opened them, and handed them out. One to the captain, one to Keetin, one to Ryan. "Drink the whole thing."

It smelled of willow bark and honey and . . .

"We don't have all day."

Ryan nodded. And they all drank.

"You six, help them onto the stretchers. You, Captain, allow yourself to be lifted. We can't deal with the most pressing problem until we reach Gateway."

"Healing," Ryan murmured a little fuzzily as strong hands laid him gently on the stretched hide.

"I was thinking bathing, but yes, healing too."

GARRETT.THEN

To Garrett's surprise, a small crowd had gathered just inside the northeast break in the rubble wall. To his greater surprise, there were two guardians with them. One of them seemed reasonably calm, the other stared around with wide eyes.

Before Uvili had finished squeezing through the too-narrow opening, a girl raced forward, and threw herself into Arianna's arms. "The Line Scouts said you were coming."

"I didn't see . . ." Garrett began.

The girl cut him off with a toss of her head. "They're scouts. They're not supposed to be *seen*." She looked past him at Malcolm and back to Arianna. "Where's . . ."

Arianna pressed mitten-covered fingers to her mouth. "They died," she said. "Now hush, Cleo."

They died—all the failures, all the questions, all the choices distilled to two simple words. Garrett hoped that someday he'd find the same clarity of grief.

"When did they arrive?" he asked, as the two guardians strode forward.

"Two days ago." The girl, Cleo, tossed her head again. "Councilor Nori made them camp inside the wall by the big gate and take food and water, but that's all she could get them to do. They're a little . . ." She rolled her eyes, the exaggerated motion showing whites all the way around. "They say they've got to talk to you, but they won't say why. Not even to Big Tam."

"Big Tam?" Garrett asked Arianna.

She almost smiled. "He thinks he's charming."

And then they were before him, dropping to one knee. That was wrong. No one knelt to the Heir of Marsan. No one knelt to the Lord Protector except when . . .

"All honor and succor to the Lord Protector who brings us safely out of fire and torment."

Garrett shook his head, but the captain continued.

"Your father, the Lord Protector, died two days after you left Marsanport, my lord."

"My sister . . ." He wasn't sure what he intended his next words to be. Fortunately, the captain filled the pause.

"Your sister sent us to inform you and to escort you back to Marsanport, my lord. She said I was to tell you . . ." He flushed. ". . . that she never wanted the flaming job and to get your ass home with the fuel before she puts her head through a wall." He swallowed. "My lord."

"That sounds like my sister," Garrett said with a laugh. And only became aware of how much like a sob it sounded when Arianna's hand closed around his arm.

"Do you," the captain began, then started again. "Do you have the fuel, my lord?"

He didn't have Norik and he didn't have Petre, but he had the fuel. "Yes."

"So, Lord Protector." Arianna stepped into the room, a green and gold shawl wrapped around her shoulders, her hair tumbling down her back in a mass of gleaming chestnut curls. "Healer Stoe tells me that you and Malcolm are a little dehydrated, but otherwise you have a clean bill of health."

Captain Ling moved between them. "Your business with the Lord Protector?"

Garrett sighed. He'd ordered the guardians into the building the council had cleared for their use while they were gone. The main floor was all one room with a rusty iron stove at one end and a barricaded flight of stairs at the other. The large open area now held a rough table and six mismatched chairs. He had no idea of what the building's original use had been, but the fireplace still worked, the tub in a small back room still held hot water, and the pallets stuffed fat with raw wool were more comfortable than the ground, so he didn't much care. Both guardians regarded the place with suspicion, uncomfortable with Gateway's survival when the scholars had taught them the city at the other end of the Mage Road had been destroyed. Garrett remembered his lot being more accepting, but they'd been focused on the search for the fuel, while he was all the guardians had as a distraction. "Captain Ling."

"My lord?"

"Go check on the horses, Captain. Take Blaine."

"My lord."

Arianna waited until the door closed behind them, then crossed to grip Garrett's arm. "How are you really?"

It didn't occur to him to lie. Not to her. "I don't know. My father and I were never close. This . . . ." He waved a hand as though the Lord Protectorship surrounded him. "It seems less real than what we faced in the Broken Lands. It probably won't be real until we reach Marsanport." He turned away, pulling out from under her touch—although the warmth lingered—and lifted a carved wooden box up off the table. "Councilor Nori brought this for the fuel. She says it's pre–Mage War and its age should help contain any mage-crafted miasma." It had lessened his awareness of the fuel, so maybe the councilor was right.

Arianna smiled. "She said *mage-crafted miasma?*"

Garrett couldn't help but return her smile. "Does it sound like something I'd say?"

She laughed. "It doesn't." A quick glance around the room. "Where's Uvili?"

"She's out back, with half a dozen children who seem to think she's a mountain they can climb. Malcolm's with her."

"She wouldn't hurt a child."

"He's there to make sure the children don't treat her like she's a thing."

Her eyes widened and Garrett basked in her look of wonder. "As someone told me, multiple times, she's a person."

"She is."

"*And* a weapon."

Arianna shrugged. "Battle axes can cut wood. Swords can slice bread. Daggers can peel apples. Helms can hold water. Shields can . . ."

He held up a hand. "I'm pretty sure I recognize that argument."

Arianna snickered, like she was twelve, not a grown woman. Like she didn't care what he thought of her making that sound. He tucked it away in memory. Then she sobered. "Saham, our animal healer, says your guardians rode hard but mindfully. He's impressed by the condition of their horses."

The guardians would be riding Norik's and Petre's horses when they left. Saham could be as impressed as he wanted, but their horses weren't ready for a charge back down the Mage Road.

Garrett sighed at the thought. "I'm not looking forward to spending the rest of this moon and most of the next in the saddle."

"There's a theory that the Mage Road is faster between Gateway and the Great Lake. Than it is between the Great Lake and Gateway," Arianna added when he frowned. "The mages weren't happy about people coming to see them, but they encouraged people to leave."

Had those whose bones still served the mages after death wanted to leave? Garrett wondered. Or had the mages given more than they took? Memory showed him Petre's face become bone and he doubted it. He shook the memory off and said, "According to the chronicle, it took Captain Marsan and the Five Thousand a full moon."

Arianna shrugged. "Then either the archives or the chronicle is wrong."

He'd never actually read the entire chronicle, only those sections the scholars used to teach the youngest children to read. He knew it, because the scholars were constantly quoting it, and he'd always meant to sit down and read it, but he'd never found the time. The Scholar's Hall had recently produced a new edition of the chronicle to celebrate the final form of their experimental printing press. The Lord Protector and his family had seen the first pages inked and later been presented with a finished volume bound in calfskin with gold lettering. It was kept on a podium next to the Lord Protector's seat in the Court. As far as he knew, no one had read it.

The scholars held the knowledge of Marsanport; they couldn't be wrong. Scholars.

His sister was often deliberately rude to scholars. "I have to get home."

"Before your sister puts her head through a wall?"

"Or someone else's." He set the box on the table. Turned. Stared at the toes of Arianna's sheepskin boots. Raised his eyes to meet her gaze. "Come with me?"

She didn't look surprised that he'd asked, but she shook her head slowly. "No."

"You have other healers here."

"Could I be a healer there?" When her mouth twisted, he knew she'd read the answer off his face.

"I . . ." He was the Lord Protector of Marsanport and he couldn't say the words. Norik would laugh at him. Norik had always been better with emotions. What would he do without him?

"You could start by manning up," said Norik's voice in memory.

"Arianna . . . please." He had no idea where that plea had come from. He squared his shoulders and said, "I love you."

ARIANNA.THEN

Arianna had been half afraid of that. Had hoped the emotion had been created by the Broken Lands and would fade once the line had been crossed. It hadn't. And now that he'd spoken, she could see it, warm and a little desperate in his eyes.

"My place is here. My people are here." She needed to give them both a little distance from his declaration.

"You could find a new place."

"With you."

"Yes."

She sighed. "Garrett, you're a good man and you're going to be an amazing Lord Protector, but while I care for you and while you and I and Malcolm will always have a shared history no one else can even imagine, I don't love you. Nor do you love me."

His eyes narrowed. "Don't tell me how I feel."

That was fair. "I'm sorry. You're right." She took a deep breath and tried again. "You don't know me. And I don't know you. The time we've spent together has been . . ." She examined and discarded several words and settled on, "Unreal. We have no idea who the other is when the worst we have to face is sour milk and a missing chicken. Or arguing advisors and potholes," she added hurriedly when it looked as though Garrett was about to protest that he had people to find chickens for him.

"We could learn," he said softly.

"How? You can't be the Lord Protector in Gateway and I can't be a healer in Marsanport."

"Was it Norik?"

Arianna took a step back. "What?"

"Did you care more for him? I saw you together and . . ."

"You're not listening to me, Garrett!" She poked him with a finger and when he caught her hand, didn't pull away. "I loved Norik the way I love you, as a friend and comrade in terror. Think for a moment, could you give up being the Lord Protector for me? Stay here, to see if you love me when I'm swearing at slugs in the comfrey? No," she said, when she saw the answer on his face. "You wouldn't even if you wanted to, you have a responsibility to your people. So do I."

He clasped his other hand around hers, holding her loosely, as though she were fragile. Or maybe, to be fair, as though what he felt for her was fragile. "So we live our lives for duty as Lord Protector and Healer?"

About to accuse him of not listening one more time, she realized it had been only two days since they'd left the Broken Lands. Four since he'd lost Norik. Six since they'd lost Petre. One day ago he'd been told his father was dead. He was filtering through more emotional turmoil than merely what he thought he felt for her.

"No person," she said, turning her hand so she held him as well, "is one thing only. You're the Lord Protector of Marsanport and you're the person who brought the fuel out of the Broken Lands. And who always puts the larger wood on the fire too soon. And who complains about the taste of dried sausage. And who mourns his friends. Not." She tightened her grip. "One. Thing. Only."

"If you say so."

"I do."

"I will always love you."

Arianna let him pull her into a hug and said, "Maybe. But that has nothing to do with me."

GARRETT.THEN

Garrett couldn't look at Captain Ling on Norik's horse. He'd have to eventually, but not now. Not yet.

All four horses carried as much trail food as Gateway could spare, dried meat and fish, dried fruit, potatoes to roast in the fire, a few hard-boiled eggs still in the shell. It seemed chickens didn't lay much at this time of the year. He hadn't known. Cleo had told him about the chickens, because Arianna had spent the last two days avoiding him. But she was here now.

He hid how he felt because he didn't want pity, not because he thought that if she noticed his feelings she might leave again. Her reactions to him weren't his responsibility.

"That has nothing to do with me."

He was beginning to understand what she'd meant.

He'd met with the council. The full council. Most of the time, they'd remembered to speak slowly enough for him to understand them. If his Court agreed, he'd declared, Gateway would be opened to trade, Marsanport controlling who and what went up the Mage Road.

"The last thing you need is to be overrun with scavengers."

"The last thing we need," had scoffed an old woman, her hair in short white locs and her eyes like a crow's, *"is a hard winter and a late spring."*

"Or worms in the sheep," one of the shepherds had added, spinning his crook between his palms.

"Could use a few strapping young men to improve the breeding stock," snickered a middle-aged woman with a wink at the shepherd.

"Enough with the colorful country-folk bullshit," Nori had snapped. *"We're open to trade if you can find someone willing to make the trip."*

He was sure he could. Their woolen cloth was amazing—clearly the weavers hadn't been taken out by the Mage War—and they'd pulled a remarkable amount of gems and precious metals out of the ruins. Gems and precious metals were of little use rebuilding a city in isolation, but they could use them to buy what they couldn't produce.

The box holding the fuel had been tied on behind his saddle, rolled in one of the thick, waterproof, woolen blankets they'd all been gifted. Three separate archivists had assured him the fuel wouldn't attract anything on the road.

On the Mage Road.

Garrett didn't entirely believe them.

Arianna stood separate from the crowd that had come to see them off, one arm around Malcolm's shoulders, their heads bent together.

Garrett suddenly realized he'd never be back again.

"Uvili."

She straightened out of her squat, picked up her pack, and walked over to him.

On the way there, she'd carried almost everything. Now she carried her own, much larger blanket, food for her, and presents from the children. What kind of a life would she be returning to? She was a horror story in Marsanport, a nightmare, a warning. *"Eat your peas or the mage-weapon will come out of the Citadel and crush you."* He remembered how he'd found her, chained, filthy, locked inside her own head. She was only just beginning to free herself.

But he was Lord Protector now and he could extend that protection over Uvili.

"Malcolm, mount up. Arianna, if you wouldn't mind."

She stood beside Uvili, frowning slightly. He smiled at her and her forehead relaxed.

After a long moment he lifted his chin and said, loudly enough to be heard by everyone watching, "Uvili. You're to stay here. Guard the Broken Line. Guard Gateway. Someday, another heir of Marsanport will return for fuel. Guard them, but guard Marsanport as well. I have no desire to own either the wonder or the horror of what's beyond the Broken Line, but we all know that when word spreads, and it will, those searching for power will come."

She stared at him, head cocked. Measuring, he realized. Measuring him. She couldn't disobey, but she wouldn't obey blindly. He could leave her without worry. Finally she said, "Yes."

"And given the temptations of the Broken Lands, make sure the Heir of Marsanport deserves the lives they'll be responsible for." He clapped a hand on her shoulder, thankful he was tall enough it didn't look awkward. "This is my last command."

Then he turned to Arianna. "Trust me?"

He smiled as she thought about it for a moment and finally said, "Yes."

Her face felt cool under his palms. Before her cheeks could warm, he bent, and breathed a word into her mouth. Impossibly guttural and sibilant at the same time, the feel of it lingered on his tongue. When she gasped, he knew she'd felt it settling into her head. Her heart. When his father had gifted it to him, it had felt like a word he'd always known, like a word he couldn't forget.

Not wouldn't forget.

Couldn't.

The word was the tension in Norik's arms before he released an arrow. The sheath over a sword. The barricade on the other end of the Mage Road.

Arianna stepped back and stared at him, eyes wide. "Did you just give me the way to control her?"

"I did."

"She can control herself!"

Garrett glanced over at Uvili, who watched them, looking amused. "Not yet," he said. "She was used as nothing but a weapon for too many years and left to rot for too many years after that. She'll need guidance."

"I can be her friend without controlling her!"

"And she can be your friend without needing to be controlled, but she *is* a weapon, like you're a healer. Would your council allow the last of the great, mage-crafted weapons to remain inside the walls if there was no way to be sure of her?"

"No." Uvili answered before Arianna could.

"You don't," Arianna began.

"No," Uvili said again.

"If she's going to stay," Garrett said quietly, "if she's going to have a life, this is the only way."

Her eyes blazed. "And yet you still should have asked!"

"I was afraid you'd refuse and then they . . ." He flicked his gaze over her shoulder at the watching crowd. ". . . would get involved and the debate could go on for days. I don't have time for debate. I have to get the fuel back to Marsanport."

She poked him in the chest, hard enough that he felt it through layers of winter clothing. "Should. Have. Asked."

"I asked if you trusted me."

"That's not . . ."

"I'm sorry." Because it wasn't the same thing, and he knew it. "I didn't ask and I stand by my reasons, but I should have."

"Don't do it again."

He spread his hands. "I'm the Lord Protector of Marsanport. I guarantee that at some point, I will have do it again."

Frowning, she tucked a curl back under her hat. Finally, she met his eyes and said, "Don't do it often."

"I won't."

"Because if I get word that you're abusing your power—any of it—I'll come to Marsanport and kick your ass."

He wanted to say that he'd look forward to it, but he knew that, even joking, it would be absolutely the wrong thing to say. Behind him, Uvili huffed out a breath of air that was almost a laugh, as though she'd known what he'd been thinking.

Not waiting for a response, Arianna pulled him into a hug. "Take care of yourself, take care of Malcolm, and remind Captain Ling that he's to use the cream *every* night."

"Cream? What for?"

"His business not yours."

"Then you shouldn't have mentioned it."

"And you shouldn't have asked." She pushed him back. "Now not knowing can drive you crazy all the way home." She'd left her hand pressed against his chest, but now she removed it. "Get going. You're wasting daylight. Send letters with the traders you'll be sending up the road." She raised her voice. "You too, Malcolm."

"I will!" he called.

Garrett took a deep breath, accepted the waterskin filled with beer Uvili pulled from her pack, and clasped her forearm. "Guard her, too."

He no longer had the word. It wasn't a command.

Uvili's hand clasped his forearm in turn, her strength gentled. "Yes."

RYAN.NOW

Ryan had half expected riders telling him his great-uncle was dead and he was now the Lord Protector. It had been five days since they'd returned to Gateway and riders hadn't come.

They had until morning.

Captain Yansav would be remaining behind with the healers. The traders would take her home with them the next time they came. Servan was staying as well.

"With your permission, my lord."

Slate had never bitten her. Ground squirrels ate from her hand. The dragon . . .

"Stay," he'd said. *"Be happy."*

The healers had taken four days to clear Keetin's lungs. When Ryan asked if they'd found tiny tentacles, they'd laughed at him.

Donal wouldn't have taken that.

He wasn't Donal and he'd laughed with them in relief.

His leg had been healed, although he'd always have the puckered scar where the hot poker had touched the wound. He hadn't felt it; the healer's cool hand on his forehead had kept him outside the pain. He'd smelled the burning flesh, though. That had been enough. He suspected he'd have a little trouble with the smell of cooking pork in the future.

He was leaning on the wall as the sun set, staring down the road toward Marsanport, when Nonee joined him. She said a few quiet words to the archers who'd been keeping a respectful distance, then came to stand beside him, too tall to lean. Too tall to do a lot of things. Large enough that everything the people around her took for granted would be too small and too delicate next to her. She wore the yellow dress and the headscarf and he understood why his great-uncle had left her in Gateway. The people of Gateway were used to the unusual. They wouldn't run in fear, fear leading to hatred and to violence. They were the descendants of those who'd built a city on the edge of the Broken Lands—the Mage Lands—who'd used mage-crafted items—who still used mage-crafted items. People who had . . . talents. Who understood the danger because they lived with the destruction. Who'd take the time to understand her before they made a judgment.

Not all of them, he acknowledged, the people of Gateway were still people, but enough.

It hadn't hurt that she'd been first accepted by a healer. Even ignoring the whole talent thing, no one with half a brain got on the bad side of a healer, not unless they were willing to drink medicines that tasted like goat piss. Or worse.

And the children loved her. The guardians had to keep chasing children off the cannon on the walls of the Citadel, and Ryan could only assume that Nonee had the same appeal—something large and powerful that they could dominate.

But if she had . . . desires, the kind of desires other people had, if the mage-craft hadn't burned them away, she could never act on them. Who would look at her and desire her in return?

"We're leaving in the morning." Stupid. She knew that.

"Yes."

"Destros, Keetin, and I." They'd come with nine. They were leaving with three. Four dead, one too injured to travel, one left behind as Nonee had been. "The Lord Protector lost half his party, I lost two-thirds."

"Captain Yansav and Calintris Servan-cee aren't lost."

"I killed Harris. And my cousin."

"You gave Harris peace. Kalyealee who-could-be-heir . . ." Her voice trailed off.

"Would you have killed her if I hadn't been able?" Ryan knew whose hands had done the deed, but the responsibility had been his. He could no more blame Nonee than he could a sword or an arrow.

"Yes."

Because she was a weapon who could wield herself and one who knew intimately the damage mage-craft could do. "Lyelee just wanted to know things. She . . ." He picked at a bit of loose mortar. "She thought that knowledge should never be silenced. All knowledge. And she thought we shouldn't deny our history."

"You shouldn't."

"But we should learn from it, shouldn't we? Knowledge doesn't exist separate from responsibility. We should look at where certain knowledge leads and decide we don't want to go there again."

"Who decides?"

He snorted half a laugh. "That sounds like a Lyelee question. She'd probably say the scholars should decide."

"She was a scholar. She decided."

"Yeah." He sighed. "But all scholars aren't like that. I mean, the Scholars of the Flesh have learned to do amazing things."

"How?"

"How?" He repeated. He glanced over at her but she was staring down the road.

"With no oversight, how often do they feel the end justifies the means?"

How much did *of the Flesh* sound like Fleshrender? Were there vats in the Scholar's Hall? For research? "Sometimes the end does justifies the means, doesn't it?"

She shrugged.

He shook his head. Denying what? "The scholars watch over themselves. Who else would understand?"

"Kalyealee who-could-be-heir valued knowledge above all. Above reason. Above lives. If the Scholar's Hall didn't create her, it encouraged her to rise."

"But they've saved lives. Tracked fish stocks. Tracked the stars. Made buildings and ships and travel and everything safer. They've taught generations of children. Lyelee was the exception."

"If the scholars watch over themselves, how do you know?"

They'd left parts out of the chronicles. Decided what parts they were willing to share. They hid information in their Archives, locked away from any eyes but theirs. "I don't."

How much had the Lord Protector faced when he was heir? Had the fog killed Norik Yeesan-cer or had the Lord Protector ended his pain? What decisions had the Lord Protector made that could have helped him had they only been shared? What had *he* seen when he broke off a piece of the fuel?

"I know why he never returned," he said. "Not because Marsanport couldn't spare him, but because he couldn't face this place again. Gateway's too close to . . ." He waved a hand in the general direction of the Broken Lands. "What I can't figure out is why he sent me. I mean, he had to have known that the fuel is only a symbol, he can't have been able to see you and not have seen that."

"You were never meant to be heir."

"I know that."

"Kalyealee who-could-be-heir was never meant to be so close to power."

"I *know* that."

"He knew his time was near and he knew you didn't have time to gain the strength you'd need more slowly, more kindly, so he sent you here to be forged in fire, as he was. And he saw the flaw in your cousin and sent her to see if it would shatter."

"That's . . ." He sighed. "That makes sense."

"Thank you."

Ryan grinned at the sarcasm, then suddenly sobered. "There's no more fuel. I'm going to have to convince the people that the Black Flame is a symbol we no longer need, aren't I? I'm going to have to tell the Scholars of the Flame that it's going to burn out and there's nothing anyone can do about it."

"The fuel burns for a long time," Nonee said thoughtfully. "Perhaps your heir will have to do all that."

"It seems that being a shithead to our heirs is a thing in my family." He traced the path of a hawk soaring over the road—at least, he hoped it was a hawk—then turned and leaned back against the wall so he could watch Nonee's face. "I wanted to talk to you because Darny told me something interesting. He says that *nonee* means auntie in one of the old Gateway dialects."

"It does."

"And that's your name?"

"No."

He waited.

Finally, she sighed. "The first children started it, then those children grew up and kept doing it. And their children did it. And their children's children. It was safer. An auntie can't be a weapon."

Ryan shrugged. "Matter of opinion. I've known some pretty dangerous aunties."

She smiled at him. He'd almost grown used to the expression. "Yes."

"Do you mind?"

Her brow creased. "Mind what?"

"Us calling you auntie, like it was your name?"

"Everyone uses Nonee." She closed her fists around handfuls of her skirt. "Except Arianna."

"That doesn't mean you don't mind. My brothers had a lot of names for me. I hated all of them." He rubbed sweaty palms on his thighs. "I want to use your name in my chronicle, your actual name." The Lord Protector had referred to her as *the weapon.* Or the scholars had. He'd have to check their archives. "I mean, if you're okay with that."

The silence stretched for a long moment. Nonee stared at him, expressionless. He forced himself to meet her gaze. "Why?" she asked at last.

Balanced on one leg, he scratched at the scar with his other foot. "Because people have names."

He could hear the archers talking quietly, sheep calling for their lambs, someone chopping wood, insects. He thought he could hear the clack and clatter of the big looms by the temple, but that was probably imagination. "It's okay if you don't want . . ."

"Uvili," she said.

NONEE.NOW

She stood on the wall with half the inhabitants of Gateway until Destros, Keetin Norwin-cee, and Ryan Heir rode out of sight. They'd left the wagon behind, but led the two work horses, carrying bundles of supplies and a tent. Trader Gils had assured him the road was faster on the way back. Ryan Heir hadn't been willing to risk starving now they were traveling without Servan's bow.

"I have a bow," Destros had protested, holding up a crossbow. Gateway had restocked his quiver.

"And if we get close enough, you can hit a rabbit over the head with it," Keetin Norwin-cee had told him.

Destros had clapped her on the shoulder like a comrade before he mounted. It would have to be enough.

Darny had offered to go with them, riding Curtin's horse, and Ryan Heir, who, after all, wasn't very much older, had considered it. Darny's mother had refused to let him go.

"You said I could go with the traders someday!"

"Is this someday? No. It isn't. Is the Heir of Marsan a trader? No. He isn't. Am I turning you loose on the world without adult supervision? No, I'm not. No offense," she'd thrown at Ryan Heir.

Ryan Heir had raised both hands and backed away.

"Mam!" Darny had wailed.

"No!"

"But . . ."

"Do you want to spend the rest of your life taking care of the chickens?"

Darny's mother knew how to win an argument.

When the road had been empty for long enough that only Servan stood beside her on the wall, she said, "Trader Gils's family will be back soon. You can always go home with them."

Servan snorted. "I am home, Nonee."

"You could hate it here."

"Possible, but I don't think so." She grinned broadly enough, the new scar on her forehead shifted. "You need archers. I like to be needed."

They stood together a moment longer, then Servan—no, Cali headed off to report to the captain and Nonee stood alone a while longer. Finally, she leapt down—easier than trusting her feet to the too-narrow stairs—and made her way to Arianna's grave.

"They're gone," she said, squatting and running her palm over the grass. She'd been afraid she'd return to a yellow rectangle of dead sod, but the children had taken turns watering the grave while she was in the Broken Lands. "Ryan Heir says he'll send a copy of his chronicle back with the traders. You'll want it read to you, won't you? He says he'll send a copy of Garrett Heir's chronicle as soon as he finds one the scholars haven't messed with."

Arianna said nothing, but then, Arianna was rotting, so although Nonee missed her like an arm or a leg or a heart, she was content with the silence.

And to let the silence continue.

"Nonee? Nonee!" Jisper raced across the grass, followed by her sister and her cousin. "You promised you'd play when you came back."

Nonee stood and brushed grass off her fingers. "Yes," she said.

ACKNOWLEDGMENTS

It's been a long four years. I'd like to thank Katherine Arcus and Michelle Sagara for keeping me going when I wanted to quit. Mostly, by demanding I send them more. Katherine with questions and enthusiasm. Michelle, by calling me an idiot. There's something very bracing about that . . .